VOWS AND HONOR. . . .

Martin rose, again meeting Judaia's eyes, candor clear in his green-gray stare. For a moment, his shielding slipped, and she caught a glimpse of deep struggle, honor against need. Then, he hurriedly rebuilt his defenses. "Yes, I *am* avoiding you."

"Why?" Surprise dispersed Judaia's anger, leaving only confusion in its wake. "I feel . . . I mean we both know . . ." Words failed her, and she discovered an awkwardness as petrifying as Martin's had seemed.

"That we're lifebonded? Yes, I know."

Judaia could do nothing but stare, jaw sagging gradually open without her will or knowledge. At length, she managed speech. "You know? Then why are you avoiding me?"

"Because I made a vow to Lyssa that she would be my one and only, that I would never sleep with another woman."

Judaia did not know which shocked her more, her own disappointment, the tie to Lyssa, or the promise like none she had ever heard before. "Are you lifebonded with her, too?"

"No."

"Then why would you make such a promise?"

Martin shrugged. "She wanted me to, and I did. Lifebonds are uncommon enough I never expected to form one."

"But it's not right!" she shouted, the agony of the thwarted lifebond writhing within her. "It's not fair."

Martin's eyes went moist, the green-gray smeared to a colorless blur. " 'Fair' is not the issue." Once again, he looked away, and this time Judaia applauded his decision to dodge her stare. "A Herald's vows," he said softly, "take precedence over desire. Honor always over right."

SWORD OF ICE
And Other Tales Of Valdemar

Edited by Mercedes Lackey

DAW BOOKS, INC.
DONALD A. WOLLHEIM, FOUNDER
375 Hudson Street, New York, NY 10014

ELIZABETH R. WOLLHEIM
SHEILA E. GILBERT
PUBLISHERS

First Printing, January 1997
1 2 3 4 5 6 7 8 9

DAW TRADEMARK REGISTERED
U.S. PAT. OFF. AND FOREIGN COUNTRIES
—MARCA REGISTRADA
HECHO EN U.S.A.

PRINTED IN THE U.S.A.

ACKNOWLEDGMENTS

Introduction © 1997 by *Mercedes Lackey*
Sunlancer © 1997 *by Philip Austin and Mercedes Lackey*
The Demon's Den © 1997 *by Tanya Huff*
Ironrose © 1997 *by Larry Dixon and Mel. White*
Babysitter © 1997 *by Josepha Sherman*
The Salamander © 1997 *by Richard Lee Byers*
A Child's Adventures © 1997 *by Janni Lee Simner*
Blood Ties © 1997 *by Stephanie Shaver*
... Another Successful Experiment © 1997 *by Lawrence Schimel*
Choice © 1997 *by Michelle Sagara*
Song of Valdemar © 1997 *by Kristin Schwengel*
The School Up the Hill © 1997 *by Elisabeth Waters*
Chance © 1997 *by Mark Shepherd*
Sword of Ice © 1997 *by Mercedes Lackey and John Yezeguielian*
In the Forest of Sorrows © 1997 *by John Helfers*
Vkandis' Own © 1997 *by Ben Ohlander*
A Herald's Honor © 1997 *by Mickey Zucker Reichert*
A Song for No One's Mourning © 1997 *by Gary Braunbeck*
Blue Heart © 1997 *by Philip Austin and Mercedes Lackey*

Contents

Introduction

My very first published story, in 1985, was a piece for Marion Zimmer Bradley's "Friends of Darkover" anthology, *Free Amazons of Darkover*. At the time, although I was working on what would become the first of a series of fifteen novels (with no end in sight), I never thought that I would be in the position to do as Marion had done, and open up my world for other professionals to tinker with.

And yet, ten years later, here it is, the *Friends of Valdemar* anthology. Some of the stories here are by names you will recognize, some by authors you will not, but the one thing that unites them all is that somewhere along the line, they actually enjoyed my work enough to want to add their own touches to the world that I created. Several of the authors in this book are protégés of mine and have cowritten other things with me; some are protégés of mine and have had work published that I had no hand in, which is, to any teacher, a source of great pleasure. You always hope that the "student" goes beyond what you can teach and finds his or her own way, own voice, and own creations that you have no direct part in.

And it is entirely possible that one or more of the authors in this volume will one day find him- or herself playing host and editor to a book of stories set in a world he or she has created.

And when that happens, I hope that they think of *me*, and ask me to come play, too!

Sunlancer
by *Philip M. Austin and Mercedes Lackey*

Philip Austin writes, "Misty Lackey is the one who made this story come alive. She deserves the majority of the credit and all my thanks. [She] has been a good friend and mentor. She's been helpful in so many ways. Through her good offers, I've been able to dream of a future. A creative future. That dream is worth more than any monetary reward."

Mercedes Lackey was born in Chicago, and has worked as a lab assistant, security guard, and computer programmer before turning to fiction writing. Her first book, *Arrows of the Queen,* the first in the Valdemar series, was published in 1985. She won the Lambda award for *Magic's Price* and Science Fiction Book Club Book of the Year for the *The Elvenbane,* co-authored with Andre Norton. Along with her husband, Larry Dixon, she is a Federally licensed bird rehabilitator, specializing in birds of prey. She shares her home with a menagerie of parrots, cats and a Schutzhund trained German shepherd.

Clarrin Mul-Par knelt below his open window and raised his face to the rising sun; he closed his eyes and felt the warmth of its rays against his cheeks, watched the inside of his eyelids turn as red as the robes of Vkandis' priests. The sun was a pressure against his skin, as real as the pressure against his heart.

Vkandis! Sunlord! he prayed. *Hear me, and guide me in what I must do. Red-priestess Beakasi tells us we do your will and bidding—should I believe her? She tells us that it is your will that we take the young ones, that your miracles show her the ones to test for your service. Must I believe her? Sunlord, all life comes by your gift; to live in your light is the old teaching, passed from generation to generation. But is this what you meant? Vkandis! Sunlord! What must I do? Give me a sign!*

He lowered his outstretched arms, letting the rays of the sun bathe him. But although they warmed his body, they did not touch the cold in his heart, nor did they ease his worry and confusion.

For the first time in his life, he doubted.

No, he told himself firmly. *No, I do* not *doubt the Sunlord. I doubt those who speak in His Name. I doubt that what they call upon me to do is truly His Will.*

And he knew exactly where to place the blame for that doubt—if "blame" was precisely the right thing to call it.

Squarely in the lap of that scholar-scribe with the terrible eyes: the guest of his grandfather, and as such, sacrosanct.

The man had been there when he arrived last night; they seemed to be old friends, and Grandfather had introduced him as such. Clarrin found the man to be a fascinating storyteller, and the three of them had conversed long into the night, in the garden pavilion, where—now that he thought about it—no one could creep up upon them to listen without being seen.

And it was the scholar's questions that had made him doubt. . . .

"Captain Clarrin Mul-Par is a wise man, I have no doubt," the scribe said in accentless, flowing Karsite that even a priest would envy. "As well as a man trusted in the Temple's service. I value wisdom, and I seek answers, answers to questions a man such as the Captain may be able to give me."

As he sat there, completely at ease in the low couch, boots crossed at the ankles and elbows resting on knees, his eyes never left the face of the Captain of the Temple Lancers. Clarrin wondered what in heaven or earth he was reading there. He never *had* learned to completely school his expression.

But he had tried not to betray his uneasiness. "What are your questions, good sir?" he replied, forcing himself to return the scribe's direct gaze. "Although you grant me more wisdom than I would claim, I will do my best to answer you."

"My first question is this—and pray, do not take offense, for I am a foreigner, and I mean none," the scholar said, with a smile that *looked* honest, leaning forward a little to speak. "Are the miracles performed by your priests and priestesses *true* miracles, or are they actually magic?"

Clarrin licked his lips, and answered carefully. "Vkandis forbids the practice of magic," he replied sternly. "It was by his will that *magic* was driven out of the land. His miracles ensure that we of Karse need no magic, and aid his holy ones to keep magic from our borders."

The scribe did not seem particularly disturbed by the implied rebuke. He sipped at the pleasant, fruity wine with appreciation, examined the crystal goblet that contained it for a moment, then looked up through the latticework of the pavilion's roof at the stars. Only then did he look back at Clarrin.

"Spoken as a true warrior of the Temple," he said, with another of those enigmatic smiles. "Yet—I have been in other lands. Rethwellan, Hardorn, even Valdemar. I have seen those who claim to be practitioners of *magic* perform feats precisely the same as those that Vkandis' priests perform. Does the Sunlord grant these people the power to work miracles as well?"

Clarrin carefully set his goblet down on the low table they all shared, heated words rising in him. "I have not seen these marvels that you *claim* to have seen, scribe," he replied, his anger giving his voice a distinct edge, "So I may make no judgment."

But his grandfather frowned. "Sharp words!" he chided. "Grandson, you come close to dishonoring my granted guest-right with your sharp tongue!"

Clarrin flushed, this time with embarrassment. He might be thirty summers old, but this was the man who had raised him, and the bright-eyed old fellow did right to remind him of the courtesies owed a guest of the house.

"I am well rebuked, old owl," he replied, with a bow of apology to the scribe, and a smile of affection for the wizened old man. "You remind me of the *proper* way to answer our guest."

He turned to the scribe. "I apologize for my discourteous reply, sir. And to answer your question with strict truth, I do not know. I have no knowledge of magic and have never seen any who practice it; we are taught that it is all trickery in any case, that the miracles of Vkandis alone are no deceit. The priests would tell you that this magic you have seen is nothing more than cleverness and misdirection."

The scribe smiled, giving Clarrin the slight bow of scholar-to-scholar, wordlessly telling Clarrin that he had shown wisdom by admitting his ignorance. Clarrin flushed again, this time feeling pleased and flattered.

"Now *this*—" the scribe said lightly. "This is a moment of true men's pleasure: to sip good wine, in a beautiful garden, on a clear summer's night, discussing the mysteries of the world. Among men who can face truth and enter debate with open minds, no apologies are needed, for all three of us are men who can acknowledge that we can *speak* the truth only as we see it. And the truth is a crystal with many facets."

A night bird began a liquid, plaintive song just as the scribe finished speaking. The scribe half-closed his eyes to listen, and out of courtesy, all of them remained quiet until it had finished and flew away.

"The ovan has other pleasures in mind," Tirens Mul-Par, Clarrin's grandfather, said wryly. "He calls a mate."

Clarrin and the scribe both chuckled. "Ah," the scribe replied. "And have you never heard the tale of the 'scholar's mate'?"

Both indicated ignorance, and he told them a roguish story of a priestly scholar who so loved to read in bed that he filled half of his bed with books and heavy scrolls every night, leaving an impression on the mattress that looked as if someone had been asleep there. This continued until his superior spied upon him to catch him in the act of bringing in a (prohibited) female, and caught him only with a "mistress" made of paper.

With the atmosphere lightened, the scribe leaned forward once more, and Clarrin told himself to keep his temper in check, anticipating another unpleasantly direct question.

He was not wrong.

"Another question comes to my mind," the scholar said. "The faithful are granted healing of ills and new injuries in the Temple, and it is true healing, for I have seen the results of it. This is said to be another miracle of the Sunlord, is this not true?"

Clarrin nodded warily. "Yes. I have received the Sunlord's Gift myself. As a young lancer I was arrow-struck during our foray into Menmellith to relieve the true believers trapped there." He tapped his left leg to indicate the site of the old wound. "One of the priests laid hands upon the wound and drew out the arrow, and there was neither blood nor wound after, only a scar, as if the injury had occurred weeks in the past."

"I am glad that you were healed that you may still serve," the scribe replied. "Yet—forgive me, but in other lands, there are healers as well. In fact, in every land I have ever been or even read of, there are healers of the flesh. In Valdemar, they are even gathered together at an early age, and taught at a great school called a *Collegium.*"

"We gather those granted the healer's touch by the Sunlord and teach them in the Temple—" Clarrin began, but stopped when the scribe held up a finger.

"True enough, but the healers in Valdemar are not taught in a temple, for there are *many* beliefs in their land, not one," the scribe said earnestly. "When these healers are proficient in their work, they are given green clothing to wear so that they may be recognized and heeded. They go where they are needed, and *all* may come to them for aid, even the lowest and the poorest. So, here again, I must ask you—if there are true healers elsewhere, does the Sunlord grant *them* this miracle of healing as well as he does here?"

Clarrin sighed. "Your question marches with the one before," he replied. "In truth, I cannot answer."

He picked up the pitcher, hoping to stave off more questions. He poured his grandfather another goblet, offered wine to the scholar and was politely refused, and filled his own glass. And in truth, he felt the need of it. This scribe had a way of demanding answers to questions he had rather not think about.

"I only have one more question, Captain," the scribe said, chuckling when he saw Clarrin's expression of resigned dismay. "Though it could be seen as more than one."

"A puzzle, then? Or a riddle?" Clarrin hoped so. He and his grandfather had often traded riddles long into the night.

"Perhaps, yes!" the scribe agreed. "A puzzle of questions."

Clarrin waited while the breeze stirred scent up from the night-blooming flowers around them, and made the wind-chimes play gently. "Your puzzle, then?" he prompted.

"Only this; why are the young ones chosen by the priesthood taken from their homes at night? Why are they tested, cleansed of all ties of kinship, and never seen again by their kin except at a distance? Why are those that cannot be cleansed of kin-ties in your temple, or those who fail the testing, cleansed instead by burning in the fire of Vkandis? Why does the Sunlord, the giver of all *life*, require the *death* of children? Is it the cleansing and sacrifice of kin-ties that give the priests and priestesses the power to perform the Sunlord's miracles, or could they perform them if they never set foot in the temple or donned robes?"

Clarrin shifted uncomfortably in his seat, but the scribe was not yet done with him.

"Is it possible," he continued, leaning forward so that

his terrible, knowing eyes bored into Clarrin's, "that the ones who are fire-cleansed are destroyed because their powers are *too* strong, too strong to permit their minds and hearts to be cleansed of the love of their kinfolk, and that if they lived, they could rival the priests and priestesses without ever having to wear a robe?"

His eyes seemed to penetrate right into Clarrin's mind, as if he were daring Clarrin to find the true answers to this "puzzle" of his. And there was something lurking in the depths of his gaze; a hint of pain, of loneliness, of half-madness that made Clarrin finally shiver and turn away.

"I—have no answers for you at all, sir scribe," he replied, rising to his feet, quickly. "I am only a poor lancer, with no head for such an elevated discourse. I will have to leave these things to men of wisdom, such as you and my grandfather. Now, if you will forgive me—" he ended, hastily, already backing away, "I have duties *early* in the morning. Very *early*—"

And with that, he beat a hasty retreat.

Tirens Mul-Par also faced the sun this morning, but not to pray. His prayer had been answered last night, and that in itself was proof enough of the Sunlord's power—and that His power, like the light of the sun, granted blessings and prayers in every land and not just in Karse.

Instead, he watched as his servants secretly readied all the horses in his stable for a long journey, and his thoughts, too, returned to the previous evening's conversation.

Clarrin beat a hasty, but tactically sound, retreat from the garden. He did not—quite—run, but it was plain enough from his posture that he wished he could. It was too bad for his peace of mind that he would never be able to run fast enough or far enough to escape those *questions* the scribe had placed in his thoughts.

Tirens watched him go, and hid a smile. This was not the first time that he had entertained the scholar who called himself "Brekkan of Hawk's Rest," but it *was* the first time he had been utterly certain of what this "Brekkan" really was.

"I fear I may have upset your grandson, Tirens Mul-Par," the scribe said softly. "It was not my intention."

The old man snorted. "It was *always* your intention—Valdemaran," he said, and watched with interest as the scribe's hand twitched a little. Interesting. A sleeve-dagger? "You *Heralds* of Valdemar do not care to see folk become too complacent, do you?"

He saw the man's eyes widen just a trifle, and smiled.

"I think you are mistaken—" the so-called "scribe" began.

Tirens held up a finger, cautioning him to silence. "If I am mistaken, it is only in thinking that a Herald would not resort to a hidden dagger up a sleeve." His smile broadened as the Herald twitched again. "But I did not make any mistakes in giving you my hospitality, nor in bringing my grandson here for you to *disturb* with your questions. He is old enough, and well-placed enough, to make a difference in this sad land."

Again the Herald moved as to protest, and again he silenced the man with a single finger.

"Your questions deserve answers, not platitudes or religious cant. But he must decide for himself what is right. I cannot *give* him answers, nor can you." He shrugged expressively. "I do not know what his answers will be, nor can I say what he will do once he finds them. That will come as Vkandis wills."

The Herald watched him with narrowed eyes, gray eyes, which marched well with his straight brown hair, the color of old leaves. You would never notice him in a crowd, so long as he was not wearing the expression he bore now. Which, Tirens supposed, was the point. . . .

"How did you know?" the Herald asked, his voice low and potent with threat.

"That you are a Herald?" The old man grinned. "I did not *know* it until this visit, when I had need to know. I have the *sight*, at need. At those times, I can sense things that are not apparent."

His guest was not in the least mollified. "Why did you grant me guest-right, Tirens Mul-Par, if you knew what I am?" he demanded harshly.

Tirens sipped his wine. "I have a granddaughter," he said. "A little above Clarrin's age. *She* has a daughter, a lovely child in my eyes, who laughs at the stories of her greatgrandsire, and who loves him as much as he loves her. She is only nine years old. A dangerous age, in Karse."

The Herald relaxed, just a trifle. "They test children in the temple at their tenth birthdays. . . ."

"Exactly so." He allowed his smile to fade. "She tells me stories as well, of dreams in the night. At times, those dreams come to pass."

The light of understanding blossomed in the Herald's eyes. "Dreams can be dangerous—in Karse."

The old man nodded, curtly. "I wish her and her mother to be taken someplace where dreams are not so dangerous. Before *we* have visitors in the night."

The Herald tilted his head to one side. "Her father may have something to say about that," he ventured.

Tirens waved his hand in dismissal. "Only if he chooses to return from the hosts at Vkandis' right hand, where the priests pledge me he has gone," he replied.

The Herald chuckled at that, and relaxed further. His hand made an *interesting* little movement, that told Tirens the dagger had returned to its home. "When?" he asked only.

"Tomorrow," the old man said firmly. "I have already made the arrangements. My granddaughter is privy to them, and just as anxious as I for her daughter's safety. They will not inconvenience you. In fact," he allowed a twinkle to creep into his eyes, "a prosperous scholar, with a Karsite wife and child, returning from visiting relatives, is not likely to be questioned by anyone, so long as he is careful to stay within law and custom. Which his Karsite wife will be sure to impart to him."

The Herald coughed gently. "I can—ah—see that."

Tirens still had not heard the promise he wanted.

"Please," he said, resorting to beggary. "Please, take them to safety. You will have no cause to regret this."

But the Herald had not been reluctant after all. "Of *course* I will," he said, a little embarrassed. "I was just— thinking for a moment! Rearranging my trip to account for a new wife and child!" But at Tirens' chuckle, his gaze sharpened. "But what of you, old owl?" he asked, using the name Clarrin had used in affection.

The old man leaned back in his seat on the couch and sipped his wine. "Oh, I shall enjoy my garden until I die," he said casually. "Life has been . . . interesting. But I do not fear to leave it." And before his visitor could ask anything more, he leaned forward with an eagerness that was completely genuine. "And now, Herald of Valdemar, since your other tales have been so fascinating—tell me of the land that my dear ones will live in!"

Clarrin put aside his doubts long enough to bid farewell to his family. It would be many more months before he had another chance to visit them, and without a doubt, by then his niece Liksani would be almost a woman. Already she had the look of his sister Aldenwin about her, and he could not help but remember all the times when it had been Aldenwin who clung to his stirrup and begged him to stay "just one more day."

But when he told Liksani, with a playful shake of his head, that there were no more days left in the visit, she let go and let him mount.

"Uncle Clarrin," she said, her pretty, dark-eyed face solemn, "I almost forgot. I dreamed a tale for you this morning, in the women's garden after sunrise prayers."

He bent down to ruffle her hair. "And what did you dream, little dreamer?" he asked, lightly, thinking it would be a request for a doll, or some such thing.

"I dreamed that a man in armor so bright I could not look at him told me to tell you something," she laughed up at him.

Clarrin went cold inside but managed to keep smiling. "And what thing was that?"

"He said to tell you that—" she screwed her face up in concentration. "—that 'the light is the life and the breath, the flame is the blessing and not life's-ending' . . ." she faltered for a moment, then smiled, ". . . and that 'children should live and laugh and play!' Then he told me to go and play in northern flowers!" she finished, giggling.

A weirding chill raised the hackles on his neck, but somehow Clarrin managed to lean down from his saddle to hug her firmly, lifting her right off her feet as she put her arms around his neck.

"Be happy, Liksani," he ordered gently. "Live and laugh and play, like the shining man told you."

"I'm *always* happy, Uncle Clarrin. You know *that*," she giggled as he set her back down on the ground.

Sunlord, keep her happy, he prayed silently, turning his horse to the gate, and leading his seven guards back toward his duty. *Sunlord, keep her always happy.*

Tirens watched as his grandson rode off down the road to the south. And two candlemarks later, he watched as his granddaughter, Liksani, and six of his seven servants rode off down the road to the north and west. With them, rode the Herald, whose true name Tirens still did not know.

He knew that the Herald was a man of honor. That was all he *needed* to know.

The sun was directly overhead, the birds singing all about his favorite pavilion, as his one remaining servant served him his finest wine from a fragile crystal goblet. He sipped it with appreciation as he turned the crystal to admire the way it sparkled in the sunlight. This had been one of a set of two, from which he and dear Sareni had drunk their marriage-wine. The shards of the other lay with Sareni in her grave.

Sareni would have approved, he thought, as he drank the last of the wine, and slipped his frail old hand into the bowl of figs where a tiny, rainbow-striped snake was curled. He stirred the figs until he felt a slight sting on his hand, then a sudden lethargy. The goblet fell from his nerveless fingers and shattered on the pavilion floor.

He lay back in his couch, watched the snake slip away under the rosebushes, and wondered if Vkandis liked gardens.

Clarrin stirred his noodles with his fork, and stared at nothing at all.

"Captain!" his Corporal-Orderly said sharply, making him jump.

"Yes, Esda?" he replied, wondering if he looked as guilty as he felt.

Evidently not. Esda pouted at him, hands on side-cocked hips, a petulant expression on his face. "Captain," he complained, "you've hardly touched your meal, and I worked very hard making it! What is bothering you?"

Clarrin grinned in spite of himself at the burly corporal's burlesque of a spoiled girl. "Esda, you lie! You never work hard at anything. Not in the ten years you've served *me,* anyway!"

Esda grinned back. "Too true, Captain. That's why *I* picked *you* for my officer."

Clarrin shook his head at his Orderly's unrepentant grin. "Here," he said, shoving the plate of noodles across the table toward Esda. "Sit down, finish my meal for me, and let me use your common sense." He made it less of an order, and more of an invitation.

Esda's grin faded immediately, and the grizzled veteran's expression was replaced by one of concern. "You *are* troubled, Captain," he observed, taking the seat, but ignoring the food, his eyes fixed on Clarrin's.

Clarrin shrugged. "I have some questions to repeat to you—and a dream to tell you about," he said, slowly.

"A dream!" Esda lost every trace of mockery. "Dreams are nothing to disregard, Captain." Esda had served the Temple for longer than Clarrin had been alive—he had seen three Sons of the Sun come and go. And he was both a skeptic and a believer; if anyone

knew where Temple politics began and true religion
ended, it would be Esda.

"Yes, well, see what you think when I am done."

For the next candlemark, Esda sat and listened without interruption as Clarrin recounted the discussion in
the garden and little Liksani's dream.

"You know we serve at the Cleansing," he finished.

"Aye, and I know you mislike the assignment," Esda
replied gruffly. "But—is it Vkandis you blame for—"

"No!" Clarrin exclaimed, cutting him off with a slam
of his open palm on the wooden table. "Never! I cannot
believe that the Lord of all Life would ever countenance
taking life, that is all! It is the priests and their minions
that I mistrust and fear! I believe they serve themselves,
not Vkandis! And I fear that they use *magic,* and call it
'miracle,' in order to puff up their own importance!"

"Well, then bugger them all, Captain!" Esda grinned,
like the sun coming out from behind a cloud. "Whatever
you decide to do, just remember that poor, overworked,
old unappreciated Esda will be there to pick up your
soiled linen!"

The roar of laughter that followed made the rest of
his personal guards turn their heads, wondering what
outrageous thing Esda had said to him *this* time.

Esda moved quietly among the guards, speaking with
them one at a time, over the next two days, while Clarrin
pretended that he did not notice. And over the next two
days, every one of his men approached him quietly, one
at a time, to offer their *personal* fealty to him. Clarrin
was touched and humbled by their trust.

But he still did not know what he was going to do.

In ten days, Clarrin was back in command of his troop
of Temple Lancers. In fifteen days, they paraded for the
Ceremony of Cleansing, conducted by Red-priestess
Beakasi. The Temple square was crowded with worship-
ers and spectators at two sides, behind the lines of the
temple guards. Clarrin's Lancers closed the third side of
the square. The low Sun Altar, flanked by priests and

priestesses in order of rank, filled most of the fourth side.

At Clarrin's signal, the lancers knelt as one at their horses' heads, lances grounded, with the shafts held stiffly erect. The red pennons at the crossbars moved lazily in the warm afternoon air.

Red-priestess Beakasi, flanked by her torch-bearers, mounted the altar-platform, and turned to face the crowd and the setting sun behind them. Her arms stretched out toward the sun, and her red robes matched the red clouds of sunset.

At that signal, lesser priests brought the two who were to be cleansed to the steps: a boy who looked to be in his early teens, and a girl somewhat younger, dark-haired, with a pretty, gentle face.

Clarrin's breath caught in his throat. *She could be Liksani,* he thought in anguish. The words of his niece's dream kept repeating, over and over, in his head.

The flame is the blessing and not life's ending. Children should live, and laugh, and play.

The boy was shoved forward onto the platform. He stood there looking frightened and confused.

"Vkandis! Sunlord!" Beakasi sang. "Grant your miracle! Cleanse this tainted one with your holy fire!"

She brought her hands together over her head, closing them on the iron shaft of a torch held there by a Black-robed priest. He let it go, and she held it high above her head, flame flickering.

"Witness the Sunlord's miracle!" she sang. "Tremble at his power!"

The torch flame flared, and grew suddenly to man-height, then bent toward the boy. He started to scream, but remained where he was, frozen with fear. Another Red-robed priest pointed, and the boy's scream was cut off; he remained where he was, a wide-eyed, open-mouthed, living statue. Flames flowed from the torch to the boy, arching overhead like water from a fountain, in a long, liquid stream. They touched him, then engulfed him, turning him into a column of searing, white-green fire that grew to three times the boy's height. A vaguely human-shaped form turned slowly in the upper half of the column of fire, as if bathing in it.

Clarrin's heart spasmed, and his gorge rose.

Slowly the flames diminished and flowed back into the torch, until it burned normally once again.

The boy was gone, and there was only a small pile of ashes to mark where he had stood.

The priestess waited until the original bearer had his hands on the torch, before she removed hers, spreading her arms wide. Looking somewhere above the heads of the onlookers, she called out into the silence.

"Hail Vkandis, Sunlord!"

"*Hail Vkandis, Sunlord!*" the crowd roared in response. Beakasi signaled for the girl to be brought forward.

"The flame is the blessing and not life-ending," Clarrin murmured, his eyes bright with tears. "Children should live, and laugh, and play!"

He was standing now, moving to his saddle in slow, sluggish motion, warring within himself.

The flame is the blessing, and not life-ending. He reached for the saddle-bow and swung up into place, feeling as if he were trapped in a fever-dream. *Children should live, and laugh, and play!*

His hand was on his lance; his horse jerked its head up in astonishment at the tightening of his legs, then stepped forward.

He kicked it, startling it into a gallop.

"*The flame is the blessing, and not life-ending!*" he screamed, the words torn from his throat in torment. His lance swung down, into the attack position. "*Children should live, and laugh, and play!*"

Red-priestess Beakasi swung around in surprise. Her face mirrored that stunned surprise for a few moments, then suddenly began chanting in a high, frightened voice, words Clarrin could not understand. Her hands moved in intricate patterns, tracing figures in the air.

Clarrin's superbly-trained mount, the veteran of many encounters, plunged up the stairs at the gallop, never missing a step. "*The flame is the blessing, and not life-*

ending!" Clarrin roared as a warcry. *"Children should
live, and laugh, and play!"*

The priestess held up her hands, as if she could ward
off the lance with a gesture. The long, leaf-shaped blade
impaled one of those outstretched hands, nailing it to
her chest as it struck her heart.

She shrieked in anger, shock, and pain. The crossbar
behind the blade slammed into her hand and chest. Clarrin took the impact in his arm, lifting her up off her feet
for a moment, as he signaled his horse to halt. He
dropped the point of the lance, and the priestess' body
slid off the blade, to lie across the altar.

Clarrin leaned down as he wheeled his horse and
started back down the stairs, sweeping the young girl
into his arms without slowing. The horse plunged down
the steps at the back of the altar, and they were away,
the child clinging desperately to him. Clarrin held her
protectively to his chest, and urged his mount to
greater speed.

So far, they had escaped, but their luck could not last
for much longer.

He heard horses behind him. Close, *too* close. He
looked back, his lips twisting in a feral snarl, ready to
fight for the child's life, as well as his own.

The snarl turned to a gape, and the gape to a grin
that held both elation and awe.

His own personal guard and fifty of his lancers, those
that had served with him the longest, were following.
Esda in the lead. Many had blood on their blades.

Clarrin slowed just enough for the rest to catch up
with him. Esda waved an iron-banded torch—just like
the ones carried by the priests. As they galloped past a
rain-swollen ditch, Esda tossed the torch into the water.
Green-yellow smoke and steam billowed up in a hissing
roar as they passed the place, and a vaguely man-shaped
form twisted and jerked in the heart of the smoke, as if
it were on fire.

Clarrin and Esda spat, and rode on, letting the evening
breeze carry the smoke away in their wake.

The pursuit, when it finally came in the wake of blame-casting and name-calling, was vicious. Clarrin felt extremely lucky that they crossed into Rethwellan with twenty-six still alive.

Or rather, twenty-seven. Twenty-six men, and one special little girl, who could now live, and laugh, and play in the warm morning sun. Without fear, and without threat.

Fifteen days later, Clarrin crossed back into Karse, his men with him, all disguised as scholars. They quickly dispersed, each with provisions and a horse, and a series of uncomfortable questions.

There were more young ones to save.

And after all, at the right time and place, a question was more deadly than any sword.

The Demon's Den
by Tanya Huff

Born in the Maritimes, Tanya Huff now lives and writes in rural Ontario. On her way there, she spent three years in the Canadian Naval Reserve and got a degree in Radio and Television Arts which the cat threw up on. Although no members of her family are miners, "The Demon's Den" is the third story she's written about those who go underground, and mines have been mentioned in a number of her books. She has no idea where it's coming from, but decided not to fight it. Her last book out was *No Quarter* (DAW, March 1996), the direct sequel to *Fifth Quarter* (DAW, August, 1995) and her next book will be *Blood Debt* (DAW, April 1997), a fifth Vicki/Henry/Celluci novel.

The mine had obviously been abandoned for years. Not even dusk hid the broken timbers and the scree of rock that spilled out of the gaping black hole.

Jors squinted into the wind, trying and failing to see past the shadows. :*Are you sure it went in there?*:

:*Of course I'm sure. I can smell the blood trail.*:

:*Maybe it's not hurt as badly as we thought. Maybe it'll be fine until morning.*: His Companion gave a little buck. Jors clutched at the saddle and sighed. :*All right, all right, I'm going.*:

No one at the farmstead had known why the mountain cat had come down out of the heights—perhaps the deer it normally hunted had grown scarce; perhaps a more aggressive cat had driven it from its territory; perhaps it had grown lazy and decided sheep were less work. No one at the farmstead cared. They'd tried to drive it off.

It had retaliated by mauling a shepherd and three dogs. Now, they wanted it killed.

Just my luck to be riding circuit up here in the Great White North. Jors swung out of the saddle and pulled his gloves off with his teeth. *:How am I supposed to shoot it when I won't be able to see it?:* he asked, unstrapping his bow.

Gevris turned his head to peer back at his Chosen with one sapphire eye. *:It's hurt.:*

:I know.: The wind sucked the heat out of his hands and he swore under his breath as one of the laces of his small pack knotted tight.

:You wounded it.:

:I know, damn it, I know!: Sighing, he rested his head on the Companion's warm flank. *:I'm sorry. It's just been a long day and I should never have missed that shot.:*

:No one makes every shot, Chosen.:

The warm understanding in the mind-touch helped.

The cat had been easy to track. By late afternoon, they'd known they were close. At sunset, they spotted it outlined against a gray and glowering sky. Jors had carefully aimed, carefully let fly, and watched in horror as the arrow thudded deep into a golden haunch. The cat had screamed and fled. They'd had no choice but to follow.

The most direct route up to the mine was a treacherous path of loose shale. Jors slipped, slammed one knee into the ground, and somehow managed to catch himself before he slid all the way back to the bottom.

:Chosen? Are you hurt?:

Behind him, he could hear hooves scrabbling at the stone and he had to grin. *:I'm fine, worrywart. Get back on solid ground before you do yourself some damage.:*

Here I go into who-knows-what to face a wounded mountain cat, and he's worried that I've skinned my knee. Shaking his head, he struggled the rest of the way to the mine entrance and then turned and waved down at the glimmering white shape below. *:I'm here. I'm fine.:* Then he frowned and peered down at the ground. The cart tracks coming out of the mine bumped down a series of jagged ledges, disappeared completely, then reappeared down where his Companion was standing.

:I don't like this.:

If he squinted, he could easily make out Gevris side-stepping nervously back and forth, a glimmer of white amidst the evening shadows. *:Hey, I don't like this either, but . . .:*

:Something is going to happen.:

Jors chewed on his lip. He'd never heard his usually phlegmatic Companion sound so unsettled. A gust of wind blew cold rain in his face and he shivered. *:It's just a storm. Go back under the trees so you don't get soaked.:*

:No. Come down. We can come back here in the morning.:

Storm probably has him a bit spooked and he doesn't want to admit it. The Herald sighed and wished he could go along with his Companion's sudden change of mind. *:I can't do that.:* As much as he didn't want to go into that hole, he knew he had to. *:I wounded it. I can't let it die slowly, in pain. I'm responsible for its death.:*

He felt reluctant agreement from below and, half wishing Gevris had continued to argue, turned to face the darkness. Setting his bow to one side, he pulled a small torch out of his pack, unwrapped the oilskin cover, and, in spite of wind and stiff fingers, got it lit.

The flame helped a little. But not much.

How am I supposed to hold a torch and aim a bow? This is ridiculous. But he'd missed his shot, and he couldn't let an animal, any animal, die in pain because of something he'd done.

The tunnel sloped gently back into the hillside, the shadows becoming more impenetrable the farther from the entrance he went. He stepped over a fallen beam and a pile of rock, worked his way around a crazily angled corner, saw a smear of blood glistening in the torchlight, and went on. His heart beat so loudly he doubted he'd be able to hear the cat if it should turn and attack.

A low shadow caught his eye and against his better judgment, he bent to study it. An earlier rockfall had exposed what looked to be the upper corner of a cave. In the dim, flickering light he couldn't tell how far down it went, but a tossed rock seemed to fall forever.

The wind howled. He jumped, stumbled, and laughed shakily at himself. It was just the storm rushing past the entrance; he hadn't gone so far in that he wouldn't be able to hear it.

Then his torch blew out.

:Chosen!:

:No, it's okay. I'm all right.: His startled shout still echoed, bouncing back and forth inside the tunnels. *:I'm in the dark, but I'm okay.:* Again, he set his bow aside and pulled his tinderbox from his belt pouch with trembling fingers. *Get a grip, Jors,* he told himself firmly. *You're a Herald. Heralds are not afraid of the dark.*

And then the tunnel twisted. Flung to his knees and then his side, Jors wrapped his head in his arms and tried to present as small a target as possible to the falling rock. The earth heaved as though a giant creature deep below struggled to get free. With a deafening roar, a section of the tunnel collapsed. Lifted and slammed against a pile of rock, Jors lost track of up and down. The world became noise and terror and certain death.

Then half his body was suspended over nothing at all. He had a full heartbeat to realize what was happening before he fell, a large amount of loose rock falling with him.

It seemed to go on forever; turning, tumbling, sometimes sliding, knowing that no one could survive the eventual landing.

But he did. Although it took him a moment to realize it.

:Chosen! Jors! Chosen!:

:Gevris . . .: The near panic in his Companion's mind-touch pulled him up out of a gray-and-red blanket of pain, the need to reassure the young stallion delaying his own hysteria. *:I'm alive. Calm down, I'm alive.:* He spit out a mouthful of blood and tried to move.

Most of the rock that had fallen with him seemed to have landed on his legs. Teeth clenched, he flexed his toes inside his boots and almost cried in relief at the response. Although muscles from thigh to ankle spasmed, everything worked. :*I don't think I'm even hurt very badly.*: Which was true enough as far as it went. He had no way of telling what kind of injuries lurked under the masking pressure of the rock.

:*I'm coming!*:

:*No, you're not!*: He'd landed on his stomach, facing up a slope of about thirty degrees. He could lift his torso about a handspan. He could move his left arm freely. His right was pined by his side. Breathing heavily, he rested his cheek against the damp rock and closed his eyes. It made no difference to the darkness, but it made him feel better. :*Gevris, you're going to have to go for help. I can't free myself, and you can't even get to me.*: He tried to envision his map, tried to trace the route they'd taken tracking the cat, tried to work out distances. :*There's a mining settlement closer than the farmstead, just follow the old mine trail, and it should take you right to it.*:

:*But you . . .*:

:*I'm not going anywhere until you get back.*:

I'm not going anywhere, he repeated to the darkness as he felt the presence of his Companion move rapidly away. *I'm not going anywhere.* Unfortunately, as the mountain pressed in on him and all he could hear was his own terror filling the silence, that was exactly what he was afraid of.

It was hard to hear anything over the storm that howled around the chimneys and shutters, but Ari's ears were her only contact with the world and she'd learned to sift sound for value. Head cocked, tangled hair falling over the ruin of her eyes, she listened. *Rider coming. Galloping hard.* She smiled, smug and silent. Not much went on that she didn't know about first. *Something must've gone wrong somewhere. Only reason to be riding so hard in this kind of weather.*

The storm had been no surprise, not with her stumps

aching so for the past two days. She rubbed at them, hacking and spitting into the fire.

"Mama, Auntie Ari did it again."

"Hush, Robin. Leave her alone."

That's right, leave me alone. She spat once more, just because she knew the child would still be watching, then lifted herself on her palms and hand-walked toward her bench in the corner.

"Ari, can I get you something?"

Sometimes she thought they'd never learn. Grunting a negative, because ignoring them only brought renewed and more irritating offers, she swung herself easily up onto the low bench just as the pounding began. *Sounds like they didn't even dismount. I can't wait.*

"Who can it be at this hour?"

Her cousin, Dyril. *Answer it and find out, idiot.*

"Stone me, it's a horse!"

The sound of hooves against the threshold was unmistakable. She could hear the creak of leather harness, the snorting and blowing of an animal ridden hard, could even smell the hot scent of it from all the way across the room—but somehow it didn't add up to horse.

And while the noises it was making were certainly horselike . . .

From the excited babble at the door, Ari managed to separate two bits of relevant information; the horse was riderless and it was nearly frantic about something.

"What color is it?"

It took a moment for Ari to recognize the rough and unfamiliar voice as her own. A stunned silence fell, and she felt the eyes of her extended family turned on her. Her chin rose and her lips thinned. "Well?" she demanded, refusing to let them see she was as startled as they were. "What color is it?"

"He's not an it, Auntie Ari, he's a he. And he's white. And his eyes are blue. And horses don't got blue eyes."

Young Robin was obviously smarter than she'd suspected. "Of course they don't. It's not a horse, you rockheaded morons. Can't you recognize a Companion when you see one?"

The Companion made a sound that could only be agreement. As the babble of voices broke out again, Ari snorted and shook her head in disbelief.

"A Companion without a Herald?"

"Is it searching?"

"What happened to the Herald?"

Ari heard the Companion spin and gallop away, return and gallop away again.

"I think it wants us to follow it."

"Maybe its Herald is hurt, and it's come here for help."

And did you figure that out all on your own? Ari rubbed at her stumps as various members of the family scrambled for jackets and boots and some of the children were sent to rouse the rest of the settlement.

When with a great thunder of hooves, the rescue party galloped off, she beat her head lightly against the wall, trying not to remember.

"Auntie Ari?"

Robin. Made brave no doubt by her breaking silence. Well, she wouldn't do it again.

"Auntie Ari, tell me about Companions." He had a high-pitched, imperious little voice. "Tell me."

Tell him about Companions. Tell him about the time spent at the Collegium wishing her Blues were Gray. Tell him how the skills of mind and hand that had earned her a place seemed so suddenly unimportant next to the glorious honor of being Chosen. Tell him of watching them gallop across Companion's Field, impossibly beautiful, impossibly graceful—infinitely far from her mechanical world of stresses and supports and levers and gears.

Tell him how she'd made certain she was never in the village when the Heralds came through riding circuit because it hurt so much to see such beauty and know she could never be a part of it. Tell him how after the accident she'd stuffed her fingers in her ears at the first sound of bridle bells.

Tell him any or all of that?

"You saw them, didn't you, Auntie Ari. You saw them up close when you were in the city."

"Yes." And then she regretted she'd said so much.

:Chosen! I've brought hands to dig you out!:
Jors released a long, shuddering breath that warmed the rock under his cheek and tried very, very hard not to cry.

:Chosen?:
The distress in his Companion's mind-touch helped him pull himself together. *:I'm okay. As okay as I was, anway. I just, I just missed you.:* Gevris' presence settled gently into his mind, and he clung to it, more afraid of dying alone in the dark than of just dying.

:Do not think of dying.:
He hadn't realized he'd been thinking of it in such a way as to be heard. *:Sorry. I guess I'm not behaving much like a Herald, am I?:*

A very equine snort made him smile. *:You are a Herald. Therefore, this is how Heralds behave trapped in a mine.:*

The Companion's tone suggested he not argue the point so he changed the subject. *:How did you manage to communicate with the villagers?:*

:When they recognized what I was, they followed me. Once they saw where you were, they understood. Some have returned to the village for tools.: He paused and Jors had the feeling he was deciding whether or not to pass on one last bit of information. *:They call this place the Demon's Den.:*

:Oh, swell.:
:There are no real demons in it.:
:That makes me feel so much better.:
:It should,: Gevris pointed out helpfully.

"Herald's down in the Demon's Den." The storm swirled the voice in through the open door stirring the room up into a frenzy of activity. All the able-bodied who hadn't followed the Companion ran for jackets and boots. The rest buzzed like a nest of hornets poked with a stick.

Ari sat in her corner, behind the tangled tent of her hair, and tried not to remember.

There was a rumble, deep in the bowels of the hillside, a warning of worse to come. But they kept working because Ari had braced the tunnels so cleverly that the earth could move as it liked and the mine would move with it, flexing instead of shattering.

But this time, the earth moved in a way she hadn't anticipated. Timbers cracked. Rock began to fall. Someone screamed.

Jors jerked his head up and hissed through his teeth in pain.

:Chosen?:

:I can hear them. I can hear them digging.: The distant sound of metal against stone was unmistakable.

Then it stopped.

:Gevris? What's wrong? What's happening?:

:Their lanterns keep blowing out. This hillside is so filled with natural passageways that when the winds are strong, they can't keep anything lit.:

:And it's in an unstable area.: Jors sighed and rested his forehead against the back of his left wrist. *:What kind of an idiot would put a mine in a place like this?:*

:The ore deposits were very good.:

:How do you know?: Their familiar banter was all that was keeping him from despair.

:These people talk a great deal.:

:And you listen.: He clicked his tongue, knowing his Companion would pick up the intent if not the actual noise. *:Shame on you. Eavesdroppers never hear good of themselves.:*

Only the chime of a pebble, dislodged from somewhere up above answered.

:Gevris?:

:There was an accident.:

:Was anyone hurt?:

:I don't . . . no, not badly. They're coming out.:

He felt a rising tide of anger before he "heard" his Companion's next words.

;They're not going back in! I can't make them go back in! They say it's too dangerous! They say they need the light! I can't make them go back in.:

In his mind Jors could see the young stallion, rearing and kicking and trying to block the miners who were leaving him there to die. He knew it was his imagination, for their bond had never been strong enough for that kind of contact. He also knew his imagination couldn't be far wrong when the only answer to his call was an overwhelming feeling of angry betrayal.

The damp cold had crept through his leathers and begun to seep into his bones. He'd fallen just before full dark and, although time was hard to track buried in the hillside, it had to still be hours until midnight. Nights were long at this time of the year and it would grow much, much colder before sunrise.

Ari knew when Dyril and the others returned that they didn't have the Herald with them. Knew it even before the excuses began.

"That little shake we had earlier was worse up there. What's left of the tunnels could go at any minute. We barely got Neegan out when one of the last supports collapsed."

"You couldn't get to him."

It wasn't a question. Not really. If they'd been able to get to him, they'd have brought him back.

"Him, her. We couldn't even keep the lanterns lit."

Someone tossed their gear to the floor. "You know what it's like up there during a storm; the wind howling through all those cracks and crevasses. . . ."

Ari heard Dyril sigh, heard wood creak as he dropped onto a bench. "We'll go back in the morning. Maybe when we can see. . . ."

Memories were thick in the silence.

"If it's as bad as all that, the Herald's probably dead anyway."

"He's alive!" Ari shouted over the murmur of

agreement. Oh, sure, they'd feel better if they thought the Herald was dead, if they could convince themselves they hadn't left him there to die, but she wasn't going to let them off so easily.

"You don't know that."

"The Companion knows it!" She bludgeoned them with her voice because it was all she had. "He came to you for help!"

"And we did what we could! The Queen'll understand. The Den's taken too many lives already for us to throw more into it."

"Do you think I don't know that?" She could hear the storm throwing itself against the outside of the house but nothing from within. It almost seemed as though she were suddenly alone in the room. Then she heard a bench pushed back, footsteps approaching.

"Who else do you want that mine to kill?" Dyril asked quietly. "We lost three getting you out. Wasn't that enough?"

It was three too many, she wanted to say. *If you think I'm grateful, think again.* But the words wouldn't come. She swung down off her bench and hand-walked along the wall to the ladder in the corner. Stairs were difficult but with only half a body to lift, she could easily pull herself, hand over hand, from rung to rung—her arms and shoulders were probably stronger now than they'd ever been. Adults couldn't stand in the loft so no one bothered her there.

"We did all we could," she heard Dyril repeat wearily, more to himself than to her. She supposed she believed him. He was a good man. They were all good people. They wouldn't leave anyone to die if they had any hope of getting them out.

She was trapped with four others, deep underground. They could hear someone screaming, the sound carried on the winds that howled through the caves and passages around the mine.

By the time they could hear rescuers frantically digging with picks and shovels, there were only three of them still alive. Ari hadn't been able to feel her legs for some time, so when they pried enough rubble clear to get a rope through, she forced her companions out first. The Demon's Den had been her mine and they were used to following her orders.

Then the earth moved again and the passage closed. She lay there, alone, listening to still more death carried on the winds and wishing she'd had the courage to tell them to leave her. To get out while they still could.

"Papa, what happened to the Companion?"

"He's still out there. Brandon tried to bring him into the stable and got a nasty bite for his trouble."

Ari moved across the loft to the narrow dormer and listened. Although the wind shrieked and whistled around the roof, she could hear the frenzied cries of the Companion as he pounded through the settlement, desperately searching for someone who could help.

"Who else do you want that mine to kill?"

She dug through the mess on the floor for a leather strap and tied her hair back off her face. Her jacket lay crumpled in a damp pile where she'd left it, but that didn't matter. It'd be damper still before she was done.

Down below, the common room emptied as the family headed for their beds, voices rising and falling, some needing comfort and absolution, some giving it. Ari didn't bother to listen. It didn't concern her.

Later, in the quiet, she swarmed down the ladder and hand-walked to where she'd heard the equipment dropped and sorted out a hundred-foot coil of rope. Draping it across her chest, she continued to the door. The latch was her design; her fingers remembered it.

The ground felt cold and wet under the heavy calluses on her palms, and she was pretty sure she felt wet snow in the rain that slapped into her face. She moved out away from the house and waited.

Hooves thundered past her, around her, and stopped.

"No one," she said, "knows the Den better than I do. I'm the only chance your Herald has left. You've probably called for others—other Heralds, other Companions—but they can't be close enough to help or you wouldn't still be hanging around here. The temperature's dropping, and time means everything now."

The Companion snorted, a great gust of warm, sweetly-scented breath replacing the storm for a moment. She hadn't realized he'd stopped so close, and she fought to keep from trembling.

"I know what you're thinking. But I won't need eyes in the darkness, and you don't dig with legs and feet. If you can get me there, Shining One, I can get your Herald out."

The Companion reared and screamed a challenge.

Ari held up her hands. "I know you understand me," she said. "I know you're more than you appear. You've got to believe me. I *will* get your Herald out.

"If you lie down, I can grab the saddle horn and the cantle and hold myself on between them." On a horse, it would never work, even if she could lift herself on, she'd never stay in the saddle once it started to move; her stumps were too short for balance. But then, she wouldn't be having this conversation with a horse.

A single whicker, and a rush of displaced air as a large body went to the ground a whisker's distance from her.

Ari reached out, touched one silken shoulder, and worked her way back. *You* must *be desperate to be going along with this,* she thought bitterly. *Never mind. You'll see.* Mounting was easy. Staying in the saddle as the Companion rose to his feet was another thing entirely. Somehow, she managed it. "All right." A deep breath and she balanced her weight as evenly as she could, stumps spread. "Go."

He leaped forward so suddenly he nearly threw her off. Heart in her throat, she clung to the saddle as his pace settled to an almost gentle rocking motion completely at odds with the speed she knew he had to be traveling. She could feel the night whipping by her, rain and snow stinging her face.

In spite of everything, she smiled. She was on a Companion. Riding a Companion.

It was over too soon.

*   *   *

:Jors? Chosen!:

The Herald coughed and lifted his head. He'd been having the worst dream about being trapped in a cave-in. *That's what I get for eating my own cooking.* And then he tried to move his legs and realized he wasn't dreaming.: *Gevris! You went away!:*

:I'm sorry, heart-brother. Please forgive me, but when they wouldn't stay. . . .: The thought trailed off, lost in an incoherent mix of anger and shame.

:It's all right.: Jors carefully pushed his own terror back in order to reassure the Companion. *:You're back now, that's all that matters.:*

:I brought someone to get you out.:

:But I thought the mine was unstable, still collapsing.:

:She says she can free you.:

:You're talking to her?: As far as Jors knew, that *never* happened. Even some Heralds were unable to mind-touch clearly.

:She's talking to me. I believe she can do what she says.:

Jors swallowed and took a deep breath. *:No. It's too dangerous. There's already been one accident. I don't want anyone dying because of me.:*

:Chosen . . . The Companion's mind-touch held a tone Jors had never heard before. *:I don't think she's doing it for you.:*

When they stopped, Ari took a moment to work some feeling back into each hand in turn. *Herald's probably going to have my finger marks permanently denting his gear.* Below her, the Companion stood perfectly still, waiting.

"We're going to have to do this together, Shining One, because if I do it alone, I'll be too damned slow. Go past the mine about fifty feet and look up. Five, maybe six feet off the ground there should be a good solid shelf of rock. If you can get us onto it, we can follow it right to the mouth of the mine and avoid all that shale shit."

The Companion whickered once and started walking. When she felt him turn, Ari scooted back as far as she could in the saddle, and flopped forward, trapping the coil of rope under her chest. Stretching her arms down and around the sleek curve of his barrel, she pushed the useless stirrups out of her way and clutched the girth.

"Go," she grunted.

~~He backed up a few steps, lunged forward, and the~~ world tilted at a crazy angle.

Ari held her uncomfortable position until he stopped on the level ground at the mouth of the mine. "Remind me," she coughed, rubbing the spot where the saddle horn had slammed into her throat, "not to do that again. All right, Shining One, I'll have to get off the same way I got on."

His movement took her by surprise. She grabbed for the saddle, her cold fingers slipped on the wet leather, and she dismounted a lot farther from the ground than she'd intended.

A warm muzzle pushed into her face as she lay there for a moment, trying to get her breath back. "I'm okay," she muttered. "Just a little winded." Teeth gritted against the pain in her stumps, she pushed herself up.

Soft lips nuzzled at her hair.

"Don't worry, Shining One." Tentatively she reached out and stroked the Companion's velvet nose. "I'll get your Herald out. There's enough of me left for that." She tossed her head and turned toward the mine, not needing eyes to find the gaping hole in the hillside. Icy winds dragged across her cheeks, and she knew by their touch that they'd danced through the Demon's Den before they came to her.

"Now, then . . ." She was pleased to hear that her voice remained steady. ". . . we need to work out a way to communicate. At the risk of sounding like a bad Bardic tale, how about one whicker for yes and two for no?"

There was a single, soft whicker just above her head.

"Good. First of all, we have to find out how badly he . . ." A pause. "Your Herald *is* a he?" At the Companion's affirmative, she went on. ". . . how badly he's hurt. Ask him if he has any broken bones."

:I don't know. I can't move enough to tell.:

Ari frowned at the answer. "Yes and no? Is he buried?"

:Only half of me.:
:Chosen, I have no way to tell her that.:
:Then, yeah, I guess I'm buried.:

"Shit." There could be broken bones under the rock, the pressure keeping the Herald from feeling the pain. Well, she'd just have to deal with that when she got to it. "Is he buried in the actual mine, or in a natural cave?"

:She seems to think it's good you're in a natural cave.:
Jors traced the rock that curved away from him with his free hand. His fingers were so numb he could barely feel it. *:Why?:*
:I can't ask her that, Chosen. She wants to know if you turned left around a corner, about thirty feet in from the entrance to the mine.:
:Left?: He tried to remember, but the cold had seeped into his brain and thoughts moved sluggishly through it.
"I—I guess so."

"Okay." Ari tied one end of the rope around her waist as she spoke. "Ask him if the quake happened within, say, twenty feet of that corner."

:I don't know. I don't remember. Gevris, I'm tired. Just stay with me while I rest.:
:No! Heart-brother, do not *go to sleep. Think, please, were you close to the corner?:*
He remembered seeing the blood. Then stopping and looking into the hole in the side of the tunnel. *:Yes. I think no more than twenty feet.:*

"Good. We're in luck, there's only one place on this level where the cave system butts up against the mine. I know approximately where he is. He's close." She reached forward and sifted a handful of rubble. "I just have to get to him."

A hundred feet of rope would reach the place where the quake threw him out of the mine, but, after that, she could only hope he hadn't slid too deep into the catacombs.

Turning to where she could feel the bulk of the Companion, Ari's memory showed her a graceful white stallion, outlined against the night. "Once I get the rope around him, you'll have to pull him free."

He whickered once and nudged her and she surrendered to the urge to bury face and fingers in his mane. When she finally let go, she had to bite her lip to keep from crying. "Thanks. I'm okay now."

Using both arms at once, then swinging her body forward between them, Ari made her way into the mine, breathing in the wet, oily scent of the rock, the lingering odors of the lanterns Dyril and the others had used, and the stink of fear, old and new. At the first rockfall she paused, traced the broken pieces, and found the passage the earlier rescue party had dug.

Her shoulder brushed a timber support and she hurried past the memories.

A biting gust of wind whistled through a crack up ahead, flinging grit up into her face. "Nice try," she muttered. "But you threw me into darkness five summers ago and I've learned my way around." Then she raised her voice. "Shining One, can you still hear me?"

The Companion's whicker echoed eerily.

"You don't need to worry about him running out of air, this place is like a sieve, so remind your Herald to keep moving. Tell him to keep flexing his muscles if that's all he can do. He's got to keep the blood going out to the extremities."

:What extremities?: Jors heard himself giggle and wondered what there was to laugh about.

:Chosen, listen to me. You know what the cold can do. You have to move.:

:I know that.: Everyone knew that. It wasn't like he

hadn't been paying attention when they'd been teaching winter survival skills, it was just, well, it was just so much effort.

:*Wiggle your toes!*:

Gevris somehow managed to sound exactly like the Weaponsmaster, and Jors found himself responding instinctively. To his surprise, his toes still wiggled. And it still hurt. The pain burned some of the frost out of his brain and left him gasping for breath, but he was thinking more clearly than he had been in some time. With his Companion's encouragement, he began to systematically work each muscle that still responded.

The biggest problem with digging out the Demon's Den had always been that the rock shattered into pieces so small it was like burrowing through beads in a box. The slightest jar would sent the whole crashing to the ground.

Her eyes in her fingertips, Ari inched toward the buried Herald, not digging but building a passageway, each stone placed exactly to hold the weight of the next. Slowly, with exquisite care, she moved up and over the rockfall that had nearly killed Neegan. She lightly touched the splintered end of the shattered support, then went on. She had no time to mourn the past.

Years of destruction couldn't erase her knowledge of the mine. She'd been trapped in it for too long.

"Herald? Can you hear me?"

Jors turned his face toward the sudden breeze. "Yes . . ." :*Gevris, she's here!*:

:*Good.*: Although he sounded relieved, Jors realized the Companion didn't sound the least bit surprised.

:*You knew she'd make it.*:

Again the strange tone the Herald didn't recognize. :*I believed her when she said she'd get you out.*:

"Cover your head with your hands, Herald."

Startled, he curved his left arm up and around his head just in time to prevent a small shower of stones from ringing off his skull.

"I'm on my way down."

A moment later he felt the space around him fill, and a rough jacket pressed hard against his cheek.

"Sorry. Just let me get turned."

Turned? Teeth chattering from the cold, he strained back as far as he could but knew it would make little difference. There wasn't room for a cat to turn let alone a person. To his astonishment, his rescuer seemed to double back on herself.

"Ow. Not a lot of head room down here."

From the sound of her voice and the touch of her hands, she had to be sitting tight up against his side, her upper body bent across his back. He tried to force his half-frozen mind to work. "Your legs . . ."

"Are well out of the way, Herald. Trust me." Ari danced her fingers over the pile of rubble that pinned him. "Can you still move your toes."

It took him a moment to remember how. "Yes."

"Good. You're at the bottom of a roughly wedge-shaped crevasse. Fortunately, you're pointing the right way. As soon as I get enough of you clear, I'm going to tie this rope around you, and your Companion on the other end is going to inch you up the slope as I uncover your legs. That means if anything's broken, it's going to drag, but if we don't do it that way, there won't be room down here for me, you, and the rock. Do you understand?"

"Yes."

"Good." One piece at a time, she began to free his right side.

:*Gevris, she doesn't have any legs.*:

:*I know.*:

:*How did she get here?*:

:*I brought her.*:

:*That's impossible!*:

The Companion snorted. :*Obviously not. She's blind, too.*:

"What!" His incredulous exclamation echoed through the Demon's Den.

Ari snorted and jammed a rock into the crack between

two others. It wasn't difficult to guess what had caused that reaction, not when she knew the silence had to be filled with dialogue she couldn't hear. She waited for him to say something Herald-like and nauseating about overcoming handicaps as though they were all she was.

To her surprise, he said only, "What's your name?"

It took her a moment to find her voice. "Ari."

"Jors."

She nodded, even though she knew he couldn't see the gesture. "Herald Jors."

"Are you one of the miners?"

Why was he talking to her when he had his Companion to keep him company? "Not exactly." So far tonight, she'd said more than she'd said in the five summers since the accident. Her throat ached.

"Gevris says he's never seen anyone do what you did to get in here. He says you didn't dig through the rubble, you built a tunnel around you using nothing but your hands."

"Gevris?"

"My Companion. He's very impressed. He believes you can get me out."

Ari swallowed hard. His Companion believed in her. It was almost funny in a way. "You can move your arm now."

"Actually," he gasped, trying not to writhe, "no, I can't." He felt her reach across him, tuck her hand under his chest, and grab his wrist. He could barely feel her touch against his skin.

"On three." She pulled immediately before he could tense.

"That wasn't very nice," he grunted when he could speak again.

She ignored his feeble attempt to tug his arm out of her hands and continued rubbing life back into the chilled flesh. "There's nothing wrong with it. It's just numb because you've been lying on it in the cold."

"Oh? Are you a Healer, then?"

He sounded so indignant that she smiled and actually

answered the question. "No, I was a mining engineer. I designed this mine."

"Oh." He'd wondered what kind of idiot would put a mine in a place like this. Now he knew.

Ari heard most of the thought and gritted her teeth. "Keep flexing the muscles." Untying the end of the rope from around her own waist, she retied it just under the Herald's arms. It felt strange to touch a young man's body again after so long. Strange and uncomfortable. She twisted and began to free his legs.

Jors listened to her breathing and thought of being alone in darkness forever.

:*I'm here, Chosen.*:

:*I know. But I wasn't thinking of me. I was thinking about Ari . . . Ari . . .*: "Were you at the Collegium?"

"I was."

"You redesigned the hoists from the kitchen so they'd stop jamming. And you fixed that pump in Bardic that kept flooding the place. *And* you made the practice dummy that . . ."

"That was a long time ago."

"Not so long," Jors protested trying to ignore the sudden pain as she lifted a weight off his hips. "You left the Blues the summer I was Chosen."

"Did I?"

"They were all talking about you. They said there wasn't anything you couldn't build. What happened?"

Her hands paused. "I came home. Be quiet. I have to listen." It wasn't exactly a lie.

Working as fast as she could, Ari learned the shape of the stone imprisoning the Herald, its strengths, its weaknesses. It was all so very familiar. The tunnel she'd built behind her ended here. She finished it in her head, and nodded, once, as the final piece slid into place.

"Herald Jors, when I give you the word, have your Companion pull gently but firmly on the rope until I tell you to stop. I can't move the rest of this off of you so I'm going to have to move you out from under it."

Jors nodded, realized how stupid that was, and said, "I understand."

Ari pushed her thumbs under the edge of a rock and took a deep breath. "Now."

The rock shifted, but so did the Herald.

"Stop." She changed her grip. "Now." A stone fell. She blocked it with her shoulder. "Stop."

Inch by inch, teeth clenched against the pain of returning circulation, Jors moved up the slope, clinging desperately to the rope.

"Stop."

"I'm out."

"I know. Now, listen carefully because this is important. On my way in, I tried to lay the rope so it wouldn't snag, but your Companion will have to drag you clear without stopping—one long smooth motion, no matter what."

"No matter what?" Jors repeated, twisting to peer over his shoulder, the instinctive desire to see her face winning out over the reality. The loose slope he was lying on shifted.

"Hold still!" Ari snapped. "Do you want to bury yourself again?"

Jors froze. "What's going to happen, Ari?"

Behind him, in the darkness, he heard her sigh. "Do you know what a keystone is, Herald?"

"It's the stone that takes the weight of the other stones and holds up the arch."

"Essentially. The rock that fell on your legs fell in such a way as to make it the keystone for this cavern we're in."

"But you didn't move the rock."

"No, but I did move your legs, and they were part of it."

"Then what's supporting the keystone?" He knew before she answered.

"I am."

"No."

"No *what*, Herald?"

"No. I won't let you sacrifice your life for mine."

"Yet Heralds are often called upon to give their lives for others."

"That's different."

"Why?" Her voice cracked out of the darkness like a whip. "You're allowed to be noble, but the rest of us aren't? You're so good and pure and perfect and Chosen and the rest of us don't even have lives worth throwing away? Don't you see how stupid that is? Your life is worth infinitely more than mine!" She stopped and caught her breath on the edge of a sob. "There should never have been a mine here. Do you know why I dug it? To prove I was as good as all those others who were Chosen when I wasn't. I was smarter. I wanted it as much. Why not me? And do you know what my pride did, Herald? It killed seventeen people when the mine collapsed. And then my cowardice killed my brother and an uncle and a woman barely out of girlhood because I was afraid to die. My life wasn't worth all those lives. Let my death be worth your life at least."

He braced himself against her pain. "I can't let you die for me."

"And yet if our positions were reversed, you'd expect me to let you die for me." She ground the words out through the shards of broken bones, of broken dreams. "Heralds die for what they believe in all the time. Why can't I?"

"You've got it wrong, Ari," he told her quietly. "Heralds die, I won't deny that. And we all know we may have to sacrifice ourselves someday for the greater good. But we don't *die* for what we believe in. We *live* for it."

Ari couldn't stop shaking, but it wasn't from the cold or even from the throbbing pain in her stumps.

"Who else do you want that mine to kill?"

"This, all this, is my responsibility. I won't let it kill anyone else."

Because he couldn't reach her with his hands, Jors put his heart in his voice and wrapped it around her. "Neither will I. What will happen if you grab my legs and Gevris pulls us both free?"

He heard her swallow. "The tunnel will collapse."

"All at once?"

"No . . ."

"It'll begin here and follow us?"

"Yes. But not even a Companion could pull us out that quickly."

:Gevris . . .: Jors sketched the situation. *:Do you think you can beat the collapse?:*

:Yes, but do you think you can survive the trip? You'll be dragged on your stomach through a rock tunnel.:

:Well, I'm not going to survive much longer down here, that's for certain—I'm numb from my neck to my knees. I'm in leathers. I should be okay.:

:What about your head?:

:Good point.: "Ari, you're wearing a heavy sheepskin coat, can you work part of it up over your head."

"Yes, but . . ."

"Do it. And watch for falling rock, I'm going to do the same."

"What about your pack?"

He'd forgotten all about it. Letting the loop of rope under his armpits hold his weight, he managed to secure it like a kind of crude helmet.

"Grab hold of my ankles, Ari."

"I . . ."

"Ari, I can't force you to live. I can only ask you not to die."

He felt a tentative touch, and then a firmer hold.

:Go, Gevris!:

They stayed at the settlement for nearly a week. Although the Healer assured him that the hours spent trapped in the cold and the damp had done no permanent damage, Jors wore a stitched cut along his jaw as a remembrance of the passage out of the Demon's Den.

Ari was learning to live again. She still carried the weight of the lives lost to her pride, but she'd found the strength to bear the load.

"Don't expect sweetness and light, though," she cautioned the Herald as he and Gevris prepared to leave. "I was irritating and opinionated before the accident." Her mouth crooked slightly, and she added, with just a hint of the old bitterness, "I expect that's why I was never Chosen."

Jors grinned as Gevris pushed his head into her shoulder. "He says you were chosen for something else."

"He said that?" Ari lifted her hand and lightly stroked the Companion's face. She smiled, the expression feeling strange and new. "Then I guess I'd better get on with it."

As they were riding out of the settlement to take up their interrupted circuit again, Jors turned back to wave and saw Ari sketching something wondrous in the air, prodded by the piping questions of young Robin.

:*I guess she won't be alone in the dark anymore.*:

Gevris tossed his head. :*She never had to be.*:

:*Sometimes it's hard for people to realize that.*: They rode in silence for a moment, then Jors sighed, watching his breath plume in the frosty air. :*I'm glad they found the body of that cat—I'd hate to have to go back into the Den to look for it.*: Their route would take them nowhere near the Demon's Den. :*That was as close to the Havens as I want to come for a while.*: And then he realized.

:*Gevris, you knew Ari wanted to die down there!*:

:*Yes.*:

:*Then why did you let her go into that mine?*:

:*Because I believed she could free you.*:

:*But . . .*:

:*And,*: the Companion continued, :*I believed you could free her.*:

Ironrose

by Larry Dixon
and Mel. White

Larry Dixon is the husband of Mercedes Lackey, and a successful artist as well as science fiction writer. Other stories co-authored by him appear in *Dinosaur Fantastic,* and *Deals With the Devil.* He and Mercedes live in Oklahoma.

Mel. White is an accomplished writer whose work also appears in *Witch Fantastic* and *Aladdin: Master of the Lamp.*

The tiny forge's flames comforted Ironrose. Its presence was a constant in his life; not always a focus of his attention, but there. Its fingers were of flame, which didn't caress him as a lover or massage him, but still provided comfort to him. The spring which fed water to its mechanical bellows was another constant, shaped by Adept magic to a simple water funnel that split off for quenching and tempering.

Tempering was another constant in Ironrose's life. He had always tempered himself, reciting oaths silently when upset, bringing his spirits up with songs when saddened. Sadness, though, had come to perch on his forge like a wingbroken vulture of late. His hard work was valued by the Clan, and his skills were ranked well above the average for Artificers. He was also well-thought-of among his Hawkbrother brethren—

—when he was thought of at all. And that was why sadness was making his temper brittle.

"Ironrose? I've brought your game."

He turned from the forge and laid down his tools. It

was Sunrunner, the lithe, strong hunter, only two-thirds his height, half his weight, and utterly unattainable. She set down an overstuffed game bag on a chipped worktable, and a sack of greens and wild herbs a moment later. She looked at him expectantly.

"Ah. Sunrunner. Ah, thank you," he stammered. How foolish he must look! The largest of his Clan, all callused fingers and strong arms, intimidated by this young hunter. And surely she knew it. How could she not? His sweating certainly wasn't from the forge's heat. He caught himself staring at her as she stood in a shaft of the late afternoon sunlight, with dust motes dancing all around her. A sudden fire burned in the pit of his stomach and he wiped his sweaty palms on his thick apron, trying to calm the sudden thunder of his heart. It was all too embarrassing, and he tried to cover it by searching for the arrowheads and bow fittings he'd made for her. They'd been put somewhere. Sunrunner stood, looking quietly at him.

Where was Tullin when he was needed?

Tullin was, in fact, behind the forge polishing an iron ring with a small file. Absorbed in his task, he hadn't noticed the hunter's entry, but he did notice when Ironrose's hammer blows stilled. That meant a visitor; someone to pick up an order or barter for the smith's services. The small *hertasi* cocked his head and flicked his tongue to taste the air. The scent identified the late afternoon visitor as the hunter, Sunrunner. Lately Ironrose had reacted like a spooked rabbit every time she visited the forge building. Ghosting up behind the smith, he tasted the air again to catch the nuances of Ironrose's scent. No doubt about it—courting pheremones. He blinked his large gold eyes in delight as he studied the scene. The lonely human had finally selected a mate: the hunter that his own mate served.

"Tullin!" Ironrose turned and found the small *hertasi* standing beside him, silently holding half a dozen arrowheads and the bow-fittings toward him. The smith accepted them with a growl and turned back to Sunrunner as Tullin collected the game bag and herbs. He identified the contents—rabbit, a tiny marshbuck, and tubers from the southern marsh—more than enough to feed the smith for two days. The hunter kept her bargain well.

Tullin watched Sunrunner trace a careful finger over the sharp edges of an arrowhead. She was a good provider: a quiet woman who appreciated well-crafted things. According to his mate, Coulsie, Sunrunner was also very even tempered. Emotionally, she was well suited to live with the shy metalsmith.

Critically, Tullin eyed her figure. Her legs were strong; her hips deep and wide; adequate for large babies—perhaps a bit too large for *hertasi* standards, but necessary for a woman of the Hawkbrothers. Tullin picked up the two bags of food and ghosted toward the rear door of the smithy. "You and she will be a very good match," he observed casually as he headed toward the kitchen. "When will you offer her a love token?"

"TULLIN!!!" Ironrose wheeled, gaping after him in outraged indignation. Sunrunner stood frozen in surprise. But all they saw of the *hertasi* was the mischievous flick of a silvery-scaled tail as Tullin vanished through the doorway.

Tullin's mate, Coulsie, was tall and stocky, with an air of quiet competence about her. She bobbed her head affectionately in greeting as he trotted in. He nuzzled her snout, tasting her warm, enticing scent.

"You take care of the hunter, Sunrunner, don't you?" he asked as he set down the bag with the rabbits. She nodded, handing him a sharp knife for skinning before selecting a knife for herself.

"My Ironrose is most interested in her. I think he needs to take her as his mate."

She slid her eyes toward him, her nostrils flared with surprise. "She is one who walks alone. She does not need a mate."

"Nonsense. Have you tasted their body scents when they are near each other? I have. They have a hunger for each other—and we both know how lonely they are.

The only thing that keeps them from courting others is
their own belief that no one would want such as they
for a mate. This sorrow over their inner selves is only
an old path that they tread. Mated, they will overcome
these things."

She gave a quick head jerk in protest, but he nuzzled
the point of her jaw and whispered softly, "Besides, what
finer service can we offer than to bring the Hawkbrothers that which they most desire?"

Sunrunner's day had been as bad as the previous ten.
Her hunting had been dismal, but she stayed by her barter with the ironcrafter and gave him the best she'd
taken. The weather had been cold and damp. The sea-
sonal dance was tonight, and she was one of the few
hunters and scouts who wouldn't be going. She cloaked
herself in bravado among her peers, taking this night on
watch "so they could enjoy themselves," but the truth
of the matter was that when it came to celebrations, she
was a gray sparrow, as exciting as tree bark. So it had
always been.

It didn't make sense, she repeated in her mind, as she
had hundreds of times before. It didn't make sense. She
was attractive enough; a hard worker, and responsible.
Yet where were her suitors? Some of the scouts were
like the rabbits they hunted, yet she was never offered
a trysting feather.

It was a vicious trap—they didn't pursue her, so she
stayed away from where they might. She left scout meet-
ings early, avoided celebrations and gatherings, and became part of the forest at the slightest indication of
direct attention from a potential lover. Besides, just any
lover wasn't really what she wanted in her heart.

It didn't make sense, she thought, for yet another
time.

But what could be done?

There was no doubt in Tullin's mind what needed to
come next. The next step, of course, was to work on
Ironrose, who was as stubborn as the mountains and as

open to subtle hints as the rocks themselves. It would take a direct line, Tullin decided as he reentered the forge room. The smith was hammering away furiously on an arrowhead. He was putting too much force into the blows.

"Is that your love token for her? Usually they like something a little less practical," he observed, his tailtip twitching with amusement.

The smith turned, scowling. "I am in no mood for *hertasi* jokes," he thundered. Tullin raised his chin, baring his throat in a submissive gesture. "I had no intent to offend," he said gently. "Only, you were in a bad mood today and so was she, and I thought that it might do you both good to go to the dance together tonight. But you would not ask, so I thought I'd prod you into action."

"I don't need your help."

"True, but you do need a bath. I will have a hot soak ready for you in a hawk's stoop," Tullin said before Ironrose could muster a decent protest. "I can see tension in your neck and shoulders, and that makes for poor work. And it's irritating your bird."

In response, Ironrose's bondbird, a very old tufted owl, opened one eye for almost an entire minute.

"I don't do poor work, Tullin, and I don't need a soak right now. I've got bow-fittings to design for Tallbush. Folding bow springs and runners, white to red and untempered. I have his drawings right here. . . ."

"Nonsense. You are tense. Your muscles are like ropes and the air tastes of your weariness. There is no one at the pools right now. You can soak for a finger's width of the moon's path and come back to work after that. It will give me time to restock the forge and to bring you the dinner that Coulsie has fixed. When you've eaten and rested, your hammer will ring truer."

Ironrose hesitated and Tullin offered his clinching argument. "Besides, a certain *hertasi* has prepared the third pool to your liking and has sent for a mug of warmed truespice tea and towels by way of an apology to you. It would be a shame to have them go to waste, you know."

Ironrose stared at him for a long moment and then, outsmarted, began removing his apron.

Sunrunner tallied her aches and bruises as she slogged down the path to the bathing pools. She'd almost gotten caught by a damned *wyrsa* while she was out today, and had scrapes and scratches that stung even after being bandaged and salved. She'd also lost three of her new arrowheads somehow, before they were even fletched onto shafts. Now she'd have to barter with the iron-crafter again. If she wasn't so sure that *hertasi* were infallibly trustworthy, she'd almost think Coulsie had taken them. Coulsie had only clucked when asked about them, though, and shooed Sunrunner off to the hot spring, promising to bring the hunter her evening meal while she rested and bathed.

She sniffed the humid air of the bathing pools appreciatively. Surely things were going to get better. She sat on a pad of moss beside a steaming pool and wearily removed her stained and sweaty clothes.

Ironrose yawned sleepily. The heat and the wine had relaxed him, and he was reluctant to go back to work in the forge. There was a slight rustle of leaves from the far edge of the pool. Tullin was announcing his presence, he thought with a grin. Usually the *hertasi* moved silently as the night, but Tullin seemed to be more aware of human needs and occasionally made small noises to alert Ironrose to his presence. He opened his eyes and met the gaze of Sunrunner.

She entered the water unself-consciously, then paused when her eyes met Ironrose's. "I . . . hope you don't mind," she faltered. "Coulsie said this bath would be unoccupied tonight. I guess she didn't speak to your *hertasi*."

"Err . . . no. I didn't mean to stay so long," he fumbled. "Fell asleep in the water." Ironrose reached nervously for his clothes, but found them missing. "Tullin!" he hissed.

"Is something wrong?" Sunrunner asked, splashing water over her sun-browned arms.

He sighed. "Only that the *hertasi* are being entirely too efficient tonight. It seems Tullin thought that my taking a bath would be the perfect chance to take my clothes to be washed and mended."

"I can pick another pool," she said with a smile.

"I'm afraid it's too late," he said wryly.

"You mean . . . ?"

Ironrose nodded. "Efficient *hertasi*. I just saw your clothes vanish. Nothing to do for it but wait till they decide to bring them back."

She glowered at the bushes, then slipped farther into the water. "Oh, well. I'm glad enough to find you here. I've lost some of my arrowheads and need to barter for more of them. Don't know what I did with them; I didn't lose that many arrows hunting."

He scrubbed at his arms with a small pumice stone. "I've got some extras at the shop. You could come by in the morning to pick them up," he offered.

"I'll need three of them," she said. "I'm down to six good arrows now and that's not enough for anything more than small game. I promised Winterstar a marshbuck in exchange for a winter blanket. I'm surprised to find anyone here," she added. "I thought everyone would be at the dance."

He lowered his eyes to his forge-stained fingers, thick from years of hammering metal. "Great clumsy thing like me? At a dance?" he said wryly. "I'd terrorize the dancers and fall on the musicians. You never saw someone so awkward and untalented in your life."

"That's hard to believe," Sunrunner said as she palmed warm water onto her face. "You create some of the most beautiful metalwork. I remember that metal buckle in the shape of a lizard that you made for Starhawk."

He groped for conversation, finding that he enjoyed talking to her, desperate for an excuse to prolong the meeting. A soft rattle at his elbow alerted him that Tullin had returned and he turned to speak to the *hertasi*. But Tullin had vanished, leaving behind a platter of steaming rabbit and herbs—and two plates.

He filled one plate and shyly pushed it toward Sunrunner. "Please . . . won't you join me? There's more than enough, and Tullin brought an extra plate."

She reached for it, smiling her thanks. From his vantage point in the bushes, Tullin blinked his eyes in amusement. Things were going splendidly.

"Move over!" Coulsie hissed, sliding into place beside Tullin. Tsamar and Shonu eeled through the bushes behind her.

"Anything happening?" Shonu whispered though whispers were not necessary. The *hertasi* language sounded like a series of hisses and snorts to the untrained human ear, and blended in with the rustle of the leaves in the wind.

"They're sharing food," Tullin said with satisfaction. "And they're talking, too, about things other than hunting and metalsmithing. It's going splendidly."

Shonu snorted softly. "Splendidly? He misses her signals completely! Look, there, how she hoods her eyes and how her hand signals 'come closer' each time she says something to him. He sits there, nostrils dilated, ready for her, frozen like a statue, afraid to move. This isn't 'splendid,' Tullin. Perhaps we should . . ." A long, clawed hand reached out and wrapped itself around Shonu's snout.

"I remember the last time you had a good idea," Tullin said with ironic humor. "We spent three weeks trying to explain the situation to the Hawkbrothers and getting them all settled down again. Bluethorn didn't speak to me for five days. I don't think we need any suggestions about Ironrose and Sunrunner."

"But . . . but just look at them. At that pace, our children's children will be having children before those two do more than say 'good morning.' Those two need help."

"I remember how well Icefalcon and Eventree fared with your help."

Shonu closed his mouth with a snap. Tullin blinked his amusement and turned back to watch the two in the pool.

"But it all grew *back*," Shonu protested in vain.

Tullin entered the smithy, blinking contentedly in the early morning sunlight. Ironrose was already there, stoking the fires of the forge. He tasted the air out of habit, noting that the smith was in a good mood this morning. Gliding over to the worktable, he examined the sketches that Ironrose had left. Today they'd begin on the new bow fittings for Tallbush. He eyed the design critically. They'd need a fairly flexible blend; one that could take a lot of stress . . . probably one of the eastern Blend Eight ingots. As he turned back toward the ingot storeroom, a scrap of parchment on the floor caught his eye. He bent and picked it up.

It was a drawing of a rose, caught at the earliest flush of bloom; a graceful spiral of stem and petals reaching upward like a promise. He studied it speculatively for a long moment, then tucked it into his tool pouch. He hefted an ingot of Blend Eight and then, on a sudden impulse, added a quarter-ingot of Blend Two to his load.

"Where are the drawings?" Ironrose frowned, pawing through the nominally organized litter on his worktable.

Tullin blinked innocently. "I set them down there, on the corner of your worktable next to the other project. It's still there. Perhaps you picked it up and put it somewhere else?"

Ironrose moved aside the metal bar of Blend Eight. "Not under them. I promised him the fittings would be finished in the next two days," he fretted. "I can't imagine what I've done with them."

"Why don't you work on your love token for Sunrunner while I look for them," Tullin suggested.

"Love token?"

Tullin pointed to the scrap of paper with the rose, lying pinned by the quarter ingot of Blend Two. "A fitting symbol; a gift more enduring than the feather, a thing of inner grace and beauty with a strong outer form. Like yourself, or like the hunter."

Ironrose stared in astonishment. "Really, she's not . . ." he began.

". . . interested in you? Your eyes fail to see what *hertasi* eyes see—how the hunter laughs with you as she does with no other; how her eyes follow you sadly when you leave. Human eyes may not note, but the *hertasi* do. Offer the token. It will not be refused." He leaned back, resting his weight on his tail, a casual pose belied by the interest in his wide eyes.

Ironrose hesitated. "If you think I am wrong, make the rose anyway. If she refuses it as a love token, say that it was only made as a gift.

"You have nothing to lose," he added, closing in for the verbal kill. "If nothing else, she'll probably give you a return gift of a marshbuck quarter."

Ironrose weighed the ingot in his large hand. Tullin blinked mildly and picked up a lightweight hammer from the workbench, silently offering it to the smith. Ironrose scowled and took the hammer and turned back to the forge, grumbling, the design for the rose in his hand.

As soon as the smith's head bent over the design, Tullin darted for the back door.

Coulsie flicked her tailtip in satisfaction as she took the day's kill from Sunrunner. Tullin slithered in the doorway behind Sunrunner, carrying two arrowheads for the hunter's bow. He nodded and touched muzzles with his mate, then handed the arrowheads to Sunrunner.

"I see you've had good hunting," he said. "Here are the three arrowheads you asked for—and two more, as a gift."

Sunrunner took them, bewildered but pleased. "For me? A gift?"

Tullin nodded knowingly. "I think Ironrose is very interested in you. He would like to offer you a courtship token, I think, but he is too afraid you will reject him— as the others have. So I bring these to you for him, though I know he would rather send his heart. He is afraid of love, but would welcome your friendship."

Coulsie hissed at him, shocked at his boldness. Tullin blinked one eye at her, his claws flexing with repressed mischief.

"Ironrose surprises me," Coulsie murmured in the *hertasi* tongue. "It is a good move, but one I thought he was too shy to make."

"I didn't say he SENT the two extra arrowheads, now did I?" Tullin said straight-faced. "Nor did I say that he made them. I said that they were a gift—and so they are. I made them for her myself."

Coulsie flicked her tongue over her muzzle thoughtfully. The Hawkbrothers relied on the truthfulness of the *hertasi* folk, and while Tullin hadn't lied, he hadn't told the full truth, either.

"Tullin . . ." she murmured.

"Trust me," Tullin whispered. "I have a plan."

"Move over, Coulsie! I can't see!" Tullin prodded. "You're blocking the view!"

She looked at him speculatively. "Is Ironrose coming?"

He nodded, wiggling to a comfortable position next to her.

"And—?"

"He finished the token. It took me a long time to talk him into bringing it with him. I came ahead to check on things here and make sure that everything was prepared."

"Shonu's got dinner for two set up. H'shama and Huli have the kitchen relay ready and Tsamar is cooling the ashdown tea over in the stream."

"Good. Good," Tullin said with satisfaction. "There's Ironrose now. He's slow tonight."

Coulsie looked sympathetically at the tall form of the smith. "More awkward than usual, and stiffer in his movements—if that's possible," she noted as the smith began undressing. "Look how carefully he folds his clothes, taking his time. This was a hard decision for him. He looks scared."

Tullin wiggled, rubbing shoulders with her. "No more scared than I was when I danced my courting dance for you. But I had tasted your scent and knew what the answer would be. Poor taste-blind Hawkbrother only has what his eyes and his heart tell him. The eyes and the heart are notorious liars. Not like the tongue. You cannot lie to the tongue." He slithered down from his perch.

"I don't see the love token he made," Tullin sniffed critically.

"The rose?" Coulsie said.

"Yes. It's not in his clothes either," Tullin said, rocking back on his heels. "He must have been afraid to bring it after all. I'll have to fix the oversight. Start the food and drinks; I'll be back in a moment!" he whispered as he slid through the leafy undergrowth.

The hunter toyed with the lacings of the smith's apron she had bartered a moon's hunting for. Tallbush had managed to keep it a secret; he was certain Ironrose would like it very much. She was not so sure, considering the circumstances her heart told her it should be given in.

Well. If he didn't seem receptive to a courting gesture, then it wasn't really one at all. Just a gift to a skilled artisan to thank him for his work. Nothing more. Easy to explain away.

Sunrunner smoothed down the outfit Coulsie had prepared for her. It seemed entirely too soft, and it fit the contours of her upper body perfectly. Below that, it draped like a hawk's tail when she walked.

At least it wasn't in some shocking color like a festival costume. It was a comfortable warm gray, speckled and smooth-seamed. The most confounding thing about it, she'd realized after it was on, was that it had lacings on the back that she couldn't reach herself.

How odd.

Ironrose cursed himself for his ineptitude. If only he was more romantic, like his brethren, he wouldn't feel like he was stumbling naked into a thornbush. He'd made the rose, thinking of her the whole time, crafting the petals with his most beloved tools. He had cooled it with his own breath, felt its heat radiating to his lips, and imagined Sunrunner's kiss. When he had polished it, he'd imagined Sunrunner's body, smoothed under his hands. And he had imagined her smile.

But now, he was as nervous as he had ever been in his life. He had mustered enough bravery to come here and meet her, but he didn't have the courage to go any further than that.

Then she appeared. He looked longingly at her, drowning in her hint of a smile, wishing that he could say or do something.

"Sunrunner. Good evening. Please. Join me."

She looked for all the world like a gray falcon flying along the ground as she came closer. When she slowed her walk, her clothing billowed around her legs like a falcon spreading its tail to land. She was grace itself in his eyes.

She gingerly laid down a pack and pulled back a few strands of hair from her eyes. "I wanted to thank you for the arrowheads. And for everything. I hope you like this."

"A . . . gift? For me?"

Her face flushed red. She nodded, then looked away.

Oh, stars above, she . . . how could I have missed this opportunity? I'll look like a fool, and she won't know that I. . . .

A small, taloned hand reached out and gently touched the smith's elbow. He turned. On a towel by the pool lay the iron rose, gleaming softly in the starlight.

Babysitter
by Josepha Sherman

Josepha Sherman is a fantasy writer and folklorist whose latest novels are the historical fantasies *The Shattered Oath* and *Forging the Runes*. Her latest folklore book is entitled *Trickster Tales*.

Thunder shook the earth and lightning seemed to shred the sky apart, and Leryn, crammed into this barely dry little cave in the middle of the gods-only-knew-where, thought wryly:

Of course. Why should my luck change now?

The whole expedition had been a farce from the start; he acknowledged that now with flawless hindsight. He was a city man, curse it, a settled gem merchant with a settled business. What in the name of all the powers had possessed him to up and leave it? To start over as a wandering merchant? (*Elenya, lost Elenya—No!*) Bad enough to go traveling among the more-or-less civilized peoples. But why had he ever been mad enough to come up here, to this cold, rocky, godsforsaken wilderness north of Lake Evendim? (*Elenya,* his mind insisted, *his dear one, and the panicky flight from a grief that would not let him rest—*No! He would *not* think of that!) Had he actually expected to start a profitable enough trade with the scattered little hunting parties, their furs for his pretty gems?

Furs, ha! What did he know of furs? Of course he'd failed! The locals had, as the saying went, seen him coming. And no one had thought to warn him about the bandits who called the wilderness home.

Leryn shivered. Of his troop, only he remained alive,

66

and that only because he'd been lucky enough to outrun those bandits.

Lucky. He was alive, yes—but thoroughly lost in the wilderness with nothing more than his belt knife and the clothes on his back. Yes, and with a storm like the end of the world raging all about him.

And did you want *to live?* a voice deep within his mind wondered. *Wouldn't it have been better to die at once and rejoin Elenya!*

"No," Leryn said aloud, then laughed without humor.

What difference did it make? He'd probably wind up dead anyhow, more slowly, of starvation or cold.

At least the horrendous storm seemed finally to be wearing itself out. A few more rumbles, one last flash of light, a final burst of rain, then . . . silence.

Almost too stiff to move, Leryn uncurled out of his cramped shelter, stretching complaining muscles. And for all the burden of chill fear within him, he stood looking about for a moment, almost in wonder. Gods, it was beautiful out here, even in the middle of all his trouble, he had to admit that: rocks and sturdy northern forest all clean-washed and glittering in the first rays of sunlight breaking through the dissipating clouds. The air was so clear and cold it made him cough.

Eh, well, all this nature worship was fine, but it wasn't helping his plight a bit. He had a goodly way till sundown, judging from what he could see of the sun, and Leryn shrugged in wry bravado. If he headed due south, he must, eventually, come out on the shores of Lake Evendim, and from there, eventually, if he followed the lake along eastward, maybe some friendly settlement.

And if he didn't, well, at least moving was better than standing around waiting to die!

But Leryn hadn't gotten very far before he let out a startled yelp and dove in the prickly shelter of a thicket. What was *that*? Something large, tawny-gold . . . a gryphon? Had he actually seen a gryphon? Leryn freely admitted he knew next to nothing about the magical, intelligent beings, other than what probably fantastic stories the locals had told him. All he could remember right now was that gryphons were definitely carnivorous!

But the gryphon ahead of him wasn't moving in the slightest, and after a wary moment, Leryn struggled out of hiding. And, much to his surprise, he heard himself gasp aloud in pity.

What a beautiful creature this was, all lovely, graceful sleekness—or rather, what a beautiful creature it had been.

The poor beast must have been caught in the storm. Either the lightning struck it, or the winds dashed it to the ground.

But why would such an experienced flyer (judging from its enormous wings) have taken such risks? Leryn saw the carcass of a deer still clutched in the gryphon's claws, and realized with a shock that it—she? The gryphon was slender enough to be a she—she, then, could only have been bringing food to her offspring. But where was her mate? Didn't gryphons mate for life?

Ah well, there wasn't anything he could do. Even if he could, by some wild chance, find where she'd hidden her young, there wasn't any way he could help them. Leryn shook his head (*his own loss, his Elenya, and the child who had died with her—No!*) and turned brusquely away. But then he turned again and hesitantly approached the dead gryphon.

"I hate to rob you, but I need this more than you."

His belt knife wasn't the best tool for the job, but at last, wincing at the messiness of the whole process (remembering days at home, when servants bought and butchered and served his meat to him), Leryn managed to cut off a good hunk of venison. What could he wrap it in? Leaves, yes, nice broad leaves like these . . . there. It made a squishy package, slung over his back like this, but at least he wasn't going to starve right away.

Feeling a bit foolish, Leryn saluted the gryphon. "Thank you. You've given me life."

He headed on, picking his careful way through a tangle of rocks.

But then something wriggled away from him. Something screamed in alarm, a long, shrill skree of fright that shot right through Leryn's head.

"What in the name of—"

The terrified screaming broke off abruptly at the sound of his voice. A bright-eyed, curved-beaked little head poking up out of the rocks. "A gryphon!" A gryphon cub, rather, or pup or—or whatever the babies were called. "You belonged to that poor creature, didn't you?" Leryn murmured, and the baby stared. "Poor little one, you can't possibly understand that she's dead."

The baby trilled softly, such a quick, inquisitive little sound that Leryn smiled in spite of himself. "You've never seen a human before, have you? No, you're probably far too young for that. Probably never even left the nest before—before this."

The gryphon trilled again, impatiently this time. *I'm hungry!* the sound seemed to say. *I'm hungry and lonely, and what are you going to do about it?*

What, indeed?

You shouldn't feed it, Leryn warned himself. *You'll only be postponing the inevitable.*

But the baby trilled yet again, wriggling out of the rocks. Leryn froze, enchanted. What a funny, chubby, furry little thing! It was about the size of a hunting hound—though no hound ever bore those silly little downy wings or that spotted, striped, yellow-brown-tan baby fuzz. The gryphon must be very young, indeed, because it was still just a touch unsteady on its too-big-for-its-body paws.

Damn. I can't *just walk away.* "Uh, well, I do have some meat," Leryn told the baby. "I only hope you can eat solid food."

Gryphons didn't nurse their young, did they? No, not when even the babies sported those sharp, curved beaks! Leryn unwrapped the slice of venison, and the baby let out its ear-splitting scream.

"Hey, stop that! I'm moving as fast as I can!" Using his belt knife, Leryn cut off a tiny sliver of meat, wondering aloud, "I hope you don't need your food regurgitated, the way birds feed their chicks. There *are* limits."

Judging from the way the little gryphon practically tore the sliver of meat from his hand, that wasn't going to be a problem. It paused only long enough to gulp down the fragment, then started to scream again.

"Hey, hey, I told you, I'm cutting it up as fast as I can!"

That didn't stop the ear-splitting complaint. Leryn tapped the baby gently on the beak with the tip of his knife, and the astonished gryphon fell silent, staring at him in innocent wonder. The man winced.

"Oh, don't look at me like that. I'll give you a good meal, but that's it. After this, you're on your own."

The baby continued to stare.

"Stop that! Don't you understand? I can't stay here to take care of you, and I can't take you with me; you'd never be able to keep up. Ha, you can barely walk steadily as it is!"

But the gryphon continued to watch him even as it gulped down meaty sliver after sliver. At last it seemed to be full, its little belly gently rounded. With a satisfied little churr, the baby collapsed on Leryn's feet, staring adoringly up at him.

"Wonderful. Just wonderful. Now what am I going to do with you?"

He reached a tentative hand down to the spotted baby down, wondering if the little beast would let him touch it. When it didn't even flinch, he stroked the gryphon gently, enjoying the fuzzy feel of it. The baby smelled faintly of spices—cinnamon, was it?—and of that delicate newness that all young things seem to have in common.

And for a moment, Leryn's hand paused in its stroking as he remembered another baby, and Elenya—

No! I will not—No! "Ah, gods," Leryn murmured to the gryphon. "I can't leave you here to die."

The baby churred again, almost as though it understood, and Leryn sighed. Maybe this would work. The little thing was about dog-sized, after all, and he doubted it weighed much more; a creature meant for flight couldn't be too heavy. Leryn sighed again, knowing he'd already come to a decision.

"All right, baby. We travel together, at least till I can find an adult gryphon to take care of you. Assuming the creature doesn't try to rend me apart first as a baby-thief!"

Ah, well, one problem at a time. The gryphon had curled up on his feet, sound asleep. Leryn continued to stroke the warm, fuzzy fur. And after a time, he realized, much to his astonishment, that he was smiling.

He stopped smiling about midway through the next day. The gryphon had tagged along after him nicely enough for a while, but it was a baby, with a baby's limited attention span and lack of sense. First, Leryn had to rescue it from a pond into which the little thing had fallen while chasing a butterfly. Then he had to pry it out from between two rocks which were just a bit too close together to allow the gryphon to pass. In between, the baby would plop itself down with a baby's suddenness, instantly sound asleep, or complaining with earsplitting pathos that it was hungry.

Leryn glanced at the rapidly diminishing chunk of venison and winced. It wasn't going to stay fresh much longer or, for that matter, judging from the gryphon's appetite, last much longer.

And what do I do when it's gone? I'm no hunter; I'm not even carrying a decent knife! Gods, I don't even have any way of starting a fire!

At least, now that that spectacular, deadly storm was past, the weather remained dry. But the air was cold, and it grew colder as night fell. Leryn tried to sleep curled up in as tight a ball as he could manage, struggling to ignore his aching, hungry body, but the earth was as chill as the air. And for all his weariness, he couldn't get comfortable enough to sleep.

But then a fuzzy little body, warm as a furnace, pushed itself against him: the gryphon, whimpering softly. Leryn drew the baby to him, glad of its warmth, and the two lonely beings at last slept.

*   *   *

Leryn sank wearily to a rock, head down. The gryphon pushed against him, trilling anxiously, but the man ignored it, too worn to care.

How many days had it been of endless walking, of hunger and aching muscles and skin chafed raw from the clothes he couldn't change? How many nights of broken sleep and cold, never-ending cold? The last scraps of the by-now-barely-edible meat had been devoured by the baby a day ago, and though the gryphon had managed to snap up enough bugs along the way to feed it—or at least keep it from that ear-splitting complaining—there hadn't been anything for a human to eat. Leryn had tried to fill his complaining stomach with spring water, but the water had been so cold it chilled him to the bone.

You knew it was going to come to this sooner or later. You knew you didn't have a chance of surviving. . . .

"I just didn't know it was going to take so long."

The gryphon cut into his bitterness, pushing anxiously against him, trilling and trilling in panic till at last Leryn roused himself from thoughts of death. He stared at the small, frantic baby. And slowly it came to him that he couldn't die, not yet, not while this small, so-very-alive creature was depending on him.

Leryn reached out a weary hand to ruffle the gryphon's fur, then staggered to his feet.

"Come on, baby. We'll see how much farther we can get."

The gryphon shrilled in sudden alarm. Leryn stumbled back, staring blankly at the men who'd come out of hiding and into whose arms he'd almost walked.

For a moment Leryn's mind simply refused to function, noting only that these strangers were warmly clad, and looked well-fed. But the gryphon continued its shrill screaming, stubby wings fluttering, trying its baby best to defend him against:

Bandits, Leryn realized through the haze of weariness. *Maybe even the same who attacked me the first time.*

What difference did it make? He certainly didn't have

anything on him of value, and if they just waited a bit, he'd probably die of hunger or exhaustion and save them the trouble of—

It was the gryphon they wanted. They were going to kill his little friend for its fur, or carry it off to captivity.

"Like hell you are!" Leryn roared (or at least thought he roared), and charged.

The first bandit was so astonished by this rush of strength from such a worn-out creature he didn't defend himself in time. Leryn tore the club from his hands and laid about with it with half-hysterical fury. The gryphon baby, shrilling a childish battle scream, fought with him—small, sharp beak nipping, small, sharp talons scratching. But of course they hadn't a chance of winning, not one weary man and one little gryphon.

At least this'll be faster than dying of hunger, Leryn thought wryly.

Thunder deafened him, wild wind buffeted him. For a dazed moment, swathed in sudden shadow, Leryn could only wonder how a storm could have struck so swiftly.

But the storm was moving, shrieking, and all at once he realized that what was looming overhead was a gryphon, two gryphons, and he forgot all about the bandits as he stared in wonder at the living golden wonders soaring down at him.

The bandits didn't waste time in staring. They scattered in all directions, racing off into the underbrush like so many terrified rabbits, and Leryn could have sworn he heard one of the gryphons hiss in soft, fierce laughter.

They landed in a wild swirling of wind and dust. The baby gryphon let out one startled little yelp and ducked behind Leryn, then took a wary step out from hiding, gaping, every line of its small body rigid with astonishment. For a long moment, Leryn stood frozen as well, staring, too weary for fright, at the savage, splendid, vibrant size of them, at the wise, keen, alien eyes watching him, at the beaks, wickedly elegant as curved swords, that could snap him in two, at the gleaming talons that could rend him apart as easily as he might tear worn-out fabric. He *should* be afraid, Leryn thought, he really should.

But the last of his desperate strength was ebbing from him. Leryn felt his exhausted body crumple to its knees.

And then he knew nothing at all.

He woke slowly, languorously, to warmth, wonderful, spicy-scented warmth. Meat was being pushed at his lips, and if that meat was raw, at least it was fresh and full of the promise of life, and he chewed and swallowed without protest, feeling the dawn of strength returning to him.

Then Leryn came to himself enough to realize he was cradled like a baby against a gryphon's side, a golden wing sheltering him, and it was a deadly beak so gently offering him food. The beings must have known he was half-dead for want of food and warmth.

Ah, warmth, yes . . . it was so good to be warm again . . . warm and fed and cozy . . .

. . . *cozy as he'd been with Elenya, his own sweet wife cuddled beside him in their bed, and the promise of new life growing inside her.*

The promise that had gone so terribly wrong.

The memories hit him without warning, hit him so hard that Leryn, still too weak to control his will, broke as he had not during all the long, empty, dry-eyed days of mourning. Broke and wept against the warm, tawny side, sheltered under the soft, golden wing while the gryphon churred ever so softly, stroking his hair with a gentle beak as though he were her child.

Her. He had no doubt of his protector's gender. And Leryn heard, or felt, or sensed, he couldn't have said how, the gryphon's own grief. She who had died in the storm had been this one's sister, long lost from the nest: too proud, too sure of herself, heeding no one's advice, taking an aging mate, one who'd died and left her and her young one alone.

Race, species were forgotten in their mingled grief. And out of mingled grief came at least the seeds of healing.

"Eleyna, Eleyna, I still miss you, and shall miss you all my life. But . . . I am alive. And I must go on being alive."

He could almost have sworn that somewhere, far beyond space and time, she'd heard, somewhere she'd smiled.

Leryn sat bolt upright. The gryphon raised her wing to free him, and he found himself staring into the wise, amused eyes of her mate.

"ssso. You live."

"You speak!" Leryn reddened. "I—I mean, of course you speak, it's just—I didn't expect—I don't know what I expected."

The gryphon chuckled. "We hardly expected you to ssspeak *our* tongue."

"Uh, no. I . . . uh . . . I'm not familiar with your kind." Leryn glanced about, seeing a neat-walled cave— no, not a cave, a ruin of some sort, human-built but plainly now the gryphon pair's nest. "But the baby!" he suddenly remembered. "The little gryphon. Where is—"

A small thunderbolt sent him staggering back into the side of the female gryphon. The baby leaping at him, churring with delight, wriggling like a happy puppy, until a quiet word in the gryphon tongue made it reluctantly settle to the floor.

"You've brought my sssisssster's child to me," the female gryphon murmured. "For that we thank you."

"You kept the little one alive," said the male. "And that," he added with a chuckle as the wriggling baby eyed then pounced on his tufted tail, "could have been no easssy thing. For that we thank you, too."

"I could hardly have let a—a child die!" A little shiver ran through Leryn at the memory of his own son, who'd never known the touch of life, but he continued resolutely, "Besides, the child kept *me* alive!" It was true enough. "Without this little ball of fur, I would have given up a long time ago."

"Yesss, but now the quessstion isss: What do we do with you?"

"Ah." What, indeed? No funds, no weapons, not even

a change of clothes. "I don't know. In my home town, I'm a merchant of gems, but—"

"Gemsss? The pretty ssstonesss you humansss like? Then thessse mussst belong to you."

"My gem pouches! Where did you—"

The male gryphon licked his talons with a lazy tongue. "I chasssed the banditsss," he murmured, eyes glinting dangerously. "It wasss good sssport. And asss they fled, they dropped everything they bore."

Leryn stared at the fortune glittering in his hands. His gems, returned to him. Ah, gods, now he could start over, and not waste the life he'd been given!

Suddenly it was all too ridiculous. Leryn burst into laughter, gasping, "I—I've come a long way just to find the—the path back to myself. And I could have managed without the hardships, thank you! But," he added, bending to stroke the baby's furry head, "I think everyone's happy with how things worked out."

"Everyone sssave the banditsss," the gryphons murmured, and gave their churring laugh.

The Salamander
by *Richard Lee Byers*

Richard Lee Byers worked for over a decade in an emergency psychiatric facility, then left the mental health field to become a writer. He is the author of *The Ebon Mask, On A Darkling Plain, Netherworld, Caravan of Shadows, Dark Fortune, Dead Time, The Vampire's Apprentice,* and several other novels. His short fiction has appeared in numerous other anthologies, including *Phobias, Confederacy of the Dead, Dante's Disciples, Superheroes,* and *Diagnosis: Terminal.* He lives in the Tampa Bay area, the setting for many of his stories.

By my reckoning, the arsonist might strike in any of fifteen places. It was sheer luck, if that's the right term, that I'd chosen to guard the right location.

When it happened, it happened fast. One moment, I was prowling the cramped recesses of the tiring house of the Azure Swan Theater. Painted actors frantically changing costume squirmed past me, glaring at the intruder obstructing the way. Their ill will didn't bother me half as much as the flowery rhetoric being declaimed on stage. That night's play was *The Bride and the Battlesteed,* a tragedy that blends mawkish sentimentality with a flawless ignorance of life on the Dhorisha Plains. Suffering through a particularly lachrymose soliloquy, I wished that the theater *would* catch fire, just to terminate the performance.

Try not to think things like that. One never knows what gods are listening.

An instant later, I heard a boom. Some of the audience cried out, and the forty-year-old ingenue ranting on stage faltered in mid-lament. Something began to hiss and crackle. I scrambled to the nearest of the rear stage entrances, looked out, and saw that a patch of thatch on the roof of the left-hand gallery was burning.

Then the straw above the royal family's empty box exploded into flame. The two fires raced along the roof like lovers rushing to embrace. At the same time, they oozed down the columns into the topmost of the three tiers of seats. I peered about, but could see no sign of the enemy I'd been hired to stop.

Shrieking people shoved along the galleries toward the stairs. Others climbed over the railings and dropped into the cobbled courtyard, where they joined the stampede of groundlings driving toward the exit at the rear of the enclosure. In half a minute, the passage was jammed.

It was plain that not everyone would make it out that way. There was a stage door in the back of the tiring house, but none of the audience had come in that way, nor was it visible from any of their vantage points, so none of them thought to use it.

Abandoning my efforts to spot the incendiary, I ran forward past two wooden columns painted to resemble marble to the foot of the stage. Though the blaze had yet to descend past the highest gallery, I could already feel the heat. "This way!" I shouted. "There's another exit!"

Nobody paid the least attention. Perhaps, between the roar of the fire and the panicky cries, no one heard.

I jumped off the platform, grabbed a strapping, tow-headed youth with bloodstained sleeves—a butcher's apprentice, I imagine—and tried to turn him around. "Come with me!" I said.

He snarled and threw a roundhouse punch at my head. I ducked and hit him in the belly. He doubled over. I manhandled him toward the stage. "I'm trying to help you," I said. "There's another way out. Go behind the stage. The door will be on your right. Do you understand?" Evidently he did, because when I let him go, he clambered onto the proscenium.

I induced several other people to head backstage.
Eventually, others noticed them going, and followed.

Which soon threatened to create a second crush, at
the rear stage doors. I sprang onto the platform and
dashed back there to manage the flow of traffic as best
I could, with pleas when possible and my hands when
necessary.

By now the air was gray with smoke. I kept coughing.
The Heavens—the machine room above me, the under-
side of which was painted to resemble the sky—started
burning. Sparks and scraps of flaming debris rained
down.

At last the stage was clear. My handkerchief pressed
to my face, I scurried toward the exit. The ceiling burst.
A windlass, used to lower the actors portraying gods and
their regalia, plummeted through the breach and struck
where I'd just been standing. The impact shattered the
floorboards.

When I escaped the playhouse, I trotted some distance
away, not only to make sure that I was out of danger but
to better survey the overall situation. Turning, I noticed
something strange.

Fortunately, the Azure Swan stood on a spit of land
that stuck out into the river. It wasn't close to any other
structure. For a while, the flames enveloping the building
swayed this way and that, as if groping for some other
edifice they could spread to. At times they appeared to
move against the breeze.

Two candlemarks later, those of us who had sought
to defend the theater regrouped in a private room in a
nearby tavern. This council of war included several
blades of the Blue political faction, which vied with the
Reds, Yellows, Blacks, and most bitterly with the Greens
for control of Mornedealth, an equal number of their
retainers, Draydech the sorcerer, and myself. And a
singed, grimy, malodorous, and surly lot we were, too.
Also present was Lady Elthea, widow of a middling
prominent Blue leader, owner of the three businesses
that had thus far burned, and my employer. Though el-

derly and infirm, she'd insisted on venturing forth from her mansion to view the site of the latest disaster.

"All right," I said, "we searched the Swan beforehand, without finding any incendiary devices. Did anyone see a figure on the roof? Or any flaming missiles?" The other men shook their heads. "Then it's magic kindling these fires, Lady Elthea. That's the only logical explanation." I looked at Draydech. "Do you concur?"

The warlock was a short fellow in his late thirties, younger than I, though with his wobbling paunch, graying goatee, and the broken veins in his bulbous nose, he looked older. He'd served his apprenticeship living rough with the nomadic Whispering Oak wizards of the deep forests. Afterward, he'd embraced the amenities of civilization with a vengeance. I'd never seen him eat a raw piece of fruit or vegetable, drink water, or go out in inclement weather. Nevertheless, he'd lost none of the skills he'd mastered in the wilderness. He was particularly adept at sniffing out mystical energies, and, despite his exorbitant fees and extortionate habits, I retained him whenever that kind of witchy bloodhound work seemed likely to be in order.

Now, however, raising his eyes from the chunk of amber he'd been staring into while the rest of us glumly guzzled our wine, he said, "Certainly it's magic. Judging from the appearance of the conflagration, someone's conjured a salamander, a being from the Elemental Plane of Fire, to do the job. But I can't *find* it."

I scowled. "Old friend. This is not the time to angle for more gold."

Lady Elthea extended her trembling hand. Her skin was like parchment, her knuckles, swollen with arthritis. "Sorcerer, I beseech you. Some of our fellow citizens died tonight. More could perish tomorrow. If you can help prevent this, don't hold back."

Jarnac, one of the Blue blades, rose from the trestle table. "I'll take care of it, Lady Elthea," he said. He was a lanky, sandy-haired youth, dressed lavishly but not tastefully in a sapphire- and ruby-studded particolored doublet with intricately carved ivory buttons. At his side hung the latest rage, one of the new smallswords, this one sporting a golden hilt. Smallswords looked elegant, and were adequate for fighting another gentleman similarly equipped. But they were apt to prove too flimsy against a heavier weapon or an armored foe, which was why I was still lugging my broadsword around.

As might have been inferred from Jarnac's ostentation, he was New Money, with a parvenu's eagerness to parade his wealth and sense of style; unlike most of his cronies in the room, he couldn't claim kinship with one of the Fifty Noble Houses. Not that that mattered to me. My birth was considerably humbler than his.

He dropped a fat purse on the table. Coin clinked. "Take it, magician," he urged. "And rest assured, there's plenty more where that came from."

Draydech gazed longingly at the money. I fancy he came close to licking his lips. But at last he shook his head and said, "I can't take it, sir, because I'm not sure I can earn it. Despite Master Selden's slander—" he shot me a reproachful glance, which, given our shared history, failed to inspire any remorse, "—I wasn't trying to inflate my price. Rather, I was attempting to explain that something odd has happened.

"We all should have seen the salamander. They're not invisible, quite the contrary. Even if its summoner veiled it in a glamour, *I* should still have spotted it. But I didn't.

"What's more, I've been sitting here scrying, and I can't pick up its trail. Apparently someone's developed a cunning new type of cloaking spell."

Sensing that he was telling the truth, I said, "And until you work out how to pierce the charm, you can't banish the spook, or guide us to its master either. Is that about the gist of it?"

"I'm afraid so."

I sighed. "What more can you tell us about salamanders?"

"A sorcerer enlists the aid of an elemental by opening a Gate to its home plane, then bartering for its services. It was probably fairly easy to recruit a salamander to start fires. They love to do it anyway. The trick will be to keep it under control, to make sure it only burns what the summoner wants it to."

Fire is a threat to any town. In Mornedealth, built all of wood, the menace was all the greater. Remembering how the theater blaze had flowed against the wind, the beginnings of a headache tightening my brow, I wondered how our problem could get any worse. The answer was immediately forthcoming.

Pivor, Lady Elthea's grandnephew and closest living kin, sprang up from his bench. He did belong to the Fifty, and no mistaking it. He had the kind of exquisite features and supercilious carriage that only generations of controlled inbreeding can produce. "Enough of this prattle," he said. "The mage has already admitted he can't aid us, so we'll have to help ourselves. We know who to blame for our troubles: the Greens." The company murmured agreement. They'd all seen the unsigned threat, written in emerald ink, that someone had tacked to Lady Elthea's door the night before the first fire. "So I say we strike back at them at once."

"No," Lady Elthea said. "I don't want—"

Pivor ignored her. "A lot of them drink at The Honeycomb. We can lie in wait in the alley that runs—"

"That's a bad idea," I said. "My gut tells me that not all the Greens are involved in this. We need to identify the ones who are. Indiscriminate slaughter would only compound our difficulties."

"If we kill enough of them, the ones who remain will be afraid to send the spirit out again."

"No, they won't," I said. "They'll merely seek to butcher you in turn."

Pivor's lip curled "I heard that when you founded your fencing academy, you swore your days as a hire-sword were over."

"You heard correctly," I said. "Twenty-five years of soldiering was enough. Unfortunately, I have a penchant for losing horses and needy friends. When the combination depletes my coffers, I accept commissions of a certain sort. Pray tell, why are we discussing this?"

"I was just conjecturing that you gave up the mercenary life because you've turned coward. For, truly, you seem afraid to fight."

No doubt he said it to shame me into supporting his strategy. But of course there was only one proper response to such an insult, and that wasn't it. Simply because Jarnac was near me, I turned to him. "Sir. Would you do me the honor of acting as my second?"

One of Pivor's friends said, "That figures. One baseborn fellow looks to the other."

Jarnac colored. "It would be better if you asked someone else, Master Selden, because I agree with Pivor. Not in his assessment of your character," he added hastily, "but about what's best to do. We shouldn't waste time trying to ferret out one man from the mass of our foes. We should wage war on them all."

Balin, one of my more promising students, said, "I'll stand for you, Master Selden."

"Thank you," I said. I gave Pivor my best killer's glare. "Then perhaps we can arrange this straightaway."

I'll give him credit, I couldn't stare him down, but he grew pale, no doubt in belated remembrance of my reputation. "Verrano, will you act for me?" he stammered.

"Stop this!" Lady Elthea said. "Didn't you all come here for the same purpose? To succor a poor old woman who needs your help desperately? Then I beg you, please, don't fight among yourselves!"

This time, Pivor chose to heed her. "You're right, of course. Moreover, this is your affair, and if you think this man should be in charge, so be it." He bowed to me. "Master Selden, for my grandaunt's sake, I apologize."

I bowed back. "And for her sake, I accept."

"If we aren't going to massacre the Greens, what are we going to do?" Draydech asked.

"The gentlemen of the Blues will keep guarding my lady's properties," I said. "Perhaps one of them will spot our human foe, lurking about the scene. You'll try to devise a magic that will locate the salamander. I'll nose around and see what I can uncover through more mundane channels. And by working together, we'll put an end to this outrage." I wished I were as confident as I was trying to sound.

I contrived to approach the house from the rear, then hid behind the stable. After a while, a maid trudged out the back door and started tossing feed to the chickens. The birds were plump and lively; she, thin and lethargic. Their feathers shone white in the morning sunlight, while her gown was drab and threadbare. In short, they looked better cared for than she was.

Which was more or less what I'd expected. Her employer was famous for the sumptuous banquets he gave for his fellow Greens, but, provided one talked to the poor as well as the prosperous, equally notorious for his miserly treatment of his servants.

I checked the windows of the four-story dwelling, making sure no one was peering out, then stepped from concealment. "Hello," I said.

The girl jumped. "Who are you?"

"A friend." I showed her the trade-silver in my hand. "With a proposition."

She looked yearningly at the money, reminding me fleetingly of Draydech. But then she scowled and said, "I'm not that kind."

"You mistake me," I said. "I just want to ask you some questions, about things you may have noticed or overheard. Though I must admit, there's a chance that something you say could embarrass your master. So I'll understand if you decline."

She glanced over her shoulder at the house, then snatched the coin. "What do you want to know?"

The racket in The Honeycomb was deafening. The tavern was packed, most of the patrons were roaring drunk, and two lunatics were playing bagpipes. We lads at the corner table had to bellow with the rest to make ourselves heard.

"And that was that," said one of my companions, a burly hire-sword with a forked beard, a broken nose, and a Green favor pinned to the sheepskin collar of his jacket. "When they saw that, armed only with a soup ladle, I'd killed eight of their band in half as many seconds, the rest of the bastards turned tail."

"Amazing," I said. I was trying to sound admiring, and truly, I was impressed by his powers of invention. I stroked my false whiskers the way I always do when I wear them, to make sure they aren't falling off. "Of course, if what we hear in Valdemar is true, it's no wonder you men of Mornedealth are master warriors. Folk say you keep in constant practice fighting one another. For instance, you Greens are at odds with the Silvers, isn't that so?"

"The Blues," someone corrected.

"Pardon me, the Blues. What's that all about, anyway? And who's winning?"

Smiling slyly, the fellow with the broken nose said, "I'm afraid that's a very long story. And my throat's already parched."

Taking the hint, I waved for the barkeep to bring another jug.

Lithe and lightning-quick, Marissa flowed through the gloomy practice hall, a dagger flashing in either hand and her short black hair flying about her head. When she finished the exercise, I said, "Your high guard is a hair too high."

"Says you," she replied. If she'd kept to her usual schedule, she'd been practicing hard for a candlemark, but she wasn't even slightly winded. "Good evening, Selden. Stop by to sign up for some lessons?"

"Who could afford your rates?" I said, sauntering from the doorway into the hall. "Well, perhaps I could if I could stay away from the hippodrome, but that's by the by. I need information about the Greens."

She shrugged. "I don't belong to any faction, any more than you do."

"But most of the Greens who study swordplay do so under you, just as the majority of the Blues train with me. I know you hear things."

"Suppose I do. Why would I betray my students' confidences to the likes of you?"

"To prevent a full-scale blood-feud. To keep the city from burning down. Either one would be bad for trade."

She smiled crookedly. "Why not say, to keep the sun from turning to dung while you're at it? You'll have to do better than prophecies of doom."

I put my hand on my purse. "How much do you want?"

"At present, I don't need money. It's been a good season. But is it true that you learned sword-and-cape fighting up north?"

I winced. A fencing master needs to hold onto a few martial secrets if he hopes to shine among his rivals. "You're a bloodsucking bitch, Marissa. You know that, don't you?" I unfastened my cloak. "All right, grab a wrap and a longer blade, and I'll give *you* a lesson."

And so it went. As myself or in disguise, I roamed the city, gossiping, flattering, cajoling, bribing, and occasionally threatening. Questing for information. Coming up empty. Meanwhile, Lady Elthea lost a lumberyard and a warehouse full of bolts of linen. The latter fire spread to a pair of tenements belonging to an inoffensive gentleman of the insignificant Reds. Another thirteen people died.

Finally, reluctantly, I went to my employer's home in the Old City to describe my lack of progress.

This time the council of war convened in Lady Elthea's bedchamber, a high-ceilinged, dimly-lit room hung with somber tapestries. Though clean, it smelled of her long illness. She lay in a canopy bed, her shoulders propped by a mound of pillows. She seemed even gaunter and frailer than the last time I'd seen her, as if some of her strength had burned along with her properties. Jarnac sat on a stool beside her, holding her hand. He looked haggard, too. Evidently the nights of futile, sleepless sentinel duty were wearing him down.

"All I'm certain of," I said, concluding my dismal excuse for a report, "is that there's no grand conspiracy among the Greens. When they discuss striking at you Blues, they talk about maneuvers in Council, sharp business practice, and the occasional duel, not magic and arson. Indeed, most of them would never even consider a tactic that could endanger the entire town. More than ever, I'm convinced that we're up against one man, acting without the knowledge of his fellows. Unfortunately, I still don't know who he is."

"And I still can't find the salamander," Draydech said morosely. "It ought to light up the psychic landscape like a bonfire. Even if they're sending it back to its own plane after every chore—and that's unlikely, given the amount of energy required—I should be able to sense the opening and closing of the Gate. And yet . . ." He spread his pudgy hands.

"Still, we're grateful to you gentlemen for your efforts," said Pivor with leaden sarcasm. He turned to his grandaunt. "Now can we try my plan? If we just keep bleeding Greens, we're bound to come to the fire-starter eventually."

"No," said Lady Elthea with unexpected firmness. "I'd rather burn in this bed, if it comes to that, than send you into the streets to slaughter people at random."

"But we can't bear to see you hurt any further," Jarnac told her.

"No," Lady Elthea repeated. "I forbid it. There has to be a better way."

"As a matter of fact," I said, "I'm not done yet. I began by making inquiries about the Greens rather than Mornedealth's community of sorcerers because the latter are proverbially closemouthed. But now it's time to look at them. After all, one of them had to conjure the spook. The question is, which?"

"Probably one of the Green House mages," said Pivor impatiently. "Or if not, any one of a host of free lances."

"No," said Draydech thoughtfully. "The sorcerers hereabouts aren't saints. In truth, a few are scoundrels. Still, we have an understanding. Certain tacit, self-imposed prohibitions. Now that I think about it, I don't believe that anyone I know would unleash a salamander inside the city walls."

"Then our man is a clandestine practitioner," said I, my pulse ticking faster. "A rogue neither your fraternity nor the authorities would tolerate if they did know about him. We can conjecture that he generally sells his services to criminals. That he lives in a bad part of town. That he hasn't been here long, or you would at least have heard rumors of his presence."

"You're about to propose another search, aren't you?" Jarnac said. "Well, I for one don't see the point. You've already turned the city upside down."

"But this time, I'll have a clearer image of what I'm hunting," I said. "Trust me, that makes a difference."

Lady Elthea said, "I believe Master Selden can find the wretch. Let's let him try."

"Grandaunt," Pivor said, "you have to understand. Devoted as we all are to your wishes and your welfare, this affair encompasses other issues. If an insult to you goes unavenged for any length of time, that reflects on the honor of *all* the Blues. And if we can't find a specific culprit to punish, it's better to chastise all the Greens than do nothing. Selden can search if you want him to, but we're not going to wait on the result."

"Year in and year out, I've watched this stupid feud claim too many lives," Lady Elthea said. "I won't to be the cause of it flaring up again. Please, child, hold off. I'm dying, you know. This is likely the last favor I'll ever ask of you."

Pivor grimaced. "Very well. I'll give Selden until midnight tomorrow. After that, the Blues will take to the streets and settle matters our way."

"Fair enough," I said. I turned to Draydech. "Finish your wine and come on. If I'm going to stalk a mage, I want you with me."

A few blocks west of Stranger's Gate, the streets narrow to twisting alleys, and the cobbles turn to muck beneath one's feet. When the City Guards patrol the area, which is seldom, they go in twos and threes, and as often as not, ignore the screams that ring from the shadowed courtyards.

Draydech and I had been prowling this warren since our departure from Lady Elthea's mansion the previous evening. A weary ache in my joints attested to the fact that it was harder for me to do without sleep than it used to be.

Still, I was in good spirits. Peering up at the narrow strip of sky visible between the steeply pitched rooftops, gauging the position of the waning moon, I judged that I had three candlemarks till midnight. Time enough to forestall Pivor's assault, if, as I hoped, I was about to net my quarry.

I pointed at a sagging post-and-beam tenement. It had a cobbler's shop and a bakery on the ground floor, apartments above. "If the kidnapper spoke true, that's the place. Can you sense anything?"

Draydech squinted. After a moment, he said, "Yes. The top story has a nasty sheen to it. Someone's worked magic up there, some of it involving torture, sacrifice, and the Abyss."

"Sounds like our lad," I said. "Is he at home?"

"I can't say. The residue of his sorcery masks any other impressions."

"Well, there's an easy way to find out. Come on." We slunk up the street, through a doorway that stank of urine, and climbed four creaky flights of stairs.

I didn't see any point in giving the man we were after a chance to ready a spell. I drew my sword and kicked his door. It flew open and I rushed through.

My violent entry served no purpose. The warlock was home, but in no condition to harm me. A bald, hook-nosed man in a hooded robe, he lay sprawled on a dark stain in the middle of the floor. The reek of feces filled the air.

I knelt beside him, and, examining him by the wan light that spilled through the open shutters, found a narrow slit on each side of his throat. I tried to flex his cool, waxy-looking arm. It resisted, but it bent.

Behind me, Draydech muttered an incantation. A globe

of sickly green foxfire appeared in the air. Its glow revealed that the one-room apartment had been ransacked. A chest stood open, and clothing lay scattered across the floor. Codices and pieces of parchment were strewn about.

"Damn!" said Draydech. "The Luck Lords hate us! Damn, damn, damn!" He kicked a stool across the floor.

Grasping at straws, I said, "Can we be certain that this man is the mage?"

"Yes. I can tell from the lingering traces of his aura."

"Shit," I said. "Well, perhaps it isn't all bad. If the bastard's dead, he can't lead us to his employer. But on the other hand, if the magician's gone, the salamander's gone, so at least we don't have to worry about the town burning down. Right?"

"Wrong. The creature's probably still around. No reason it shouldn't be. I suspect the mage commanded it to obey his patron. Otherwise, Mornedealth would already be in flames. But without the wizard's power bolstering the Green's control, the elemental could slip its reins at any time. The threat of a conflagration is actually greater than before."

"Wonderful," I growled, rising. "We'd better search this place ourselves. I don't know what the murderer was looking for, but—"

"Watch out!" Draydech cried. To this day, I don't know what he could have seen or heard that I missed; it must have been his mystical senses that alerted him. He sprang at me and knocked me away from the window.

An instant later, there was a quarrel in his back. He tried to speak and then he was gone, just like that, death's ghastly conjuring trick that stuns and appalls no matter how many times one sees it played on a friend.

Fortunately, though my thoughts were frozen, my reflexes weren't. I threw myself to the floor. Another bolt whizzed through the air above me. The marksman, who must be shooting from the window directly across the street, had had at least two crossbows loaded and ready.

I didn't see much reason to stand back up and find

out if he had a third. It would be wiser to slip out of the apartment. I crawled to the door.

Onrushing footsteps clattered up the stairs. The crossbowman's colleagues, without a doubt. It sounded as if there were half a dozen. Long odds even for a fencing master, especially if one had to worry about taking a quarrel in the back while one fought.

I wished I could lock the door. That might at least buy me a few seconds. But, cunning fellow that I was, I'd broken the latch. And as long as I was taking stock of my ill fortune, it was a pity I was too high to leap from the window to the street. If I tried to climb down the wall, the marksman would shoot me for certain.

I crawled back to the window, pulled off my cloak, stuck it on the end of my sword, and raised it. Another bolt thrummed overhead. Instantly, discarding the makeshift lure, I scrambled up onto the windowsill and leaped.

Though the street was narrow, it was an awkward jump, and I didn't land gracefully. I slammed down on my belly on the marksman's windowsill, half in and half out, legs dangling. My attacker, a skinny, coppery-bearded fellow, smashed an arbalest over my head.

For a moment, I blacked out. When I came to, he was pushing me backward.

I grabbed the windowsill with one hand and whipped out my dagger with the other. I thrust. The blade scraped a rib, then plunged deep into the marksman's chest. He groaned and flopped on top of me.

I shoved him off, then hauled myself into the empty apartment he'd been shooting from. When I examined him, I saw that Draydrech was avenged.

My knees were weak, my crown throbbed, and blood trickled down my forehead. I wanted to sit and rest, but I knew I mustn't give my remaining assailants a chance to figure out where I'd gone and tree me again. I dragged my dagger out of the redhead's breast, then hurried out the door.

*　　*　　*

By the time I reached Lady Elthea's mansion, I felt a little better. Perhaps in recognition of the noblewoman's disapproval, Pivor's miniature army, if one cared to dignify it with that name, was awaiting midnight outside in her garden. He'd gathered about a hundred men, those who'd stood watch over his kinswoman's holdings plus some new recruits. Casks of ale and wine sat on trestles beside a dry fountain, and the cool night air smelled of drink.

Working my way through the throng, I spotted Pivor drinking from a tankard. "Good evening," I hailed him.

He pivoted. Squinted. "You're hurt."

"A scratch," I said. "You can send the mob home."

He frowned. "Are you saying you found the magician?"

"More or less. I'm sure you can appreciate that no one should hear my tidings before my employer." I waved down a passing footman. "Please tell your mistress Selden is here."

I thought he'd return and usher me into her presence, but instead, leaning heavily on a gleaming bronzewood staff, she hobbled out onto the marble steps beneath the porte-cochere. At her appearance, a hush settled over the crowd.

I bowed. "My lady. I know your enemy's name." The Blue blades jabbered excitedly. "I deduced it not a candlemark ago. Truth to tell, I should have realized before, but I'm like everyone else in Mornedealth. I'm so wearily familiar with the enmity between Blue and Green that it was difficult to think beyond it."

Pivor gaped at me. "Are you saying the incendiary isn't a Green? What about the threat?"

"Anyone can buy green ink. The letter was merely a ruse to divert suspicion from the real culprit. Think about it: Lady Elthea isn't active in public life. Even her late husband didn't make himself any more obnoxious to the Greens than many another member of your faction. Why, then, would a Green choose to persecute her and her alone of all your number? Wouldn't it make more sense to attack a genuine Blue leader such as you?"

Pivor opened his mouth, then closed it again.

"While you ponder that," I continued, "you can chew on this as well. Lady Elthea, we all worried that you would indeed burn in your bed, but, in point of fact, the salamander never came here. Instead, it devoted its attentions to your commercial ventures. Once again, if your foe intends your destruction, one has to wonder why.

"Here's what I think. You have a wealthy friend. Like me, he started common and shinned his way up into the lesser gentry. Unlike me, he yearns to rise higher still. In Mornedealth, that isn't easy, so he decided to ruin you, then offer to cover your losses if you'd adopt him. Or perhaps he wouldn't have been so crude; he might have relied on your gratitude. Either way, he expected to gain a title and membership in one of the Fifty Noble Houses." I turned. "Isn't that right, Master Jarnac?"

Jarnac glared at me. "This is absurd."

"Is it? Once we started standing watch, every building that caught fire did so while you were guarding it. Moreover, Draydech and I found the mage who conjured the salamander slain. By a thrust from a thin blade like yours. No Green knew we were hunting the warlock, but you did. You were here when we hatched the plan. Since the man could identify you, you got to him first, silenced him, and ransacked his quarters to make sure that he hadn't written your name down anywhere. Afterward, you found you were still afraid. Maybe you were worried that your search had missed something, or that Draydech's sorcery could make a dead man speak. In any event, you hired a band of assassins to lie in wait for us. Perhaps, in the moments of life remaining to you, it will console you to know that only I escaped."

Pivor said, "Hold on. How do you know that the fire wizard died after you left here yesterday?"

"As a corpse cools, it stiffens," I replied. "But after the better part of a day, it starts to go limp again. The body was at that stage when I found it."

Jarnac's forehead glistened with sweat. His voice breaking, he said, "You can't prove a single thing against me."

"True," I said. "Not to the satisfaction of a court of law. But I don't have to. I've cast aspersions on your honor, and you're supposed to call me out. If you don't, I'll challenge you, and you'll still have to fight. It's time you learned: there are drawbacks to being an aristocrat."

He turned. "Lady Elthea, I swear—"

Her old eyes glittered. "You vile *thing*."

Jarnac's face crumpled. "All right. I confess. I surrender. Send for the City Guards."

I couldn't help feeling disappointed. Though I was confident that the authorities would behead him in due course, I wanted to kill him myself. But I also figured we needed him alive for the nonce, to help us deal with the salamander. "Tell us about the elemental," I said.

"As you wish," he said. He opened his collar and pulled out a round brass medallion on a chain. "That will be the true consolation, getting rid of the beast." He lifted the chain over his head. "You can't imagine how it's been. I didn't mean to harm anyone. But the thing kept *pushing* and *squirming*—"

His sandy hair burst into flame.

An instant later, fire blazed out of his eye sockets and silently screaming mouth. His skin shone dazzling white, like molten metal, and wisps of blackened cloth flew away from his body. Crying out in shock and terror, the men around him recoiled. For a moment, he reeled about in manifest agony, then dropped into a truculent crouch.

At last, too late, I understood why Draydech had never been able to find the spirit. Its summoner had somehow hidden it *inside* Jarnac. And now, seizing control, it had transmuted their mingled substance into something more nearly resembling its native form.

I drew my dagger and lunged. Heat seared me. My point plunged into the salamander's breast. Seemingly unhurt, it lifted one fiery hand to seize me.

I sidestepped its grab and slashed at its other hand. The dagger snagged the chain, and I ripped it out of the elemental's grasp.

Evidently, it had been a good idea, because the sala-

mander snarled and tried to snatch the medallion back.
I surmised that in the hands of a mage, it might have
the power to subdue the creature.

Wishing that I were a sorcerer, wincing at the blistering touch of the metal, I gripped the chain securely
in my fist, wheeled, and ran. The panicky Blues parted
before me, clearing my path to the street. The salamander lumbered in pursuit.

After a few steps, it became apparent that the creature
couldn't catch me. Perhaps it would have been slow in
any world, in any form, but more likely it was clumsy
using Jarnac's legs. Foolishly, I imagined that for the
next little while, my primary problem might be making
sure that it didn't abandon the chase.

The air around me grew warmer. I glanced back, but
the salamander, now entirely enveloped in a corona of
hissing blue flame, was still several yards back. For another heartbeat, I still failed to grasp what was happening. Then I remembered how the spirit had kindled fire
at a distance, simply by willing it.

I dodged, an instant too late. The blast hurled me
through the air and smashed me down on the cobbles.
Though stunned, I started to scramble up, then noticed
that my left sleeve was on fire. I rolled over and over
till the blaze went out, then jumped to my feet and
dashed on.

From then on, my progress was a nightmare. Explo-
sions blinded and deafened me. Gasps of hot air charred
my throat. By zigzagging, I managed to prevent the salamander from centering a blast on me, but only at the
cost of eroding my lead. All things considered, I was
reasonably certain that I'd never reach my destination.

But I was wrong. Eventually I staggered around a corner and there it was, the ground on which I'd chosen
to make my stand. I ran a few more feet, drawing the
salamander to where I wanted it. Then I sucked in a
deep breath, spun, and charged.

Perhaps the maneuver surprised it, because it didn't
even try to get out of my way. I grappled it and bulled
it backward. It wrapped its blazing arms around me.

The next moment seemed to last an eternity. I felt my skin crisping, my tunic, breeches, and eyebrows catching fire. Then the salamander and I plunged off the riverbank.

As I'd prayed, the elemental's halo of flame went out when we splashed into the stream. But its flesh was still hot. The water around it started to boil. I imagined that in time it could cook me like a crayfish.

But now that I had the elemental submerged, I wasn't about to give it a chance to come up for air. Clinging to it, I stabbed it again and again. As far as I could tell, these new wounds didn't trouble it either. Meanwhile, it tried to thrust me away.

Though no one could have seen much in the dark water, I still sensed my vision fading. My ears rang and my chest ached, the compulsion to gulp a breath becoming insupportable.

And then the salamander stopped struggling. Its body turned soft, crumbled and dissolved in the current, as if it had burned itself to ash.

I dropped the knife and amulet, then, with the dregs of my strength, floundered to the surface. After filling my lungs several times, I paddled to the shore, only to discover that my arms were too feeble to drag me out of the river.

Gauntleted hands gripped my wrists and hauled me onto the grass. "I came after you," Pivor said.

"I'm afraid you missed all the fun," I wheezed. "They're dead, the spook and Jarnac both." I started coughing. I wondered vaguely if it was from swallowing smoke or water.

"You need a Healer!"

"That would be nice. Not that I'm dying, but I could definitely use some ointment for my scorched parts. Just let me lie here a minute, and then, I think, I'll be able to walk."

After a pause, Pivor said, "Thank you for bringing us the truth. I keep thinking about things my grandaunt has always said. And all the blood I nearly shed, for nothing.

Do you think there might be an honorable way to end the feud? I mean, without killing all the Greens."

I smiled, which hurt my face. "It's worth considering," I said.

A Child's Adventures
by Janni Lee Simner

Janni Lee Simner grew up in New York and has been making her way west ever since. She spent nearly a decade in the Midwest, where the recent floods formed some of the background for this story; currently she lives in the much drier Arizona desert. She's sold stories to nearly two dozen anthologies and magazines, including *Realms of Fantasy* and *Sisters in Fantasy 2*. Her first three books, *Ghost Horse, The Haunted Trail,* and *Ghost Vision,* have been published by Scholastic.

When the Companion first appeared in the marketplace, Inya hoped it had come for one of the grandchildren. Such a thing wasn't unheard of, even in a village as small as River's Bend. Companions were said not to care about rank, or about where people were born.

The people milling around the square froze at the sound of those bridle bells, at the sight of the graceful white creature, too perfect to be a horse, trailing silver and sky-blue trappings. The Companion had no rider, and everyone knew what that meant. She had come searching, maybe for one of them.

Lara fidgeted at Inya's side, and Inya squeezed the girl's hand. Mariel stood beside them, large-eyed and still. Lara was too young, but Mariel, just sliding into the awkward lankiness between childhood and adulthood, was not. Companions came for children Mariel's age all the time. Anyone who spent an evening listening to a tavern minstrel knew that.

The Companion tossed her head, mane falling down

her back like soft winter snow, sapphire eyes scanning the crowd. Then she started forward, bells jingling, steps light and quick. Inya heard Mariel catch her breath. After all, she'd heard the minstrels, too.

But maybe, just this once, the stories would turn true. The Companion stepped toward them, until Inya saw her breath, frosty in the late autumn air. Another step, and she would be within reach. Another step—

A wet, silky muzzle nudged Inya's chest. She looked down, startled. The Companion looked back at her, through eyes bright and very deep. Inya felt herself falling, drowning in that endless blue. At the bottom waited friendship, and welcoming, and a life without loneliness. The world tilted crazily around her, but for a long moment she didn't care.

The moment ended. Inya pulled herself away, flinging the Companion's reins to the ground. She hadn't even realized she was holding them. The ground steadied beneath her; the world came back into focus.

The Companion kept staring at her. Something brushed Inya's mind, soft as a feather. *:I Choose you:*, a voice whispered. *:After all my searching, I Choose you:*.

As a child, Inya had dreamed about hearing that voice. But that was a long time ago. She didn't have time, now, for a child's adventures. She had a farm to keep up. She had grandchildren to raise. And someone had to look after the girls' father, too. The Companion had made a mistake. Inya couldn't run off, not now.

"Go away," Inya whispered. She twisted a gray strand of hair between her fingers. "I'm too old. You're too late. Go away."

The Companion shook her head. *:You:*.

"Take one of the children. They're who you're looking for, not me."

The Companion snorted, a surprisingly horselike sound. She knelt beside Inya, inviting her to mount.

"No!" Inya turned from the Companion's sapphire eyes. Her foot slipped on a loose stone, and pain shot through her knee, so sharp she caught her breath. She

stood still for several minutes, waiting for the pain to
fade.

Even if she could leave her home and her family, she
couldn't follow the Companion. Who ever heard of a
Herald with bad knees, with joints that ached whenever
it rained?

She felt warm breath on her neck. The muscles down
her back tensed. "Go away. You've made a mistake."

"I wish mistakes like that would happen to me."

Inya turned to see Mariel standing beside her, the bag
with their purchases swinging from one shoulder. The
girl's face had a twisted, angry look. *:You should have
come for Mariel:,* Inya thought again. She sighed, taking
Mariel's hand. She had to get home, to start on dinner,
to clean the house. Whatever dreams she'd had as a
child, she didn't have time, now, to argue with
Companions.

Lara came up at Inya's other side, and Inya took her
hand, too. People lingered in the square, staring. Inya
ignored them. She started past the jumble of stalls and
vendors, toward home.

Lara twisted around and looked over her shoulder.
"She's following us." The girl giggled, as if the idea were
terribly funny.

Mariel dropped Inya's hand, turning to look for herself. "You have to stop," she said. "You can't just leave
her there." Mariel's voice was fierce. "You can't."

"It's not your place to tell me what I can or can't do,"
Inya said sharply. "Now come along."

She kept walking. Mariel followed, but she wouldn't
take Inya's hand again.

All the way home, Inya didn't turn around. Even
though she heard the Companion's steps, light as snow-
fall, behind her.

By the time they got home, an icy rain was falling, turning the dirt road to mud. Inya shivered, dropping Lara's
hand to pull her cloak close around her shoulders. Over
the steady patter of the rain, Inya no longer heard the
Companion's hoofs. Maybe she had finally gone away.

Lara started to run, and Inya, unable to keep up, let her. Mariel followed her sister, the two of them racing for the house.

Inya skirted the edge of the fields, where the girls' father was working. Jory nodded as she walked past. He was splattered with mud, brown curls plastered to his face. Beside him a dappled brown horse was hooked to the plow, deep in mud itself.

Beyond their land, through the trees, Inya saw the dark band of the river. Even from where she stood, she could tell the water was rising. Tongues of water lapped at the trees.

Inya kept walking, past a battered barn and on to the house. She started a fire in the kitchen hearth, and made the girls change into dry clothes.

Mariel avoided Inya's eyes. She wouldn't talk to her, and she ran back outside as soon as she'd changed, muttering something about helping her father. Inya sighed.

She started on dinner, Lara by her side, trying to help but mostly just getting flour in her face and short curls. The fire quickly took the chill from the room, and the smell of simmering soup made the cold outside feel even farther away. Inya kneaded the smooth, hard dough beneath her fingers, trying to forget the Companion's bottomless eyes, trying to forget the silky whisper in her head.

Jory and Mariel came in just after dark. They ate in silence. Jory wolfed down his food, face tired and tight. Mariel didn't eat at all, just stared at Inya with an unreadable expression. Outside, the wind picked up, whistling through the gaps around the door. One of the hinges was wearing loose. Inya needed to fix it before winter.

Jory looked up. "I spoke to old Caron today." Jory's tangled curls fell into his face. Lara looked a lot like him. Mariel was the one who looked like their mother—Inya's daughter. She couldn't believe Anara had been gone almost a year.

Inya fixed her gaze on Jory. "What'd Caron say?"

"He offered me half again what he'd offered before—

more than this farm's ever going to make on its own."
Jory buttered a thick slice of bread. "I said I'd think
about it."

Inya stiffened. "It's not your decision to make." The
farm had been in her family for generations, since before
River's Bend was more than a few scattered houses, before the village even had a name.

"Well, maybe you should think about it, too," Jory
said.

They'd had this discussion before. Caron had first approached Jory nearly two years ago. The farm, once a
candlemark's walk from the next nearest house, was now
close to the village. The merchant wanted to build a
tavern there, and maybe a couple of shops.

At first Jory had refused, just as Inya expected him
to. Then Anara had died, giving birth to a child who
died a few hours after her. After that, Jory took Caron
more seriously. "My heart isn't in this place anymore,"
he'd told Inya once.

Jory's family had moved to River's Bend when he was
a child. He didn't know what it was like to be in a place
for hundreds of years, to stay with it through good times
and bad.

"We could move up to Haven." Jory had finished the
bread and reached for the ale pitcher. "With what Caron's willing to pay, we could start all over again."

"This is our home."

"Anywhere can be home." Jory's voice rose. "Unless
you're too foolish to let it be."

"Jory." Inya kept her own voice low. She wouldn't
yell in front of the children. "What would you do in the
city? You're a farmer."

"My grandfather worked leather. It's a trade I could
learn, if I set my mind to it."

"We belong here."

"You always say that!" Suddenly Jory was standing,
yelling across the table. "We belong where we can make
a living!"

Mariel silently left the kitchen. Lara followed her into
the bedroom. Inya let them go. It was bad enough they'd

lost their mother. They shouldn't have to worry about losing their home, too.

"You're a fool," Jory said, but he didn't say anything more. Somehow, with the children's leaving, the argument had ended.

For now. Inya sighed and started clearing the table.

She'd just finished the dishes when the door flew open and Mariel staggered in. Her clothes were soaked through; water streamed from her hair. She shivered. Thunder rumbled outside.

Inya hurried her to the hearth. She hadn't seen Mariel leave; the girl must have climbed out one of the bedroom's shuttered windows. Inya winced. Had the argument with Jory upset her so much that she didn't want to go through the kitchen again?

Mariel stared at the flames. Her face had a strange look, eyes very large and dark. Inya hoped she hadn't caught a chill. She put water on for tea.

"What do you think you're doing, running around in the rain like that? You'll make yourself sick."

"I had to feed the animals." Mariel's teeth chattered.

"Your father would have done that."

"I had to do it."

The tea boiled. Inya poured Mariel a steaming mug of it, then added a spoonful of honey. Mariel took the cup eagerly. Inya poured herself a cup, as well. Just listening to the wind made her shiver. Her joints were stiffening with dampness; she knew she wouldn't sleep well.

She sipped the hot tea, staring at Mariel over the cup's rim. Mariel's clothes and hair were drying; she'd stopped shivering, too.

She looked a lot like her mother had at that age, from the dark eyes to the long, stringy hair. For a moment Inya thought she saw Anara sitting there, not a married woman but a girl, halfway between childhood and adulthood, staring at her through serious eyes.

"Grandma? Are you all right?" Mariel's voice brought Inya back to the present.

Inya brushed a hand across her face. "I'm fine. Are you warmer now?"

Mariel nodded.

"Why don't you go on to bed, then?"

"Come with me." Mariel sounded suddenly young.

"I'll be along in a moment." Inya watched as Mariel left the room. Then she stood, wincing at the weight on her knees. She walked slowly to the door, examining the worn-out hinge. She felt a tingling at the base of her skull. Some instinct made her undo the latch. She opened the door, staring out into the cold, wet night.

The wind had died. The moon shone through the dark clouds, lighting the field. And something stood beneath that moon, too perfect to be a horse. Its white hide shone, brighter than any moon.

Inya slammed the door shut again. The hinge creaked in protest.

She realized she was crying. :*I can't follow you. Don't you understand?*:

The Companion didn't answer, and Inya didn't open the door again. She banked the fire and stumbled into bed.

That night she dreamed of half-grown children—Mariel, Anara, even herself as a girl. Only all the girls had blue eyes, bright as sapphire. Inya knew that wasn't right, though in the dream she couldn't think why.

Inya woke in the dark, not sure what had stirred her. Rain crashed against the roof; thunder rumbled. She crawled out of bed. The dirt floor was cold and damp beneath her feet, even through heavy socks. Her knees and ankles ached. She walked slowly toward the kitchen.

Jory stood by the door, holding a lantern. The yellow light cast shadows on his face. His shoulders were tight, hunched together. He looked tired.

Inya tensed. "What's wrong?"

"It rained harder than I thought last night. The river's rising fast. If it doesn't crest by the end of the week, the farm'll flood out. Sooner, if the rain keeps up."

Inya bit her lip. She'd known the water was high, but she'd thought they had more time.

There hadn't been a flood since she was a girl. People had come from the village, then, helping her parents build floodwalls of mud and wood. Together, they'd held the water back.

Jory ran a hand through his hair. "Soon as the sun's up, I'm going to start digging."

Inya nodded, suddenly wide awake. "I'll send the children into town with word that we need help."

Jory nodded. He opened the door again. The sky was dark, still more black than gray. Rain fell in icy sheets. There was no moon, no Companion standing in the field. Perhaps she had given up and gone away.

Jory stepped back out, closing the door behind him. Inya went to wake the children.

Mariel was already up. Lara poked out from under the blankets, yawning and rubbing her eyes. Inya explained, as quickly and calmly as she could, while the sun rose and thin light crept around the shuttered windows.

"Will we have to swim?" Lara sounded so worried that Inya didn't know whether to laugh or cry.

"Of course not." Inya spoke as gently as she could. "We're going to sit down and have breakfast, same as always. Then I'm going to send you into town with a message for the mayor." As a child, Inya had taken a similar message to the mayor's grandfather. River's Bend hadn't had a mayor back then, but there had been a village council, and he'd been on it.

While the girls munched on reheated soup and cold bread, Inya wrote the message. Then she bundled Lara and Mariel into warm clothes and followed them outside. The rain had let up, and pale yellow light filtered through the clouds. The warm rays felt good on Inya's face.

She didn't have time to stand around, though. The dishes needed washing, and the door needed mending. She had to check for new leaks in the roof, too. And with Jory and the girls out all morning, she needed to make something warm for lunch.

She went back inside, closing the door behind her.

*   *   *

The rain started again soon after the girls left. No thunder this time, and not much wind; just a steady drizzle that stole all the warmth from the air. Inya found herself shivering, even inside. She worked slowly, knees and ankles complaining as she did.

Lara didn't return until well past noon. She pulled off her boots, sat down by the hearth, and stretched out her feet to warm them.

"Where's Mariel?"

"She's—" Lara hesitated. "She's outside helping Dad."

Inya nodded. She put water on for tea, then sat down beside Lara.

"They made me wait a long time," Lara said. "They wouldn't let me see the mayor, but they took the note to him, and came back with an answer. It's in my pocket." Lara pulled out a sheet of wet, crumpled paper.

The ink ran, but Inya could still make out the writing. She read the letter slowly. Then she read it again, unable to believe the words.

Much of it was formal, meaningless prose, thanking her for writing and expressing concern for her family. But two lines told her what the message really meant.

While we share concern for your property and safety, the village has not gone unaffected by this rain, and our own affairs occupy most of our time. I can make no promises, though we will send what help we can, when we can.

Anger blurred Inya's sight. *What help we can, when we can.* That meant there'd be no help at all. And, *our own affairs.* That meant the farm's affairs were not the village's affairs, not their concern at all.

Things had been different when Inya was a girl. The farm and village had worked together; in her grandmother's day, the farm had even been the larger of the two. There'd been no question, then, about whether the villagers would help hold the water back. They had helped. Just like Inya's family had helped the villagers, during hard winters, supplying food and charging only what they could afford.

Inya wondered when things had changed. She wondered why she hadn't noticed. She'd been busy—raising children, raising grandchildren, working on the farm—but how could she have missed what was happening around her?

She threw the message into the fire. The wet paper hissed, then burst into flames, turning to ash as she watched.

She found Jory by the river, ankle-deep in mud, leaning on his shovel and staring at the water. A wall of dirt and wood began upstream, beyond the house, and extended to where he stood.

The current swirled swiftly by, carrying tree branches, loose reeds, clumps of grass. Something that looked like a broken chair floated past. Inya shuddered.

Jory shook his head, splattering water around him. "I can save the house," he said. His voice was hoarse. "But not the barn and the rest of the land. Not without help."

"There won't be any help." Inya told him about the mayor's note.

Jory brushed a hand across his dirt-streaked face. "Doesn't surprise me. That's how people are, you know. Watch out for themselves first, and for everyone else if they have any time left over."

But people weren't like that, Inya thought. Not everywhere. They hadn't been in River's Bend, not when she was a girl. She stared at Jory, not sure what to say. If he assumed people only cared about themselves, no wonder he wanted to move. One place was the same as another, if you saw the world like that.

An awful thought crossed Inya's mind. If the people in River's Bend didn't care, did that mean it was time to leave, to find a place where they did?

"I'll finish securing the house tonight," Jory said. "And see what I can do about the fields in the morning."

Inya nodded. "At least you've had Mariel helping you."

"Mariel?" Jory squinted. "I haven't seen her all day."

"What do you mean?" Ice trickled down Inya's spine. "Lara said she was with you."

Jory shook his head. "I'll go look for her. You talk to Lara."

Inya hurried toward the house, boots squishing in the mud. She slowed down when her legs began to ache. Sweat trickled down her face, in spite of the cold. She threw the door open and went inside. Lara still sat by the fire.

"Where's your sister?"

Lara started. "I promised not to tell."

"Lara—"

"She's in the barn." The girl's words tumbled over one another. "It's not my fault. She made me promise."

Relief washed over Inya. Of course Mariel was all right. She'd been silly to think otherwise. The girl had probably run off to be alone. Anara had done the same at Mariel's age.

"How long has she been there?"

"All day."

Well, Inya would have to talk to Mariel about that. The girl had no right to send Lara into town alone.

"Don't tell her I told," Lara begged.

Inya didn't answer. She gulped down a mouthful of warm tea and went back outside.

She found Jory in the barn, staring at the ground. Mariel was nowhere in sight.

"Look at this." Jory's voice was strained.

Cold dread settled in Inya's stomach. She followed his gaze.

The muddy barn floor was covered with Mariel's boot prints. But there was a second set of prints, too, and those weren't human.

Hoof prints. Inya knelt to have a closer look. The prints were large, larger than any horse Inya had owned. She examined a print more carefully. Short, white hairs were scattered in the mud. They were bright and fine, and even in the mud hadn't gathered any dirt.

Inya caught her breath. The Companion had left—and

had taken Mariel with her. Inya smiled, though she felt a tinge of sadness, too.

"You see anything down there?"

"Yes." She told Jory about the Companion, leaving out her own role in the tale. It was Mariel's story now, after all. As it should be.

Jory didn't smile. In a thin voice he asked, "Do you think she's all right?"

Mariel was Chosen, Inya thought; of course she was all right. But she realized she didn't really know what happened after someone was Chosen. The Companion would head to Haven and the Collegium, but that was more than a week away. What would Mariel eat? Did she have warm clothes? Why had she left without saying good-bye?

Inya examined the prints again. They led out of the barn, toward the river. Mariel never mounted, just continued alongside the Companion. Didn't Heralds always ride?

Probably everything was all right. Probably Inya was just a crazy old woman, worrying too much. But probably wasn't enough.

"We have to find her. Bring her some food. Make sure she's all right."

Jory nodded. But then he looked back toward the river, and Inya knew what he was thinking. If he went after Mariel, they might lose the farm.

"I'll go," Inya said.

"That's crazy." Jory brushed his hands against his breeches.

"No it isn't." Inya spoke fast, afraid she might believe him if she didn't. "On horse I can make decent time, even with my knees. What I can't do is keep the farm from flooding out. You can."

"It'll be dark soon."

"I'll bring a lantern. I can carry it and walk, once the sun goes down." Inya didn't know how long she could manage on foot, but she'd worry about that later. She stared at Jory, hoping he'd see that she was right.

"I don't like it." Jory looked at Inya through tired

eyes. He needed to rest, much more than Inya did. He'd been building walls all day, after all. "I'll take another look around the farm," he said. "Maybe she hasn't gone all that far."

"I'll start packing," Inya told him.

By the time she was ready to leave, the sun was low, casting gold light through the drifting clouds. Jory hadn't found Mariel—both her boot prints and the Companion's hooves followed the river, disappearing upstream.

Jory didn't argue any further. He saddled the dappled horse and helped Inya mount. Her knees ached, unused to being twisted out for riding, but she gritted her teeth and ignored the pain. Her hips complained, too, at the way they stretched across the saddle.

Inya reminded Lara to listen to her father, reminded Jory that there was some reheated soup on the fire. Then she left, following the tracks past the edge of the farm.

The sun soon dipped below the horizon, but the light stayed with her for a while. The moon rose above pink and orange clouds. Inya's breath came out in frosty puffs.

The scattered trees grew thicker beyond their land, until Inya rode at the edge of a forest. The mud deepened, and she had to slow down.

Inya stopped just as the last light faded. She didn't want to dismount, but she needed to rest and get something to eat. Better to go slow than to wear herself out.

She eased herself out of the saddle. Her legs wobbled as she hit the ground. She hadn't realized that getting off would hurt more than getting on.

She ate by yellow lamplight, munching on some bread while the horse grazed nearby. By the time she was ready to move on, the moon had slipped behind a cloud.

Taking the horse's reins in one hand and the lamp in the other, she started walking.

Inya tired much more quickly on foot. Every candlemark, it seemed, she had to stop, rest, and eat something.

Small swirls of water appeared in the mud, and the swirls turned into puddles. Mud coated her boots; water soaked through her socks. Cold air numbed her face and fingers. She pulled out the scarf and gloves she'd packed. The next time she stopped, she'd change her socks as well. She was glad she'd packed extra clothes. When she was younger, she probably wouldn't have bothered. But back then she could have managed, in spite of her foolishness. She didn't have that luxury now.

The puddles widened, until Inya had to veer into the woods to get around them. She lost track of how long she walked.

Then she saw that the sky had turned from black to dark gray. It was almost morning. The very thought made her tired. She stopped to rest, wondering how much farther Mariel had gone.

The gray sky lightened; a thin band of color appeared along the horizon. Birds chirped across the treetops. There was another animal, too, farther away, but Inya couldn't hear it as well. It made a low sound, more like a cry than anything else.

A child's cry.

Fear tingled down Inya's spine. "Mariel!" She took off upstream at a run.

Her legs protested, but she ignored the pain, shut it away to deal with later. In the growing light she saw that the ground had turned uneven. In spots the water surrounded small islands of land.

She found Mariel on one of those islands.

The girl stared at the water, eyes wide. Her clothes were rumpled and muddy, as if she'd slept on the damp ground. The water wasn't very wide, but it was still—and therefore deep.

"Grandma!" Mariel looked up, red-eyed. "I fell asleep. There wasn't any water when I fell asleep."

Inya wanted to reach out and hug her. Instead she just called out, "I'm here, Mariel," as calmly as she could. A distant corner of her mind wondered where the Companion had gone. She'd worry about that later, after she got Mariel off the island.

"You'll have to swim. You can throw your shoes across to me first; that'll make it easier."

"I can't." Mariel choked on a sob.

"Of course you can. I'll be right here, waiting for you."

"No." Mariel began to cry. "I can't swim. I don't know how."

For a moment Inya didn't believe her; she was sure she'd taught Mariel to swim herself. But no, Anara was the child she'd taught. She'd assumed Anara had taught her children in turn.

Inya might be able swim to the island herself, but she couldn't make it back, not while carrying someone. And the damp logs on the ground were too soft and slippery to walk across.

In the distance, the dappled horse let out a nervous nicker. If the horse could swim, it could carry them both across, but the mare had a terror of water that no one had broken.

"Grandma?" Mariel shivered, drawing her arms around herself. Inya felt cold too—frozen, unable to move, unable to think what to do next.

Her skull tingled. There was a sudden flash of sapphire, bright and deep, gone before Inya was certain she saw it. The sky was gray, with pale streaks where the light filtered through.

Somehow, that flash of blue unfroze her, allowed her to think again. She couldn't use the dappled mare, but maybe she could call someone else. Someone who had no right to have left Mariel in the first place, but she'd worry about that later.

:Thea.: Inya didn't know where the name came from, but she knew it was right. *:Thea, I call you.:*

For a moment the air was still, the birds in the treetops silent. Then Inya heard a sound—like a nicker, only higher, lighter, more graceful. Hoofs hit the dirt lightly, with only the faintest whisper of noise.

And the Companion stood before her. Mud splattered her saddle, but the white coat was bright. Beneath the overcast sky, the creature seemed to glow. And her eyes—

No, Inya wouldn't look into her eyes. She wanted to be able to let her go when she was through.

The Companion snorted, pawing one foot against the ground. She almost seemed impatient.

All right, then. :*Thea. You're the one who left Mariel stranded. Now you're going to help get her out.*:

:*I did not leave her. She ran away on her own. I only followed because I was worried about her safety.*: But Thea knelt, inviting Inya to mount.

The Companion was larger than the dappled horse, and wider; Inya's hips stretched painfully across the saddle. Yet Thea moved more smoothly than any horse; when she stepped forward, Inya barely felt the motion.

She almost didn't notice when Thea stepped into the water, not until the water came up to her feet and soaked through her breeches. Water sloshed over the saddle, and the Companion used her strong legs to swim. Inya clutched the wet mane, drew her legs more tightly around the saddle.

Then the water turned shallow again. Thea stepped up onto dry land, and Inya shivered as the air hit her wet clothes.

"Grandma!"

Inya eased her way out of the saddle and took Mariel in her arms.

"She wouldn't take me," Mariel sobbed. She buried her face in Inya's shoulder. "She was in the barn, and you didn't want her anyway, but she wouldn't take me."

Inya whirled to face the Companion, glaring. "How dare you get a child's hopes up like that? How dare you follow her this far and not Choose her? You lied to her, that's what you did!"

:*No. I never claimed to Choose her, though she begged me to. I did not know my presence on the farm would bother her so. I did not know she would run away. I went after her, but I could not persuade her to return.*:

:*So Choose her now. It's not too late.*:

:*No. I Choose you.*:

:Damn you!: Inya turned away, facing Mariel again. *:She's still young—young enough for a child's adventures. She has an entire life in front of her.:*

:There is no right or wrong age for such things.:

Inya laughed, a bitter sound. *:You don't know much about the responsibilities that come with adulthood, then. Or about the ailments that come with old age.:*

Thea snorted. *:I know that you've had the strength to keep your family together, through death and hard times. You've had the strength, too, to travel through the night, steadily and in spite of pain, to rescue a child. These are not small virtues. They are virtues that would serve a Herald well.:*

:That's not enough,: Inya said.

The Companion stamped a foot; it squished against the mud. *:I know, also, that you're more sensible than a child would be. You packed extra supplies, made sure you stopped to rest before you collapsed from exhaustion. You would never die for the stupid reasons young people die. Your age makes you more likely to be taken seriously, too, in negotiations and other diplomatic matters. There are a thousand reasons. Need I list them all?:*

Inya felt anger again, not for Mariel's sake, but for her own. She brushed hot tears aside with one hand. *:Why in all the Havens didn't you come sooner? Why didn't you come when I could still leave?:*

Thea came up behind Inya, leaning a silky muzzle against her neck. Inya turned to look at the Companion.

And made the mistake of meeting her eyes. She felt herself falling, drowning in a field of endless sapphire blue.

:I Choose you. Don't you understand? Now neither of us will ever be alone.:

:I need to take care of Jory and the children. I can't just follow you away.: She knew, though, that Jory would welcome the chance to move to the City. And the villagers would hardly notice they were gone.

:I couldn't come sooner. I was not yet in this world, and then I was too young. I've come now. Will you have me?:

Inya took a deep breath. Her next words surprised her. "I don't know."

"Don't know what, Grandma?"

Inya looked down to see Mariel staring at her. She hadn't realized she'd spoken aloud.

:I can wait while you decide.:

There was the farm to take care of. The water to hold back. And the land had been in her family for so long. No matter how hard the villagers turned their backs, Inya wouldn't walk away without thinking a good, long time. *:How long are you willing to wait?:*

:As long as you need.: Thea met Inya's eyes again, but this time, Inya didn't drown in them. Instead, something rose up from the Companion, a warmth that surrounded her, made her understand what it truly meant to never be alone. She was crying again, but this time she didn't even wipe the tears away.

She knew, then, what her answer to the Companion would be. She'd wait a while to give it, but she knew.

"Grandma? Are you okay?"

:Your grandmother is fine.:

"Grandma!" Mariel's face lit up. "She spoke to me! Did you hear? She wouldn't Choose me, but at least she spoke. That's something, isn't it?"

"Yes, that's something." *:You should have taken Mariel,:* she thought again, but she didn't know whether she meant it. Something brushed her mind, feather-light. Inya smiled. She reached out and hugged Mariel.

Thea did not speak again, not then and not for a long time afterward. The Companion knelt down, letting Inya and Mariel mount.

The three of them crossed the river, and together began the long journey home.

Blood Ties
by Stephanie D. Shaver

Stephanie Shaver is a twenty-something writer living in Missouri. In her spare time, she works on the obligatory novel and short stories, but most of her time is taken up attending school, where she's majoring in Computer Science, and writing code for an online games company. She has worked at *Marion Zimmer Bradley's Fantasy Magazine,* and considers it one of the great experiences of her life. Of this story, she says, "I wrote this story for the anthology a long time ago, back when I was still in my 'Angry Young Woman' phase. Misty has always been a strong force in my life, beginning at the age of thirteen. I can only thank her for introducing me to a world of magic and wonder, a feeling I hope to someday breathe into my own works."

Dedication:
to Mr. Brian Devaney—
respected teacher, good friend,
and one of the few true Heralds in this world

"Rivin."

From where he sat at the table, the boy looked up at his father. He had been rubbing his fingers—near to blistering from chopping wood all day—trying to get the ache out of them.

Holding so hard to the ax handle I forgot how to let go, he thought, reminding himself of a quote his older sister, Sattar, was fond of.

Rivin looked around to see Sattar clearing the wooden trenchers for washing, Danavan—his younger sister—

smiling her sweet, undefiled smile and vanishing after Sattar, and Nastasea squalling as she tried to catch up with her two older siblings. In his concentration on his pain, he had forgotten that dinner was over.

"Is—something wrong, sir?"

For a small man, Delanon Morningsong had an enormous presence about him. Strict and solemn, dedicated to purist beliefs, he was a refugee of the famine that had caused his family to flee from their native land of Karse.

Rivin had not been part of the flight that had carried his father, mother, and their extended families to Valdemar, but he had heard enough stories about it to be happy to no longer live in Karse. While he had been pelted with his father's beliefs since before he could speak, his daydreaming and slightly absentminded attitude had mostly helped him to escape the rigid mindframe of most of his father's teachings—and had also caused him great bodily harm in the area of thrashings and penance.

"You chopped that wood?"

"Aye, sir." Rivin smiled, not wincing as he ran a hand through his short black hair. His eyes were gray, like his mother's.

"All of it?"

"Yes, sir."

The dark brown eyes of his father flickered.

"Good," he grunted at last. "I have another task for you."

Rivin groaned inwardly. He had estimated one week until he began planting in the fields—usually that week was a lazy, vacationlike existence where he performed menial tasks and occasional chores, a break before the longest season. But Delanon had been piling jobs on him since weather had permitted, and Rivin feared his father might be trying to put the yoke of "responsible manhood" upon him.

Well, I am nearly thirteen . . . I suppose he'll be thinking about marriage, too, soon.

Outwardly, Rivin's face remained neutral, neither smiling idiotically nor showing contempt toward further work. One would have been considered mockery, the other insubordination.

But the words Delanon had to say were hardly what his son expected, and it was all the boy could do to keep the shock and joy from showing on his face.

"I want you to go into town and buy some things. Sacks, candles, Sattar says she needs a new spindle as well." His serpentine eyes turned thoughtful as he appraised his son. Rivin blinked in surprise. This was no chore! He was going into *town*! Away from the farm! Away from work! Freedom and fresh air!

"In addition to that, Sattar and I have decided that we can no longer support having Nastasea and Danavan. I talked to my sister, and she said she'd be more than happy to take them—she being no longer capable of having littles and all."

Surprise again, and relief as well. Rivin and Sattar had been conspiring long and hard to get Nastasea and Danavan out of the house, if only to avoid having to endure a life of poverty and their father's harsh rules . . . now it seemed their plans would come true.

"After all, they'd only be a dowry fee and a nuisance," he added casually. "And we don't have the money your aunt does."

Probably because Aunt has the sense to let some of her fields lie fallow, while you plant more than you could ever hope to harvest! Rivin had heard his father's excuses and complaints many times, and had long ago stopped believing them.

Delanon raised a glass filled with water to his lips and drank. His father had long ago forsworn spirits and beer, sticking to clean water and berry juice, or cow's and goat's milk.

"Any questions?" the older man asked, wiping his mouth.

Rivin shook his head, and then said, "No, sir."

"Then get to bed. You'll be leaving in the morning."

Rivin bowed his head. "Thank you, sir."

The soft pad of his feet as he left the house for the

stables was all the sound Rivin could make to express his joy.

Though clouds had built up the night before, the promise of rain had not come through. Rivin awoke in the barn, surprised to find the hay he was lying in (with a scrap of cloth thrown over to take away the itch) was not damp with early moisture. Indeed, the day was clear and the sky blue as the Morningsong excursion began— Nastasea and Danavan behind and Rivin leading in a steady walk. In a way, he was grateful for the clear weather. It meant that the trek would be easier. But dry weather wouldn't make planting less difficult, and he hoped that it would cloud over after he dropped off Nastasea and Danavan with Aunt Rianao.

I don't care if I get drenched, but the girls are still too delicate. They'd probably die of pneumonia, and gods know what hells I'd go through trying to forgive myself— as well as the suffering Father'd *put me through. Not like he'd need to do anything. I'd probably kill myself if I let one of them die.*

Time whittled away as they moved, Rivin's feet taking well to the walk. He glanced back only once, when they got to the top of the hilly slope that overlooked the farm. He thought he saw Sattar standing in the doorway, hands tucked into her apron, the wind stirring her hair lightly. She was a mirror of their father—dark and sharp—except that her eyes were not solemn, they were sorrowful. Ever since their mother had died a month after Nastasea's birth, she had taken on the tasks of housewife and sister, moving like a steady ghost through the house and tending to their needs. He felt a stab of sadness as he disappeared over the ridge, as if he were leaving her forever. . . .

But I'll be back before the moon turns full. Why do I feel this way?

Sunzenith rose over the windy farmlands, and Rivin took the time to rest and feed his sisters on bread and cheese and cool water. He himself fasted, knowing that in three candlemarks there would be a good meal waiting at Rianao's. Besides, he would need to keep a tight watch on his rations if he were to make it to Kettlesmith and back.

By a candlemark and a half, he was carrying Nastasea, who had begun complaining—*"feet!"*—to mean that her feet hurt. Though nearly five years old, she still talked like one of the littlest littles. Sattar said that they had all been like that, and that this would pass.

Aye, just like the fears of monsters in the well and colddrakes in the dark. And me—with my fear of the barn. Still get kind of nervy when I go in there at night to sleep. Ah, well, time will cure.

A thread of wind tickled his face, and Nastasea giggled a little, playing with a digit of his hair.

Rivin nodded to himself. *Time always has before. . . .*

Rivin rubbed his shoulder—weary from holding the burden of his younger sister—trying to massage the pain out of it. His back leaned against the wood-built wall of his aunt's fore-room, his left side toward the cheery fire that was burning steadily in the hearth. He took a long drink from his milk-filled tin cup, grateful for the cool liquid, and smiled when Rianao walked by.

His aunt's establishment was larger than his home, being the dwelling of numerous children (called Rianao's Brood) as well as a crew of work hands, seven large wolfhounds, and five cats.

On the other side of the room was an enigma. Seated in a high-backed, armless wooden chair and dressed in white tunic and side-split, white leather riding skirt was Lisabet Morningsong, the Herald-Mage of the family, and distant cousin to Rianao. She didn't look much like a mage—with needlework on her lap and her face lost in concentration as she pulled up a knot—but there was a slight aura about her that spoke of control, restrained power, and authority.

She looked up at him upon noticing his eyes on her, and smiled slightly, inclining her head at him just a little before reaching into the basket at her side and hunting for a new color of thread.

"She's here on vacation," he heard a voice say, and looked up at the looming form of Rianao's fifteen-year-old son Tileir, who had met the Morningsong pack as they arrived at Rianao's farm. "Some vacation—haw!" The older boy shook his head as he slid down on the floor next to Rivin. "She's just 'bout as old as Ma an' looks like she was Ma's daughter! They say," his voice grew to an undertone, "that it's the *magic* tha' does't."

"I never heard of magic doing that," Rivin murmured back.

"Neit'er I until m'cousin Kentith told me."

"And what does *Kentith* know?" Rivin had only met Kentith once or twice, but had, from first encounter, disliked the boy for some strange reason.

Tileir gave a braying laugh. "Why, boy, didn't ya hear? *Kentith's* been Chosen, too!"

Rivin went silent with shock. "Kentith? Kentith Ravenblack? *Our* cousin?"

"Why are ye so surprised? If Lisabet, why, then, whyn't another?"

Rivin shrugged. "Do'know. It's just . . ." he trailed off, shook his head. "Never mind." He could see Tileir was going to push the subject, so he said, "Where am I sleeping tonight?"

Tileir considered for a moment, his caravan of thought rerouted with this new line of questioning. "Why—most prob'bly wi' me."

Rivin winced, feeling a strange panic build inside. Panic not so much of having to sleep with Tileir, but of what Tileir might do to him.

Why am I thinking like this? he rationalized to himself in bewilderment. *Tileir wouldn't do anything to me! Lady—I think I'm going mad!*

Across the room Lisabet's head lifted, and she cocked her head to one side, as if trying to hear something she couldn't quite catch. She swept the room with baffled eyes, pausing only momentarily to look at him before going on.

It was then that Rivin heard the thin wail coming from outside.

"... *No! no! no! no!* ... *won't! won't! won't!* ...
DON'T WANT BATH!*"

Rivin ran outside, stopping when he saw Rianao
standing over Nastasea. The child was snarling up at
her aunt, her little face streaked with tears and broken
with anger.

"Won't, won't, WON'T!"

"Now, 'Stasea—" Rianao said soothingly, moving
forward.

"NO!" the child shrieked, hands curled into white-
knuckled fists at her sides, eyes squeezed shut.

"Aunt—here, let me." He moved forward, past the
round, horse-faced body of his aunt, and knelt in front
of Nastasea.

" 'Stasea," he said, touching her fists.

"No!"

His ears rang as her scream echoed around him. In a
soft voice he gentled her, watching as her short-lived
tantrum drained away, her expression remolding again,
except now it was confused and tear-filled.

"Want *Mamma,*" she whimpered, using her word for
Sattar.

"Mamma's not here anymore, 'Stasea. Rianao's going
to be your new mamma."

"No!" The shriek went up again.

"Yes," he said firmly, pulling her into his arms. "Yes."

He stroked her hair lovingly as she sobbed against his
shoulder, stuttering out *"Mamma"* every third word. He
could feel Rianao's curious gaze on him as he spoke to
his sister. He kept his own eyes fixed on the steaming
tub in front of him.

"Let Ria give you a bath?" he asked at last, patting
her back with a note of finality.

She sniffed and nodded, her eyes downcast.

"Good." He turned to his aunt. "All yours."

She looked a bit shocked as he handed her his sister.
"I thank ye," she said, blinking owlishly at him as he
stood.

" 'Twas nothing," he said as he walked away from

them, going back into the house, masking his face with false cheer.

But between his brows was a headache, between his shoulders tight muscles, and his arm once more hurt from holding on too hard to his sister.

Night!

He woke with a start, his breath heavy as his eyes strained to adapt to the absence of light. Next to him, Tileir dreamed on, his heavy snoring sending discordant ripples into the pearly pre-dawn silence of the room.

Rivin wiped his hands over his brow, surprised to find it dry. He had been flushed a moment ago, he was sure of it. The room *must* have been stifling hot—

But it wasn't. The window was open, letting the cool air in, letting the hot air out. Slowly, so as not to wake Tileir, Rivin stood. He picked up his belongings, cast one last unnecessary, fear-inspired glance back, and then exited.

Rianao's home was silent save for the sound of the sleepers. The chairs were empty, the sewing set aside, and Rivin found himself thinking, *I guess mages sleep, too.*

He purloined a loaf of the oldest bread he could find, then moved outdoors and filled his leather skin with water from the well. His aunt wouldn't mind, he knew, but she would probably be disappointed when she found him gone before she woke. So would Nastasea and Danavan. Rivin had to remind himself that they were only half a day's ride from his father's, and that it would be easy to come and visit . . . just as soon as he finished planting . . . and harvesting . . . and trading . . . and planning for winter . . . but then they would be snowbound for all the winter, and then. . . .

Rivin realized with a sinking heart that it would be a very long time before he saw his sisters again.

Silent with guilt, he loped down the road.

Two days later, he was ruing his wish for a storm.
While the precious items he had bought in town were

securely wrapped in layer upon layer of lavishly waxed skins, *he* had no such protection, and was drenched to the core when finally he reached home, letting himself into the barn to change and then go via the adjoining, *dry* overhang into the house proper.

"Rivin?" he heard, low and soft from his right, and he spun—panic catching him off guard—only to see Sattar, sitting in a golden pile of hay with her knees drawn to her chest and her arms wrapped around her legs. She looked up at him, and he noticed the dark rings around her eyes.

Somewhere inside him, despite her appearance, he felt a deep weight lifted, and relief flooded every pore.

She's alive, he found his mind sighing.

"Sattar—" He swallowed. "You scared me."

She nodded, and he noticed a haunted look in her eyes.

"What's wrong?" he asked, kneeling next to her. Concern tinged his voice.

She flinched as he touched her, her muscles clenching spasmodically, and then the emotion smoothed away as she took rigid control of her body. She smiled at him, her lips tight, if not pained. One hand sought his hair and the other went around his shoulder in a gesture that reminded him keenly of his mother.

"Sa . . . sa . . . sa," she murmured. "How was your trip, Rivin?"

He shrugged, wrapping his arms around her and placing his cheek against her shoulder.

"How did you convince Da about the girls?"

" 'Twas nothing. Da is very easy to talk to if you—catch him in the right mood."

He heard loss and something he knew but could not name lace her words, but he ignored it, instead closing his eyes and being content to listen to her heartbeat.

"You know I would've rather stayed—" he started.

"Sa, sa," she interrupted. "We all must have our freedoms, fledgling. I would not limit you yours."

He sat up, shaking droplets from his hair. "Look, I'm

soaked. How about I put on some of my dry things and
you take the packs inside?"

She nodded, smiling. "I'll get to stoking the fire—
Father can complain if he wants, but the rain is a good
omen and you're cold. The wood is worth it."

With brisk efficiency, she took the packs and went
inside.

It took him a while to realize that she had never told
him what was wrong, and he cursed himself for not recognizing the same tactics he had used on his cousin.

Rivin watched the scythe slide over the grain, listening
to the whisper of the wheat as it cut. He blinked rapidly,
exhaustion blurring his vision. He had been working sun
up to sun up for the past two days, with one more day
to go. Harvest week was crucial to the prosperity of the
crop—if they didn't reap it in time, the wheat would
spoil along with their profits.

While he was used to this sort of work, he wasn't so
sure of his sister. She was some hundred yards away,
working her section of the field, cutting with slow, even
strokes. In the past months since the planting season had
started, she had grown more and more anxious—worried
almost—with lines of fatigue growing around her eyes.
Rivin had no idea why she felt this way—the crop was
growing well, and they should be able to harvest enough
to make a large profit. But, still, the state of despera-
tion—almost depression—she had fallen into made him
wonder, and agitated him no small amount.

He did not know what made him stop and look up.
He thought that he heard a soft voice call his name like
a lost spirit on the breeze, but he was never sure. One
moment he was biting his lip to keep himself awake, the
next his head had snapped up and trained on Sattar,
who had fallen motionless in the field.

"Sattar?" he called, dropping his scythe and running
over.

Rivin knelt when he came to the body of his sister,
and was shocked to see blood staining the heavy layers
of her skirts. A claw of pure fear gripped his heart, and

he glanced toward the scythe she had been using, fearing
that she had fallen on it.

But, no, the blade shone like a clean moon, the silver
edge dulled, perhaps, by the work it had been doing, but
not bright red with fresh gut-blood. Than what . . . ?

"Move away, boy!" Delanon roared, coming out of
nowhere, and Rivin was pushed back by surprisingly
strong hands.

"Sattar?" he heard his father say, panic in his voice.
The man shook her, rolling her over and staring into her
pale face. Even from where he lay in the ripe crop, Rivin
could see the sweat on her clammy skin, could almost
feel the chill coming off her cool body.

"Should I—should I get the Healer?"

"Yes! Now!" his father roared, picking her up and
cradling her tenderly, like a lover. His jaw was clenched
tight, his eyes downcast, and Rivin could clearly hear
him say, *"Don't die, girl. Papa loves you. Don't die now.
Not yet."*

And then the boy was running—not for his life, but
his sister's.

"Let me see," said the Healer, his face blank as he
bent over the unconscious form of Sattar.

Rivin was still breathing heavily as he leaned against
the doorway to his sister's room. The Healer lived a full
hour down the road, but it had seemed to Rivin to be
a thousand miles he traveled before he finally arrived at
the old man's house, banging on the door and screaming
at the top of his lungs as if the Hounds of Hell were on
his heels. It had taken another thousand years to saddle
the Healer's horse, and then a thousand leagues to ride
back, with Rivin gasping the whole way.

Now, safe at home, he watched in anxious concern as
the Healer drew back the covers and examined his sister.

After a moment he looked up, giving Rivin and Delanon a severe look and saying, "Please leave the room."

The two men filed out, Rivin panting now from increased fear as well as exertion.

The door shut with an ominous *thud*.

Rivin waited, shifting nervously from foot to foot. After a moment, he felt an iron hand on his shoulder, and turned to look into Delanon's dead eyes.

"Go," he said, pointing out the door, toward the fields.

Rivin's jaw dropped, and it took all his will not to scream, *You've got to be joking!*

"*Now,*" Delanon said, leaving no question of authority.

Rivin submissively lowered his head and walked out the door.

In the field, he picked up his fallen scythe, looking at the only-half-harvested crop, blind to the fact that the profits this year would be slim.

The silent whisper of the scythe was the only sound he heard, gasping like the laboring death-rattle of a dying person.

"Ho—boy."

Rivin stopped his work, dumbly turning toward the Healer who was standing in the stubble of wheat-trail that Rivin had made.

"We must speak.'"

Mute still, and shivering from sweat-chills and weakness, Rivin leaned on his scythe, waiting.

"How is she?" he asked bluntly.

The Healer shook his head. "There is a sore deep inside her that my Gifts and knowledge can't seem to reach. I am going to try and summon help, but I fear I may not be quick enough."

Rivin scrubbed his face, pretending that the dampness this action left on his hand was sweat, and not tears.

"Why has this happened?"

The Healer frowned, a line of worry between his brows. "Did not you know, boy? She has miscarried. The babe could not survive the strain of the work she was doing. Some can, but she was too frail." A note of disapproval entered the man's voice.

Rivin blinked, the chill in his body suddenly concentrating and finding a focus in his breastbone.

"Do you know the father?" the Healer went on.

Rivin stared at the man, feeling a numb balm wash him. In that moment, he felt separate—from his body, from the situation, from the questions the old Healer asked. He was above it all—all laws and vows, all beliefs and blood ties that had bound him to his family and his father. The chill in his heart began to radiate outward, and he felt it enter his gaze.

The Healer must have seen it, for his own blue eyes widened and he stepped back, slowly, first one step, then another.

"I—" the old man began, and then broke into a run, waddling flat-footed toward his horse, mounting, and galloping off into the night.

In his belly—even apart—Rivin felt a colddrake uncoil, stirring.

Go, the Rivin that walked apart from Rivin thought. *Summon your Healers. They may be able to help my sister, but there is none who can save my father.*

Carefully, Rivin felt himself lay the scythe down. He would not need its edge. He turned to the farm, and took one step—

The movement was like a trigger. He *Felt* the tremble of inner blocks crack, fracture, and start to collapse. Revulsion, that sense of broken trust, panic—the source of all those emotions had overflowed its dam. The walls disintegrated—

And . . . he remembered. . . .

So long ago, as a child—a baby. The warm trust and love he had once held for the man who loomed above him, who he called Da. He remembered the day he had been playing in the barn and his mother had been down at Rianao's, on an errand with Sattar, heavy with Danavan. He remembered looking up, and seeing Delanon—

He remembered pain, and screaming. He remembered the ripping sound of his clothes as they were torn from him, and he remembered begging, pleading, "No—no—please, Da, no—"

He remembered being beaten, and then told that if he

told anyone, anyone, *his father would kill him—or kill Sattar. And it would all be Rivin's fault if that happened.*

And he had made himself forget. To keep that from happening, he had built up walls, drowned the memory, weighted it with stones and thrown it down a well—

But now he knew. Now he was soaked with memory. All the groundless fears had a base. His vision was clear. The denial was gone. Now he knew—

His father had raped him.

The door to the farm did not open, it *exploded.* He Felt himself reaching for the chill fire that had now spread to his palms, and he Felt it buoy his spirit higher. He Felt the hunger for revenge—*cleansing at last!*—sweep him as he opened the door to Sattar's room, and stared down at his father.

Who was sitting in a stool, holding his daughter's hand, bent double.

There was no pity, no remorse at that moment. There was no doubt as to who was the father of Sattar's baby. He had heard the unknown element in Sattar's voice that rainy night he had returned from his excursion to the city, and now he knew a name for it.

Shame.

Delanon stood, a frown on his brow, his eyes dark. With a sweep of his hand, Rivin felt raw power roar through his body and pick his father up, slamming the older man against a wall.

There was a *crack* and a scream as Delanon's rib cage broke and his pelvis shattered, and Rivin felt a rivulet of sheer exhiliration trickle into him. *Retribution,* he thought, and Reached for *more.*

"No!" the disembodied boy heard. He saw realization in his father's eyes, a desperate plea—horror—fear—*good!*—*"Stop! Please—oh—gods—I'm sorry—"*

Rivin did not waste the breath to tell his father that there was no way he could excuse what he had done, nor words enough to apologize. There wasn't even the *time* for words. Only the time for destruction. Only—the solution—

Fire exploded from the boy, smoking through his body

and out of his hands in a burst of light and energy. He
Felt the agony as his father screamed, writhing and twisting.
The fire sloughed off flesh, burned away blood, burrowed
into marrow and bone. Rivin screamed his hatred—his
burden of *shame*—into the winds he had summoned,
feeling his mind snap and crackle beneath the new burden of magic.

And then it was over, leaving behind only a char-
black, greasy smear on the wall, and ashes on the floor.
Rivin swayed, staring down at his hands, amazement in
his eyes.

With a popping sound akin to that of a dislocated joint
being reset, he came back to himself.

What have I done?

He sank to his knees, sanity returning, the cold ban-
ished, weakness and a strange inner emptiness making
him tremble. The air was stifling. He felt flushed. When
he ran his hand over his forehead, he pulled sweat away
from his face.

What have I done?

Slowly, he stood, turning his eyes from the glassy-slick
mark on the far wall, turning to the shutters of the window, fumbling to open them, to let this foul, foul air
out—to purify—deep, clean, breaths—clean, cleansing
air.

His body was racked with sobs when he finally pushed
the shutters open and nearly collapsed against the win-
dowframe. He was a murderer—a killer of men—he was
foul—slimy—caked in dirt—stained in blood—blackened
by ash.

He was just like his father.

Like father. Like son.

:*No.*:

The voice was assertive, female. He trembled, fear
consuming him again, making a fist around his belly. He
shook his head against the voice, choosing to disbelieve.

Killer. Defiler. Damned. What have I become?

:*No!*:

The voice again, and he screamed in the silence of his

soul, *Don't you see what I just did? Don't you know what I have done? Don't you understand?*

:I see. I know. And I understand.:

He looked up, for a moment blinded by a light akin to the sun, though it was an hour until dawn. And then he saw her—the graceful line of her white neck, the glancing blue-stream brilliance of her eyes—like fire, but kinder.

Shock gathered him up in its prickly folds, and then plunged him into an endless field of blue that was as textured and soft as a satin robe, and as all-encompassing as the closing surface of water. But he had no fear of drowning. Nor did he want to. All he felt—was—her—

And her name was Derdre, and he was her Chosen.

Lisabet gently pulled the covers over the bed that had held the corpse of the girl, tucking everything into neat order. The undertaker had carried the body of Sattar Morningsong off two days ago, and buried it yesterday. They had had to wait that long just to let Rivin rest from the exhausted state he had fallen into.

The man that the regional Healer had brought from Maidenflower stared at the bed and then turned away. He had stayed around in case any other—accidents— had occurred.

"It didn't have to end like this," he murmured, glancing out the window toward the boy, leaning against his Companion, head buried in her slender neck.

"It didn't have to start either," Lisabet replied grimly, glancing at the mark on the wall that no amount of washing had removed. "Gods damn it—I should have *known!*"

The Healer, a man by the name of Yiro, put a hand on her shoulder and shook his head. "Stop it now, Herald. Sometimes it's almost impossible to tell. Even Delanon's sister said that she thought he was a tad harsh, but never . . . well. . . ."

"Those kids carried that secret well."

"Or else they thought it was normal to be treated that way."

They stood in silence for a time.

Then: "Why would someone do that to their own children?" she whispered.

"I've asked myself that same question before. The best answer I have is that they like the . . . power. The pleasure of a helpless victim. The dependence. They get a feeling of control. Some even think they're doing the child a favor. If nothing else, they try to justify their actions."

Quiet. Outside, the Herald could hear Derdre take fidgety steps, the tall grass whispering softly. Then, "And the other two?" she asked.

"I've already called in one of the best MindHealers in this district. She'll check them out, live with them for a while. They're young. With luck, she'll be able to Heal them."

After a moment, Yiro clasped her in a quick hug. "Cheer up, sister. Things'll get better. The boy will most likely heal, if not today, then tomorrow. If not tomorrow, then the next day. It will take a lot of time, but hopefully, it'll happen. He'll realize . . . and then maybe he'll even forgive."

"But not forget."

"No. He already forgot once, from what we got out of him. He must have blocked that incident for years. I've heard of it."

But the Healer's words were fading away as Lisabet moved out of the room and toward the figure in the fields.

Gently, she placed a hand on his shoulder, remembering what she had seen from her view out the window of her cousin's home when Nastasea's bathtime had come up. A child comforting a child.

And now I am doing the same. Aren't we all just children at heart?

She enclosed him in her arms, petting his hair, holding him as he began to cry.

"Sattar," he whispered, weeping into her shoulder.

"She's gone," Lisabet replied.

"Want *Sattar*," he said, echoing Nastasea's words.

"Sattar's gone now. It's time to let go, Rivin."

The boy neither agreed nor rejected her words. Instead, he turned and mounted his Companion, his face a cast-granite mask of sorrow. Lisabet checked the shields around him, looking for leaks and holes. No use letting *that* powerful a new-born Mage-Gift get out of hand.

Satisfied, she called Raal over, and pulled herself into her own saddle. With one trembling hand on her Companion's neck, she led the way down the road toward Haven.

Gods—mage-power coming to life like that scares me. The boy didn't even know what he was doing—didn't even realize it was magic—until it was too late. It was only luck that this was my circuit and that I was close by when he first Reached. I don't think that I would have wanted a stranger taking care of him. She shivered. *There was so much* anger *in him. . . .*

:Thus, the nature of madness,: Raal said, his voice heavy and dusky in her mind.

:I'll never figure it out.:

:Some things we were never meant to figure out.:

:Like Companions?: Lisabet asked slyly.

She heard a dry chuckle. *:Like Companions.:*

A wind chuckled by, catching her hair. She saw Rivin's head jerk up, as if he had heard something, and then he shook himself, falling back into his mournful brooding.

It was then—when he lifted his head—that she noticed the worryline now chiseled between his brow. She noticed his taut neck muscles, the lines around his eyes. But most of all, she noticed the way he held his arm and rubbed his shoulder as if it ached with the pain of a hard grip that had, for a long while, forgotten how to let go.

... Another Successful Experiment

by *Lawrence Schimel*

Lawrence Schimel is the co-editor of *Tarot Fantastic* and *Fortune Tellers,* among other projects. His stories appear in *Dragon Fantastic, Cat Fantastic III, Weird Tales from Shakespeare, Phantoms of the Night, Return to Avalon,* the *Sword and Sorceress* series, and many other anthologies. Twenty-four years old, he lives in New York City, where he writes and edits full-time.

They resembled nothing so much as ill-proportioned hammers, but Chavi was pleased with them. No, he decided as he held one aloft and the weight of the tiny head on the end of the broomstick-length handle caused it to quiver slightly, he was more than just content.

"They're perfect!"

Gathering the other five from his bed, he tucked them all under one arm and went in search of his year-mates.

Chavi had spent the last week hidden in his room constructing these strange items. An air of mystery had naturally developed around them as Grays and sometimes even full Heralds stood outside his door listening to the curious sounds of their creation. Locking himself into his room was always the first clue that mischief was afoot, and that another of Chavi's (in)famous experiments would soon be unveiled. Therefore, as Efrem wandered down the hallway and noticed the door ajar, he could not resist the temptation to peek inside, hoping for a glimpse of the latest invention. Finding it empty, not only of marvels, but of the mischief maker himself, he went in search of him, knowing it would be worth his while, in laughter if nothing else.

Whether it was simply a lucky guess, or the fervent hope that Chavi was not foolish enough to premiere one of his experiments indoors again, his search led him—after a brief stop in the kitchens—to Companion's Field, where Chavi and his Companion Tecla waited for his year-mates to arrive.

The first person to show up was not, however, one of Chavi's year-mates. A tall, lanky man in the red-brown of a Bardic trainee came by and leaned against a tree, facing Chavi and Tecla. Chavi was of a mind to ask him to "Move along," then decided it might be good to have a Bard on hand to immortalize his success. He was sure it would be a success, too, and did not even consider that the experiment might fail.

The second arrival, however, gave Chavi pause. Efrem was a fellow Gray, who had been chosen two years before him. While Chavi did not at all dislike the Herald (he doubted it was even possible for a Herald to actively dislike another Herald), his presence made Chavi nervous. Had he been wandering by and noticed them, Chavi wondered, or had he known to come to Companion's Field now? If one of his year-mates had let slip that they would unveil his latest experiment. . . .

Just then, Gildi arrived with her companion, Fedele. With them came an older woman in Healer's green, her hair just turning to frost.

"I *knew* it," Chavi admonished, even as he hugged his year-mate in greeting. "I told you not to tell anyone." He glanced meaningfully from the Healer to Efrem and the Bard.

"I've been part of your experiments before, Chavi, and felt having a Healer on hand was a precaution worth taking. But *I* didn't tell anyone."

"*Someone* must have" he said, glaring at the pair of bystanders.

"Oh, don't sulk, Chavi. What harm is there in having spectators to revel in your latest crowning glory?"

He grinned at her. "Well, when you put it that way. . . ."

Tecla warned him that he was in for a surprise when he turned around. Nervously, Chavi looked behind him. His year-mates Sorne and Grav had arrived with their Companions.

:That's not it,: Tecla told him.

Chavi looked again, and this time saw what Tecla had meant: a group of three full Heralds coming toward them. "Aaaarrgggh! Why me? Why? All I ask for is a little peace and quiet in my life!"

Gildi could not stop laughing at that last comment until the three Heralds had reached them. Their Companions had come in from the Field to greet them. That must be how Tecla had known they were coming, Chavi realized.

"So who told you?" Chavi asked with a small grin, by way of greeting to the three Heralds.

All three of them laughed. "I'm afraid you can't keep a secret that involves six Companions," one said.

Chavi looked sternly at Tecla, about to ask her if she had told, but then decided he really didn't want to know. He was sure she had read his thoughts and knew what he had meant to ask, but she kept silent, aside from her usual comforting presence at the back of his mind.

Chavi sighed. While he was interrogating, he might as well do them all. "And how did *you* find out?" he asked the Bardic trainee.

"One of the servants told me."

One of the servants, Chavi thought. And how did *they* know? Did he have no privacy whatsoever around here, or what?

Chavi turned to Efrem. "You?" He was getting very tired of this question very quickly.

"No one."

"No one?"

"We all knew you were making something in your room, since you could hear the noise even from the cellar, practically. When I noticed your door was open again at last, but the room empty, I knew there was a sight to be seen somewhere, if only I could find it. One worth risking Mero's wrath by skipping out on preparation." Efrem smiled. "But I found a way around that."

"Oh?" Chavi asked, very curious as to any new techniques he might learn, for getting out of chores. "Pray tell, how was that?"

Before Efrem had a chance to explain, the answer walked into sight. Mero carried a basket stuffed with food in each hand, the three Grays in tow carried chairs and a table. They would work outside, and therefore *all* get the chance to watch the spectacle.

"This is ridiculous!" Chavi exclaimed as they began setting up the table and chairs. "You'd think I had invented entertainment for the first time."

Kem and Fiz chose that moment to show up with their Companions. "Are we charging admission or something?" Fiz asked.

"Then neither of you told?"

"Chavi. Really." Kem struck a melodramatic pose. "That you could even doubt us."

Chavi turned to Gildi. "Now you see why I didn't want spectators? Put him in front of a crowd and he's incorrigible."

"You're just jealous of my charm and good looks," Kem replied.

In answer, Chavi picked up one of his inventions and held it aloft. Advancing on Kem he said, "I can take care of those looks."

But once his actions had gotten enough laughter, Chavi lowered the creation again and turned serious. He turned to face the crowd. "I'll bet you're wondering why I've brought you all here," he began, earning boos and catcalls from his year-mates. Chavi looked down his nose at them, even though he was shorter than all save Grav. "Now where was I . . . ? Oh, yes, today's demonstration. You are very privileged to witness here today the birth of a new sport. A game of skill that will enchant spectators, and also," Chavi turned toward the three Heralds, "help train the participants in equitation and combat."

"You don't intend to spar with those things while riding Companions?" one of the Heralds asked.

"Hear me out." Chavi turned to his year-mates and began passing out his creations, one to each. "The rules are simple. Mount your Companions and I shall explain."

As they climbed into their saddles, Chavi whispered to his year-mates, "Now I have no idea if this is going to work." Gildi and Kem exchanged knowing glances, for Chavi never made disclaimers like that unless he was sure of success. "But let's at least put on a good show, eh?"

Switching back into a performer's voice, Chavi continued explaining the rules. "I'm sure you are all familiar with the games of stickball and football played by children? What we are about to play is a mix of both." From one of Tecla's saddlebags he brought forth a small wooden ball wrapped in leather and tossed it to the ground. "That is the object of our pursuit. To manipulate it, we use these." Chavi held aloft his creation in demonstration and, swinging down, gave the ball a solid crack which sent it rolling off through the grass. There was a burst of applause from the audience, in response to which Chavi stood in his stirrups and bowed to them, before continuing.

"The game is played by two teams of three players each. Why this number? Because more Companions and Heralds than that on the field of play at once would be disaster." He smiled. "There are also that number among my year-mates and myself, and since I am inventing this game, that is what I decided. Besides, it takes forever to make the mallets.

"Sorne, Kem, and Gildi are one team; your goal is those two trees over there marked with yellow ribbons. Grav, Fiz, and myself guard the goal on the other side of the field marked by blue ribbons. Points are scored by knocking the ball through the opposing team's goal." Chavi paused to let all this information sink in and smiled out at the assembled crowd. They were listening raptly for his every word, and Chavi exulted in the sensation while his year-mates made practice swings with their mallets, testing the distance between themselves and the ground.

"Are there no precautionary rules?" the Healer nervously asked at last, breaking the silence.

Chavi smiled kindly at her, wondering what Gildi had told her of his earlier experiments. "Indeed there are. While our Companions are quite capable at taking care of themselves, and us, we shall not put them at unnecessary risk. No hitting Companions or riders with your mallets or fists, although I would hazard to say that leaning heavily against someone as you rode them off would be fair, so long as your hands stayed over your own saddle. No sticking your mallet under or between the legs of a Companion, even for the sake of hitting the ball. Furthermore, no lifting the mallet head higher than your shoulder, so you don't endanger those of us topside. And finally, the rider who has control of the ball (with his mallet—touching the ball at any time with your hands will result in a penalty) the rider who has the ball, also has the right of way to follow after it for a second swing. This means you cannot ride in front of him, in a perpendicular path, and stop there. The object of the game is not to get injured, nor to wind up with all our Companions smacked into each other.

"Now, is everyone set on these rules?" His year-mates nodded, and the Healer looked content. "Then let's play ball."

Chaos quickly descended upon the field, and had it not been for the precautionary rules (which the Companions remembered, reminding their riders whenever they forgot) all six players would have wound up in the House of Healing after the first five minutes of practice, never having the chance to move into full fledged play. Grav's first swing at the ball was so wild he fell from the saddle. He turned as scarlet as a Bard's garb, but climbed back on and tried again.

"If you stand up in the stirrups like this," Chavi advised, "and lean from the waist, you should find it easier to keep your seat." Chavi had, of course, taken all his tumbles days ago when no one was around to see them.

Grav followed Chavi's instructions and gave the ball a nice, solid whack, knocking it over the bystanders' heads.

"Careful there!" the Bardic trainee shouted as he ducked the projectile.

Grav apologized, but he was feeling smug as he turned to Fiz and said, "Your turn."

Fiz fared slightly better than Grav, in that he did not fall off his horse on his first swing. However, he did not hit the ball. After his seventh missed swing, the crowd was wild with laughter that far exceeded what Grav's fall had earned. The expression of frustration on Fiz's face each time he swung was enough to redouble their mirth. As he was winding up for an eighth swing, Fedele brought Gildi alongside of him and she blocked his mallet's arc with her own.

"I would have hit it that time!" Fiz screamed, sending the crowd of onlookers into hysterics.

Gildi merely gave him a sarcastic look and tapped the ball out of Fiz's reach. However, when Fedele walked up to it and she took a second swing, she missed too. Grav lost no time in riding behind her, standing up in his stirrups as Chavi had told him, and giving the ball another good, solid crack. It sailed into the audience once more.

"That's twice," the Bardic trainee said as he ducked again.

Just then, Efrem lost control of the potato he had been peeling, and it slipped out of his hands. With a mixture of shame and curiosity he watched its arc as it left his hands and knocked the trainee in the back of the head, where he knelt in "safety" behind a bush.

"Herald, thy days are numbered," the Bardic trainee thundered as he turned to face his assailant-from-behind. "Thy lack of skill with a blade shall henceforth go down in the annals of history in the 'Ballad of How Efrem Lost the Battle of Potato Picnic.' Let thy infamy precede thee wherever thou go." He sat down with his back to a nearby tree and began composing verses as he watched the rest of the game.

"You know, he's right," Eladi told Efrem after they had all laughed heartily. She handed him some of her carrots to peel, hoping he would have more luck with them. "I mean, if Alberich had seen you—" She shuddered, the thought too unpleasant to contemplate.

"What do you mean _if?_" a voice behind them asked. Eladi turned to find the weapon's master standing behind them. Efrem did not need to look to know who it was; the overwhelming feeling of impending doom was enough.

The game was as exhilarating as Chavi imagined it would be, once everyone had mastered the rudiments of play and the actual game was underway. It moved at a remarkably fast clip, the entire thrust shifting to the other side of the field as a backhand swing sent the ball arcing toward the other goal.

Gildi served as a highly efficient captain for her team, masterminding a myriad of strategies which Chavi took careful note of. She was less concerned with scoring the most points herself than in helping her team to the most points. Her favorite tactic was to ride up alongside someone as he was about to take a shot and block his mallet with her own. Then, one of her team mates, who had been instructed to follow her, took the ball back toward the other goal. Through Mindspeech, team members were only a thought away as strategy decisions were relayed to them by their Companions.

Fiz proved to be an excellent backhand, although he still had difficulties with his forward shot. Grav was the powerhouse hitter, often sending the ball arcing out of bounds (usually toward the audience). Kem and Sorne were both adequate players, but they never really excelled at anything in particular. Chavi kept worrying that they weren't enjoying themselves.

:You're daydreaming again: Tecla warned him. _:Keep your eyes on the ball. We're going for the shot.:_

Chavi relinquished his musings to the game. He focused on the ball, stood up in his stirrups, and swung. He connected, and a moment later whooped with delight as the ball rolled into the unprotected yellow goal.

Chavi held one of his creations aloft and decided that, yes, he was more than just pleased with them. He was elated. The game was seen as a general success by one and all. The Bardic trainee had begun a second ballad about the day's events, featuring Chavi as its hero. Chavi was grateful that he had changed his mind before asking the man to "Move along." As the game progressed and she was not called upon in her official function, the Healer let herself relax enough to enjoy the sport. Word had spread quickly once the game was underway, and the audience had swelled to five times its original size. Even the Queen herself showed up to watch. Aside from thinking it looked like fun, Heralds were interested in the game for the combat training and equitation skills it provided.

Everyone wanted a mallet of their own. Chavi was beside himself with pleasure.

As his tired but happy year-mates dismounted and re-linquished their mallets to other Heralds who wished to try them, Chavi began congratulating himself. "Yes, yet another successful experiment brought to you by the one and only Chavi the magnificent, inventor of innumerable wondrous inventions, including the—"

Gildi Mindspoke to Fedele, who passed the message on to Tecla, who dumped Chavi into the river.

"All right, all right," Chavi said, as he dragged himself, soaking wet, onto the shore, where his year-mates waited, ready to toss him back in depending on his attitude. "So I had a little help from my friends."

Choice
by Michelle West

Michelle West has written two novels for DAW, *Hunter's Oath* and *Hunter's Death*, and, with any luck, is finishing her third, *The Broken Crown*, by now. She likes the Heralds, but couldn't imagine being one—she's the only fantasy writer she knows who's never been up on the back of a horse for fear of breaking her arm in three places when she came off it. Not that she lets cowardice rule her life, of course. Well, not often.

When Kelsey saw the white horse enter the pasture runs, she stopped breathing for a moment and squinted into the distance. Then she saw the Herald Whites of the man who walked just beside it, and with a pang of disappointment she continued across the green toward the inn. Shaking her head, she grimaced just before she took a deep breath and walked through the wide, serviceable doors.

"Kelsey, you're late. Again."

"How can you tell?" She pulled her dark hair back from her square face, twisted it into a makeshift coil, and wrapped it up with a small swathe of black silk—a parting gift from a friend who'd left the town to join a merchant caravan. It was the finest thing she owned, and the fact that she used it in day-to-day wear said a lot about her. Not, of course, that she had very many other places to wear it.

"Don't get smart with me," Torvan Peterson snapped, more for show than in anger. He had very little hair left, and professed a great resentment for anyone who managed to retain theirs, he was obviously a man who liked food and ale a little overmuch, and he owned the very practically named Torvan's Tavern. Children made games with that name, but not often in his presence. "Not," he added, "that I would disparage an improvement in your intellect." He stared at her expectantly, and she grimaced. "Well, out with it, girl. If you're going to be late, you can at least amuse me with a colorful excuse."

She rolled her eyes, donned her apron, and picked up a bar rag. "We've got a Herald as a guest."

"Chatting her up?"

"He, and no."

"Hardly much of an excuse, then. All right. The tables need cleaning. The lunchtime crowd was rather messy."

She could see that quite clearly.

On normal days, it wasn't so hard to come and work; work was a routine that added necessary punctuation to her life. She saw her friends here—the few that still remained within reach of the inn—and met strangers who traveled the trade routes with gossip, tales of outland adventures, and true news.

But when a Herald rode through, it made her whole life seem trivial and almost meaningless. She worked quickly, cleaning up crumbs and spills as she thought about her childhood dreams, and the woman who had—while she lived—encouraged them.

"You can be whatever you choose, Kelsey," her grandmother was fond of saying. *"You've only to put your mind and your shoulders to it, and you'll do us all proud."*

Kelsey snorted and blew a strand of hair out of her eyes. I can be whatever I choose, but I'll never be Chosen. In her youth she'd believed that to be Chosen by one of the Companions was a reward for merit. She'd done everything she could think of to be the perfect, good little girl, the perfect lady, the little hero. She had forsworn the usual childhood greed and the usual childhood rumbles for her studies with her grandmother; she had learned, in a fashion, to wield a weapon, and to think her way clear of troublesome situations without panicking much. Well, except for the small stampede of the cattle back at Pherson's, but anyone could be expected to be a little bit off their color in the midst of their first stampede.

She had done her best never to cheat or lie—excepting those lies that courtesy required; she shared every bounty she was given; in short, she had struggled to lead an exemplary life.

And for her pains, she had drifted into work at Torvan's Tavern, listening to her friends, encouraging and supporting their dreams, no matter how wild, and watching them, one by one, drift out of her life, either by marriage, by childbirth, or by jobs that had taken them out of the village.

She had her dream, but it was a distant one now, and it only stung her when she came face to face with the fact that someone else—some other person, through no work, no effort, no obvious virtue of their own—was living the life that she had dreamed of and yearned for ever since she could remember.

Still, if the Heralds—they never traveled alone—came in for a meal and left their Companions in the pasture runs, she could sneak out for a few minutes and watch them, and pretend. Because no matter how stupid it was, she couldn't let go of her dream.

It was clear from the moment he walked into the tavern that something was wrong. Heralds were able—although how, she wasn't certain—to keep their Whites white and in very good repair, and this Herald's Whites were neither. He was pale, and the moment he stepped out of the glare of the doorway, she saw why; his arm was bound, but bleeding, and his face was scraped and bruised.

"Excuse me," he said, in a very quiet, but very urgent voice, "I need help. My Companion is injured."

Heralds seldom traveled alone. Kelsey tucked her rag into her apron pocket and made the distance between the table and the door before Torvan had lifted the bar's gate.

"What—what happened?"

He shook his head, and it was obvious, this close up, that he was near collapse. She put an arm under his arms—she was not a weak woman—and half-walked, half-dragged him to a chair. "Don't worry about me," he said softly, his face graying. "She's hurt, and she needs help."

"Why don't I worry about both of you?" Kelsey replied, mimicking the stern tone of her grandmother in crisis. "Torvan—send Raymon for the doctor, and send Karin for the vet!" The Herald started to rise, and she blocked him with her arm. "And where do you think you're going?"

He opened his eyes at the tone of her voice, and studied her face as if truly seeing her for the first time. Then he smiled wanly. "Nowhere, ma'am," he replied. It was then that she realized that he was probably twice her age, with gray streaks through his long braid and two faded scars across his neck and cheek. His features were fine-boned, unlike her own; he looked like the son of a noble, except it was obvious that he was used to doing his own work.

"Good. What are you smiling at?"

"You. You remind me of my grandmother." The smile faded as he winced; his expression grew distant again. She knew that he was seeing not only the loss of the Herald he traveled his circuit with—for she was certain that that Herald must be dead—but also the fear of the loss of his Companion.

She brought him an ale and made him drink; he finished most of it before the doctors—human and animal—arrived.

"If you make her travel on the leg, you can probably get a few more miles down the road, but you'll lame her," the vet said, staring intently at the cleaned gash across the knee. "I don't know much about Companions—but I do know that if she were a horse, she would never have made it this far." That he didn't offer more, and in the lecturing tone that he was wont to use, showed his respect for the Herald.

The Herald—who called himself Carris, although that was clearly not his full name—nodded grimly and wiped the sweat absently from his forehead with a handkerchief. His uniform was safely in the tub in Kelsey's room, and he wore no obvious weapons, although a sword and a bow were in easy reach. "How long will it be until she can travel safely?"

"Hard to say," the older man replied.

Carris nodded again, absorbing the words. The doctor had been and gone, and Kelsey had been forced to rather harsh words with both doctor and Herald before an uneasy truce had been reached between them.

"You don't interfere with His Majesty's business," she'd snarled at Dr. Lessar. "And you—what did you think we called the doctor for? He'll bind and treat that arm—and those ribs—even if you feel it's necessary to go out and break them again. Is that clear?"

The doctor laughed. "And you're telling me how to talk to a Herald?"

Oddly enough, the Herald laughed as well. And he did submit to the doctor's care, electing to more quietly ignore most of the doctor's subsequent advice.

Torvan accepted Kelsey's desertion with as much grace as he could muster during the season when the trade route was at its busiest and the tavern could be expected to have the most traffic. She did what she could to lend a hand between the doctors' visits with Carris and his Companion, but it was clear that she felt them both to be her concern, and clearer still that the Herald was almost in bad enough shape to need it, so he gruffly chased her out of the dining room and told her to finish off her business.

Her business took her to the stables, where, in the dying light, the orange flicker of lamps could be seen through the slats of the door. *That's odd,* she thought, as she lifted her own lamp a little higher. It wasn't completely dark by any means—but the stables tended to

need a little light regardless of the time of day—and she
shone that light into the warm shadows.

Carris was kneeling at the feet of a pinto mare, gently
probing her knees. She nickered and nudged him, and
he nearly fell over as he spun quickly to face Kelsey.

"What are you doing here?" they said in unison.

Then Carris smiled. "You know, lass," he said, although she'd passed the age of "lassdom" five years
back, "you should consider a career in His Majesty's
army. You've the makings of a fine regimental sergeant."

"Thanks," she replied, feeling that he meant to tease
her, but not seeing anything in his words that could be
viewed as perjorative. "You haven't answered my
question."

He chuckled, and it added wrinkles to his eyes and
mouth that suggested he often laughed. "No, lass, I
haven't. What do you think of her?"

"Of—" She looked at the horse, and then realized
that it wasn't. A horse. "That's your Companion."

"If she forgives me for the indignity and the desertion,
then, yes, she is."

"Why—why have you done that?" She lowered her
lamp, as if to offer the Companion a little more privacy.
Her tone made it clear that she thought it almost
sacrilegious.

"Don't you start as well," Carris said, mock severely.
"I've done it," he added, his voice suddenly much more
serious, "because I've a message that must be deliv-
ered—and I can't take her with me, but to leave her
here, as an obvious Companion, is to risk her life."

Kelsey let the seconds tick back while she figured out
exactly what he meant. Then she lifted the lamp again.
"Are you crazy?" she said at last. "You can't ride with
your arm like that and your ribs broken—you'll pierce
your lungs for certain!"

The Companion bobbed her lovely head up and down
almost vigorously.

"Don't start," Carris said again. "We've already covered that ground, and I've made my decision. She knows
it's the right one." He stood slowly, but winced with

pain just the same as if he'd jumped up. "Kelsey, you've done as much as any girl can to help me—but I've one more favor to ask of you."

"W-what?"

"I want you to take care of her."

"Of . . . her?"

"My Companion, yes," he replied. "Her name is Arana." He waited for her to answer, and after five minutes had passed, he said, "Kelsey?"

She couldn't even speak. Instead, she walked past him, holding the lamp as if it were a shield. She approached the dyed Companion, met her eyes, and held them for a long time. Finally, she remembered that she wasn't alone, and had the grace to blush.

"I meant to tell you that dinner's been laid out for you. It's probably cold, but you should still get to it while you can."

"Kelsey?"

"I'll have to think about it," she replied, not taking her eyes off of Carris' Companion.

That night, with the moon at half-mast, it was dark enough that she stubbed her toes twice on the path to the stable. The lamp that she held was turned down as low as possible—she didn't want to attract attention from the field mice and the rats.

She wanted to look at Arana again, without Carris intruding upon the privacy of her old dreams and her old desires. Could she watch the Companion. Could she take care of her. Ha!

She opened the doors, paused as the smells of the hay and the horse scent hit her nostrils, and made her way in. Usually Companions weren't stabled like this—but Carris had insisted that Arana be as horselike as possible.

"Does she like sugar?"

Carris had laughed. "As much as a real horse."

She hadn't snuck into stables since she was child, but she'd lost none of her old instincts. She made her way, unerringly, to Arana's stall.

She wasn't particularly surprised to find Arana waiting for her. "Hello," she said softly. The Companion, as expected, didn't answer. A pang of disappointment, like a slightly off-key chord, rippled through her and vanished. "I'm Kelsey."

Arana lifted her head and nodded.

~~"I suppose you've met a lot of people like me. I—I~~ always wanted to be a Herald. I've always prayed that one day, a Companion would Choose me. It's never happened," she added ruefully. "And I don't suppose you'd be willing to tell me why."

Arana put her head over the stall's door and let Kelsey scratch her. It was easier than scratching a normal horse; the Companion seemed to be more sensitive. "Doesn't matter. Carris wants me to stay here, with you, while he does some fool thing on his own, injured, without anyone to look after his back. What do you think of that?"

Arana said absolutely nothing, but she became completely still. Kelsey shook her head and lowered the lamp. "That's what I thought as well. Here. I brought you some sugar."

"Where do you think you're going?" Carris, dressed like a well-to-do villager, frowned as Kelsey let her backpack slide off her shoulders to land on the ground with a thump.

"Talked it out with Torvan," she replied, around her last mouthful of bread and cheese, "and he says it's a go." She swallowed, wiped her hands on her pants, rolled her hair into its familiar bun, and shoved her coin bag into the inner reaches of her shirt.

"What's a go?" Carris asked, suspicion giving him an aura of unease that made Kelsey want to laugh out loud.

"I'm going with you, Carris." She checked her long dagger, and then picked up her wooden bat. Made sure she had a hat, and a scarf to keep it attached to her head.

"That's preposterous," he replied. "You are doing no such thing."

She shrugged. "Whatever you say."

"Kelsey—"

"Look—what did you think you were going to do? Dress like that, but pick up a fast and fancy horse that'll take you to the capital?"

He looked taken aback.

"You'll stand out like a scarecrow. You're afraid that someone following you would recognize Arana, and if that's the case, you'll be recognized if you travel as you'd planned. Trust me."

"I wasn't aware that you'd studied the arts of subterfuge. You certainly haven't mastered the art of subtlety."

"Ho ho ho." She bent down and picked up her pack; slung it over one shoulder, and then bent down for his. "Don't argue with me," she said, not even bothering to look up. "I'll take the packs. You take your arm and your ribs. Oh, damn."

"What?"

"I almost forgot."

"What?"

"The hair. It has to go."

Carris was in a decidedly less cheerful mood when they finally departed the inn. "Look, Kelsey," he said tersely. "You may not believe this, but that hair was my single vanity."

"A man your age shouldn't be beholden to a single vanity," she replied sweetly. "Now come on. You've come at a good time—I've a friend who guards one of the caravan routes, and they're always looking for new hands."

"As a caravan guard in this territory?" Carris raised an eyebrow. "You do realize that with the upsurge in banditry lately, he's just asking for trouble?"

Something about the way he said the word "banditry" caught her attention; she pursued it like a cat does a mouse. "What do you know about the bandit problems?"

He didn't reply.

"This have something to do with the message you need to deliver?"

He nodded, but no matter how she pressed him, he would say nothing else.

Well, it's King's business, not mine, Kelsey thought. *And probably better that I don't know.* She knew enough, after all, to know that as a Herald he was trustworthy, and that anyone who tried to kill him was as much the King's enemy—and therefore her own—as a stranger could be. Still, she felt a twinge of envy; she knew that were she a Herald, they'd talk openly of their mission—like equals. Comrades.

As if he could read her thoughts—and it was rumored that some Heralds could—he said, "It isn't that I don't trust you, Kelsey."

"Don't bother with explanations. I can come up with a dozen good ones on your behalf and you don't even have to open your mouth." She paused, and then stopped. "You can wield that thing, can't you?"

"Both of them, yes," he replied, smiling.

"Good."

"What did you intend as a weapon?"

"This." She pulled her bat out of her pack and swung it in a wide circle. "I call it a club."

"You're going to sign on as a caravan guard wielding a club?"

"You've never seen me wield a club before," she assured him. Then she laughed. "You should see your face. Yes, I intend to sign on, but I'll probably do it as cook or a handler. If a person's willing and able to work, there are always jobs on the trade routes. Especially now." She started to say something else, and then stopped. "Are you in pain?"

"Yes," he said, but the word was so soft it was a whisper.

She studied his pale face for a moment and then grimaced. The death of his friend wasn't real for him yet, but in bits and pieces it was becoming that way. Kelsey was almost glad that she wouldn't be with him when he finally completed his mission—because she was certain that when he did, he'd collapse with grief and guilt.

She'd seen enough hurt men and women come through Torvan's place to know the look of it.

"That's the life of a Herald, dear," her grandmother would tell her.

"I know," she told her grandmother's memory. *"But I want it just the same."*

David Fruitman had the look of a barbarian to him. His face was never closely shaven, but never full-bearded, his brown hair was wavy—almost scruffy—and long, and his carriage gave the impression not only of size, but of the ability to use the strength that came with it to good advantage.

Kelsey waved and shouted to catch his attention.

When he saw her, he rolled his eyes. "What, you again?"

Carris hung back a bit, unsure of the larger man's reception, but Kelsey bounded in, slapped him hard on the upper arm, and then dropped the two packs she carried to give him a bear hug. She called him something that was best left in the tavern among friends who had had far too much to drink, and then swung him around.

"Carris, get your backside up here. David, this is Carris. Carris, this is David. He's what passes for a guard captain around here."

David looked at Carris, raised an eyebrow, and then looked down at Kelsey. "There's a problem, Kelse," he said.

"What?"

"His arm's broken."

"So? It's not his sword arm."

Carris and David exchanged raised brows. "Shall I explain, or shall you?" Carris said.

"You do it. I'm not getting enough danger pay as is."

"Very funny, both of you. David—can I talk to you in private for a minute or two?"

"Is this like last time's private—where you shouted loudly enough that this half of the caravan lost most of their hearing for the next two weeks?"

"Very funny." She scowled, grabbed his arm, grabbed

her packs, and nodded frantic directions to Carris. It all
came together somehow, and they made their way to the
wagon that David called home while he was recruiting.

"Well?"

"Carris is a Herald," she said, dispensing with pre-
tense and bluster—although the latter was hard to get
rid of. "His partner's dead, his Companion's injured, and
he's got a message that he's got to get to the capital as
fast as possible. He can't ride—don't argue with me,
Carris, you heard what the doctor said—and he's being
hunted."

"Hunted by who?"

"He can't say."

"I can't hire him, then."

"David—he's a Herald."

"That doesn't mean the same thing to me as it means
to you," David replied. "Look—the people who hunt
the type of guards I hire are cutthroats that I know how
to deal with. The people who hunt a Herald . . ."

"David!" She reached out, grabbed the front of his
surcoat, bunched it into two fists and pulled. Even Carris
recoiled slightly at the intensity of her tone. "You-are-
going-to-hire-us-both."

He raised a brow, not in the least put out. "Or?"

"Or I will tell Sharra about the time that—"

He lifted both of his hands in mock surrender, and
than his expression grew graver. "Is it that important,
Kelse?"

"More. Trust me. We need you."

"All right. Let go of my surcoat and pray that the
entire encampment didn't just hear that. I'll take Carris
on,—but we've got to strap a shield to that shoulder."

"Can't you just say he was injured in the line of
duty?"

"Sure. But who's going to ask me? Most of the guards
here are the same as I started with, and they'll know
he's a stranger if they're asked. We've hired five men
here, and he'll just be another one of those—but he's got
to look the part, even if he's not going to act it. Clear?"

She said something extremely rude. "Yes. Clear."

"Good."

"Captain?" Carris said softly.

"What?"

"Thank you."

"Don't. Thank her. I owe her, and it's about time she started calling in her debt."

"I hope you appreciate this," Kelsey said to Carris as they set up their tents. Her hands were stiff and chapped, and she was busy nursing a blister caused by peeling carrots and potatoes for a small army. When he didn't answer, she looked across the fire.

"What's wrong?"

"It's Arana," he replied at last, weighing his words. "You travel for this long with a—a very dear friend, and you really notice when she's gone."

"You aren't used to being separated?"

"No. I'm used to being able to hear her no matter where I am." He was quiet, and she let the silence stretch between them, wondering when he would break it. Fifteen minutes later, she realized he wasn't going to.

"Is it everything they say it is?"

"Pardon?"

"Being a Herald. Having a Companion. Is it everything it's cracked up to be?"

He smiled. "It's harder than I ever imagined," he replied, leaning back on his elbows, and then wincing and shifting his weight rapidly. "And it's the most rewarding thing I could ever dream of doing." He laughed, and the laugh was self-deprecating. "It wasn't what I'd intended to do with my life—and both of my parents are still rather upset about it, since it significantly shifts the family hierarchy."

"Do you know why you were Chosen?"

"Me?" He laughed again. "No. If I had to Choose, I'd be the last person I'd ask to defend the kingdom with his life." He sobered suddenly. Rose. "Kelsey, I don't know how to thank you for everything you've done, and I know that leaving you to the campfire alone isn't the way to start."

She waved him off. "Everyone needs a little space for grief," she told him firmly. "Even a Herald. Especially a Herald."

But after he was gone, she stared at the fire pensively. By his own admission he'd done nothing to be considered a worthy candidate—why had he become a Herald? Why had he been Chosen? *Don't start, Kelsey,* she told herself sternly, *or you'll be up at it all night.*

"You look awful," David said, as he ducked a flying handful of potato rinds.

"I didn't sleep very well," she replied. "Are you here to annoy me, or should I just assume that you already have?"

He laughed. "I wanted to see how you were faring. The caravan's got a few extra mouths this time round; if I was going to choose KP, I wouldn't have done it for this stretch of the route."

"Thanks for the warning," she said, and heaved another handful of rinds. Then she wiped her hands on her trousers, set her knife aside, and stood. "Why is the caravan so bloody big this time?"

"It's well guarded," David replied, lowering his voice. "Well guarded. We've done our buying for the season, and we're doing our damned best to protect our investment."

"How bad has it been? We'd heard rumors that—"

"It's been bad." His face lost all traces of its normal good humor. "If you hadn't insisted, Kelse, I wouldn't have taken your friend on. There's a very good chance he'll get to see action whether he's up to it or not."

"Oh." She blew a strand of dark hair out of her eyes. "Is there some sort of drill?"

"Meaning?"

"What should the noncombatants do if the caravan is attacked?" She waited for a minute. "Look, stop staring at me as if I've grown an extra head and answer my question."

"Well," he replied, scratching his jaw, "if I were in that position, I'd probably hide under the wagons."

Great. "If I'd wanted an answer that unreal, I'd have asked a Bard." She picked up her knife and went back to potatoes, carrots, and onions. Onions. That was the other thing she was going to have to find a way around.

Carris took to taking it easy about as well as a duck takes to fire. He was grim-faced and impatient, and he watched the road and the surrounding wooded hills like a starving hawk. David had decided that the best watch for Carris was the night watch; under the cover of shadow and orange firelight, he could pass for a reasonably whole guard. He carried his sword and his bow—although Kelsey pointed out time and again that the bow was so useless it was just added encumbrance—and wore a shield that had been strapped to his front as well as possible given the circumstances.

What he did not do well was blend in with the rest of the guards. It was his language, Kelsey reflected, as she listened to him speak. He didn't have the right cadence for someone who had fallen into the life of a caravan guard. Never mind cadence, she thought, as she dove into the middle of a conversation and pulled him out—whole—he didn't have the vocabulary, the tone, the posture. He did, having been on the road without being able to shave himself, have the right look.

"Stop being so nervous," she said, catching his good arm in hers and wandering slightly away from the front of the caravan.

"Kelsey, do you know what this caravan is carrying?"

"Nope. And I don't want to."

"Well, I do. We're going to see action, and I can't afford to see it and not escape it alive. We've lost four Heralds to this investigation, not including Lyris, and we'll lose more if I don't get word back."

"We'll get word back," she said, assuring him. But she felt a twinge of unease when she finally left him. Dammit, he's even got me spooked. She went to her pack, found her bat, hooked it under her left arm, and walked quickly back to her place among the cook's staff.

*   *   *

"What is that?" A familiar voice said.

"Don't ask her that." Marrit, the older woman who supervised the cooking, looked a tad harried as she glared in David's general direction.

"It's a bat."

"I know what it is."

"Then why did you ask?"

"Don't be a smartass, Kelse. Why are you carrying it around?"

"It's as much a weapon as anything else I own."

"And you need a weapon on kitchen duty?" David laughed. "Marrit, I didn't realize that you'd become such a danger over the past few days."

"Look—don't you have something to do?"

"I'm off duty. I've got nothing to do but sit and visit." He smiled broadly and took a seat. He even managed to keep it for five minutes. Marrit didn't say one disparaging word about her cook's lax work habits when Kelsey dropped her knife into the potato sack, turned, and pushed him backward over the log.

Two days passed.

Carris was edgy for every minute of them, except when he spoke of Lyris. Then his emotions wavered from guilt and grief to a fury that had roots so deep even Kelsey was afraid to disturb them by asking intrusive questions that stirred up memories too sharp and therefore too dangerous. This didn't stop her from listening, of course. She managed to infer that Lyris was the Herald who had traveled with Carris, and further that Lyris was young, attractive and impulsive. She knew that he had come from the wrong side of town, just as Carris had come from too far into the right side, as it were.

Never anger a noble, her grandmother used to say. Especially not a quiet one. Although it was a tad on the obvious side, it was still good advice.

"Kelsey, why must you take that club everywhere you go?"

Given that she'd just managed to hit his rib with the

nubbly end, it was a reasonable enough question—or it would have been had she not heard it so often. "Don't start. I thought if there was one person in camp I'd be safe from, it'd be you. Why do you think I'm carrying it?"

He shrugged. "I don't know. Everyone here seems to have their pet theory."

"What do you mean, everyone?"

"Guards," he said, offering her the gleam of a rare smile, "have very little to talk about these days."

She blushed. "I'd better not catch them talking about me, or I'll damned well show them what I'm carrying it for."

Carris actually laughed at that. Then he stopped. "I know I'm unshaven and unkempt, but have I done something else to make you stare?"

"Yes," she replied without thinking. "You laughed." She regretted her habit of speech without thought the moment the words left her lips; the clouds returned to his face, and with them, the distance.

"And there's not much to laugh about, is there?" He said softly, his right hand on his sword hilt.

Kelsey was at the riverside, washing more tin bowls than Torvan owned, when she heard the screaming start. A silence fell over the men and woman who formed Marrit's kitchen patrol. Fingers turned white as hands young and old clenched the rims of tin and the rags that were being used to dry them. No one spoke, which was all the better; Kelsey could hear the sound of hooves tearing up the ground.

Horses, she thought, as she numbly gained her feet. *The bandits have horses!*

"Kelsey!" Marrit hissed. "Where are you going?"

Kelsey lifted her fingers to her lips and shook her head. She motioned toward the circular body of wagons. Marrit paled, and mouthed the order to stay by the riverside, where many of the cooking staff were already seeking suitable places to hide.

It was the smartest course of action. *Of course,* Kelsey

thought, knees shaking, *that's why I'm not doing it.* She swung her bat up to her shoulder and began to run.

In the confusion and chaos, panic was king, and the merchant civilians his loyal subjects.

The wagons, circled for camping between villages too small to maintain large enough inns and grounds, provided all the cover there was against the attackers. People—some Kelsey recognized, and some, expressions so distorted by fear that their faces were no longer the faces she knew—ran back and forth across her path, ducking for cover into the flapped canvas tents, the wagons, or the meager undergrowth. The guards on watch had their hands full, and the guards off duty were scrambling madly to get into their armor and join the formation that was slowly—too slowly—taking shape.

She counted forty guards—their were forty-eight in total—as she scanned the circular clearing searching desperately for some glimpse of Carris. No sign of him; maybe he'd finally shown some brains and was hiding somewhere under the wagons.

Ha. And maybe the horses she heard were a herd of Companions, all come to ask her to join them. She took advantage of a scurry of panicked movement to take a look under a wagon. She saw the horses then.

Funny thing, about these bandits. They weren't wearing livery, and they weren't wearing uniforms—but they looked an awful lot like a Bardic description of cavalry. The horses were no riding horses, and no wagon-horses either. She didn't like the look of them at all, and she loved horses.

They sure make bandits a damned sight richer than they used to, she thought, clenching her teeth on the words that were choking her in a rush to get said. *And a damned sight more organized.* She had a very bad feeling about this particular raid. And when the blood spray of a running civilian hit the grass two feet from her face, she knew that if there were any survivors to the raid at all, it was going to be a minor miracle.

*   *   *

A flare went up in front of the lead wagon; fire-tipped arrows came raining from the trees, and shadows detached themselves from the undergrowth, gaining the color and height of men as they came into the fading daylight.

Kelsey knew she should be cowering for cover somewhere, but the tree that she'd managed to climb was central enough—and leafy enough—that it gave her both a terrific vantage point and a false sense of security. She counted the mounted men; there were ten. She couldn't get as good a sense of the foot soldiers—bandits, she corrected herself—but she thought there weren't more than thirty. So if one didn't count the cavalry as more than a single man each, the caravan guards outnumbered them.

It made for a tough fight, but the horses were too large to be easily maneuvered around the wagons, and if the merchants and their staff were careful, the caravan would pull out on top. She smiled in relief, and then the smile froze and cracked.

For on horseback—a sleek, slender riding horse with plaited manes and the carriage of a well-trained thoroughbred—unarmored and deceptively weaponless, rode a man in a plain black tunic. At his throat, glowing like a miniature sun, was a crystal that seemed to ebb light out of the very sky.

This was the threat that Carris wouldn't speak openly of. This was what he had to reach other Heralds to warn them about. This was the information that the King needed. Kelsey gripped both her bat and the tree convulsively as the Mage on horseback drew closer to where she sat, suddenly vulnerable, among the cover of leaves.

His was a power, she was afraid, that dwarfed the power of all save a few Heralds—and she was certain that Carris was no Herald-Mage, to take on such a formidable foe.

Damn it, she thought, holding her breath lest a whisper rustle a leaf the wrong way. *Carris was right. I shouldn't have brought him along with the caravan.* Then,

*And he'll probably die just like the rest of us—they won't
know he's their Herald, and they won't care.*

One of the mounted soldiers rode up to the Mage.

"That wagon," he said, pointing. "Food supplies, but
nothing of more value."

"Good." The Mage gestured and fire leaped up from
the wagon's depths, consuming it in a flash. The circle
was broken, and the ten mounted horseman, pikes readied, charged into the encampment.

She heard the shouts and then the screams of the
guards and the civilians they were to protect. People fled
the horses and the hooves that dug up the ground as if
it were tilled soil. They didn't get far. Kelsey saw,
clearly, the beginning of a slaughter.

Sickened, she shrank back, closing her eyes. *There's
nothing you can do,* some part of her mind said. *Hide
here. Maybe they won't notice you.*

"Captain! 'Ware—they've got a Mage at the center of
their formation!" It was Carris' voice, booming across
the panicked cries and painful screams of the newly
dying. In spite of her fear, she gazed down to see him,
sword readied, shield tossed aside and forgotten. The
blade caught the fire of the camplight, and it glowed a
deep orange.

You see? Another part of her taunted. *You wouldn't
have made a decent Herald after all.* She hid in the trees,
and Carris, broken arm and cracked ribs forgotten, stood
in the center of the coming fray, his sword glowing dimly
as it reflected the light of the fires.

No. She took a deep breath. Watched.

The guards met the bandits, but the bandits attacked
like frenzied berserkers, and it was the caravan guards
that took casualties. Kelsey could not make out individual faces or fighting styles—and she was thankful for it.
What she could see was that somehow, the blows that
the caravan guards landed seemed to cause no harm.

It was almost as if the enemies were being protected
by an invisible shield. Magic. Magic.

Another horseman rode in, and stopped three yards
from the mage. "Sir," he said. "We've got a group of

them hiding by the riverside. Possible one or two have managed to cross it."

The Mage cursed. "Get the archers out, then," he snarled. "We can't afford to have anyone escape."

"Can't you—"

"Not if you want to be safe from steel and arrow tips," he replied grimly. "Go." He gripped the crystal around his neck more tightly.

Get down, Kelsey. She shivered as she saw the Mage close his eyes. Now's your chance. Get down. But her legs wouldn't unlock. Her hands shook. She watched the ground below as if the unfolding drama was on a stage that she couldn't quite reach.

Carris came out of the wings. She saw him, close to the ground, and nearly cried out a warning as the mounted soldier departed. But she bit her lip on the noise. He used the shadows, Carris did, and he moved as if he had no injuries. An inch at a time, he made his way to the Mage who sat on horseback, concentrating.

The horse shied back, and the Mage's eyes snapped open. Carris leaped up from the ground, swinging his sword. It whistled in a perfect arc; the Mage didn't have time to avoid it. The sword hit him across the chest and shimmered slightly. That was all.

The man laughed out loud. "You fool!" He cried. "Did you think to harm me with that?" Carris swung again, and again the Mage did nothing to avoid the strike. "Why, I think I know you—you're the little Herald that escaped us. It's probably best for you—you wouldn't have enjoyed the fate that you consigned your friend to suffer alone."

Carris' next swing was wild, and it was his last; three foot soldiers came up, slowly, at his back. But the Mage lifted a hand, waving them off. "No, this one is mine, gentlemen. Unfinished business." He smiled. "Don't you have merchants to kill?"

The soldiers nodded and stepped back almost uncertainly. If Kelsey had to guess, the Mage had probably killed one or two of them to keep them in line; they weren't comfortable with him; that much was clear.

"You can't think that you'll get away with this," Carris said. It was, in all, a pretty predictable thing to say—and not at all what Kelsey would have chosen as her last words.

Something snapped into place for Kelsey as she thought that. *I can't let him die with that for an exit line, she told herself, and very slowly, watching her back as* much as possible, Kelsey began to shinny down the tree.

"I know we will," the Mage replied, all confidence. "Are you sure you don't want to continue your futile line of attack? It amuses me immensely."

Carris lowered his sword.

"You could try the bow—you can wield it, can't you? It would also amuse me, and perhaps if I'm amused, you'll die quickly. I was embarrassed by your escape," he added, his voice a shade darker. "And have much to make up for to the Baron."

Carris said nothing.

"Come, come. Why don't you join me? We can watch the death of all of your compatriots before we start in on yours. You see, you have a larger number of guards— but they aren't, like my men, immune to the effects of sword and arrow. It's a lovely magic I've developed, and it's served me exceptionally well. Come," he added, and his voice was a command.

Like a puppet, Carris was jerked forward.

"Watch."

It was almost impossible not to obey his commands. Kelsey looked up—and what she saw made her freeze for a moment in helpless rage. David was fighting a retreat of sorts—but he was backing up into another cluster of the enemy. He seemed to understand that the swords that the caravan guards wielded were only good for defense, for he parried, but made no attempt to strike and extend himself to people who didn't have to worry about parrying anymore.

A guard went down at David's side.

Kelsey bit her lip.

And then, because she was her grandmother's daughter—and more than that besides—she swallowed, took a deep breath, and crawled as quickly as possible to where the Mage sat enjoying the carnage.

She wanted to say something clever or witty or glib—but words deserted her. Only the ability to act remained, and she wasn't certain for how much longer. She lifted the bat, and, closing her eyes, swung it with all the force she could muster.

She had never heard a sound so lovely as the snapping of the Mage's neck. She would remember it more clearly than almost any other detail of the attack. Almost.

He toppled from his horse as the horse reared. She watched him crumple and fall, watched his body hit the ground. Then she lifted the bat and began to strike him again and again and again. Carris shouted something—she couldn't make out the words—as she began to try to shatter the crystal that hung at the Mage's neck.

Then she felt a hand on her arm, and swung the bat round.

"Kelsey, it's me!" Carris' face was about two inches away from hers. There was a bit of blood on it—but she thought it wasn't his. Couldn't be certain. "You did it," he said. He tried to pry the bat out of her hands, but her fingers locked tighter around it than a merchant's around his money chest. He let go of her hands and smiled. The grin was wolfish.

"We've got them, Kelsey. Thanks to you, they don't know that they can die yet—but they're about to find out the Mage is gone." His teeth flashed. "And they've been walking onto our swords because there's no risk to them."

"Remind me," she said faintly, "not to make you mad."

He looked down at the corpse at her feet. Laughed, loudly and perhaps a little wildly. "You're telling me that?"

An hour later it was all over. People lay dead in pockets of blood across the width of the encampment. The merchants buried and mourned their own, but they left the bandits for carrion. The mounted men had fared the best, once they realized that they were vulnerable, and three at least had fled the arrows and bolts that the guards used against them. The rest joined their unmounted counterparts.

David, injured, was still alive. Kelsey was glad of it. She watched his wounds being bound by the doctor—the merchant Tuavo always traveled with a good physician as part of his caravan—and swung her bat up onto its familiar shoulder-perch. "Hey," she said.

"I know, I know. So we never make fun of strange barmaids who carry bats around the kitchen. Okay?"

She smiled. "That's not what I'm here for. It's about my position as a caravan guard."

"As a what?"

"Look, I'm a bit of a hero for the next hour, and I'll be damned if I don't use it to get out of peeling potatoes and onions for the next two months. You're going to vouch for me—is that clear?"

He laughed. "As a bell."

"Hello," Kelsey said, as she caught Carris' shadow looming over her shoulder. "Aren't you late for your shift?"

"The captain excused me. I've been," he added, lifting his arm, "injured in action." He grinned and Kelsey laughed. She'd done a lot of that lately.

Carris returned her laugh with a laugh of his own. He seemed both taller and younger than he had when she'd first laid eyes on him in Torvan's place. A little more at peace with himself.

Still, there was something she wanted to say. "I—I've been meaning to apologize to you."

"To me? For what?"

"The Mage." She looked up, and her eyes, dark in the fading day, met his.

Carris shook his head almost sadly. "Was it that obvious?" He took a deep breath, and ran his fingers through his short, peppered hair. Very quietly, he gave her her due. "I've never wanted to kill a man so badly in my life."

"I would've felt the same way."

"You got to kill him." He looked into the fire, and she knew he was seeing Lyris. She reached up and caught his hand, felt his fingers stiffen and then relax as she pulled him down to the log.

"Tell me," she said, in the softest voice he had yet heard her use. "Tell me about Lyris."

He did. He talked for hours, letting his tears fall freely at first, and then returning to them again and again as an odd story or an old, affectionate complaint brought the loss home. He talked himself into silence as the fire lapped at the gravel.

Then he did something surprising. He turned to her in the darkness and said, "Now tell me about Kelsey."

She was so flustered, she forgot how to speak for a moment—and Kelsey was not often at a loss for words. *Well,* she thought, as she stared at the crackling logs beyond her feet, *what do you have to say for yourself? About yourself?*

His chuckle was gentle. "Should I start?"

"Go ahead."

"Kelsey is a young woman who, as a child, very much wanted to be a Herald."

It was dark, so he couldn't see her blush. "H-how did you know that?"

"It's a . . . gift of mine. And as a Herald, you get used to spotting people who hold the Heralds in awe. Or rather," he added wryly, as he touched his short hair again, "hold the position in awe."

She shrugged.

"You asked me if I knew why we were Chosen—but what you really wanted to know was why you weren't."

She couldn't answer because every word he spoke was true.

"I don't know why." He slid an arm around her shoulder and it surprised her so much she didn't even knock him over. "But having met you, I can guess."

Here it comes. "What? What would you guess?"

"Kelsey—I told you that I was the son of a noble, and as it's not important, I won't tell you which one. But if

Arana hadn't come to me, hadn't Chosen me, I would have become embroiled in the politics of the nobility, and would have done very little of any good to the people of the Kingdom as a whole. I like to think I would have ruled my own people well, but . . . it's not easy.

"And Lyris? Much as I love him, he'd have probably wound up as a second-rate thief—or a corpse. Not much good there either."

She was very quiet.

"You don't have a Companion, yet if not for you, the people of this caravan would have been slaughtered like sheep at the Crown Princess' wedding." He caught one of her hands in his good one. "I've got to get some sleep, if I can. So do you. But think about it."

"I will."

Kelsey had spent many sleepless nights in the cold of a dying fire, and this one was to be no exception. What did it mean? What did it really mean? She looked at her hands, seeing both the calluses and the dried blood of the injured that she'd helped the doctor with. They were good hands, strong enough to do what was necessary.

I'm not a Herald, she thought, as she stared at them. *And I never will be.* She turned it over in her mind, and for the first time in her life, she accepted it without sorrow. *I never will be Chosen.*

She stood up as the embers faded. *But if I can't be one of the Chosen, I can be one who chooses. And I choose to do what I must, when I'm needed.*

Heralds couldn't do everything for themselves; she knew how to run an inn—maybe, if she proved worthy of it, she'd be allowed to run a school. Everyone needed to eat—surely the Heralds would need a cook? And that close to the thick of things—that close to Heralds, Companions, possibly the King himself—there was certain to be a lot for Kelsey to do.

She smiled; the sun was on the fringe of the horizon. "Carris!"

If she expected him to be sleeping, she was wrong; he

was awake, and a strange little smile hovered around the corner of his lips. "Yes?"

"I'm coming with you to the capital, and I won't take no for an answer. You're still injured, you probably still need someone to watch your back, and you—"

"And I'd love your company."

He didn't, come to think of it, look at all surprised. Made her suspicious, but it also made her, for the first time that she could remember, completely happy. She had done with waiting; it was time to start the life that her grandmother had always promised her she could choose to live.

Song of Valdemar
by Kristin Schwengel

Kristin Schwengel is an avid fan of Mercedes Lackey's work, and leaped at the opportunity to write about Valdemar. This story is her first published work. She lives in Green Bay, Wisconsin with her fiancé, John Helfers, whose work also appears in this collection. They have no cats (yet), but they do have a collection of wolf and wildcat paraphernalia, which will have to do for now.

"Revyn," Eser called quietly, "I need some more of those bandages over here. And a splint."

The young trainee trotted over to the Master Healer, arms full of soft fabric, fingertips barely clutching the smoothly carved pieces of the splint. Eser took the wood from his hands just before he dropped it, smiling gently.

"Now, lad, I don't need you bringing so much that you lose it before you can do any good with it," he teased, a smile lighting his faintly lined face. Revyn smiled thinly back at him, acknowledging the mild rebuke, and watched with feigned disinterest as the Healer carefully set the broken leg.

"Do you think you could do the same, hmm?" Eser asked when he had finished, glancing up at his pupil.

Revyn avoided Eser's eyes as he lifted his shoulders slightly, carefully hiding the surge of affirmation that raced through him.

"I—I'm not sure. It seems easy enough, but . . . I wouldn't want to cause more harm than is already done." He spoke awkwardly, trying to seem all nervousness and uncertainty.

Eser's lips thinned as he stood smoothly, stretching his back to straighten out the knots that he got from hunching over the pallet. He still moved with a fluidity and grace belying his forty years, but every so often his body chose to remind him of his true age. He studied Revyn's averted face carefully. What was wrong with the young man? Was there more than he himself was aware of? Eser shrugged mentally, knowing that answers would come eventually, one way or another. Now, they had more important things to take care of. Eser gestured to his apprentice to follow him and moved down the halls of the House of Healing to the storeroom.

"Well, Revyn, you're going to set a leg now. Teral wasn't the only one caught in that rockslide. More bandages and another splint, lad, and follow me."

Revyn nearly gasped aloud at Eser's words, staring at the older man's parting back. *What if he finds out?* he thought frantically. *I can't hide much longer, but I can't keep refusing either.* Taking a large breath to relax his nerves, he scurried along the halls of the House of Healing after his teacher, nearly spilling the extra bandages again in his haste.

Finally, Eser stopped and gestured for Revyn to precede him into the sickroom. Revyn paused in the hallway to allow his heightened breathing to slow to a normal pace. *"Never enter a sickroom in a hurry or in obvious panic,"* he heard Eser's voice in his head, *"for that is the best way to hinder the Healing you wish to encourage."* Gently, he laid his hand on the door and slowly pushed it open. The well-oiled hinges made barely a sound as the two of them slipped into the room and closed the door carefully behind them.

Glancing at the blanket-covered figure on the low pallet, Revyn was barely able to contain a low gasp of shock and surprise. It was just a boy! A boy, no older than his sister Chylla. The lad was clearly fevered, for he tossed his head restlessly under the effects of the herbs that had taken away his pain and put him to sleep so that the Healers could work on him. Looking uncertainly up at Eser, Revyn received no encouragement other than a small nod. Taking a deep breath, he knelt on the floor by the side of the pallet and lifted the blanket from the boy's thin legs.

Carefully, Revyn moved his hands gently over the skin of the broken leg, exploring the shape of the bone and determining how much movement would be needed to line up the two edges so that the splint and bandages could do their work. Thankfully, he had just to pull slightly on the boy's foot to straighten the bone, and the pieces moved easily into place, seeming to straighten almost of their own accord. Silently, Eser crouched next to him and maintained the tension on the foot so that Revyn could place the splint and swiftly bandage the leg tightly, making sure the bone would heal as straight as before. Standing, he met the Master Healer's eyes and was surprised and intensely pleased by the approbation he saw there.

"He will sleep easier now that his bones are in line, and the healing herbs can take better effect. Well done," Eser said softly. "We are finished here, but I would speak with you."

Revyn was no stranger to the sudden sinking feeling in his stomach. He had often felt this way before one of his older brother Myndal's chastising sessions—those that had involved swift beatings and usually the destruction of at least one of his own precious treasures, few though they were. He had thought he had done well with the young boy's leg—no, he *knew* he had done well. Eser's own words had told him that. What could have gone wrong? He followed the Healer out of the House, trying to control his concern.

Eser slowly shut the door to his room and turned to face his student, a swift touch to his temples easing the tension headache that was already building.

"Why, Revyn?" he asked. "We both know that you have a strong Healing Talent. Why do you resist it so?"

Revyn looked down at the floor, shuffling his feet slightly. How could he put it so that the Healer would understand? He didn't *want* to be a Healer, at least he *hadn't* wanted to until— He broke off his thoughts and tried to answer.

"I—I don't know. I just don't want to . . . hurt anyone when I try to help them. And I seem so clumsy sometimes that it seems that all I can do is just to make a mess of what I put my hands to, and . . ." The hurried flow of his speech stopped as he ran out of words, and he glanced uncertainly up at Eser. The older man had turned to look out the window at the autumn golds and reds in the garden, just visible beneath the dusting of the second snow.

"Revyn, you've been here at Haven for almost a year now, and most of that time you have spent with the Healers. You should be farther along in your studies than you are now. Your skill today, handling that broken leg without even asking advice, proves that you are not as clumsy as you say. Yes, I know you nearly dropped the splint this afternoon," Eser laughed, holding up a hand to stop his student's protest, "but that was only because you took more than you could easily carry, through no fault of your own."

The Healer paused for a moment, thinking, then turned to look his student straight in the eye. "Just because one dream won't come true for you doesn't mean that you should stop dreaming, should stop thinking of the good you can do for yourself and others." He would have continued, but Revyn, choking as if the words he wanted to say were stuck in his throat, had already turned and fled.

How can he know? Revyn thought furiously. *He's just a Healer.* He ran to his room, paused only to snatch his letters from his desk and stuff them inside his tunic, and hurried out to the garden. *He only knows Healing. He wouldn't know who has the Gift and who doesn't. "But Bard Keryn would,"* a small voice in his head reminded him, a voice that he crushed as he had so many times before. *Keryn could be wrong,* he told himself. *Sometimes Gifts don't show until later, like with the Heralds. Some of them aren't Chosen until they're older than I am. There's still a chance that I could have a Bardic Gift,* he told himself, refusing to listen to the voice that told him otherwise.

Revyn settled himself in a private grotto in the garden, the one farthest from the buildings, and pulled the two letters, each with the seal of Hold Elann, from the front of his tunic. Even though he had been receiving these letters roughly every month since he had come to Haven, each time he opened them his heart raced in anticipation.

> *My dear son,*
>   *It is good to hear that you have learned so much in your time in Haven. Perhaps soon you can return to us. Your brother Myndal seems to have come to terms with your leaving, as he allows us to write to you openly now. If you come back to us, surely he would respect your skills with your professional training.*
>   *Your sister writes you as well, so I will not speak to you of her, save that she misses you greatly. We are all well here in Hold Elann, though we miss your music. Myndal begins to speak of finding a wife and raising children to carry on the mastery of Elann. He hopes for a daughter of one or another of the nearby landowners. Young Aislynn, whom you surely remember, grows ever prettier. If you were to return soon, before someone else snatches her up, I think the two of you could make a match of it.*
>   *The dogs are well, though Tygris is aging. I fear she has raised her last batch of pups this summer, for she will likely not survive the coming winter. I run out of paper, and so I close with best wishes for your continued health and hope that you return soon, the Bard I always knew you could be.*
>   *Your loving Mother*

Revyn bit his lip, wishing that there were some way he could tell his family what his situation truly was. How could he say that he was no longer a Bardic student? That he was now in the Healer's Collegium? Chylla would be so disappointed. She had always wanted him to compose a song for her when he tried to reach Master Bard rank. She wanted him to write a ballad about Valdemar, a song that put everything that was best about their homeland into words. On his journey to Haven he had begun a draft of it, but ever since that interview with Bard Keryn he had tried to forget about it, the sheets of paper covered with his brief notations buried in the back of his desk.

His mind flashed back to that day Keryn had spoken with him, only a few weeks after he had come to Haven and been brought from an inn to the Bardic Collegium by Keryn herself.

"Revyn, you'll make a superb Minstrel, better than most even here in Haven. You're one of the most talented students we've ever had. But I'm afraid that you don't have the Bardic Gifts. Some of us think that you might be Gifted in Healing, however, and . . . Revyn, I'm sorry," Keryn had said softly.

The hurt of hearing Keryn's words still tasted bitter in his mouth, even months later. She had tried to be kind, tried to tell him about his Healing Talent, but it had all added up to the same thing. He could never be a Bard. Those first few weeks of living and studying in the Bardic Collegium had easily been the happiest time of his life. Hearing Keryn affirm his worst doubts and fears had torn his joy away from him, leaving an aching empty spot where his long-cherished dream of being a Bard had been, a spot he had thought could not be filled. And then Eser had come and taken him to the House of Healing. . . .

Revyn brought his mind back to the present with a quick mental shake, avoiding the thought of being a Healer as he had tried to avoid it for the past year. He broke the seal on the second letter with a smile, thinking of his fair-haired sister, and her laughter that sounded like summer's golden sunshine would.

Revy—
   Oh, how I miss you still. Hold Elann isn't the

same without you. You probably said that when Minstrel Des died, didn't you? Well, now I know how you feel. Did Mother tell you? Myndal is letting us write you openly. Maybe that means you can come back soon.

Speaking of Myndal, that oaf actually thinks he can find a girl stupid enough to marry him. He tried for Aislynn, but she had too much sense for him. Besides, she told me she wanted to wait for you to come back. Even though she's two years older than me, she doesn't act like it, and we're still friends.

I think Myndal also wants to set up a marriage for me, it being as I'm getting to be old enough. Think of it, Revy, your Chylla the matron of a household—at fourteen and a half! Sometimes I can't think of it for laughing. I hope he goes to Hold Gellan. Edouard, the younger son, is unmarried and only a few years older than you are, so he's not too old for me. And he's handsome, too!

Your horse misses you, the dogs miss you (Tygris has faded in health ever since you left), Mother misses you, and I miss you most of all. I hope you get to Journeyman rank soon, so you can come to see us.

Love and hugs, your own Chylla

Revyn leaned back against the sun-warmed stone of the grotto, closed his eyes, and smiled, laughing with his merry sister. He could see her now, just the way she had been on the day he told her he was leaving Hold Elann.

"But what will Mother and I do without you?" Her lips were quivering, and she bit them so hard he was sure she would cut them. She looked at the ground then, turning away from him so he wouldn't see her tears.

"You'll have to take care of Mother for me, Chylla. You know how hurt she'll be when you tell her where I've gone." He smiled and gently touched her thin shoulders. She turned abruptly back to him, taking a deep breath.

"Take me with you, Revy. Please. I can cut my hair.

You can tell the traders I'm your little brother. Please don't leave me here, not alone with Myndal."

"Better that you stay with Mother," he had answered gravely. "Mother will need you more than you will need me. Besides," he said, smiling cheerily, "I'll come back for you, little one. You know I will, and everything will be fine."

If only she could be here with him now, everything *would* be fine. She would understand about him being a Healer if she just saw him, if he could just talk to her and show her how he felt, but he didn't know how he could write it to her. It seemed to him that to tell his family would make everything just that much more final. Telling them that he wouldn't be a Bard would mean that he would have to give up his dream and become a Healer.

"You know you want to be a Healer, too," came the insistent voice in his head, the second self that chose times like this to scold him. This time, however, he didn't slap it away as he would a biting gnat. *"You have Talent. You know it, Eser knows it, the rest of the Healers know it, too. You're just afraid."*

Revyn thought about that one for a while. *What would I be afraid of?* he asked himself.

"You're afraid of losing your last hope of being a Bard. As long as you stay in the House of Healing without making any progress in using your Healing Talent, there's a chance that a Bardic Gift might show up. If you become a full Healer, you might have to leave Haven, and you couldn't continue your musical studies like you have been. Like Eser and Keryn have indulgently allowed you to."

The voice was a sting of conscience, sharply reminding him of how ungrateful he had been to those who were trying to help him and teach him. He squirmed suddenly, trying to avoid his self-recrimination. But the voice, once unleashed, refused to be fettered again.

"You know it's just your own pride. Keryn said you could be a good Minstrel—and you already are one, even if it is 'just' around the circle of other Healing students.

And a Healer who can play music to soothe and calm the nerves is a rare thing. You're just too stubborn to accept that. You won't accept being anything less than the best, anything less than what you decided you had to be without even knowing what you could and couldn't be. You—"

~~*Enough!* he "shouted" at the voice, squelching it into~~
silence. *You've made your point. Leave me alone for a while. I just need to think, to figure out what I want.*

Some weeks later, Revyn hurried down the hallway of the House of Healing ahead of Eser, anxious to get to young Seldi's room for a few quick minutes of conversation in the course of the morning rounds. The boy's broken leg had been healing well, and Revyn expected that Eser would soon allow the lad to return to his family's holding with his older brother, who had arrived in Haven this day to fetch him.

"Good morning, Seldi," he said cheerfully as he entered the room, smiling at the first patient he had ever treated on his own.

"Hi, Revyn," the younger boy said, grinning. "I hear my brother's come t' pick me up. 'S it true? Will I be goin' home soon?"

Revyn glanced in mock warning at the door. "I wouldn't say that too loudly when you know Healer Eser is coming. He's liable to keep you here just to dash your hopes."

Eser smiled at the sound of the two boys' laughter as he entered the sickroom.

"Well, Seldi, how do you feel today?"

"I'm itchin' t' go home, Healer Eser, sir. I hear m'brother has come t' fetch me."

"He has, and he'll be in to see you soon. But it seems you might not be getting away from us for good, after all."

Revyn shot Seldi a quick "I-told-you-so" look, then turned his attention to what the Master Healer was saying.

"You, my boy, have a slight Talent for Healing. Not

enough to make you a Master Healer, so don't worry about being trapped in my job," Eser said, smiling at his own expense. "But what you have, if trained, would be very useful back on the farm to help with the livestock and small injuries."

"What, *me,* a Healer?" Seldi gaped at Eser, eyes wide with disbelief.

"Yes, in certain things, if you choose to come back when you're a little older, for training. You probably wouldn't be strong enough to save lives, but you could save a good deal of the pain from small things—the little hurts that you get often enough on a farm. And you could learn to set legs, too."

"In case anyone else is fool enough t' go climbin' the crag so soon after the first snow, y'mean?" Seldi grinned.

"Something like that," Eser smiled. "Would you like to be able to do that?"

"Would I! Ma 'n' Da are allus sayin' how much we need a Healer down nearer t' the village—we can't allus be runnin' t' Haven. An' if I could take care of what we need, well, that'd save us time and gold. Sure I'd come back!"

Eser smiled again at Seldi's infectious enthusiasm.

"Well, then, we'll just have a look at your leg and I'll talk with your brother and we'll see if we can get you sent off home to finish knitting up that bone." He turned and nodded at Revyn, who slipped quietly into his accustomed place beside the cot, lifting the blankets and laying his hands gently over the bandages.

Carefully, he let his mind sink into the leg, beneath the bandages and the splint, until he could See the white of the bone buried deep within the flesh. The joining of the two pieces was a complete, though fragile, network of bone and ligaments. The break had healed straight and clean. He withdrew his awareness and looked up at Eser, nodding slightly.

"It's clean," he said quietly. Eser bent down and touched the leg briefly, checking Revyn's Sight against his own, and nodded back at his student.

"Well, Seldi, you're doing fine. I'll just have a word

with your brother and we can send you home in good health. Mind you don't try walking too soon, now, or you might bend the bone."

"Thank you, Healer Eser, sir," Seldi murmured breathlessly. "I'll be back before you know't."

Eser slipped out the door, leaving Revyn alone with the younger boy.

"I'm t' be a Healer like Eser an' like you, Revyn. Can you believe't?"

Revyn grinned at his friend, sharing his delight.

"Who'd've thought this would come of me breakin' me leg tryin' t' get me Mum the last of the ferril flowers?"

"Was that what you were doing, Seldi? You never said."

"Oh, aye, a stupid enough thing, eh? I allus promise t' pick the last ferril flowers I can find for me Mum, and I hadn't gone and got 'em this year. So after the first snow, I decided to take a last look up the crag t' see if'n I could find some. When the snow started again, Teral came up to look for me, an' we both went down in that rockfall." Seldi became quiet and looked down at the blanket, absently picking at its weave.

"Well, you never can tell when good'll come to you, right?" Revyn asked cheerily, standing and heading toward the door to join Eser and continue the morning session.

"Nay. Sometimes, good comes even when you don't get what you want—or when you don't even get what you promised yourself an' somebody else, too."

Revyn turned suddenly, staring at Seldi in shock. *Sometimes, good comes even when you don't get what you want,* he repeated to himself. *Havens, I think I must be the fool here. Seldi's climbing the crag to pick flowers for his mother is no stupider than what I've been doing here for the past year.*

He smiled and said his farewells to the young boy without really paying attention to what he was doing, his mind still repeating what the lad had said. Without even knowing it, Seldi had done more for him than a year of Eser's teachings.

Passing into the hallway, Revyn nearly ran into the Master Healer, who was just returning, a tall strapping youth with a striking resemblance to Seldi following in his wake.

"Ah, Revyn, there you still are. I will just take Derem in to see his brother and we can finish visiting our patients. I know you'll be in a hurry now."

Revyn gave his teacher a questioning glance and saw the smile crinkling the corner's of Eser's eyes.

"I have letters for you from Elann," he said, opening the door to Seldi's room and gesturing for the other boy to enter, then going in after him.

Revyn stared at the closing door, then turned and hastened down the hall to the next occupied sickroom, not even bothering to wait for Eser to finish talking to Seldi.

Revyn took the two letters from Eser's hand and hurried out to the garden, ignoring the midwinter cold. He always read letters from home in the privacy of what he had come to consider "his" grotto, bad weather notwithstanding.

Brushing the snow off of the small bench, he sat down and studied the envelopes. The first he recognized as his mother's handwriting, and he expected the second to be from Chylla.

Revyn nearly dropped the second letter in surprise when he saw that the second letter was addressed in the awkward, blocky script of his brother. Why hadn't Chylla written him? Why would *Myndal,* of all people, write to him? He decided to read Myndal's letter first—it would surely be the shorter, and would probably only be a tirade against him anyway.

Revyn—
   Your sister took sick a fortnight ago, going outside in the snow like the fool she was. She said she was going to find you, but I think she was running away from the decent marriage I had arranged for

*her. Anyway, she took sick real badly after we
found her and brought her back. She died last week
at a candlemark before midnight. I thought you
ought to know, but we don't expect you back soon,
so we buried her right away.*
   Myndal

Hot tears flooded from Revyn's eyes as he read the
last lines, trying to force his mind to accept them. Chylla,
his beloved golden sister—gone! No, it wasn't true. It
couldn't be true. Gods, why Chylla? Why couldn't it
have been—he stopped that thought before it completely
formed. No. He couldn't wish death on anyone, even
Myndal. Healers weren't allowed—again, he stopped his
thoughts before he touched that which he feared and
wanted so much. He folded the page before his tears
splotched the ink beyond legibility, tucking it absently
into his tunic. Hurt raged inside him as his mind cried
her name in agony.

Long minutes later, he broke the seal of his mother's
letter and slowly unfolded it.

My poor, dear son—
   *I weep as I write this, weep for your poor sister,
and weep for your foolish brother. Ah, if the gods
only knew how I suffered. I am sure Myndal has
told you what has happened, but I doubt me that
he told you all. He had arranged a disagreeable
marriage for poor Chylla, wanting to wed her to a
rich man my own father's age, simply to combine
our lands. I could do nothing to stop his plans, nor
could your poor sister. Ah, me, how foolish I was.
I should have dissuaded her from her attempt to
flee to you. She left just before a great storm came
up. Myndal was furious and set out with hounds
and men after her. They brought her back half-
frozen and sick. The fever set in, and Myndal refused to send for any Healers, saying Chylla would
be fine and that she deserved a little sickness for her
disobedience. I sent for the herb-healer, but she was*

helpless. Finally, Myndal sent to Hold Gellan, for
they have a full Healer, but by then it was too late.
Ah, poor Chylla. My heart grieves for her, my son,
as it does for you. As soon as you are able, come
home to me, for I fear I need you more than ever.
    Your ever-loving Mother

Revyn's tears began again, but this time he felt awash
in a feeling of guilt. If only he hadn't stayed to be
trained and to continue his Bardic schooling. If only he'd
gone home when he knew he couldn't be a Bard, Chylla
would still be alive. He could have stopped Myndal from
marrying her off to an old weakling. He could have
helped her. He should have brought her to Haven with
him. He should have— A sudden thought struck him,
and he turned back to the letter. Yes, his mother had
said that Myndal had refused to get a Healer until it was
too late. Gods, his fault again!

He'd been resisting the Healers, holding back on his
training, trying to give any Bardic Gift at all as much
chance to emerge as possible, hoping against hope that
he could still be a Bard. If he had taken the training as
it had come, maybe he could have been home, and if
Chylla had gotten sick anyway, he could have Healed
her. He had a strong enough Gift, he now knew that
instinctively. Now he accepted it, now that it was too
late for Chylla. Twice and three times a fool! Twice and
three times his fault!

He tucked his mother's letter next to the other inside
his tunic, folded his arms across his knees, bent his head
down, and wept furiously, shaking with sobs as he re-
viled himself for his stupidity. He grieved for his sister
and blamed himself for his grief. The tears soaked the
arms of his winter cloak, chilling him as the snow seeped
into his bones, but he didn't care. Chylla was dead, and
it was all his doing. Nothing would ever matter again,
not without Chylla there for him.

Much later, Revyn was only vaguely aware of Eser
and some other Healers running toward him with blan-

kets. They snatched him up and brought him in, warming him and giving him the Healing teas that he had so often helped to brew. Thoughts of Chylla raced through his fevered mind, until finally he slept.

He was back at Elann, standing outside the gardens on a foggy spring day. Hazy clouds swirled around him, and his head throbbed painfully. Somewhere, he heard music. Then he heard the golden music of Chylla's laughter. A sharp pain stabbed deep into his heart when he heard the joyous sound.

"Chylla!" he cried, "I'm sorry!" He ran into the garden maze, calling her name, following the laughter that rang in his head. "Chylla, come back to me!"

Suddenly, he rounded a corner, and there she was, rosy as ever, her golden hair spilling over her shoulders, her bare feet buried in the fresh green grass.

"Chylla," he gasped, "I'm sorry, so sorry. It's all my fault."

"Oh, be quiet, Revy," she said affectionately. "Maybe Myndal was right, maybe we are both fools."

"But, if I could have been there, I could have Healed you, if I'd accepted my training . . ." Her laughter rang out again.

"If you'd been there, it would have happened differently. But don't you see? It doesn't matter now. The Havens are so bright, so wonderful. They sent me back to wake you up. It's not your fault, silly. I'll be fine."

"But, Chylla . . ."

She stepped forward and put a golden fingertip across his lips. "No more of that, now. Tell Mother I love her, and that I'm happy. She always worried about the ending of life. Tell her it's just a new beginning." She danced backward and began to head toward another of the maze pathways. Just before she disappeared, she turned to face him.

"And, Revy, don't worry about that song you were going to write for me. Just keep Healing. It's a different music, but it's all connected." She slipped back into the maze, and the shrubs began to disappear into the haze around him. Rooted to the spot, he cried out her name, trying to bring her back to him.

"Revyn, wake up," Eser murmured again, holding the student's head in one hand and a mug of tea in the other.

"Eser?" Revyn said, wonderingly, turning his head slightly to look at his teacher.

A smile lit the Healer's face as he raised the cup to Revyn's lips. "Drink," he said, "and rest. Your mother only needs to grieve for one child at a time."

Revyn nodded and drank obediently, then slipped back down under the quilts. The dream of Chylla was still so strong, so clear in his mind and his heart.

Eser smiled again and nodded to himself. The lad would heal soon, and then they could talk again about his resistance to the training. He stood and slowly headed towards the door. A weak voice stopped him.

"Eser? How long before I can resume my training in the House of Healing?"

The Healer tried unsuccessfully to hide the happiness in his voice as he turned to the bed again. "You won't be able to visit the sickrooms for at least another week, until your strength is back. We can still give you some lessons here in your room, though. Would you like your lute? You can begin to practice again in a few days."

"No, I don't think so," Revyn said drowsily. "Chylla told me I was better off playing a different kind of music."

The School Up the Hill
by *Elisabeth Waters*

Elisabeth Waters sold her first short story to Marion Zimmer Bradley for *The Keeper's Price*, the first of the Darkover anthologies. She has sold short stories to a variety of anthologies. Her first novel, a fantasy called *Changing Fate,* was awarded the 1989 Gryphon Award, and was published by DAW in 1994. She is a member of the Science Fiction and Fantasy Writers of America and the Authors Guild. She has also worked as a supernumerary with the San Francisco Opera, where she has appeared in *La Gioconda, Manon Lescaut, Madame Butterfly, Khovanschina, Das Rheingold, Werther,* and *Idomeneo.*

The voices were particularly loud today. All day the instructions, unspoken and impersonal, were dinned into her brain. "This is how to make it rain . . . now you do it." She spent the entire day resisting, trying to block them out.

These voices weren't so bad, though; at least they weren't men wanting her to do things she had no desire to do—men who saw her as a thing, not a person with feelings.

Then twilight came. She had always hated twilight, when her mother's customers started arriving. She had never liked her mother's customers and had resolved at a young age that she was going to find some way to live without selling her body. And that was before she started hearing what they were thinking.

Some of the customers wanted her in addition to her

*mother—or instead of her mother. And when her mother
started thinking that it was time she began earning her
keep, she ran away, as far and as fast as possible, until
she found a place where she felt safe.*

*But still twilight made her uneasy, and her resistance
to the commands weakened. . . .*

Myrta lay back in the tub in her room and relaxed.
Maybe it was a bit self-indulgent, but she really enjoyed
a bath in the early evening, before she had to busy herself with the rush of customers the inn got every evening,
particularly in the bar. The town of Bolthaven had been
built around the winter quarters of a mercenary troop.
When the Skybolts moved out, their garrison had been
taken over by a mage-school, the largest White Winds
school in Rethwellan. Now instead of drunken mercenar-
ies, the bar got student mages.

Sometimes this created problems: a mercenary could
be asked to leave most of his weapons back at the bar-
racks, but a mage's abilities were always with him. And
if the mage was young enough for practical jokes and/
or foolish enough to get too drunk. . . . Well, the school
had a policy for that; they'd send down a teacher to stop
whatever was going on, and the school would pay for
any damage done.

Myrta heard running footsteps in the hall and a quick
tap on her door. One of the barmaids dashed into the
room before Myrta had time to say "enter."

"Excuse me, Mistress, but it's raining in the kitchen!"

Myrta surged out of the tub, splashing a fair amount
of water around the room as she half-dried herself, threw
on the nearest garment, and ran for the kitchen.

It was indeed raining in the kitchen. A thin layer of
cloud had formed just below the ceiling, and rain
dripped steadily from it. Fortunately, the brick floor in
the kitchen sloped slightly to a drain in the center, so
that water was running out as fast as it fell; and the stew
for tonight's dinner was cooking in the fireplace, so the
rain wasn't falling into it. But the floor was getting rather
wet and slippery, and the biscuits the cook had been

rolling on the center table were a total loss. The table's surface was being rapidly covered with flour-and-water paste, and the cook was cursing steadily. Serena had been a Skybolt until an injury left her with a permanent limp. Myrta counted herself very fortunate to have Serena in the kitchen; she was a wonderful cook, and she wasn't frightened by the occasional magical mishap. Frequently angry, but never frightened. The new scullery maid, on the other hand, was cowering in the corner by the fireplace. She looked wet, miserable, and terrified.

Poor girl, thought Myrta, *she's not used to the hazards of Bolthaven yet, and she can't be more than thirteen years old—if that.* "Serena, I think both you and Leesa had best go get into dry clothes. I'll send up to the school and have them deal with this."

Serena stalked out, still grumbling. Leesa scuttled after her, hugging the wall, trying to stay as far as possible from everyone else. Myrta closed the door behind them, sent the barmaid back to her regular duties, and went out to the stables.

"Ruven!"

"Yes, Mistress?" The stable boy, a stocky lad of seventeen, appeared from one of the stalls.

"I need you to run up to the school. Present my compliments to Master Quenten, and tell him it's raining in our kitchen."

"Raining in the kitchen, right." Ruven wasn't terribly bright about anything but horses and mules, and thus he tended to accept everything, however outrageous, as normal.

He dashed off, and Myrta returned to the bar to wait for help to arrive.

Elrodie, one of the teachers at the school, was there within half an hour. In addition to being an earth-witch, she was also an herbalist. "Master Quenten wasn't certain how much salvage would be required for tonight's dinner," she explained, greeting Myrta. "Let's go see the damage."

The two women stood in the doorway. It was still

raining, but the fire under the stew still burned, and the stew did not seem to Myrta to have scorched.

"I think the stew will be all right," Elrodie said, confirming Myrta's opinion, "assuming I can get the rain stopped quickly." She sighed. "That shouldn't be too difficult; the apprentices have been practicing weather magic all week. By now I think I could stop rain in my sleep."

"Thank you, Elrodie," Myrta said. "I'll leave you to work in peace, then. I'll be in the bar when you're ready for me."

Elrodie nodded absently, already rooting in her belt-pouch for supplies.

The rain was stopped in short order, the kitchen cleaned up, and Serena even managed to finish a new batch of biscuits in time for dinner. Myrta went to bed in the early hours of the next morning believing that life was back to normal.

This belief lasted until the next evening, when she was interrupted just as she was about to get into the tub.

"Mistress?"

"What is it, Rose? It's not raining in the kitchen again, is it?"

"No, Mistress." The barmaid took a deep breath and said nervously, "This time it's fog."

Myrta put her gown back on and went down to the kitchen. Everything was normal in the other rooms, but at the kitchen doorway the air turned misty gray. The visibility in the kitchen was less than an arm's length, as Myrta discovered when she stuck her arm into the fog and her hand vanished. Cursing from the center of the room informed her that Serena was still managing, after a fashion. "I'll send for help," she informed the cook.

Elrodie arrived and surveyed the scene with a teacher's eye. "Yes, this is today's apprentice lesson, all right. And someone has done a very nice job of it."

"But why is it in my kitchen?" Myrta asked.

Elrodie sighed. "Either it's a practical joke, or we've got an apprentice whose control needs more work. I'll clear this up for you, and then I'll have Master Quenten put a shield around your building for a few days so that no external magic can get in here. That should give us time to sort through the new apprentices and find out who's doing this. I'm truly sorry for the inconvenience, Mistress Myrta."

Myrta shrugged. "These things happen, and it could be a lot worse. Just fix it, so that the cook can see what she's doing. A shield around this place should certainly take care of the problem."

She broke out of his grip and ran, terrified, into the first hiding place she could find. What he wanted was only too clear—he wanted her to do what her mother had done, but he wasn't even planning to pay her. She remembered what her mother had said to her when she was a little girl, the one time she had spoken of wanting to do something else when she grew up. "What else are you good for?" her mother had asked. Mother had been so angry that she had never mentioned the subject again, but she had resolved that she would rather die than be a harlot.

But maybe she was one; maybe if your mother was, you didn't have any choice, no matter how hard you tried. After all, why else would he treat her like that? It must be her fault somehow.

The air around her was turning colder and darker. Now snow was starting to fall. She huddled against the wall, her face pressed into her knees, and just let the snow cover her as the tears froze on her face.

Myrta walked into the bar to find Ruven complaining to Rose and Margaret.

"... I don't know what she made such a fuss about— I barely touched the girl. I wasn't going to hurt her."

What girl? Myrta wondered. *Please don't let it be anyone with protective or influential parents.*

"Ruven," Rose said patiently, "you scared her. And you *were* going to hurt her."

"What do you mean?" Ruven asked. "I never hurt you two."

Margaret sighed. "Rose is eighteen and I'm nineteen. Leesa is twelve, much smaller than you, and a virgin. You *were* going to hurt her if you continued with what you were doing."

Myrta's relief that this problem was confined to her own household was cut short by a stream of curses coming from the kitchen.

She hurried there at once. The kitchen looked normal enough, but when she joined Serena at the entrance to the pantry, she saw a great cloud of white before her eyes. For an instant she thought that someone had dropped a bag of flour, but then she realized that all the white stuff was coming straight down from the ceiling and it was cold.

"Ruven!" she called. "Go tell Master Quenten that it is snowing in my pantry, and I would greatly appreciate it if he would give the matter his personal attention, since this appears to have come through *his* shields!"

Ruven ran out immediately, but it took a while for Master Quenten, who was not a young man, to come down the hill. By the time he arrived, everything in the pantry was covered with six inches of snow.

"I apologize for the delay, Mistress Myrta," he said mildly. "I stopped to check my shields on the way here, and they are intact. It's beginning to look as though whatever is causing this is here, not at my school."

"Here?" Myrta said incredulously. "Do you think I hire mages to wait on my customers?"

"Not knowingly, I'm sure," Master Quenten replied. "But tell me, who was in the building when this started?"

"I was," Myrta said, "along with the two barmaids, the cook and the scullery maid—and I believe that Ruven was indoors at the time as well."

Ruven looked as if he would rather not have been anywhere near the house. "I didn't do anything to her, honest!"

"To whom?" Master Quenten inquired, raising his eyebrows.

Ruven stared at him dumbly, and Rose answered for him. "The scullery maid. It seems that Ruven fancies her, but she doesn't fancy him."

"Indeed?" Master Quenten turned his attention to Rose. "How old is this girl, and how long has she been here?"

"She's twelve," Rose said, "and she's been here about three weeks."

Master Quenten looked around the kitchen. "And where is she now?"

Margaret looked worried. "I thought she was in here. She ran out of the bar crying when I came in and Ruven let her go."

Myrta silently resolved to pay a lot more attention to Ruven's activities in the future.

Serena frowned, trying to remember. "She ran in here crying, and . . . I think she went into the pantry."

Master Quenten hurried into the pantry. The snow stopped falling as soon as he crossed the threshold, and the clouds just below the ceiling thinned and vanished. The snow on the floor melted away from his feet as he walked the length of the room and reached down to grasp what appeared to be a sack of grain covered in snow—until he pulled the girl to her feet and began gently brushing snow off her hair and shoulders. "I think we've found our mage," he said calmly.

Leesa looked even more incredulous than Myrta had at the suggestion. "That's silly," she said. "There aren't any mages—except in old ballads. My mother said so."

"Indeed?" Quenten asked. "Where are you from, child?"

Leesa looked at the floor. "Haven," she said softly.

"Valdemar," Master Quenten said. "That explains a lot. Until recently there were no mages in Valdemar; it was certainly the most uncomfortable place for a mage to be." He shuddered at the memory. "I was there once, briefly, and as soon as I crossed the border it was as if there was something watching me all the time. I got out as soon as I could."

He looked Leesa over carefully. "So if you were born in Valdemar with a Mage-Gift, which you were—believe me, anyone with Mage-Sight can see it—you would never know you had it as long as you stayed there. But when you came to Rethwellan, whatever it is that inhibits magic in Valdemar would stop affecting you."

"If it's so obvious that I'm a mage," Leesa said disbelievingly, "then why didn't that teacher who came here the last two days notice it?"

"That is a good question," Master Quenten said approvingly. "Elrodie has no Mage-Sight, so she would not have noticed—and I imagine you kept out of her way as much as possible, didn't you?"

"Yes," Leesa admitted. "Being around mages makes me feel funny—they're so noisy, yelling about how to make it rain, or how to make fog, until I feel like my head is going to burst."

"You heard the instructions on how to make rain two days ago and how to make fog yesterday, right?"

Leesa nodded. "I don't like hearing voices all the time. It was nice when they stopped."

"So you didn't hear anything today?"

Leesa shook her head. "No. Not until Ruven came in and grabbed me. Then I could hear him really loud." She shuddered. "At least my mother's customers paid her to do stuff like that!"

Master Quenten turned a measuring eye on Ruven. Myrta glared at the boy. "Can't you tell when a girl is not interested?" she asked. "Or don't you care?"

"He doesn't care!" Leesa said, suddenly furious. "I told him to stop and I tried to get away from him, but if Margaret hadn't come in then . . ."

"You probably would have killed him," Master Quenten finished calmly, "and quite possibly leveled the entire building while you were at it."

Leesa looked at him uncomprehendingly. "I'm not a harlot," she said. "I'd rather die than be one."

"Well, that explains the snow," Master Quenten said.

"What do you mean?" Myrta demanded.

"She turned her perfectly justifiable anger at what was being done to her inward instead of outward. Part of her wanted to die, and part of her put the weather lessons of the last two days together. Precipitation and a low enough temperature generally produce snow."

"Lessons?" Serena said.

"Leesa," Quenten said, "fog occurs in nature when—"

"—the ambient temperature approaches the dew point." Leesa finished the sentence automatically, with the air of a student who had heard the lesson more times than she wanted to.

"You're a quick study," Master Quenten said approvingly.

Leesa just shrugged. Compliments made her feel uneasy. Since her own mother had never seen anything to praise in her, she figured that anyone who was nice to her wanted something in return. But she couldn't read this man; he didn't broadcast his thoughts the way most men she had encountered did. "What do you want?" she asked him suspiciously.

"I want you to come up the hill to my school, to live and study there, so that you can learn how to use your abilities without hurting anyone."

"I haven't hurt anyone!" Leesa protested.

"You're hurting yourself," Master Quenten pointed out. "You are standing here in dripping wet clothing, and by my reckoning this is the third day you've managed to soak yourself to the skin. Keep this up and you'll be sick. Do you have any dry clothes left?"

"Well, no," Leesa admitted after a moment's thought. "Everything I own is still damp."

"Come on upstairs," Margaret said, "and Rose and I will find something to fit you. We weren't in the kitchen during any of the incidents, so our spare clothes are dry."

"Good idea," Rose agreed. She glanced at Master Quenten to see if he had any objections, then took Leesa's hand. The three girls went up the stairs to the large attic room they shared.

"What you said about her leveling the building," Myrta said as soon as the girls were out of earshot, "you were exaggerating, weren't you?"

"No," Quenten said, as Serena shook her head. "She really could have done it. It's fortunate for all of us that the lessons the last few weeks have been basic weather magic, rather than say, how to summon a fire elemental." He looked at Ruven. "You, young man, have had a very narrow escape. And I wasn't joking about her killing you. If you hadn't let her go, if she had felt truly cornered and desperate, you *would* be dead by now. Think about that next time you're tempted to treat a girl worse than you would treat a horse."

"But horses are different!" Ruven protested.

Serena snorted. "Yes, they're bigger than you are, and they kick harder. Go back to the stables, Ruven."

"Shouldn't he apologize to her?" Myrta asked.

"Not if she can read thoughts," Serena said. "That's why I always say exactly what I'm thinking—I spent enough of my time in the Skybolts around Master Quenten and his mages to learn that you're much safer around mages if your behavior matches your thoughts. Since Ruven obviously doesn't understand what he's done wrong, any apology he attempted to make would be perceived by Leesa as an insult—and he's insulted her more than enough already."

"I see your point," Myrta said. "Ruven, you can go back to the stables now, and I suggest that you stay there."

Ruven, still looking bewildered, shrugged and went out.

Meanwhile Quenten was conferring with Serena. "You've worked with her for several weeks. What's your impression?"

"She's smart, determined, and a hard worker," Serena replied promptly. "I'll be sorry to lose her; it's not often you get help that diligent. But she's running scared from something—probably her mother's way of life."

" 'I'm not a harlot,' " Myrta quoted softly. " 'I'd rather die than be one.' "

"Exactly," Serena said. "And if 'I'd rather die' had been 'I'd rather kill,' we'd have a real mess on our hands. The sooner she's moved up to the school, the better."

"You're sending me away?" Leesa stood in the doorway, looking stricken. The fact that she was wearing clothes too large for her made her look even more like a helpless and frightened child.

To Myrta's astonishment, for Serena had never struck her as the motherly type, Serena limped over to Leesa and held out her arms, and Leesa took the step that closed the small distance between them and clung to Serena.

"Master Quenten is an old friend of mine," Serena said quietly. "We were Skybolts together, and I've trusted him with my life many times."

"Almost as many as I've trusted you with mine," Master Quenten pointed out.

Serena ignored him. "He's good people, and the school he runs is one of the best. You'll have a room of your own there, with a lock on the door—"

Leesa looked sideways at Master Quenten, who nodded.

"—and you'll have people to teach you how to use your powers. There are a lot of jobs that mages can do, and I think that you're going to be a very good mage."

"I think so, too," Quenten said, smiling at her.

"What's the catch?" Leesa asked, still suspicious. "Am I going to be a prisoner up there?"

"No, you won't be a prisoner," Master Quenten assured her. "Students are not allowed to leave the school grounds without permission, but permission is routinely granted when you have free time." He chuckled. "How many of our students do you get in your bar here every night?"

"Quite a few," Myrta said, "and even more on holidays."

"And I'll come up and visit you, too," Serena said reassuringly. "You're not going to vanish into a dungeon. Once you reach Journeyman status, you can go out and get a job if you're tired of studying. And by then, you won't have to worry about anyone's trying to rape you—you'll be able to defend yourself from idiots like Ruven."

Leesa looked up at her. "Truly?"

Serena nodded. "Truly."

"And you promise you'll come visit me?"

"I promise."

Leesa chewed on her lower lip, then decided. "All right, I'll go."

"Excellent," Master Quenten said. "You can share my horse on the ride uphill."

Leesa's eyes sparkled. Riding a horse was a real treat.

"But promise me one thing, Leesa," Serena said. "Even when you've learned how, don't turn that idiot Ruven into a frog. It's a waste of energy."

Leesa laughed. "I promise."

Chance

by Mark Shepherd

In 1990 Mark Shepherd began collaborating with Mercedes Lackey in the SERRAted edge urban fantasy series with the novel *Wheels of Fire,* (Baen Books). Also available from Baen is another collaboration with Mercedes, *Prison of Souls,* and a solo project, *Escape from Roksamur,* both novel tie-ins based on the best-selling role-playing computer game *Bard's Tale.* His first published solo work, *Elvendude,* appeared on the *Locus* bestseller's list. In the works is a sequel, *Spiritride,* to be published in 1997.

He is not what I expected, and everything I expected, Guardsman Jonne thought as he made his way back to the camp. *What I didn't expect was that he would look so tired.*

It had been a candlemark since making the acquaintance of Herald-Mage Vanyel, and already Jonne was convinced that the gods had sent him to this place for a reason.

It certainly took Haven long enough to send a Mage; here on the Karsite border the battle had been raging for some time, and until recently had been limited to the more "conventional" elements of warfare: arrows, swords, knives. These were the things Jonne knew well. Levin-bolts and mage-lightning, these were better left to the magicians.

But Vanyel, he is no mere magician. If the stories I've been hearing are true, he could level the entire town of Horn with a glance.

Jonne walked with a lightness in his step and a glad-

ness in his heart, both of which were unfamiliar feelings
in this war-torn land. He'd grown up in the area, with
Karse just on the other side of the valley, and he'd become accustomed to the Karsites' occasional war threat.
But Jonne and his family, comrades in arms and friends,
had never felt as vulnerable as they had this war. Jonne's
family owned a good piece of the land bordering Karse,
including a number of crystal mines that were relatively
untouched, so he had a personal interest in defending
the border, as well as a patriotic one; lately the war had
gone badly, and this was most certainly one of the reasons why Vanyel the Herald-Mage had been sent.

Perhaps there was another reason, which had nothing
to do with the war, the Kingdom, or even with Vanyel's
magical abilities.

Perhaps, Jonne thought, *we were simply meant to meet.*

There were other stories, about Vanyel's lovers, one
in particular. They said he was *shay'a'chern,* that his
loves were all young men. Jonne was in his thirtieth summer, had never married, but had also been drawn to the
males of his village from an early age. He knew what
he was long before puberty breathed new life into his
body while torturing it with growth, but only recently
he'd had a name for it: *shay'a'chern.* His experiences in
youth and early adulthood were awkward, brief, and
scarce, and had never grown into anything other than
fumbling adolescent experiments. The last, of a few
years before, with a young farmer having marital problems, might have become more than a single night. But
the farmer had second thoughts, guilty thoughts connected to his religion, and had pushed Jonne out of his
life and declared the whole affair a moment of weakness
that he would *not* repeat. Jonne accepted the reaction,
and his fate, resigned to a life of loneliness.

Then he started hearing stories about others, this
Herald-Mage in particular, and he began to wonder if
perhaps he might meet someone like himself, who would
want *more* than a single night of physical pleasure. When
his captain asked for volunteers to be the Herald-Mage's
guide, he raised his hand immediately. Given Vanyel's

mysterious and frightening reputation for destroying armies at a glance, no others offered their services. Which was just as well, as Jonne was the only one who knew the area, having grown up in this very forest.

Vanyel and other important Valdemaran officers had made camp on a hillside. Jonne looked back at the camp, now visible as a campfire in the forest; when Jonne had asked them why the camp was so far from the troops, Vanyel had replied that it was to draw any magical attack toward him, the Herald-Mage, and away from the troops, who were ill equipped to deal with such an attack. Jonne thought this a great act of bravery, or stupidity; since he had little experience in magical warfare, he withheld judgment. After all, he was a mere country lad, trained as a soldier, whereas Vanyel was a full Herald, and a Mage to boot, educated at the Collegium and, it was rumored, a close friend of the King himself.

Vanyel has survived many battles, magical and otherwise. He must know what he's doing, Jonne reasoned. *Or he would not be here, filling in for* five *Herald-Mages.*

After his brief introduction to Vanyel, the guardsman sensed something familiar behind the younger man's eyes. It was a look, a spark of recognition, that Jonne had seen maybe a dozen times in his life. It was a lingering gaze, normally brief between most men, but between *shay'a'chern* the gaze lasted a moment longer, just long enough to let the other know that *yes, I know you, too. We are both . . . different.*

The Guardsman also felt Vanyel's power behind the sexuality; Jonne had a slight Gift for Empathy and Mindspeech, but it was so unpredictable that he did not qualify for training. Occasionally the Gift would surface when his emotions were charged, as they were this evening.

Jonne bid him good evening with promises to return the next day. *Yes, he knows. He is,* he thought, trying not to let his joy show to the others gathered there.

The next day they would properly scout the Karse border, and perhaps catch a glimpse of the enemy, way off in the distance. War seemed to be a distant prospect now, as more pleasant thoughts occupied his mind as he made his way back to his company. Nearby was a system of caves he would show the Herald-Mage.

The path Jonne had taken passed along a ridge, below which was a sea of tents housing Valdemar's forces. Here and there was the occasional revelry, as this was Sovvan, which some insisted on celebrating despite the circumstances. The tents looked like shingles on a tiled roof, reflecting pale light from a full harvest moon. His own tent was down there somewhere, and as he began the descent to the valley, he even fantasized that some night very soon he may not be sleeping in it alone.

So long, Jonne thought. *So very long.* The Guardsman didn't want assume too much. After all, Jonne was no spring chicken anymore, and he had no way of knowing if the Mage would find an older man attractive, even if he was only five years his senior. Many years of sword training and a dislike for wine left him leaner and younger than his years; he made a point of staying in shape, not only to maintain his strength and stamina, but to keep himself physically appealing for that special man, wherever and whenever he might happen along. Jonne wanted so much to believe that Vanyel was that man.

The path led downward, into a thicker part of the forest where the shadows darkened. Jonne hesitated before starting down it. Something felt wrong, very wrong . . . the hair on his neck stood up.

Above the hill where Vanyel's group was camped, a dark stormcloud blotted out the moon. Lightning raced from it, striking the ground, rippling through the sky. There had been no sign of rain a mere hour before; wind whipped up from the south, racing up the valley and through the forest. Trees swayed around him, and he felt a surge of magic, evil magic, coming from Karse.

Jonne saw the magic for what it was, an attack from the south. *On this night, of all nights, when we would least expect it,* he thought in panic.

His first duty was with the company, but the rest of the army was still some distance away, and Vanyel's tent was much closer. Something called to him, drawing him back the way he came. From the thunderclouds came another streak of lightning, followed by an enormous fireball, which struck the hillside, sending a cloud of sparks high in the air.

Gods, was that their camp? Jonne thought, breaking into a run. *Have they been destroyed?*

He didn't want to consider the possibility that Herald-Mage Vanyel was injured. But when he reached the camp, he knew *someone* had been hurt. Three of the tents were ablaze, and other Guardsmen were scurrying about, trying to put out the fires. The hair on the back of his neck raised again. Guardsman Jonne dropped to the ground and covered his head.

The concussion hammered through the ground he lay against. A wave of heat blazed over him, scorching the back of his hands covering his head. Behind him someone was screaming; another Guardsman was on fire, and others tried to wrestle him to the ground.

"Lord and Lady, what is attacking us?" someone shouted, but in the chaos Jonne didn't see who.

Jonne started to get up, but before he was fully on his feet, a voice resounded in his head:

:Guardsman, come help us,: came the distraught words. In the shadows cast by the flickering flames, Jonne saw a shape, which moved toward him. What he first took for a large man in Herald Whites turned out to be a white *horse.*

No, not a horse, Jonne thought. *That is a Companion.*

He knew enough about the Heralds and their partners to know that this was no mere horse, and was as intelligent as any man.

:Vanyel is injured,: the words sounded. *:Come help us now.:*

At the mention of the Herald's name, Jonne stood straight up.

"Vanyel?" he called out. "Where is he?" Then he knew he was speaking to the Companion.

:This way,: the Companion answered, moments before the next explosion hit.

Jonne heard nothing as a flash of light illuminated the

entire area. The light came from behind him, as it cast his long shadow on the ground before him. The explosion threw him forward, into his own darkness.

Something solid nudged him solidly in his ribs. When he opened his eyes, the Companion was standing over him, looking down.

:You survived,: the Companion Mindspoke. *:You, and Vanyel. The others are dead.:*

Again, Jonne got up. The camp had been leveled by whatever struck them last. All that remained of the tents were wisps of burning fabric. A forest fire raged, spanning outward, burning away from them, filling the air with thick smoke. The Companion appeared to be singed, and smelled of burned hair, but for the most part unhurt. Items of Jonne's own clothing continued to smolder, and the Guardsman batted them out. He moaned when he touched the back of his neck and hands, the only parts of him that were burned.

"The others," Jonne murmured, then he saw them. *Burned,* unmoving bodies lay about like discarded dolls. Then, *"Vanyel.* Where is he?"

:This way,: the Companion said, and led Jonne to a clearing just beyond the tents. Above, lightning continued to flash, casting brief moments of visibility on the area. Still, no rain had fallen, but threatened to at any moment. Vanyel lay in the center of the clearing, and the Companion went to him, nudging with her nose.

:He's alive,: the Companion Mindspoke. *:But he is injured. Help him onto my back. This is not a safe place anymore.:*

The Guardsman sniffed the smoky air, remembering that whatever sent that last blast was still out there, somewhere, and was probably getting ready for another attack.

Jonne easily picked up the Herald, noting his slight weight as he propped him up on the beast. Vanyel muttered something unintelligible as he found his balance on the saddle.

:*He can ride,*: the Companion told him. :*Take us to safety, please, Guardsman.*:

Lightning struck the campsite, several paces behind him. The blast spattered them with dirt and pebbles, and in reflex Jonne shielded his face with his arm.

Time to go. Now.

"There are caves nearby," Jonne offered. "Will that—"

:*Take us to them,*: the Companion ordered. :*While you still can.*:

Jonne led the Companion and her barely conscious rider to the mouth of one of the hidden caves. In the distance, he heard battle, and felt an urge to go join it. Torn between his duty to his company and his new assignment to Vanyel as his guide, he had little trouble choosing his course of action.

This Herald is injured, and if I don't take him to safety, we will lose him, and all will be lost, the rational part of Jonne's mind told him. But beyond his duty, he felt a link to Vanyel, as if they were part of the same brotherhood: the brotherhood of *shay'a'chern.*

Jonne had chosen this cave because it had a hot spring pool near the mouth, and also because it had a few provisions they would need, which he'd stored down here in case of an emergency. The Guardsman led the Companion a few paces into the cave, where he paused to light a torch mounted on the cave wall. The sudden light revealed a pair of straw mattresses, lanterns, candles, and a cabinet which, assuming it hadn't been disturbed, had medicines and supplies he would need.

As he helped Vanyel down, he saw, in the blazing torchlight, the burns. They were three lines, slicing through his Herald Whites, reaching from his neck down past his waist. Jonne gently cradled Vanyel in his arms, hoping he wasn't injuring him more by moving him.

Lord and Lady, what did this to him? he thought, but deep inside he already knew. *Mage-lightning. What was he taking on, out there in that clearing?* As he lowered him to the mattress, Vanyel opened eyes wide with alarm.

"Easy, easy," Jonne said, suddenly concerned for his own safety. "I'm Guardsman Jonne, and I'm here to help you:"

The brief words seemed to do the trick. Vanyel visibly relaxed, and allowed the Guardsman to ease him onto the mattresses.

Vanyel's Whites practically fell apart as he lay him on the mattress. The mage-lightning had sliced through his clothes. Jonne reached into the cabinet for some ointment he hoped was still in there; it was, and when he opened the ceramic jar, Jonne found Vanyel eyeing him with a mixture of admiration and, something else, an emotion Jonne couldn't readily identify.

"We were under attack," Vanyel said. "The camp . . ."

The Campanion stepped forward, nuzzled Vanyel affectionately, and the Herald looked directly into her deep blue eyes.

"All of them?" he asked sadly. Jonne realized they were communicating, and the Companion had just told him about the camp. Then, "I have no energy left, Yfandes." A pause. "Yes, I will stay put—ouch!"

Vanyel had moved sideways on the mattress, raking his arm across his burns. He looked down at his ruined Whites, "I guess this uniform's had it," he said. "That makes the second this month."

Vanyel sat up on an elbow, regarding Jonne thoughtfully, wincing at the evident pain. "Where is this?" he said, looking around the cave.

"This mine belongs to my family," Jonne said, kneeling down beside Vanyel. "We are safe for the time being. How do you feel?"

Vanyel shrugged, leaned back on the mattress. "Dreadful, after that last round," he said. Jonne waited for him to continue. "I wasn't ready for that attack. We had no idea Karse had mages that powerful."

"Those burns look nasty," Jonne said, looking over Vanyel's mostly naked body. "Mage-lightning?"

"The worst," Vanyel said, but his tone had changed,

from that of a powerful man to a meek boy. "It got
through my shields somehow. Just wasn't ready."

"Lean back," Jonne said, "I'll put some of this on."

Jonne smoothed the ointment on, starting from his
neck and working down to his ankles. Vanyel looked
down at himself, then gave an embarrassed laugh.

"Don't take offense," Vanyel said, through obvious
embarrassment. Jonne tried not to laugh, and continued
to ignore Vanyel's excitement. "I'm *shay'a'chern*," he
said, flustered. "Sometimes I don't have any control
over it."

"Don't worry about it," Jonne said, suppressing a grin.
"So am I."

Vanyel sat up. "You're *what*?"

"I'm *shay'a'chern*, too," Jonne said, but Vanyel still
looked stunned.

"Are you sure?"

"I'm thirty years old," Jonne said, as he continued
spreading the ointment. "I should think I would know
by *now*, wouldn't you?"

Vanyel looked too tired to discuss it further. "I would
never have known," the Herald said distantly.

"And neither would I, if your reputation hadn't pre-
ceeded you. But, given your condition, I doubt you're
feeling very romantic," Jonne said reluctantly. "I'm not
suggesting anything. At the moment."

Vanyel reached over and touched his wrist. "But *I
am*."

Some time later they had submerged themselves in
the hot springs near the mouth of the cave; Van took a
little more time to get in, wincing as the waters touched
his wounds, but in moments he had surrendered to the
pool's warmth, and allowed Jonne to wrap his arms
around him. The shallow pool was only waist deep, but
had a smooth rock surface beneath, and a natural bench
for them both to recline on. Steam rose from the surface
of the water, forming clouds around their heads.

If my life ended right now, I would consider it fullfilled,
Jonne thought as he held Vanyel closer to him, avoiding

the worst of the burns. Fortunately, the injuries were bad only above the waist.

"I should feel guilty about leaving the war right now, but I don't," Vanyel said, snuggling closer to Jonne. Yfandes had politely excused herself before things had gotten too involved, and Vanyel said he was keeping in touch with her. The Companion had recently returned from a brief recon of the area, and her news had been good. All magical attacks had ceased, and the regular army was on alert, ready for any conventional invasion.

"The Karsite Mages may think I'm dead," Vanyel said casually. "In which case, I had better keep my head low, and in this cave. I suspect this place is shielding me from them." He shook his head. "All those men, dead. Why was I the only one to survive?"

Jonne didn't know how to answer him, so he remained quiet. *Something dark and sinister haunts this man, and if I pry too much, he's likely to shut me out completely,* Jonne reasoned. *He will tell me when he is ready. If that time ever comes.*

"You survived so you could be with me," Jonne teased, and nibbled on his right ear. "Otherwise, who would I have had to sleep with? My horse?"

"Your *horse,*" Vanyel said, with a smirk, "would have had more meat on his bones than I. Not to mention . . . well." Van turned, and gave him a long, slow kiss. Afterward, he proceeded to wrap Jonne's arms around him again, holding them tightly. "How can you find me attractive?" Van said, after a long pause. "I've lost so much weight in the last year, I'm practically a skeleton."

The question confounded Jonne. *How can I find him attractive? How can I not! I haven't felt this good bedding someone since I was twenty.*

"You are a most beautiful man, Vanyel," Jonne said. "I suspect that you're not very good to yourself." The Guardsman almost regretted saying that last; this was getting into an area Vanyel probably didn't want to explore. But Van said nothing, at first.

"Savil would agree," Vanyel said at last. "Tell me, Jonne, have you ever had a lover?"

What, exactly, does he mean by lover? he wondered, and since he didn't want to seem thick, he didn't ask. *A one night fling, or a year-long relationship?* The farmer he'd known was the closest thing to being a lover, his marriage to a lady notwithstanding. Jonne told Vanyel about him, and the day or two they'd spent in each other's intimate company.

"It was not what I would have preferred," Jonne added. "But it was what was available." He held Van tighter, as if to emphasize their present situation. "It was better that, than nothing at all." Jonne hoped that he didn't sound cheap; it was how he felt, and he assumed honesty is what Vanyel wanted.

"Then I suppose I must consider myself fortunate, to have had Tylendel as long as I did," Vanyel said, with only a hint of sadness. "This is Sovvan. The anniversary of his death."

That was his lifebonded, Jonne thought. *The one he lost. The pain must have been. . . .* He searched, but could not find the words to describe what he though Van might have felt.

"It was a long time ago, but it still feels like a part of me left when he did. I don't expect to replace him—"

"But you don't have to be *alone* the rest of your life either," Jonne blurted, uncertain where his words were coming from. "I don't know what the gods have in mind for me, but I do believe we were meant to be together tonight, and perhaps tomorrow night as well."

"And after that?"

Jonne carefully turned Vanyel around and looked directly into his eyes. "Does *anyone* know?"

Afterward they slept, and when they woke Yfandes had returned well fed from another trip. The enemy had left the area, as near as she could tell, but Van was uncertain. The brief time he'd spent with Jonne had helped him recover more energy than he said he'd expected, and he appeared to be ready to take on the entire Karsite army.

"As you are a mage, there is something I must give

you," Jonne said, pulling on the last of his clothes. They had made temporary repairs to Vanyel's Whites, but he would still have to replace them as soon as they got back to the camp. "But you must promise to tell no one about this place, because this mine is a family secret, and needs to remain that way. If Karse knew what was down here, they would have invaded in force long ago."

"Mine?" Vanyel said absently, but Jonne had already ducked back into one of the dark tunnels. Moments later he reappeared, concealing something wrapped in cloth.

I don't know if I'll ever see him again, Jonne thought, even though he doubted last night would be a one night stand. *The Fates can be tricky sometimes.*

Vanyel opened the cloth, revealing a massive, perfectly formed rose quartz crystal the size of his fist. The Herald-Mage stared at its perfection for a long time before saying anything.

"This is the largest rose quartz crystal I've ever seen," he said. "Are you certain you want to part with it?"

Jonne beamed with pleasure. "I'm certain, Herald-Mage. Just, whenever you see it, think of me, would you?"

Vanyel looked like he was about to cry. Instead, he took Jonne's hand in his own, then wrapped his arms around him in the tightest embrace yet.

"I will *never* forget you, Guardsman," the Herald-Mage whispered in his ear.

Sword of Ice

by Mercedes Lackey
and John Yezeguielian

Hailing from the Chicago area, John Yezeguielian began his writing career at 14, when an article of his was published in a local paper. Since then he's written a music review column and various other pieces of journalism. This short story marks his first published fiction. Previously he has worked in fast food, owned and operated three businesses, trained animals, programmed computers, and been a bodyguard to celebrities and princesses. His hobbies include sailing, scuba diving, motorcycling, aviation, Aikido, and falconry. (Yes, he's a real-life Hawkbrother.) Prose and music, however, remain his highest passions. He lives near Tulsa with a cougar, a bobcat, two German shepherds, and, of course, a mews full of hawks and falcons.

:Downwind,: the voice in Savil's head demanded, and Savil followed in the direction of the falcon as it changed trajectories. The huge bird pulled its wings in tightly now, an arrow slicing through the sky.

:Hurry!: the raptor pleaded, and Savil felt the urgency in the falcon's mental message.

If only it could give me more than vague concepts. Savil mumbled imprecations under her breath as she scrambled over yet another boulder in this miserable craggy landscape.

All at once, as if in answer to her unspoken wish, Savil's mind flooded with images. Sensations of speed overwhelmed her as her vision was superseded by the bird's point of view as it twisted and gyrated, plummeting recklessly from the heavens. Vertigo swept Savil's footing from beneath her. She scrambled blindly now, her fingers clawing desperately at the granite face, struggling for purchase as she slid down the side, dangerously close to a ledge.

Shut it down. Center, she reminded herself. *This is novice stuff. Regain control.* In an instant, Savil was back in charge of her perceptions. Then she slowly let the bird's sendings back in, until they were vaguely superimposed on her true sight.

She couldn't see a man yet, but from the bird's eyes she could see what lay over the next rise. Rock scorched and molten, trees burst, their trunks still smoldering. The scene was one of rampant havoc, implying power turned loose to run wild in a way that sent atavistic chills up her spine. And then the falcon swiveled around one last boulder. Kicking its feet out before its body, the bird flared its long, pointed wings and set down gently upon firm ground.

Or what? In her mind's eye, Savil could see the falcon looking in what must be her direction, the raptor's sure, steady gaze finding her amidst the mass of upthrown debris, still quite some distance off. But the bird's vision was wavering, rising and falling. And then the falcon cast its gaze downward, and Savil saw the burned face of a man.

The rising and falling must mean she's perched atop his chest. He's alive and breathing, though the gods only know why.

Her resolve hardened, Savil reached out with her special Gifts, locating the man and probing swiftly and delicately at his mind. Gently, she pulled back a layer of unconsciousness, moving deeper, and pulled back as if stung. This man, this strange one somehow linked with a hawk, was able to function while the full, raw power of a major node of magical energy flowed in and through his body. Though still young, Savil was decidedly a master, a full Herald-Mage, and she could not do that for even an instant. He must be like a sword of ice to channel such power and still be alive, Savil thought to herself.

Still wondering what peculiar sort of being it was which she was being called to aid, Savil scrambled across the tops of the last few boulders and began climbing down into what used to be a mountain glade.

:Tayledras, beloved,: Savil's Companion spoke into her mind. *:This is a Hawkbrother.:*

Until Kellan had Mindspoken, Savil had all but forgotten her Companion amidst the excitement and shock of a bird's-eye view of flight. As she was reminded, Savil realized Kellan's voice had been conspicuously absent during the usurpation.

:I was blocked,: Kellan pouted, feigning a sulk, *:by your whirlwind rapport with that bondbird creature.:*

Oh? Really? And just how did that come about? Savil thought to question her Companion further, but the descent was over and she had other concerns now. Before her were the charred, breathing remains of the only Hawkbrother she had ever seen.

So badly wounded was he that Savil was barely certain where to start. Something had ripped down the Hawkbrother's side, scorching and cauterizing flesh as it apparently continued from his shoulder to the ground. It seemed to be a lightning strike, but that was simply not possible. No man could have survived even that one blow, let alone the other tears and rips in this man's flesh and the agonizing burns across his skin.

As Savil's hands cleared his clothing from the wounds, her mind sent him energy—healing energy essential to his survival, though she was no Healer. The going was slow as she gingerly pulled the fabric from the Hawkbrother's devastated form. The power was still flowing through him somehow, and Savil knew better than to attempt to touch him or his fragile, dangerous mind again.

Without warning, the bird let out a scream from deep within its throat. Startled, Savil pulled away and turned to look at the huge falcon. When she looked back again, the Tayledras' eyes were open, breathtaking ice-blue eyes surrounded by a mass of seared flesh which was healing, changing right before her eyes. The Hawkbrother's gaze met hers for a brief moment, then his eyes closed again. Through the aura of pain which she now realized she'd been feeling from him the entire time, she could have sworn she'd felt the faintest of smiles.

A myriad of sendings from the bird confirmed what Savil had begun to suspect—that the Tayledras could heal himself better if she'd just remain to protect him and continue to transfer energy to him.

"Well," she said aloud, looking down at him. "It looks as though you and I are going to be together for a while. At least I was ahead of my schedule and there won't be anyone missing me for a couple of weeks." Then she waited for Kellan to catch up with her, picking his own way through the rocks, and prepared for a long vigil.

Throughout the rest of that day and the next, she remained close to the stranger, imparting as much healing energy as her own reserves would allow. She left his side only to gather wood for the nighttime fires, and to step behind a boulder to relieve herself.

She could see a gradual but marked improvement over that first day. By the end of the second, she sensed he had recovered enough for her to bathe him. Savil's gentle hands lifted the Hawkbrother's head and washed his neck and face with the meager supply from her waterskin. Even more carefully did she move his body from side to side to wash it, removing his tattered garb and replacing it with a clean set of Whites of her own. At no time during those two days did the Hawkbrother make movement or sound, and his eyes remained shut, as if he were locked in a very deep sleep.

Early in the morning of the third day, Savil's routine of preparing breakfast was interrupted once more by the falcon's scream. When she looked over at the Tayledras, he was struggling to rise to his elbows. Savil rushed to help him.

:*Thank you, but you have already done more than enough,*: the Tayledras said to her in clear and coherent Mindspeech. Then, though not entirely steady in his movements, the Hawkbrother rose carefully to his feet. His bondbird began chittering pleasantly at him. His eyes closed again for a moment, and he nodded, a warm smile upon his lips.

:My friend has been telling me of your vigilance these past few days. It would seem that I am in your debt. . . .: It was a question phrased as a statement.

The Tayledras were reclusive by nature, even hostile toward strangers. That she knew, though little else. Even though Savil had helped him, and perhaps she had even saved his life, he would probably be suspicious of her motivations.

By the customs of some of the strange people who dwelled in this wilderness, the fate of one not of one's own tribe was usually left to the gods; it was not for anyone else to interfere or concern themselves with what happened to strangers. That might be the case with the Hawkbrother. It could be that while he was grateful for her assistance, he would also wonder why she had done so, and be suspicious of her motives.

Savil noticed his wary mood, and was quick to recognize the skepticism in his tone of voice.

:You may start your repayment by telling me the name by which I am to call you,: she said, smiling, knowing that to some folk, asking for a personal name was tantamount to asking for a weapon to use against them.

:I am called Starwind,: he said with much dignity, *:And the falcon you have been in rapport with is my bondbird; you might refer to her as my familiar.:*

Savil stole a quick glance in the direction of the bird and thought to herself that she wished she'd had some bit of meat to offer the hawk. As if it had heard her, the bird launched itself from the stone it had been perched on, taking to the sky with swift, powerful beats of its wings. Soon it was circling high above them. Then, all at once, the bondbird dropped its head, folded its wings, and fell, scorching straight downward from the sky toward the quarry its powerful vision had spied. Excited by the hunt, the impressions the bird sent were intense. Once again, Savil was swept up in the bird's aerial pursuit.

But not enough so that she was unaware of her companion. Starwind, too, appeared caught up in the bond-bird's sendings. His eyes narrowed, a hint of fiery temper behind the hooded lids, as he watched through the bird's keen eyes. When the falcon made impact with the prey, Starwind's fingers clenched just as the bondbird's talons closed on the duck's neck. For another few moments, Savil knew that she and Starwind were sharing in the bloodlust the falcon felt in the kill. She found she was salivating along with the bird, in anticipation of the rich, red feast quivering beneath the falcon's talons.

This was such a unique experience, that Savil allowed herself to remain caught up in it a little longer. Starwind was first to break from the trance, and as she slowly disentangled herself, she noted by his reaction that he had suddenly realized that Savil had been linked with the bird during the kill as well as he. At the same time, his knees gave out, and he sat down abruptly on the boulder beside him.

She made no move to help him, as it was possible that such a movement could be misinterpreted. He stood up again, slowly, clearly taking stock of himself. Then, as though he'd decided something of great importance, Starwind gathered himself and faced Savil directly.

:If I may trouble you a bit more, Sister,: Starwind said, looking deeply into Savil's eyes. *:I fear I am yet too weak to return to my* ekele *without help.:*

:That's hardly surprising,: Savil said gently as she looked back, awestruck by the strange beauty of this man. *:I'm more than a little amazed that you are able to stand at all. And I'd be happy to help you get to your. . .?:*

:My ekele? *My home.:* Starwind confirmed her guess.

:Your ekele, *then,:* Savil continued,*: and you need not call me "Sister" to convince me to do so.:* She flushed a little, wondering how he was reacting to *her.* *:In fact, I'd rather that you not . . . think of me . . . as your sister.:*

Though hardly innocent, Savil had never been so forward with any man before. But there was something about this one, something exotic and compelling about this Starwind that had her heart beating fast, her palms breaking a sweat. She supposed she'd seen it in him the first time he opened his eyes, but she'd been too busy tending to his wounds then to pay it any heed. Now, though, his face all but healed, his elegant movements, those ice-blue eyes, and that mane of snow white hair combined to make an irresistible package.

Or perhaps it was just that she had been out on circuit for a very long time.

Or perhaps—

Starwind seemed very well aware of her reaction. :*It is the fever of the bondbird, Sister,*: he said gently, but firmly. :*And I would call you otherwise, if I had your name.*:

She sighed—but made a little resolution that the game was not over yet. :*I am Savil, Herald-Mage of Valdemar, Chosen by Kellan . . . and at your service.*:

Over the next couple of days, Starwind and his bond-bird, Savil and Kellan wove their way carefully through the mountains back to Starwind's home, the place where his Tayledras clan lived. When they finally arrived, they were met by a small group of Tayledras, Starwind's people, all similarly exotic, most with the same white hair and ice-blue eyes. They greeted Starwind with warmth and relieved enthusiasm, obviously glad for his safe return, but kept Savil at a goodly distance. Starwind spoke with them in a light, musical language at once similar and different to the few words of Shin'a'in she knew, apparently explaining how he'd come to be hurt and how Savil had rescued him. At one point in his telling of the tale, he must have said something shocking, because all of the welcoming party turned at once to look at her, their eyes wide in disbelief. The group then quickly disbanded, leaving the four of them alone again.

On the way to Starwind's home, Savil had explained the nature of the relationship between Heralds and Companions. Starwind had not seemed overly surprised, explaining that his people had stories of Valdemar and even kept some fluency in the tongues of other peoples. Accordingly, Starwind directed Kellan toward a meadow rich with herbs and grasses for him to eat before accepting Savil's assistance in the monumental ascent to the Hawkbrother's home.

That home! It was lodged somewhere up in the branches of a tree so huge she could hardly believe her eyes, and to reach it, one had to clamber up a contrivance that was more ladder than staircase. Savil's one real fear was of heights, but somehow she managed to put on a brave front, showing no signs of her fear in climbing up into the *ekele*. After only one look out the window though, she decided she'd prefer to seek lodgings on firm ground. The vertigo she experienced while in the lofty *ekele* was simply too much for her.

Starwind chuckled quietly, but unkindly.

:You have the Tayledras' ability at rapport, but not our love of the heights? It is merely foreign to you. Remain here a few days, and you will come to cherish the here-above as we do.:

The mere idea was appalling. *:A few days? If I remain here a few days, I'll be in worse shape than you were when we met!:* Savil was already quite dizzy from the climb, and getting more nauseous by the moment. She could not help it; now that she was no longer moving, she felt a jolt of fear each time the *ekele* moved with the wind. Starwind took pity on her, probably because although she could conceal the more obvious signs of fright with jokes, she could not conceal her increasing pallor.

:As you wish, then. I would not care to dwell in a deep cave below-ground either,: he said. *:The* hertasi *keep some rooms here-below, and you are welcome to make your stay in one of them. There are some matters I must attend to—affairs of my people.:*

With that, Starwind guided her back down from the *ekele* and to an oddly constructed building surrounding the trunk of the huge tree, which somehow incorporated a warm spring and much green foliage. As they walked, Starwind explained to her about the *hertasi,* and how the sentient, elusive lizard-people tended to the Tayledras' needs in exchange for protection. Then he left her to her own devices, promising to return within a couple of candlemarks.

Savil used the time to rest and think, to take in and shelve away all of the strange wonders she'd discovered in the past few days. She Mindspoke with Kellan about it all. While he carried on a lively conversation with her, Savil made note that her Companion didn't seem unduly surprised by any of this.

:There are a great many things we know of, my love, which we are not at liberty to share with you before it is time to do so,: he said, in that infuriatingly patronizing tone he very occasionally used with her. It reminded her of her father and brother—and how they used to pat her on the head and tell her that she would be told about something "when she was old enough." And then, of course, having dismissed the mere female, they would go on about their business and never tell her anything at all.

Savil was about to send Kellan a scorching retort when all of the exertions of the last few days caught up with her. It seemed like far too much effort to go to, and besides, she wasn't in the mood for an argument. So instead of retorting, she ignored him, even to the extent of partly blocking him out of her mind while she searched for a place to lie down. It didn't take long to find a kind of couch, built among all the leaves and foliage, and she fell into it, and then into a deep and sudden sleep.

The meeting of the Tayledras clan had been going on for hours. Starwind had been severely chastised for having brought Savil into the midst, not only of k'Treva's holdings, but into the very heart of the Vale. Outsiders were *never* brought this far; at the most, one allowed them a little way into the fringes of Clan territory before dismissing them. It had caused no small commotion when Starwind had argued that he'd done no such thing since Savil was not an outsider, but one who deserved the title of Wingsister. The elders had called it nonsense, and accused Starwind of making up such an outrageous claim to justify his actions, claimed his desire for this Herald was the true cause of his behavior.

While Starwind did have strong feelings for Savil, it was not the lust the elders suspected, although he himself could not have explained the insistent feeling that he *must* bring this stranger into the very center of k'Treva. He could only feel it, and without facts to bolster the feelings, could only rely on thin logic to convince the others.

"I bring this woman," he cried out defiantly, "because she *is* one of us. Have I not told you of her rapport with my bondbird? What greater testimony can there be than this? Tell me, when has such a thing happened before?"

There began a quiet murmuring amongst the elders. Though relatively young, Starwind had proven himself and his worth on numerous occasions. He could only hope that they would decide that it would be unfair to take his word lightly.

"It is not that we do not believe you," one elder finally confessed, "but that we have no precedent for such a thing. We are an ordered people, as well you know. Never has anyone who was not of our cousin-Clans, the Shin'a'in, ever been granted the title of Wingsib. This woman has not even a drop of shared blood with us!"

He set his jaw. "Do we share blood with *hertasi*? With *tervardi* or *kyree*? With *dyheli*? Yet all of these are welcome here!"

The elder sighed. "Starwind, you are young and eager for a change that you see as a clear necessity, but we are not comfortable when someone wishes to make things change so suddenly. This makes us unwilling to accept that which brings changes, and . . . it frightens us to think of how different we may one day become."

The honest wisdom of the elder held them all in silence for some time. Starwind's mind was running the whole while. He had seen inside of Savil, knew her good heart. How could he convince them of this, or even get them to depart from the strictness of their ways long enough to look at her objectively? The silence was deafening. Starwind knew if he did not speak up, convince them somehow, that they would retreat back into the safety of their routines.

"Savil should be—no, *is!*—Wingsister to k'Treva. She has proven her worth with her rapport with my bond-bird, and earned her place by the acts of charity she performed for this member of the clan. I speak for her in claiming that place, and challenge you to examine her spirit and say why this should not be so."

How could he tell them the things he only felt, but had no reason to feel? That he *knew*, without doubt, that this stranger would be important to the future of k'Treva, and that k'Treva would be instrumental in shaping, not only her future, but that of many, many people outside of the Hawkbrother lands, people that Starwind would never see and who would probably never even dream that Tayledras were anything but a fable. He had never shown any trace of ForeSight; never been able to look into the future without the aid of one who did have that talent. He knew he was taking a chance that all of his actions for many years to come would be regarded with suspicion and mistrust if he could not convince them. But he knew what he was doing was right, and trusted in the wisdom of the elders to overcome their fears.

"How can we know that you are not simply seeing what you wish to see?" the first elder asked.

"She sleeps, and she is too weary to awaken if you do not alarm her," Starwind said. "She trusts us. You may touch her mind now, and from there see into her heart. Read what you see there, see what it is she represents for her own great Clan k'Valdemar, and then tell me if she is not indeed worthy to be named our Wingsister."

"Even if we find it so," another elder spoke, "what difference will it make? Tell me, Starwind k'Treva, why we should bring her into our clan? She has people of her own, and the Heralds of Valdemar are different from us in more ways than they are similar. We do not eat the same foods, speak the same tongue—we do not even swear by the same gods!"

"She should be made one of us because she is one of

us, she and her kind differ from us only in the names
by which we swear, not to the spirit behind those
names," he replied stubbornly. "And because we can
learn much from each other, the k'Treva and this
Herald-Mage. In many ways, our magic is much greater
than theirs. Yet there are things they can do which we
cannot. It is my belief that what we learn from each
other—the combination—will be greater than any that
we can each of us perform apart."

Another long silence followed. Each of the elders was
considering what Starwind had said. Surely they knew
he was right that the k'Treva could not live isolated in
the Pelagirs forever. There had even been visions, Fore-
Sight some of them had experienced, which suggested
that events in the future would require that they learn
to broaden their ways. Finally, the first elder spoke.

"It will cost us nothing to look at this Savil you bring
us. We must at least look before we judge."

Savil's sleep was interrupted by dreams, memories,
and nightmares. In them, she relived experiences from
the years since she had first donned Whites, the moment
that Kellan had Chosen her, battles fought in the service
of Valdemar, even passionate feelings for those loved
and lost. Then came a dream of a test—a decision she
was forced to make three times, one which left her
frightened, exhausted, and drained. Countless hopeless
scenarios presented themselves to her. Over and over
again she was forced to decide how to react. Just as her
decision was made, the scene would fade, and another
would take its place. Each was progressively worse than
the last, more hopeless, more futile, and in it she and
those around her were suffering greater and greater loss.
Only when the scenario required that she sacrifice Kellan, her Companion, did she wake from the nightmare,
unable to make the impossible choice.

She woke with a start, her own voice screaming to be
left alone, tears streaming down from eyes wide open in
the darkness.

:It was only a dream, dearheart,: Kellan consoled her,

:*A hideous, ugly, necessary dream. I am fine. Return to your sleep.*:

She was too sleep-fogged to take in anything except Kellan's reassurance, too exhausted to question anything Kellan said. Relieved to have Kellan's voice in her mind, she fell back into the embrace of the strange bed, and slept until morning. If she continued to dream, she didn't remember any of it.

When she awoke, she found Starwind sitting beside her, his hand resting gently on her shoulder. She could feel the soft tingle of power as it flowed through him to her.

:*Good morning, Wingsister,*: he said cheerfully. :*Wind to thy wings.*:

:*Wind to thy wings, Starwind k'Treva,*" she answered automatically, her head throbbing. She wished, vaguely, that he wasn't being so damned cheerful. :*Gods, but I've one miserable headache!*:

He sobered, and looked both contrite and a little guilty. :*Forgive me, Wingsister. The elders felt it was necessary.*:

She frowned. :*What have the elders to do with my headache?*: Then she sat up, her own suspicions flaring. :*Were your people messing about in my head?*:

Starwind closed his eyes and spoke quietly into her mind. :*Remember all, little sister. There is nothing to fear.*:

With that touch, Savil suddenly recalled the dreams and sendings she'd gotten after the nightmare of sacrificing Kellan, the knowledge slowing coming forward to her consciousness. In a single flash, she knew as much about the Tayledras as they knew themselves, as if she had studied them and their ways all her life.

The history of the k'Treva, their philosophies, their purpose as entrusted to them by their Goddess, their mysterious bond with their birds, everything given to her, including Starwind's own memory of the meeting last night, every newly gifted memory, all rose up and became a part of her. As they did, her headache dulled and then faded. Savil lay there unmoving, sharing Starwind's loving gaze for quite some time. They may have lain there for hours longer, basking in the communion, if a *hertasi* had not crept in quietly to bring them some fruit.

Without conscious thought, she thanked the *hertasi* (who was already leaving,) in Starwind's own tongue. Then she laughed out loud of the pleasure and strangeness of it all.

Once before in her life she had known the incredible, indescribable joy of finding that she *belonged* somewhere, that there were people in the world who welcomed her as one of their own. That had been when she became a Herald—and now it had happened again.

"So this is what it means to be one of you," she whispered.

"Not entirely, *shayana*," Starwind replied, "but you now share the most of it."

Savil's eyes had been alight with the joy of the newfound knowledge and abilities of these strange and wondrous people she knew she could now call her own. She was overwhelmed by the all-pervasive sense of the *peace* of this place, of the serenity of those who lived here. After all the conflicts within and besetting Valdemar, k'Treva Vale seemed like a vision of paradise, and she wanted to remain here forever.

And as soon as she had that thought, she knew it was impossible. For a moment, her eyes stung with tears.

"You know I can't stay. You must know that I'm a Herald first, and always will be so."

"Of course, *ashke*, of course," Starwind patted her hand to console her. "It was that which finally convinced the elders of the trueness of your heart."

"But I *want* to," she confessed desperately, as Starwind's elegant fingers brushed a tear from her cheek. "I want to stay here, live here in this peace."

"We each have our duties, Wingsister. Mine is to the land, yours to your people. Neither of us can fully understand the other, yet it is so. But we can revel in that which we share. I believe that this sharing, this exchange between us, will be of great importance in times yet to come."

Savil nodded, understanding, remembering the certainty she held in memories now her own, shared with him. Neither of them knew why—but the certainty was there, as real as if they had absolute facts to prove it to be true.

"There is much yet to learn, Wingsister, and far too little time to learn it in. We are now your clan, as you are one of us. Every member of k'Treva will do what he can to help you gain the skills that are ours, and we know you will share willingly of your ways as well. And I feel this will not be the last time that those of k'Treva and k'Valdemar will share their wisdom."

She thought about her duty—but she had been far ahead of her schedule, and there was time. A little, but there was time. "Where do we start?" Savil asked. "With your lessons, or mine?"

He smiled. "Where both our powers flow from, at the nodes."

Then Starwind took her hand, guiding her to her feet, and their journey toward knowledge was begun.

In the Forest of Sorrows
by John Helfers

This story marks John Helfers' fourth fiction sale.
Other stories of his can be found in *Phantoms of the
Night, Future Net,* and *A Horror Story A Day: 365
Scary Stories.* When he's not writing or editing, he
enjoys role-playing games and disc golf. He lives in
Green Bay, Wisconsin, with his fiancée.

Treyon scrambled over the top of the small foothill and
raced down the other side, never once glancing back. He
could hear the sounds of pursuit behind him, the shouts
of men and thuds of galloping horses growing louder.

The forest loomed before him, a thick green mass of
trees and underbrush. Treyon ran for the treeline, his
side aching. Seconds later, he heard a shout from the
foothill.

"There! There he goes!" The hoofbeats started
pounding again, and Treyon knew he was down to his
last bit of luck. The brigands seemed to be right behind
him, and that thought drew a bit more energy from his
nearly exhausted body. The dull ache in his ribs grew as
he increased his speed. With a surge of energy, he dove
into the brush and started crawling deeper into the forest. Behind him, he could hear the horses panting and
neighing with fear as they stopped short of the trees.
The voices of the men were fading as Treyon extended
his lead, but he could still hear them.

"What's the matter? Get in there after 'im!"

"The Hells I will, that's the Forest of Sorrows, ya
stupe!"

"You idiot, it's just a piece'a woods. Nothing gonna

225

happen in there except he's gonna get away. You know what Ke'noran'll do if we don't bring him back. Would'ja rather face her?"

"I'm telling ya, I ain't going in."

"Look, it's possible death in there, or death for sure if we come back without him. Now let's give the others a chance t'catch up and we'll go in together. Boy's moving so fast he'll leave a trail any moron could follow. We'll grab him and be gone before anybody even knows we're here."

The voices grew fainter as Treyon pushed deeper into the woods. It grew darker as he pressed onward, the trees dwarfing him and swallowing the available sunlight until it seemed he was walking in twilight. When he could hear no sounds of pursuit, Treyon paused for a minute to catch his breath, leaning wearily against one of the huge trees surrounding him. Looking around, he wasn't surprised to discover he had no idea where he was.

Better lost and alone than found by them, he thought, shivering as he remembered their conversation. Although he didn't know any more about the forest than the bandits did, he knew one rumor they didn't.

"Only those with no evil intention may enter the Forest of Sorrows and live." He repeated this to himself like a mental prayer, almost trusting his belief in the legend to keep him safe more than the legend itself.

"All right, Treyon, enough of this. Time to find your way out of here." Hearing his own voice, even whispered, heartened him. Looking up, he tried to find the sun to figure out which direction he had to go. Unfortunately, the trees were blocking most of the available light, making the attempt impossible. Shrugging his shoulders, Treyon found a suitable tree and began to climb. *Well, at least I'm not scouting trade caravans for them anymore,* he thought, that having been his primary job with the bandits, besides general whipping boy.

A few minutes later, he was among the topmost branches of the tree he had been leaning against, feeling the cool wind on his face and looking in every direction.

Once he had gotten his bearings, he started down. About halfway to the ground, his foot slipped and, as he was already committed to his next step, he started to fall. Suddenly, his feet landed on a thick branch, the jarring stop giving him enough time to wrap his arms around the tree trunk and stay there until his heart stopped threatening to leap from his throat.

Once he had calmed down, he looked at the branch he was standing on. Although this was the route he had used on the way up, he didn't remember this limb at all. Shrugging, he continued downward. *The surest thing now,* he thought, *is to get my feet, as well as the rest of me, back on the ground and get moving.*

Shinnying down the tree trunk, he jumped the last few feet—and landed to stare at the battered boots of Caith, the leader of the trackers who had been chasing him. The bandit had stepped around from his hiding place behind the tree and, before Treyon could move, grabbed his tattered shirt and drawn him close.

"Little coney sprouted wings and tried flyin' to the trees, eh? Not good enough. I've pulled the same trick myself a couple o' times." Keeping a tight hold on Treyon, he raised his head and whistled a series of notes twice. Within minutes, the rest of the brigands had rejoined their leader.

"Found the little bastard. Now let's go, Ke'noran ain't gonna be pleased with the delay." Making sure Treyon was in front of him, Caith pushed him forward and the group began retracing his path back out of the forest.

The forest was ominously silent, making everyone more nervous than they already were by just being in the supposedly cursed woods. They had been traveling for a while when Caith's advance scout held up his hand. The brigand group froze immediately, each hand on a weapon, every ear and eye alert for danger. Despite himself, Treyon craned his head to try and see what was going on. Soren, the bandits' best scout, crept back to Caith and whispered, "Horse in the clearing up ahead."

"What in the Hells is a horse doing in these woods? One of ours?"

"Not hardly. Snow white and clean as a stew bowl after dinner. Looked right at me."

"This doesn't sound right. Forest dead as a grave and now a horse comes out of nowhere? I want a look." Taking a stiletto from a sheath behind his neck, Caith put it to Treyon's throat. "One sound outta you, boy, and I'll open yer neck where ya stand. Now move." Pulling Treyon along, the bandit leader moved silently up to the head of the column.

In a small clearing about ten paces ahead was an animal that took Treyon's breath away. The scout's description did not even begin to do it justice. Its coat was the color of new-fallen snow, with a mane and tail that shone even in the wan sunlight. The horse's light-blue eyes regarded its audience with amusement, but it didn't take flight or move at all, except to lower its head to crop at the strangely lush grass.

Caith crouched down, dragging Treyon to the ground with him. Motioning the other bandits closer, he whispered hurriedly, "Here's our chance to make up for losing the runt. A horse like this 'un will hopefully make Ke'noran more forgiving. Toren, circle round that way, yer brother will take the other side, and get yer lariats ready."

The two scouts looked at each other, then at the horse, nodded, and slipped into the brush like ghosting deer. Despite his fear, Treyon wondered for an idle second what kind of ability the brothers had that let them communicate without speaking like that. His attention was quickly drawn back to the ambush before him.

The brothers made no more noise than the slight breeze rustling the leaves, and Treyon quickly lost sight of them, so well did they blend in with the trees and bushes.

The horse was munching a thick clump of grass, seemingly unconcerned about the huddled group of ragged men nearby. Treyon couldn't help wondering what it would be like to ride such an animal, sitting on its sleek back as it raced full out across the plains. It would probably be the closest thing to pure freedom he could imagine. Thinking about what Ke'noren would do to it made him almost ill. At that moment, Treyon knew he had to warn the horse somehow.

Looking up, he saw Caith was watching his two men who were almost in position. His dagger, although still under Treyon's chin, had relaxed its pressure a bit, allowing him to swallow without feeling the scrape of cold steel.

Noticing a large dead branch next to him, Treyon subtly shifted his position until he had moved the branch under him. Pretending to overbalance, he stepped directly on it, bearing down with all his weight.

The branch snapped loudly, causing everyone to freeze for a moment. The horse's head jerked up, looking directly at Treyon, who wanted to scream at it to run, get away, escape. He remained silent, however, locked into the animal's stare, watching as it did a very strange thing.

It winked at him.

Before Treyon could wonder what this meant, he was rocked by a blow that came out of nowhere. Already overbalanced after stepping on the branch, he swayed dizzily after the punch, held up only by Caith's grip on his shirt. Looking up again, he saw Caith glaring at him, his mouth curled in a feral snarl.

"By the Gods, boy, if you cost us that horse, I'll take it out o' yer hide."

Treyon just hung there limply, knowing the brigand didn't make idle threats.

The two turned their attention back to the horse, Caith keeping a tight hand on the boy's shirt. The bandit waited patiently, knowing the brothers would spring their trap with perfect timing.

And so it would have been, if not for their target. As one, the two men flicked out their loops of tough woven rope, their hands steady, their aim true, both lassos flaring out to settle around the neck of their quarry.

Or would have, if the horse hadn't danced out of the way of the snares with a graceful ease, as if it had known exactly where they were all the while. Treyon exhaled in relief. Caith, noticing the boy's reaction, cuffed him again.

The horse neighed, the noise sounding like laughter in the silence, then turned and slowly trotted off through the trees.

Caith stood up, grimacing, and called out. "By the Hells, I want that horse! Toren, Soren, take two men and run it down, damn it. Don't come back without it." *Another fool's errand to send them off on, just like finding the boy,* he thought.

The twins stood, one of them pointing to two other men, and the foursome set out after the shrinking white figure. Caith put his back against a tree as he waited with the last two bandits. He looked around, then snorted, "Don't know why that horse is here when our own horses wouldn'a come in. Haunted forest, my arse."

One of the other men, a newer arrival whom Treyon didn't know, spoke up, "Maybe it's a Companion."

"Oh? Is it? Where's the bleedin' Herald? Hells, no," Caith snorted again, "Just got a little more horse sense than usual. Living in the wild'll do that to an animal sometimes. What better place for a horse to live than here, eh?"

"Breeze's dying down." the other bandit remarked.

Treyon had been standing as well, pulled to his feet when Caith had risen. Looking around, he also noticed the lack of wind. Which made what else he saw even more unusual, easily passing into terrifying.

With barely a rustle, the trees around the bandits were slowly bending their branches down toward each of the men's heads. Treyon remained motionless, not wanting to attract any attention to himself. Caith and his men continued their idle conversation, unaware of the movement until Caith looked again at Treyon.

"Here now, what are you lookin—" His voice trailed off as he followed Treyon's gaze to the surrounding foliage, which quivered, then suddenly lashed out.

Caith, his reflexes quicker than the other two, released Treyon and dove to the ground, thinking to find safety there. When he hit the ground, thick roots erupted all around him, completely wrapping his body in brown tendrils and drawing him slowly underground, his screaming face the last thing to vanish.

The other men, caught completely by surprise, fared just as badly. One never got a chance to move, impaled by a thick limb that burst from his stomach like a third arm. The other managed to get his dagger out before several tree branches wrapped around his neck and jerked him, struggling and strangling, into its leaves, his knife arm flailing uselessly as he disappeared from sight. A few seconds later, the dagger skittered down the tree trunk and fell to the ground underneath it.

Treyon watched all this without moving, without even blinking. He just stood there, until the screams finished echoing through the woods. Finally, all was silent again, the only sign of disturbance being the impaled bandit's body still standing grotesquely upright. Treyon straightened up and took a hesitant step forward, then another, then another, and took off again, running through the forest until his legs would carry him no farther. Sinking to the ground under another large tree, heedless of the cursed forest and what might happen to him, Treyon fell asleep almost before he hit the ground.

The cracks and pops of a fire slowly woke Treyon. The first sensation he had was of pleasant warmth surrounding him. The second was the unmistakable smell of something cooking, making his stomach clench with hunger.

Treyon slowly blinked the last bits of sleep away, aware that he was still tired, but too concerned with trying to figure out where he was to rest any more. He flexed his hand slowly, feeling the mat of dry grasses he was laying on. Overhead, a canopy of trees blocked out the sky.

Meaning I'm still in the forest, Treyon thought. Moving his head slowly to the side, he looked first at the trees which surrounded him, trees that grew so close together they made natural walls encircling the small clearing, although here and there small gaps of darkness showed through. Treyon shuddered as he remembered the attack of the forest again.

The only opening was a small break on the opposite wall of trees, past the fire in the middle of the room and the cloaked form crouched in front of it.

Treyon gasped in surprise, for his bandit-trained senses hadn't noticed the figure until just a few seconds ago. Sitting upright, he tensed to bolt for the small exit. A few steps and a dive and he would be free.

"Finally awake, I see?" the indistinct shape said in a clear, gentle voice, still facing away from him. "If you wish to leave, by all means, there is no one here to stop you. Of course, there is no one here who wishes you harm, either."

Treyon flattened himself against the tree wall, his eyes still upon the figure who had appeared seemingly out of nowhere. The bandit part of his mind was still screaming that this was a trap. The being continued, apparently unmindful of Treyon's fear.

"Of course, I'd rather you stayed a bit and dined with me. It has been far too long since a stranger found his way to my doorstep, such as it is. And it would be a shame to waste most of this stew."

At the mention of food the rich stew smell floated into Treyon's nose again, reminding him how painfully hungry he was. It had been so long, if ever, since he had eaten a meal that was more than scraps and leavings from the brigands. The part of his mind that was still wary of a trap was quickly being overpowered by the demands of his stomach. *but,* Treyon thought, *if—whatever it is—had wanted to, it could have done anything to me while I slept. I should have woken up bound or held somehow. Hells, even if this is a trap, it'll be worth it for a full stomach.*

Summoning up the scraps of manners he knew, gained mainly from watching the bandits beg and scrape to Ke'noran, Treyon got up from the bed of grass and stood. "Can I have some food, then?"

The figure turned toward him, pushing back its hood and Treyon saw a man, his face unlined yet somehow looking very old, framed by a mane of fine silver hair. The ageless face smiled gently, and the man extended an already full wooden bowl. "Of course, child."

Snatching it away, Treyon hunched over the bowl protectively and tried to scoop out a handful, only to yelp in pain as he burned his fingers. The man winced as Treyon blew on his injured hand and held out a spoon-shaped piece of wood, not carved, but looking like it had been naturally formed. "Try this."

Gingerly Treyon took the spoon, scooped up some of the stew and blew on it for a few seconds, then popped it into his mouth. Chewing fast, he sucked in air to further cool the hot food. All the while, his arm was curled protectively around the comfortably warm bowl.

The stranger said nothing, just watched him eat and refilled his bowl when it was held out. After Treyon had finished his third helping, he belched and asked for something to drink, receiving another bowl already filled with clear spring water.

His stomach full and ready to face whatever was asked of him, knowing it would be easier to take if he was prepared, Treyon squared his shoulders and looked at the man. "What do you want?"

The man looked up from stacking the bowls in a corner, the question clear from the expression on his face.

Treyon continued, "For the food and shelter. Work, or anything else you want. It's all right, I'm used to it. Just tell me."

The man's head lowered again, his shoulders shaking silently. Treyon thought he might have been laughing, but when he raised his head again the tears on his cheeks gleamed in the firelight. "By the Gods, boy, you're only twelve or thirteen at the most. What has been done to you?" Taking a deep breath, he wiped his face. "I don't ask anything of you other than your company." Seeing the look on Treyon's face, he added hastily, "Just talk, that's all."

"Oh." The word turned into a yawn as his comfortably full stomach and the warmth of the fire made Treyon sleepy.

"Why don't you rest some more, and we can talk in the morning." The man said quietly. Treyon found himself growing sleepy just listening, but he wasn't convinced of his safety quite yet.

"What about the trees?" he mumbled as his eyelids drooped.

"Nothing will harm you, not while you're with me." the man replied, turning back to the fire.

Feeling he had nothing to lose anyway, and now wanting to sleep more than he ever had in his life, Treyon crawled over to the grass mats and was soon curled up, breathing rhythmically in slumber.

The stranger stood, stretched, and walked to the wall near the small opening. He looked back to ensure that the boy was sleeping soundly. Satisfied, he walked straight through the trees, his body encountering no resistance from the wood. Once outside, he looked up through a break in the trees at a small patch of night sky.

"Over thirty years in the forest now, and I'm still finding boys in trouble."

Treyon awoke to dappled sunlight streaming in through the small gaps in the trees. He blinked several times, unsure if he was awake or still dreaming. When no coarse shouts or heavy kicks jerked him out of bed, he relaxed a bit, remembering where he was.

Breathing deeply, Treyon felt the bite of the crisp morning air on his face. The rest of his body, however, was comfortably warm, mostly because of the gray woolen cloak covering him. Throwing it aside, Treyon got up and stretched, trying to get moving before the cold could soak into his bones. He walked toward the opening to the small tree-shelter and crawled out, freezing in place as soon as he was outside.

Directly in front of him, the white horse was grazing contentedly. Even though Treyon thought he hadn't made a sound, the horse raised its head and looked at him. Caught in its gaze as he had been the day before, Treyon felt like the animal was reading his mind. He didn't move a muscle, content to hold its eyes with his own steady stare. He felt proud that he wasn't compelled to look away in fear or submission. It was almost as if the horse were evaluating him, and apparently liking what it saw.

The horse looked beyond him for a moment, then neighed, wheeled around, and cantered off through the woods again, only this time with no bandits in pursuit.

A noise behind him made Treyon whirl in a defensive crouch before he could stop himself. The silver-haired man held his hand up in a calm gesture. "Good morning."

Straightening, Treyon mentally cursed his reflexes. "Hello."

The man gestured toward the horse's retreating back. "What do you think of her?"

Treyon turned to look at the horse again. "She's beautiful. Yours?"

"Not exactly. We're very good friends, though."

"I'd give anything to ride something like that."

"Well, I don't know. You'd have to ask her. Her name's Yfandes."

Treyon looked up at the man who had come up beside him, and was now watching him without a trace of humor on his face, as if talking to horses was something he did every day. Not knowing quite how to respond, Treyon kept silent. There was a not-quite-awkward silence for a few seconds until the man spoke again, "Are you hungry? I'm afraid all I can offer is more of the same as last night, if you don't mind."

The memory of the savory vegetable stew brought a smile to Treyon's face, "Fine, if you have enough."

"Always." The man started to go inside, then paused, "I'm sorry. I've fed and sheltered you and I don't even know your name."

Treyon paused before heading back into the shelter. "It's Treyon."

The man nodded. "And you can call me Van."

Treyon's head snapped up. "As in Vanyel Demonsbane?"

The man smiled as if he heard that question a lot.

"The name is similar, but the Herald-Mage Vanyel has been dead for over thirty years. He died around here, as a matter of fact."

"You know of him?"

Van grinned. "Bits and pieces I've heard here and there. After all, I haven't lived my whole life here. Come inside and I'll tell you more over a hot meal."

Treyon hurriedly scooted through the break in the trees. Van started to follow, but stopped for a moment as a familiar voice carried clearly in his mind.

:Don't embellish too much while telling your "bits and pieces" now.:

:'Fandes, I'm shocked you would even accuse me doing something like that. If he wanted embellishment, he should talk to Stefen. But I do think he should get his information straight from the "legend's" mouth, don't you?:

:As long as I get to correct you on parts you may be a bit fuzzy on. Deal?:

Van smiled. *:Deal. Except I wish I had his gift with children. He's much better with them than I am.:*

:Well, dear, if wishes were Companions, then everybody would have one. You'll just have to make do.:

:Yes, yes, but . . . I have the feeling that this boy is a harbinger of something evil to come. You sensed him, didn't you?:

:Of course. Why do you think I went after him?:

:All right, all right, Van grinned again, *Pardon me for trying to figure out your mind.:*

Van could almost see Yfandes' smile. *:Over five decades together and you're still learning, dear. Are you going in? That boy needs to talk:*

:Right away. Keep watch for anything unusual, particularly from the North. This may take a while.:

:Understood.:

". . . and that was how Vanyel earned the name "Shadow-Stalker." Van leaned back against the wood of the shelter, watching Treyon finish the last of his meal.

"Boy, it sure must have been exciting." Treyon said

after he had swallowed the last mouthful. "Riding all over Valdemar, protecting those who needed help, battling evil wherever it appeared."

A wry grin appeared on Van's face. "I don't know. I doubt it was all adventure and romance. I mean, you're from around here, right?" Treyon nodded. "So you know how cold it gets at night, how hard the winters are. I'm sure Vanyel spent many days cold, hungry, and tired while he was protecting those who needed him."

"Yeah, but he was the most powerful magician of all. He leveled armies, battled hundreds of demons at once, cut through mountains like they were soft butter. He could do anything. Why would he be cold and tired when he didn't have to be?"

:Funny, that's what his Companion said more than once.: Yfandes Mindspoke, along with a gentle laugh. Shaking his head at both of them, Van continued.

"Treyon, it wasn't, and still isn't, that easy. Often times Vanyel was probably battling other mages, with power as strong, or even stronger, than his. Sure, he could have used magic to keep himself warm and fed, but that would have been just like sending a signal to the other mages, telling them where he was, like a torch on a dark night."

"Oh. You seem to know a lot about magic." The statement was meant as just that, but Van inferred something more behind it, as did Yfandes, who commented, *:The boy's quick.:*

"Well, before I settled down here, I picked up some training in it. But times changed, and I ended up here, where I've been ever since."

"Oh." Treyon stared into the fire for a time, then said quietly, "It's too bad Vanyel isn't still around. But that's just wishful thinking, I guess. I mean, why would a legend concern himself with one person?"

Since Treyon was still looking at the fire, he didn't notice Van stiffen at his tone, or the pained expression on his face as he replied.

"Well, Treyon, I'm sure if Vanyel was still alive, he would still be helping those who needed him."

At those words Treyon looked at the older man sharply. Seizing the moment, Van continued, "Treyon, why were you in the forest?"

After a long silence. "I was running away."

"From whom?"

"Bandits. I was sold to them a long time ago, I don't even know who my mother and father are." Under Van's level gaze, Treyon felt compelled to tell him as much as he could.

"So you didn't want to be a bandit?"

"No, of course not. Running and hiding all the time, never sure where your next meal is coming from, always in fear of your life." Treyon paused as a thought struck him. "Maybe Vanyel and I had more in common than I thought."

The boy is *quick,* Van thought as Treyon continued. "But I didn't see any way out of it. I mean, I don't know anything other than banditing. Sure, I could go to a city, but what would I do there but end up stealing to eat again. So I thought banditing was what I was gonna do forever, till Ke'noran came along."

"Ke'noran?"

"Yeah, she's a wicked woman if'n I ever saw one. Knows lots 'bout magic, too. She took over the group by killing Trold, who'd been the leader. She appeared one night, said she was leading us now, I mean, I was still with them then. Trold got up and started walking toward her, talking 'bout how no woman was taking over his band. She just looked at him, and he started bleedin' everywhere, his eyes, nose, ears, and mouth. He ran into the woods, 'n we never saw him again. She's led ever since, and now most of the men actually respect her. Not just because she could kill anyone who opposed her, but she actually made life a bit better for us. We even ate pretty regularly after she took over."

"Did she make you leave?"

"Yeah, but she didn't kick me out or nothing. When she first saw me, it was like she was looking into my head. She always gave me the creeps. Well, one night I had a dream, and in it I was tied to this big rock, and

Ke'noran was standing over me with this sharpened stick with strange marks carved on it. She was leaning over me and saying something, bringing the stick closer to my head, and then I woke up. I don't know how to explain it, but I knew that if I stayed there any longer, what I saw was gonna happen to me. So that night I headed for the border, hoping to get to a town or city somewhere. Just as I got out of the mountains, they caught up with me. I ran for the woods, and here I am." Treyon said, omitting the part about the trees.

:*Did you catch all that, dear?*: Vanyel asked.

:*Yes, Van. Sounds like a textbook blood-magic sacrifice to me, just as Treyon's dream sounds like ForeSight. But what's puzzling is why she would take him so soon. I mean, Treyon has the potential for two, maybe three Gifts, but he hasn't even been trained in them yet. What could she want with this boy, when an ordinary peasant would power the blood-magic just as well?*: Yfandes replied.

:*There must be a reason. Perhaps she's found a way to tap into the magical energy of another's mind and use that as her own, as well as the life forces. It would be a powerful augmentation,*: Vanyel thought worriedly.

:*Hmm, that's very possible. But what you said about augmentation gives me an idea. What if she's found a way to take untrained Gifts into herself, and use them as if they were her own?*:

:*Which could only be accomplished by the sacrifice of the victim, ensuring the magic is released for her to absorb at the moment of death. Yfandes, I think you've got it.*: Vanyel was careful to keep his face calm as the conversation continued.

:*Well, I guess we'll know soon enough. We didn't get all of the bandits. One of the group that was chasing me managed to get away, and I'm sure is warning his leader by now.*:

:*Why didn't you tell me this before?*: Vanyel asked, a hint of anger coloring his thoughts.

:*Vanyel, dear, we've had bandits crawling around the borders of these woods for so long, another group just didn't seem very important. However, once this came to light . . . :* 'Fandes trailed off.

:*Of course, 'Fandes, I'm sorry. Well, that means she'll probably be on her way here. Good. To be perfectly honest, fighting the same bandits all the time gets rather boring.*:

:*It sounds as though you miss the old days.*:

Vanyel thought for a few seconds before answering. :*I don't know, sometimes it just doesn't feel like we do enough for Valdemar here. I mean, I don't regret my choice, but after the Battle of the Ice Wall, there hasn't been much of anything from the North, even in the past few years.*:

Yfandes sent an image of herself snorting in amusement. :*I don't think I would try anything, even years after word of what happened got back.*:

:*Anyway, if we're right, and this Ke'noran can do what we think, then she's a threat that must be dealt with.*:

:*Vanyel, a mage-battle could destroy a large part of the forest. While bandits may be boring, they also don't have the power to level acres of trees. It could get out of hand if you're not careful.*:

:*True, very true. Well, we'll just have to contain her as much as possible. Most likely she's more educated about the "legends" of the forest, and will be more loath to come in here.*: Vanyel replied.

:*We'll see. You had better warn Treyon about this. He's not going to like it.*:

:*No doubt. By the way, beloved, I'm sorry for referring to you as a horse in front of him, but it seems easier than trying to explain what we really are.*:

Yfandes smiled in his head. :*Understood and accepted. He's waiting, I think.*:

The Mindspoken conversation had only taken a few seconds, so Treyon hadn't even guessed at what was going on. Van looked at him again, smiled, then began speaking calmly.

"Treyon, Ke'noran is going to come after you here. Apparently one of the bandits got away and has most likely warned her by now. If she Gates in, she could be on the edge of the forest already—"

"No, no, she'll kill me! Please, you've got to hide me, help me get away from her!" Treyon was frantic with fear, looking around as if they were already surrounded by her men.

Realizing he had said too much too fast, Vanyel tried a different approach. "Treyon, I'm going to help you. She's not going to take you back, I promise."

But now fear had taken hold of Treyon completely, and he stared at Vanyel wildly. "You, you're just one man. She's got a dozen with her. She's skinned them alive for failing her, or burned them to ashes. I've seen it happen. What can one man do against that?"

"And a horse, don't forget."

The statement was so ridiculous that it broke through Treyon's fear and made him look at Vanyel as if he wasn't sure which one of them was crazier. Vanyel broke the silence.

"She won't take you, Treyon, I swear it."

The words hung in the air, Vanyel's silver eyes meeting Treyon's brown ones, with the promise between them. Finally, he slowly sank to the ground and nodded. "I believe you. I don't even know why, but I do."

"All right. You should know why she wants you so badly. First, you have potential for Gifts in you—"

"Me?" Treyon's incredulous snort interrupted Vanyel, who nodded.

"Everyone has it, buried deep inside their minds, but not everyone has the ability to bring the power to the surface and use it. Your powers, as I said before, lie in the area called Gifts, which are more or less mind-powers, contacting people with your thoughts, bringing objects to you just by thinking about them moving, and so on. Ke'noran wants those untapped abilities, we—I think, to use for herself. And that's why we have to stop her."

"Because if she does that to me, she could do it to others?"

:When this is done, this boy's Haven-bound,: Yfandes thought.

Nodding to both statements, Vanyel said, "Exactly. I think the safest thing to do will be to keep you here while I go find Ke'noran—" He trailed off, seeing Treyon shake his head.

"I don't want to be left alone if she's anywhere nearby."

"Treyon, I can protect you much better if you're in the middle of the forest—"

"What if she does this Gate thing into the forest and grabs me while you're someplace else, huh?"

Vanyel started to reply, then stopped, aware that he couldn't answer the question in a way that would satisfy the boy. Or himself, now that Treyon had exposed the flaw in his plan. As long as he had Gift potential, she could eventually find him. And a mage would have ways around the forest's defenses.

:*Most probably starting by burning the place to a cinder,*: Yfandes Mindsent.

Sighing in defeat, Vanyel turned his attention back to the conversation. "All right, you're coming with me. But you must do *exactly* what I say. Yfandes and I should be able to shield you magically, but if she has those brigands or constructs looking for you, it's vital that you stay hidden, exactly where I place you, understand?"

Treyon thought for a moment, nodded, then asked, "Constructs. What're those?"

"Cruel mockeries of life, created by magicians and fueled by magic. They can be given limited powers by their creators, but are still dangerous." Vanyel fell silent as he remembered one of the few he had ever seen, the raven-beast that had killed his Aunt Savil decades ago. The form of that particular monster was still clear in his mind, as if he had seen it yesterday. His thoughts were interrupted by Treyon.

"I . . . think Ke'noran has one."

"Oh? Have you seen it?"

Treyon shrugged, trying to put what he knew into words. "I'm not sure. Sometimes, when she's talking to the men at night, I catch a glimpse of something behind her, in the shadows. Man-sized or a little shorter. It never comes into the light and she never refers to it, but something's there, all right." A sudden thought occurred to Treyon while they were on the subject. "Van, what if she's got things huntin' in the woods right now?"

Vanyel shook his head. "Don't worry, there aren't. If there were, they'd have been dealt with long before they got here. My guess is that she wants to be here to recover you personally, since the bandits couldn't finish the job. No doubt she probably also wants to investigate the forest, to see if there is anything here she can use for herself."

:Man-sized, eh? This one must have a fair amount of power, to keep something that big alive.: Yfandes thought worriedly.

:Yes, I know.: Vanyel thought back distractedly.

"But you're going to stop her, right?" Treyon asked, a familiar light in his eyes.

Vanyel smiled. "Yes, I promise."

The sun was just below midpoint among a scattering of clouds when Vanyel, Yfandes, and Treyon reached the northern edge of the forest. From their vantage point in the treeline, they could see up and down the border of the forest. As expected, there was a contingent of men waiting about a hundred paces away. Most were dressed much like Treyon, in ragged shirts and vests, tattered and patched breeches and wearing shapeless, well-worn boots, rough sandals, or nothing on their feet at all. The force of men was split into two groups, about half a dozen on each side of the central figure, who had to be Ke'noran.

She stood at least a hand-span over most of her men, more in some cases, less in others. Unlike the bandits, she was dressed well against the cold fall afternoon, in dark gray robes and a dazzling white fur cloak, complete with the claw-studded paws of whatever animal the pelt had come from holding the cloak in place on her shoulders. Her skin matched the tone of the fur, stark white, with red-irised eyes like ruby chips glittering in a snowdrift.

She was standing near a cairn of stones piled long ago by someone who had buried another while traveling in or out of Valdemar. As he looked at the scene before him, Vanyel hoped he wouldn't have to make another smaller pile before the day was out.

:*A Cheldaran*.: he heard Yfandes muse, *I didn't think they came down this far*.:

Vanyel squinted, trying to examine her more closely. :*I've never seen anything like that before. What do you know of them?*:

:*Just that you should be wary, beloved. She may be more formidable than you think.*:

Vanyel focused his Mage-Sight on the tall woman for a minute, than replied, :*Actually, I don't think she's formidable, I* know *she is. Look for yourself.*:

Yfandes silently stepped up beside him and stared for a second, her blue eyes widening in disbelief. :*Does she have what I think she does?*:

Vanyel nodded. :*She's found a way to tap the Mage-Gift as well. She's connected to a node out there.*: He tried not to think of what else she could have waiting and addressed Yfandes again. :*Do you know anything else?*:

:*Just rumors, that's all. Supposedly one of the many barbarian groups to the far north. But it's said that of outland magicians, these white-skins are more closely attuned to their powers than most.*:

:*Thanks for the confidence builder.*: Vanyel groaned in his mind.

As if she could hear their conversation, the pale woman called out, "Spirit of the Forest, hear me. One of my own has become lost in your woods. I know of you and what you are. Return him to me, and the forest will be left unharmed. Hide him from me, and I will find him, no matter what it takes. I will not wait long upon your answer, for I know you are nearby."

Her gaze swept the line of trees, pausing for a moment as her eyes passed over the three figures in the treeline, invisible to all save her. A humorless smile creased her mouth, then disappeared as she crossed her arms and waited.

Vanyel contacted Yfandes. :*I'm going out.*:

:*Van, you can't. What about Treyon?*:

:*Someone has go out and give her what she wants, or she'll make her threat real. You're going to have to stay here and watch over him. 'Fandes, you're my back-up. If that construct is out here, you'll have to guard Treyon while I deal with her.*:

:*Well, what if something gets by both of us?*:

:*Then we'll just have to play it by ear, I guess. This could take a while, she's stored up a lot of power, both in blood-magic and from the node.*:

:*Worried?*:

:*No, just angry at all that destruction.*:

:*Vanyel . . . be careful.*:

:*Always.*:

Turning from them, Vanyel started to step around a tree, but was stopped by a hand on his arm.

"Where are you going?" Treyon whispered.

"To face her."

"Alone? Are you crazy? You're one against more than a dozen."

"No, this will be between me and her. Stay here with Yfandes."

"What do you want me to do if . . . something bad happens?"

Van looked at him. "I don't suppose you can ride?" Treyon shook his head. Vanyel thought for a moment, than continued. "If something does go wrong, I want you to run into the forest as fast and as far as you can. Yfandes will stay with you as long as possible, but you should be safe enough until I can find you afterwards, just keep moving. And no matter what happens, I'll make sure Ke'noran can't come after you, all right?"

Treyon nodded, looking past him at Ke'noran and her brigands, "Van, I don't see the construct anywhere."

Van nodded, pleased the boy was still able to think clearly, even when so obviously frightened. "I don't either, but I don't sense him anywhere as well. Either she's not using it for this, or it's shielded so well I can't sense it. Either way, trust Yfandes to protect you, for she will, with her life if necessary."

Treyon nodded silently as the silence of the forest was cut by the sorceress's voice. "Spirit, I grow weary of waiting for you. Return him, or I will begin the search. And I will leave no rock unmoved, no tree living where I look."

Vanyel winked at Treyon, then stepped around a large oak and disappeared. Treyon looked for him walking through the forest, but in vain. A gentle touch on his cheek from Yfandes' warm nose brought his attention back to the plains and the bandits before him.

Suddenly, there he was, standing just outside the forest's boundary, the sunlight making his silver hair flash and glitter. All was quiet save the two magicians, so their conversation easily carried to Treyon and Yfandes.

"I am here." Vanyel said.

The Northern sorceress' ice-blue eyes narrowed for a moment, then she smiled again. "You are not a simple forest spirit. There is much power within you. But I am sure neither of us wishes for conflict, so I will be blunt. You have what I want, forest-walker. Give him to me and I will leave in peace. Deny me, and be destroyed."

Both Treyon and Yfandes watched silently, hanging on every word. Vanyel was impassive. "If I give my life in defense of another, so be it. What you want from this forest you shall not have, for he is under my protection."

"Then once you and this forest fall, he shall have no protection." With that Ke'noran swept her arms outward and a wall of mage-fire appeared, not anywhere near Vanyel, but for dozens of paces on either side of the two mages. Driven against the wind into the forest, the blue-green flames began to grow rapidly as they licked at the trees and underbrush.

Surprised by the unorthodox attack, Vanyel hesitated a bit before beginning his defense. Quickly he weather-magicked the nearby clouds to grow, making them suck up the water vapor in the atmosphere, swelling into gray thunderheads that covered the sky. With a flick of his hand, the water poured down, drowning the flames in the forest. Fully on guard now, Vanyel went on the offensive, calling all of the power at his command and sending it at the woman before him.

As soon as Treyon saw the flames appear at the forest's edge, his bandit's intuition knew that a trap had been laid and they had walked right into it.

A whinny of alarm turned his head toward Yfandes, just in time to see a dark, blurry shape, all claws and teeth, leap out of the surrounding woods at him.

:VANYEL!:
"Van!"

Until he heard the mind-cry and shriek of terror simultaneously, Vanyel had actually been enjoying the battle. Ke'noran was extremely strong, but it was the strength of blood-magic, easily gained and stored, but not so easily replenished once used. Eventually, if he and Yfandes had read her right, the Mage-Gift she had siphoned from some unfortunate soul would eventually be exhausted, and he could make her forget all about using blood-magic forever. That had been the plan, but Ke'noran had seen fit to change the rules.

Boosting his shields enough to hold off Ke'noran's next assault, Vanyel turned at both cries, one of alarm, one of pure terror, and saw something explode out of the forest in a spray of leaves and branches. It would have been as tall as a man, save for its hunched back. It moved as fast as a *wyrsa,* but on two legs, and appeared to be a mix of human, bear, and wolf, with ursine features and thick, gray-brown fur. What was most frightening was what it carried in its mouth. Treyon, the collar of his shirt tangled in the beast's teeth, was being borne toward the battle with magic-fueled speed.

Behind the beast, but at a safe distance, galloped Yfandes. Vanyel thought he had never seen her look so frustrated.

:Vanyel, she's going to get him.: she sent angrily.
:Can't you stop it from reaching her?: Vanyel asked.

:*No,*: came the fear-tinged reply, :*I can't even get close
to it. She's laid a trap-shield on the construct, and now
Treyon's inside, so it's around him as well.*:

:*Trap-shield?*: In that instant Vanyel realized just how
ruthless Ke'noran really was, remembering that if any
magical or physical attack was directed at the construct,
the shields would react instantly, destroying whatever
they surrounded by lethal backlash. :*Great good Gods,
maybe I can Fetch. . . .*:

:*No, Vanyel, any Gift will set it off, even mind-magic!*:
Yfandes sent.

:*Hells, that thing moves fast. Come to me then. She
may have the ability to steal these powers, now let's see
if she knows how to use them:*

In the time the two had Mindspoken this much, the
construct had already reached Ke'noran, and had been
admitted inside her shields. Vanyel bit his lip in frustration and he saw Ke'noran take the boy as she snapped
a guttural word at the construct, causing it to sit back
on its haunches, its hooded eyes becoming glassy. With
his Mage-sight, Vanyel saw the sorceress' shields flare
even brighter now as she added the power the construct
had been using to her own protections.

By this time, Yfandes had swung away from her pursuit and ran over to Vanyel, coming around to stand
behind him. Vanyel put one hand on her mane as he
watched the barbarian.

:*Get ready to give me power on my signal,*: he sent
to her.

:*I hope you know what you're doing.*:

:*Now that she has him, it's the only way. I just need a
little more time . . .*:

Ke'noran slammed Treyon down on the cairn, knocking the wind out of him and effectively preventing any
struggle. Holding him down with one hand, she reached
underneath her cloak with the other and brought out a
dagger-sized wooden wand covered in rough runes and
glowing brightly with power. Ripping open Treyon's
shirt, she touched the focus to Treyon's chest, outlining
his heart, the wand leaving a glowing trail wherever it

touched the boy's skin. Looking up, Vanyel once again saw her feral smile as she said, "Spirit, you have defied me, and for that you will be destroyed. Once I have taken this one's Gifts, I will take everything else you hold dear."

"Ke'noran, hold!" Vanyel threw out his hand as if offering it to an unseen person. Recognizing the gesture, Ke'noran looked down at Treyon, who was still lying motionless beneath her. Her head snapped up to look at the silver-haired mage before her. At that moment she felt her shields actually buckle as the impact of Vanyel's magic hit them. For a moment, everything stopped as the two mages' gazes met. Vanyel smiled as he saw the sorceress' eyes widen as she realized what was about to happen.

Ke'noran recovered quickly, however. Raising the wand about her head, she screamed the final word of the spell out as she plunged the stake down at Treyon's unprotected chest.

The wand ripped through the empty air where Treyon's body had been a moment before to shatter on the rocks of the cairn. Now uncontrollably released, the magic contained by the wand surged back though Ke'noran's body. Held in by her shields, it redoubled in intensity, arcing and snapping as it contacted the restraining magic walls. Ke'noran didn't even have time to scream. In seconds the wild energies had destroyed everything in the area of the sorceress' shields. As her protections vanished, all that remained was a circle of burned ground and two small piles of ash and bone.

Vanyel watched, unblinking, cradling Treyon to his chest, burying the boy's head in his chest to prevent him from watching. When it was over, Vanyel just held him while glaring at the brigands, who had watched the fight at a safe distance. Under his stare, they quickly broke and left for the hills, and silence once again fell over the Forest of Sorrows and the small plain.

"Vanyel . . . I can't breathe." Treyon gasped from his shirt. Standing up, Vanyel slowly let go of Treyon, watching all around him as if waiting for Ke'noran to suddenly appear from the grave and wreak more havoc. When nothing happened, his shoulders slumped as he relaxed, slowly fading into translucence.

Seeing this happen, Treyon quickly stepped over to Vanyel, meaning to hug him. But when he tried to wrap his arms around the other's slim body, he met nothing but air. Off balance, Treyon just managed to avoid falling over. Before Vanyel could speak, Treyon waved an arm through the middle of Van's body, watching it pass through the misty form as if there was nothing there at all.

Treyon was hesitant to say it, but he did anyway, "What happened . . . I thought you defeated her." His eyes overflowed with tears again as he thought he realized what had happened.

Vanyel, realizing what Treyon was thinking, was quick to correct him. "No, no, Treyon, that's not what happened. Using so much power so quickly can drain even a legend for a time." Seeing Treyon's expression as comprehension dawned, he added, "Yes, I am the Vanyel of the legends and songs. I have been like this," he pointed a hand toward his insubstantial body, "for decades. I have been a part of this forest for over thirty years, guarding the northern border against bandits and mages like Ke'noran. In a way, I *am* the forest around me, every tree, every plant, every gust of wind that moves through the brush, I feel it, react to it, as far as I can see. And to things that enter the forest. Ke'noran couldn't kill me or Yfandes, not without destroying every last bit of the woods around us, and that, I think, is next to impossible. But she almost got you, and that was something I never wanted to happen. I had no plans to put you in danger. You deserve better than that."

"Why?"

"Why? Just because of who you are."

"What, I'm just a boy, that doesn't make me anything special."

"Well, then, how about what you can give back to Valdemar."

"As what, a brigand? Vanyel, how can I help Valdemar?" Treyon was growing more and more exasperated.

"As a Herald," came the soft reply.

"What? A Herald? Me?" Treyon's mouth was gaping like a fish.

For the first time since the battle had ended, Vanyel smiled. "Don't you remember me telling you about your Gifts? You need training to use them effectively, and, as you happen to be about the right age to begin, you should get started right away. There's a way station about a half-day's journey from here. Usually a Herald passes by every few days, on patrol for the outlying villages, and he can take you to Haven."

"Training? Haven? Gifts? But I don't know anything about anything. How can I be a Herald? Who's going to believe that I can be anything but a brigand?"

Vanyel let his hand drop to Treyon's shoulder, and for several seconds, the boy actually felt the older man's hand steadying him. "I do. Treyon, you can't stay here, not with us," he said, cutting off Treyon's startled protest. "You need to be around others, to learn all that Yfandes and I don't have time to teach you. Besides, Haven is the place where you're needed, not here."

"That's all well and good, but what about my needing someone?" Treyon said, sniffing back his tears and looking away at the ground.

Vanyel knelt down beside him, catching the boy's downcast stare with his own gaze. "I'm not going anywhere. Granted, Haven is far away, but if your Gifts manifest like I think they will, pretty soon you'll be able to Mindspeak with me as if I were standing beside you. And by that time, maybe you'll have been Chosen by a Companion of your own."

Treyon was silent for several seconds, then raised his head again, feeling truly hopeful for the first time since he had entered the forest. "I guess we'd better get going, then."

"Let's not rush off quite so quickly. You'll stay with us another night, and we'll set off in the morning." Vanyel said, smiling.

Treyon smiled in return, and the trio walked into the forest, leaving the charred patch of dirt, and the new leaves of grass that were already sprouting behind.

Vkandis' Own
by Ben Ohlander

Ben Ohlander was born in Rapid City, South Dakota, and has since lived in eight states and three foreign countries. He graduated from high school in 1983, after spending a period of time in military school for various infractions. He enlisted in the Marines, where he served for six years as an intelligence analyst and translator in such places as Cuba and Panama. He has since completed a degree in International Studies, been commissioned as an Army Intelligence Officer, and works as a freelance writer. His hobbies include chess, rugby, fencing (the kind not involving stolen goods), and politics. He has coauthored novels with David Drake and Bill Forstchen for Baen Books, as well as several short stories. He is currently developing several independent projects.

Author's Note: This story takes place after the events chronicled in *Arrow's Fall* and before *Storm Warning*.

Colonel Tregaron, commander of His Holiness' Twenty-First Foot, was hot, tired, and very pleased as he surveyed the long line of marching infantry. The regiment had made good time, in spite of a sun hot enough to boil a man's brain inside his skull, thick clouds of choking dust that rose with every step, and short water rations. It pleased him that he had yet to lose a single trooper to the heat, even after nine days crossing the badlands, and another twenty trekking from the Karse-Rethwellan border. Most caravans, fat with water and rich food, couldn't make that claim.

He shook his head, grimly amused that His Holiness

would transfer regiments in High Summer when "Beastly" was the gentlest adjective useful in describing the heat. Still, when the Son of the Sun called, the army marched.

An infantryman, seeing him grin, hawked and spat. "You like eatin' dust, Colonel?"

Tregaron raised his hand, one soldier to another. "It can't be any worse than your *hummas,* Borlai. I'm surprised your squadmates haven't strung you up as a poisoner." The troopers around the luckless soldier laughed as he mimed taking an arrow in the chest. "I'm struck!" Borlai cried.

Tregaron made a mental note to eat with First Battle that evening, the better to ensure no lasting insult came from his ribbing. Morale had remained high, in spite of the miserable conditions, and he had no desire to see even a small wound fester for want of tending.

He glanced over each rank as it passed, looking for the small signs and minute sloppiness that marked declining morale or increasing fatigue. Some pikes sloped a little more loosely than the prescribed thirty-degree angle and an occasional head drooped, but that was to be expected, considering each soldier carried, in addition to a full fifty-pound kit, three days' extra field rations, water, extra throwing spears, and either a mattock, pick, or shovel to dig fortifications. It was no wonder Karsite soldiers called themselves "turtles," for they all carried their houses on their backs.

Several veterans, seeing Tregaron, raised their fists in salute as they passed. A weak cheer rose from the ranks as he doffed his plumed helmet and returned the gesture.

"Aye, lads," he said. "Save your wind for the walk. We've a bit to go before you can laze about." That drew a laugh. There was trouble on the Hardorn border, bad trouble, and even the rawest recruit had heard the rumors of massacred caravans and slaughtered villages. He knew, sure as night followed day, that there would be hard fighting along the frontier before the fall rains swelled the Terilee River and blocked passage. *Vkandis willing,* he thought, *we'll make the Terilee by nightfall and be dug in before the bastards know we're there.*

He unrolled the grimy travel map he used to plot their daily course. Its scale was too small for any real detail now that they were close to their destination, but the scouts had provided good reports of what lay ahead.

He ran one dirty finger across his short, pointed beard as he studied the map. The Terilee River, hardly more than a stream this time of year, marked the border between beloved Karse and Ancar's Hardorn. It had seen its waters colored red more than once in the past year as the Usurper's bandits raided across its brackish waters. Bodies from those fights were said to have floated as far as Haven, in distant Valdemar.

His staff, walking alongside the regiment, joined him as he rerolled the small map and bent to pick a stone out of his sandal. Cogern, the Twenty-First's Master of Pikes and responsible for the order of the regiment, stopped beside him. Tregaron saw backs stiffen and pikes straighten. They might respect him, but they *feared* Cogern.

It was well they did. The sergeant had a truly horrible visage. The Pikemaster had been lucky his helmet's gorget and bar nasal had deflected the Rethwellan's blow, or he'd have received more than a maiming and a harelip. Tregaron, then a green lieutenant, had fully expected the Master to feed the sacrificial Fires. He remembered his quiet amazement when the old soldier had not only recovered, he'd returned to duty.

He shook his head. *That* fight had been almost twenty years ago. *He* would never see the south side of forty again. Cogern had fifteen years on him, yet the older man did his daily twenty miles, hit the pells, and led the charges with more energy than men half his age. Tregaron had no doubt that twenty years after he was wormfood, Cogern would still be offering tithes to Vkandis Sunlord and defeating Karse's enemies.

The Commander and the Pikemaster stood silently together a long moment, while the staff waited patiently. Their horses, led by cadets, shifted and fidgeted in the hot, dry air.

"They look good," Tregaron ventured.

Cogern spat and grinned. "They'd better," he lisped, "if they know what's good for 'em." He took off his helmet and ran his hand over his scarred head. Runnels of sweat, trapped by the helm's padding, ran down his face, cutting tracks in the caked dust. Drops fell from his chin to stain his rich scarlet sash. "What idiot moves a regiment across the northlands in summer?" he asked scornfully.

Tregaron smiled. "When the Son of the Sun says 'March,' " he started.

Cogern snapped his fingers. "Bugger the Son of the Sun," he snorted. "The fat bastard's lapping up chilled wine and making doe eyes at the acolytes while we grunt along out here."

Tregaron laughed at the aptness of the blasphemy. "You'd best lose that notion before a priest hears you."

"Bugger them, too," Cogern repeated, but softly and with a quick look around.

"How are the recruits holding up?" Tregaron asked, moving the conversation back onto safe ground.

Cogern rubbed his forehead. "This stroll's melted the city fat offa'em faster than drill and pells." He paused, weighing his words. "Their weapons drill ain't upta' par, but it ain't bad either. Not for pressed troops, anyway."

Tregaron didn't envy the "recruits" who filled out the Twenty-First's ranks. They'd used their victory parade through Sunhame to "volunteer" some of the capital's less wary citizens into Vkandis Sunlord's service. Many of the newest lambs had lost their stunned expressions and had settled into the regiment's training routine, which for them included fighting drills and weapons practice *after* marching a full day and *after* building the night's camp and surrounding fortifications.

Two lambs had keeled over dead so far, and Cogern had reported they'd probably lose another before they got to the border. The press-gangs were supposed to only draft hale men and a few women, but were also given quotas and limited time. Occasionally, they cut corners, placing the burden on the trainer. The training process usually weeded out the hopeless cases *before* the

fracas started. It pained him to lose troops for any reason, but having them die due to sloppy recruiting ran-
kled him.

One cadet holding the horses mumbled to another.
They laughed together. Tregaron stared at him a mo-
ment before he remembered the lad's name. The boy,
Dormion, was the son of a southlands freeholder sent to
the army to avoid the Tithe and, very possibly, the
Flames.

"Eh?" Cogern snapped, "what was that?"

"Um, I said," said the lad, visibly unhappy to have
drawn the Pikemaster's undivided attention, "that they
don't, uhh, have press-gangs in Valdemar." He paused
uncertainly. "Sir," he concluded lamely, after the silence lengthened.

Cogern feigned a look of utter surprise. "How would
you know anything about Valdemar?" He stared at Dormion with the horrified intensity of a man watching a
large and potentially deadly insect crawling up his arm.

The other cadets sidled away, leaving Dormion, gulp-
ing and pale, alone. "I read it, Pikemaster, in the
Chronicles."

"In Val-de-mar," Cogern said, drawing out each sylla-
ble sarcastically, "they don't have to fight. That gives
them certain luxuries we can't afford." He looked dis-
gusted. "A reading cadet. What will they think of next?"
The old sergeant glared at the boy with an expression
fierce enough to cow the bravest veteran. "This ain't
Valdemar, boy, and you'd best get that through your
head! Now get back in your place."

Dormion, pleased to have escaped with little more
than a tongue lashing, scuttled away to rejoin the
other cadets.

"I'm surprised you let him off so easily," Tregaron
said softly. "Usually you just cuff them flat."

Cogern scratched his nose with one ragged nail. "Most
of 'em 'are fish. Not real bright, and just waitin' for
hooks in their mouths and knives in their guts. Once't a
while you get one who sees beneath things. Them's
worth keepin' an eye on." He sighed. "I just wish't I

could keep him out of the damned books. He's got too much to learn in too little time for that folderol."

He met Tregaron's eye. "I saw the same thing in another lad some years back. Even took a sword for 'im, just to give 'im a chance't grow up."

Tregaron, embarrassed, took the worn rope reins from the cadet and led the gelding toward the standards that followed the lead battle. The regiment's flags marked both the commander's location in the formation and the relics that were the unit's pride.

The lacquered ivory boxes contained the femur of the regiment's first commander, a lock of hair from Torlois the Prophet, and a finger bone from Vkorion, who, before he had become Son of the Sun three centuries before, had struck off his own hand as a tithe for Vkandis. Each relic box also contained a certificate of authenticity signed by a senior priest. Tregaron suspected one pedigree was more the result of bribery than accuracy; Vkorion would have to have had at least a dozen fingers on the severed hand alone to accommodate all of the "verified" relic bones.

Pride stirred in his chest when he saw the regiment's stained and tattered banner. The standard, a gold sun bursting on a scarlet background with the number 21 in blue thread stitched across the center, was flanked by the smaller gold, scarlet, and blue guidons of the regiment's three battles. A fifth bearer carried the pole to which the tokens and names of the Twenty-First's thirty-odd victories had been affixed.

Behind that, by itself, came the Oriflamme, the cloth-of-gold standard that was the mark of His Holiness' favor. The regiment had paid in blood for the right to carry the 'Flamme, but it was a distinction that Tregaron would just as soon have forgone.

Beneath Vkandis' Stainless Banner clustered three flint-eyed Sun-priests, the Oriflamme's guardians when it went into the field and the source of Tregaron's worries. Two were from the capital, sent as much to counter Hardorn's magic as they were to protect the flag from dishonor. They wore full priestly regalia, their golden

Sun-in-Glory medallions glinting against their black court robes.

The third was a woman, a fact itself of some note in Vkandis' patriarchal priesthood. She wore the simple red cassock that marked her a common parish-tender, even though she was alleged to be at least as powerful a mage as the Black-robes.

Tregaron knew little about her—only that she had been a provincial prefect drafted when the third member of the capital's troika had died of apoplexy. Darker campfire rumors suggested he had died while demon-summoning, a common enough practice among the Black-robes, even if Tregaron didn't believe the story. The Black-robe Priests *had* warded the northern borders with summoned creatures until Ancar's magi had driven them back.

The tension between the woman and the Black-robes from Sunhame was thick enough to slice and serve on flatbread. He knew the church hierarchy was rife with factional strife, but seeing it made him nervous. All three were above his authority, and he had no doubt that each had the clout to forward a report that, if bad, could cost him his regiment, if not his life.

His worst nightmare was that if the woman reported well of him, the others might speak poorly, to spite her, or vice versa. In either case there would be a black mark against him with His Holiness, and no amount of military skill or booty would erase the stain. He hoped they would judge him only by how he did his duty, but he couldn't be certain their acrimony wouldn't affect their judgment where he was concerned.

He nodded to the three. The woman pleasantly returned his greeting, making a small gesture of blessing. He found her handsome, though with a mannishly square jaw and sharp features. Her eyes, though not as soft as liked, were warm and friendly, and her generous mouth seemed more given to smiles than frowns.

The Black-robes, by contrast, looked stonily forward, their expressions set in harsh disapproval. Tregaron kept his face expressionless. In small things could big things be judged. The provincial had been arguing with her counterparts. Again. *Great,* he thought dryly, *and I thought the army would keep me OUT of politics. Fool.* He felt like the man in the proverb who, when caught between fire and flood, ran back and forth, unable to decide whether to burn or drown.

"I still don't see how all of this skulking and sneaking benefits Karse," the woman said waspishly, continuing what Tregaron was certain was a long-running argument. "Ancar's troops raid us at will, and we do nothing!"

The Fighting Twenty-First isn't "nothing," lady, Tregaron thought, even though generally he agreed with her. Hardorn *had* been testing them, and their response so far had been tepid. It seemed a bit inconsistent that a raid from Rethwellan merited a six-month campaign by a dozen regiments while Hardorn earned—one foot-sore command.

The older Black-robe made a rude face. "His Holiness predicted peace, Solaris," he said to her, as though addressing a small child. "So peace there shall be!"

"You know as well as I that Lastern couldn't scry for a sunny day, much less Ancar's intent," Solaris replied, her voice dripping scorn. "It's a meaningless augury and a meaningless peace. Ancar's eventually going to conclude we're too timid to fight—and then you'll have a full scale war. Try to hide that under a proclamation!"

"You go too far!" Havern hissed. "Continue your blasphemy and I'll have you before an Ecumenical Court."

Tregaron, overhearing more of the exchange than he wanted, blanched. She had spoken treason, and his life might very well stand forfeit for it. She could have him killed to cover her lapse, or Havern might order him executed to snuff the chance he'd repeat what he'd heard. *Fire and flood indeed,* he thought grimly, *flaying and the rack is nearer the mark.* Cogern turned away, mumbling something about adjusting the trumpeters. Tregaron followed, but wasn't quite quick enough to miss Solaris' quiet laugh.

"I'm sorry, Havern," she said, her voice quiet in what might charitably be called contrition had her voice not

dripped scorn. "I overstepped myself." Her speech
changed, becoming singsong as she recited the liturgy of
the Word and Will of Vkandis. "His Holiness is His
Holiness, anointed by the hand of Vkandis, and is the
Son of the Sun, and His avatar on earth." Tregaron
guessed her retreat to the liturgy had more to do with
survival than religion. Still, the very effusiveness of her
recitation argued that even in this, she was poking fun.

Havern appeared unconvinced. He peered at her a
long moment, as though trying to see inside her soul.
"You country priests have had it too much your own
way for too long. I see that certain, ah . . . distortions
and baseless rumors have taken root in the provinces.
Come to my tent this evening and I will instruct you in
the methods by which you might return to orthodoxy."

Solaris shook her head ruefully. "I'm sorry, Havern.
I've already promised to minister to the Third Battle
this night. I gave my word to the Colonel."

Tregaron wasn't happy she had brought up his name,
especially as she had promised to do no such thing. He
sighed to himself. No matter how hard he tried to remain
neutral, it seemed they were determined to draw him
into their feud.

Havern shrugged. "Well," he said easily, as if the matter were of no importance, "I'd like to be reassured of
your orthodoxy before I make my report to His Holiness. Perhaps we can work something out." Tregaron
backed away, trying to put distance between himself and
the three priests. Vkandis' servants were under no obli-
gation of celibacy, but hearing what amounted to extor-
tion embarrassed him.

Solaris flushed, two spots of color forming high on her
cheeks. She opened her mouth to speak when a distant
shout and pounding hooves drew their attention.

Tregaron, relieved at the distraction, trotted toward
the regiment's standards. The mounted scout galloped
down the line and reined in his horse with such savagery
that stones and grit sprayed from beneath its hooves and
flecks of foam flew from its lathered sides.

"Report!" Tregaron snapped, pleased to turn his attention to a problem he could handle.

"Cavalry, soir!" the scout replied, his upcountry accent emphasized by his stress. "Two full regiments, soir, less'n half an hour north of here, 'an movin' toward us."

Tregaron took a single deep breath, calming himself and giving him a moment to order his thoughts. "Do they know we're here?"

The scout looked chagrined. "Aye, more likely than not. We tripped over three o' their outriders while we was on our way back. We got two. The third gave us the slip."

Tregaron sucked air though his teeth, a southlands expression of disapproval. "Well," he said, "what's done is done." He ignored the excited chatter as word of the approaching enemy made its way along infantry column. His staff clustered close, eager to hear the report. "Did you see who they were?"

"One regiment had a boar's head mounted on a pole, soir, with ribbons hanging from its tushes. I din't see the second."

"That would be Reglauf's lot," Cogern said. "He led a regiment under Ancar when they made their try against Valdemar. Word has it he didn't do much except plunder farms."

It didn't occur to Tregaron to question Cogern. The sergeant was *supposed* to know such things. "Word also has it," the old man lisped, "that he cut out early, before they'd properly lost."

"How many troops?" Tregaron asked the scout.

The man pulled a string out of his tunic and counted the knots. "Five battles, soir, about three hundred riders each. I'd guess about the same in the t'other regiment."

"Three thousand cavalry," Cogern spat, "two-to-one, or thereabouts."

"Just like Selenay in Valdemar," Dormion chirped, earning a black look from Cogern. "From the Battle of Border, in the Chronicles. Ancar had them two-to-one as well, and they whipped him."

Cogern sighed, the air of man beset by fools.

The brat doesn't know when to shut up, Tregaron thought.

Cogern growled something obscene and crooked his finger at Dormion. "Come here, child. It's high time I took a *personal* interest in your education."

Dormion swallowed heavily, his mobile features still. "Um, Pikemaster . . ." he began. He looked at Tregaron.

"You tickled the bear, Ensign," Tregaron laughed. "Now you dance with him."

"Selenay," Cogern said with heavy dignity as he ticked off points on his fingers, "had the advantages of Mindspeaking Demon horses, superior terrain, time to pick her battlefield, better-trained troops, and Ancar for an opponent. Not to mention her troops were defending their homes and were backed by a substantial number of defectors, including Hardorn's best Guardsmen."

He paused to switch hands, having long since run out of fingers. "Ancar only had numbers. He needed at least three to one to beat her on *open* ground, and probably six to one to best them on that turf. He had, maybe, three to two, and most of *them* were rabble, not real soldiers a'tall. Hell, only about half his force even had the gumption to attack."

He closed his fist an stuck it in Dormion's face. "Ancar," he finished, "didn't have a prayer. So don't draw false comparisons, especially ones gleaned from books written by the winning side." He exhaled heavily. "Here endeth the sermon. Now get back to your units. All of you."

The cadets scattered.

Tregaron looked at Cogern. "Do you think he heard you?"

"Damn that Bard-written tripe," the Pikemaster replied, "Selenay could have held that hilltop with a company of recruits and a detachment of washerwomen. Demon horses, magic, and good writing don't make up for sound tactics and superior strategy."

"I don't know," Tregaron said, "Selenay's done all right for herself, by all accounts."

"Not you, too!" Cogern snapped, his expression torn

between shock and betrayal. He crossed his arms across his chest, muttering about tyros who read more books than was good for them. Tregaron, laughing, mounted his horse and scanned the field for a good place to make his stand.

"There's a shallow stream up ahead, soir," the scout said, pointing. He had wisely kept his mouth shut while Cogern ranted. "It's about five-hundred paces from here."

"Do you want to form behind the water course?" Cogern asked, his voice and manner now all business.

Tregaron considered a moment before answering. "No, I don't want to give them any excuse to go toward our flanks. A nice long feature like that might encourage them to get creative."

"You're expecting them to come right for us?" Cogern asked in a neutral voice.

"Yes," Tregaron answered. "When Ancar assassinated his father, he put Alessander's generals to the sword as well. He lost anybody he had with troop-handling skills, and the rabble he recruits aren't much for the discipline that goes with good tactics." He smiled sourly. "Not that they've needed it. They've been riding right over the local militia for a while now. I'm betting it's been a while since they've faced regulars. They'll go straight for our throats."

He straightened his shoulders. "We'll put the stream hard by our right and use it to anchor our flank on that side. We'll assume an open field defense and meet them in that high grass over there." He pointed to the open area beside the streambed.

"All right," Cogern said, turning to the cluster of runners and trumpeters, "what are you waiting for?"

The staff members scattered to execute the orders. Horns blared. Under officers shouted as the lead battle, company by company, shifted their pikes and picked up a clumsy trot. The regiment's company of mounted skirmishers thundered past, their riders adjusting bows, quivers and heavy sacks. They disappeared in a trice over a low brow to contest the Hardornans' passage.

Tregaron knew a hundred archers weren't enough to stop the invaders by themselves, but he hoped they'd be enough of an irritant to make Reglauf deploy his forces prematurely.

The vanguard had just drawn even with the streamlet when a single horn blew in the distance. Tregaron followed the sound and saw a thin dust plume rising above the bluffs. "That would be our guests," Cogern said, his flat voice calm. Tregaron studied the thin brown column. Infantry dust tended to spread as it rose, making a ground-hugging haze rather than a rising tail. Yes, definitely cavalry.

He turned in his saddle to address the trumpeters. "Play: Form line of battle—left."

The horns skirled. Trumpeters farther down the line answered the calls, acknowledging the orders.

"Front Northwest!" Cogern shouted, his bass voice cutting the din. In such moments all hint of his lisp vanished. "Debouch by companies!"

The battles' officers and sergeants amplified the commands as the regiment dropped its packs and began to smoothly deploy into the serge alongside the dusty road. Tregaron heard the crack of a whip and snapped his head around to see one sergeant coiling his badge of office back into his hand. He rode over as the man raised it for another blow. "You are a fine sergeant, Gren," Tregaron said through clenched teeth, "but you are no longer in the Seventeenth. If you raise that starter to another one of my lambs without good cause, I'll have you flogged back to your old regiment. Is that clear!"

The sergeant, his face pale, nodded silently. Tregaron jerked his horse's head around and rode to take his position with the standards, by then positioned on the left-center of the line. The battles' guidons had long since returned to their units.

Front-rankers aligned the regiment into four neat rows, using pikestaves as guideposts. The pikemen in the first two ranks took their intervals, setting their shields between them to provide cover if the cavalry stormed them with arrows. The rear ranks, composed of swordsmen each equipped with two heavy javelins, marked off their running distances and prepared their gear.

The javelins were cunning weapons. The swordsmen wrapped lanyards around the middles, which, when held between the casters' fingers when throwing, imparted a spin on the spear. Spinning spears flew farther and more accurately than straight-thrown, though no one knew why.

The javelins' heads were attached to the shafts with weak glue or brittle pins. When the weapon hit, the glue usually failed or the pin broke, making the thing useless for a return throw.

The regiment's longbow company moved quickly out in front, ready to act as skirmishers and contest the ground in front of the regiment with long range fire. Two scouts galloped across the field, plunging white-washed stakes into the ground at hundred-pace intervals to mark the boyers' ranges.

The farthest scout turned, and using his last stick as a goad, pounded back toward the readied regiment.

Cogern cantered up beside him. "As for tactics, sir," he asked, "butterfly wings?"

Tregaron nodded. "If they let us. Have Luhann double her leftmost companies. If they try to turn our flank, her side'll be the most likely place they'll try."

Cogern passed the instruction to a runner. Most battlefield situations were too complex for trumpets. Runners gave more precise messages, but were slow and often got lost or were lost.

Cogern smiled the easy grin of man with a secret. Tregaron rarely saw the Pikemaster as happy as he was before a fight. Vkandis knew *his* guts always knotted up beforehand.

"Your horse, sir," Cogern said. Tregaron dipped his head and dismounted. Mounted officers made easy targets.

They gave their animals to an orderly to take behind the line.

"Where's the damned Oriflamme?" Tregaron snapped. "It should be here."

"Here, Colonel," Solaris said, stepping through the ranks to join them. Tregaron saw she wore no mail and carried no weapon.

"Where are your cohorts?" he said, a little more harshly than he'd intended, but only a little.

She made a wry face. "They've decided to support your fight from back there." She pointed toward the area behind the regiment, where the horses, gear, and a few noncombatants waited.

"That'll do 'em no good a'tall if'n they get behind us," Cogern said. He looked at Solaris. "Do you have a weapon?"

She held up the Oriflamme. "I have this."

Cogern looked closely at her a long moment. "Then what are you waitin' on, girl?" He pointed to the Stainless Banner. "Show 'em what we're fightin' for."

She grinned and hefted the pole, raising the 'Flamme high above their heads. She waved it about, swirling its swallowtail in a gentle arc. The center battle cheered. The shouting built as each battle fought to outdo the others.

The skirmishers' reappearance quieted the noise. The horsemen paused at the hill crest to fire one final volley at their pursuers, then fled across the open ground. They opened the sacks tied to their saddles and tossed handful after handful of small black objects into the grass behind them.

"What are those?" Solaris asked, lowering the 'Flamme and grounding the haft.

"Caltrops," Cogern said with malicious glee, "four sharpened pieces of iron welded together. No matter how they fall, one prong always points up—a little dainty for a horse's hoof."

The first mass of Hardornan cavalry crested the hill, a black tide that quickly covered the facing slope. Tregaron heard the thin voice of the archers' commander. "Take your aim—four hundred paces. Loose!" A thin iron sleet rose and fell. Some arrows struck home, here and there felling a horse or rider. The range was a bit long for accurate fire, but Tregaron hoped the harassment would goad the Hardornans into leaving.

The mass reacted by spurring their horses and charging.

"They've got no order at all!" Cogern sniffed, sounding offended. Tregaron knew he hated inefficiency, even when displayed by an enemy.

"Three hundred paces!" the archer leader yelled, timing his fire so the riders would cross the stake just as the arrows arrived. "Loose!"

The toll grew heavier as arrows found their marks or pierced armor. Horses pulled up and fell, screaming and thrashing, as the cruel iron caltrops pierced their hooves. Most riders scrambled to their feet, but here and there one lay still, either knocked witless or themselves victims of the spikes hidden in the grass.

"Two hundred!" More riders fell. The Karsite horse archers added to their toll with their shorter-ranged bows as they moved to the flanks to cover the ends of the formation. Here and there a Karsite fell, arrowstruck, but the Hardornens' volleys were erratic and largely ineffective. The cavalry's thunder grew louder as they galloped down onto the waiting Karsite line.

"One hundred!"

Cogern turned, cupped his hands around his mouth, and bellowed. "Set to receive cavalry!"

With a wordless shout, six hundred pikes came down in a single glittering arc, their bitter edges bright in the noonday sun. The rear ranks gave way a pace, ready to hurl their javelins on command. The archers scampered for the rear.

Cogern grabbed the regimental standard and raised it over his head. At the instant he dropped it, the battles' commanders dropped their swords and six hundred javelins smashed into the onrushing horses. The cavalry slowed, their charge blunted by the heavy spears. A second volley crashed home an instant later, cutting down the lead ranks like a scythe through wheat. The rear ranks piled over the dead and dying and pressed home the attack.

The crash of the horsemen hitting the readied pikes roared over Tregaron like a tide of sound, a breaking wave of iron-shod hooves and slashing, cursing soldiers. His world retreated to a circle five yards across. A Hardornen, her horse gutted by a pikeblade, bowled over the front ranks and plowed into the command party. One orderly slashed the animal across the knees, bringing it down and throwing the rider. Two officers plunged their blades into her before she could rise, the second twisting his weapon to gore her before withdrawing it. She collapsed, dead, blood fountaining from her mouth and nose.

The lead Hardornen was dead, but the gap she'd forced in the line filled quickly with other horsemen, slashing and stabbing as they tried to widen the breach. Horns blew in alarm on either side of the command party as squads detached from the flanking units to help seal the break in the line. Tregaron, looking for more troops to throw at the Hardornens, whipped his head around and saw Solaris using the Oriflamme's staff to fend off one horseman while Cogern moved to his flank. The Pikemaster stabbed deep, driving his sword deep into the horse's barrel, dropping it in its tracks. He then brained the rider with his sword pommel and ran him through with a quick thrust as he tried to rise.

Karsite swordsmen flooded the area, surrounding the horse troops and attacking from all sides. Their grim intensity and lacquered red-and-black armor made Tregaron think of ants swarming a moth.

Distant horn calls announced the arrival of the second regiment. He craned his head toward the sound and saw it advancing over the hill crest in slightly better order than the first. The newcomers made a token effort to dress ranks, then charged across the caltrop-littered ground. A few fell to the hidden spikes, but the charge went home almost unblunted.

Pikemen fell, lanced through or scattered like ninepins as the horsetroops plowed into the center of the Twenty-

First's line. Swords slashed and stabbed. The din drew louder and the center units, beset by the fresh Hardorn regiment, sagged under the pressure. Trumpets blew frantically as under officers fought to hold the line. The battle hung in the balance, a race between whether the pikemen could reknit their formations or the Hardornens could split the regiment and roll it up.

Cogern took half the remaining swordsmen in the command party and went to shore the line where the fighting was thickest. Solaris followed, keeping the Oriflamme aloft. The soldiers, seeing the woman and the banner, both now stained with blood, fought harder. The pressure intensified, the battle growing more desperate as units lost cohesion. The thick, coppery smell of blood, mixed with the stink of loosened bowels and horsedung, threatened to overwhelm Tregaron, as did the clouds of dust as thick as smoke that obscured much of the field.

Twice the pressure on the command party built, and once Tregaron himself had to swing his sword against the enemy. More horncalls sounded from the right, calling for assistance. Tregaron looked around frantically. The entire right half of the line was engulfed and all reserves on that side were already committed. He had to launch a counter, something to take the pressure off the beleaguered center and right before it cracked under the Hardornens' hammerblows.

"This'll have to work," he said to himself as he summoned his remaining trumpeters. Most were dead, killed defending the relics. He pointed to two. "Go to Captain Luhann. Tell her to prepare to attack *en echelon.* She's to commence when she's ready. Don't wait for a signal. We're counting on her to take 'em in the flank and grind 'em into powder. Repeat."

The runner cleared his throat. "Attack *en echelon* when ready. Don't wait for signal." Tregaron checked the message with the other runner, then sent them to the left. He repeated the same message with two more and dispatched them to the right, though he doubted that wing of the regiment could comply.

He fretted in the minutes that followed, afraid his

order had come too late, or that the Hardornens would break the line. He peered anxiously to where he could see the Oriflamme, still bravely waving. He worried about what was going on there even as a Battle or two of horsetroops made another try for the regiment's banner. More blood and more dead followed in a sharp little fight.

The Hardornens finally broke, driven from the standards by a volley of arrows fired from *across* his line of sight. The dust cleared and he saw the archers on the extreme left complete the echelon movement that gave them a clear shot along the regiment's long axis. Each pike company stepped off in turn, marching forward a few paces, then wheeling to the right. In the distance, Luhann made it look like a parade ground maneuver. He distantly heard her voice through the din, using a leather megaphone to yell orders to her troops. Her voice didn't have Cogern's carrying power, but she compensated well.

He considered Luhann his best triumph. The army, the fighting arm of a *very* male god, was as thinly populated by women as the priestly ranks. He remembered the laughter of his counterparts when he'd accepted her as a cadet. The crisp precision of her troops was all the proof he'd ever need that he hadn't been daft in appointing her to command.

A runner panted up to him. "Pikemaster Cogern sends 'is respects, sir, and asks if you're ready to close the wings yet? He says he's hanging on by 'is teeth."

Tregaron gathered his thoughts a moment before answering. "My compliments to the Pikemaster. Tell him the left has already started. He's to lure them deeper, if he can." The runner repeated the message and scampered away.

Tregaron had little to do but fret. Victory and defeat looked a lot alike in those moments, while the center remained vulnerable and the flank attack developed. His smaller force was strung out around three-quarters of the compass while a numerically superior enemy held the center. His regiment could be easily shattered and there was not a damned thing he could do about it.

He sent several squads he couldn't afford to give up to back Cogern, who had began a slow retreat in the center. The Hardornens pressed forward, sensing victory. Just when he thought the battle could get no louder, he heard a crash and clatter on the far right. The sounds of fighting there intensified. A slight breeze stirred, moving the thick dust, but not clearing it. Had the Hardornens broken through? Was all lost?

Distant trumpets sounded. The trumpeter beside Tregaron closed his eyes, listening intently to the distant signal. "First Battle reports: Attacking *en echelon,* Left Wheel, sir." Tregaron tried not to whoop with glee.

More trumpets blew, this time on the left. Luhann's entire battle, pikes in hand and its blood up, finished pivoting on its right heel, paused, aligned its ranks, and *charged.*

They crashed into the disordered Hardornens, crushing one side of the mass and working a fearful slaughter as the cavalry tried to flee. The horse archers, briefly visible though the murk, rushed to seal the trap, covering the opening between the two wings like a lid on a pot.

The bulk of two regiments were trapped. Tregaron knew his own forces were spread much too thin to hold the enemy inside, so it was time to kill as many as they could before the Hardornens broke free.

"Sound General Advance," he yelled at the remaining trumpeter. The boy nodded, blatted into his horn a few times, then sent the final command in pure ringing notes. The troops on either side of Tregaron advanced, carrying with them their standards and cheering. They smashed the weakening resistance, killing horses and riders with equal abandon.

A portion of the rear regiment cut through the thin screen of horse archers and burst out of the trap. The Hardornens scattered like wind-blown leaves as each rider fled to preserve life and health. A hot gust of wind swept the dust away, giving Tregaron a glimpse of the carnage. The entire field before him was littered with dead and dying horses and soldiers, piled three deep in some places. Hardornens cried for succor in a dozen languages.

He saw, as he walked forward across the torn and bloody field, that the leading regiment had gotten trapped between Cogern's and Luhann's units. Badly weakened by the javelins, robbed of its momentum and best fighters, it was caught in the jaws of an implacable foe. He looked at the trumpeter. "Play: No Mercy." The boy looked grim, but complied.

Ancar took no prisoners in Karse and showed no mercy. Now the favor was returned. Luhann gave the final command and Reglauf's regiment vanished under a wall of pikes.

Later, Tregaron walked among the troops laid out in groaning, screaming rows where the regiment's hedge-wizards labored to save as many as they could. He adjusted his turban, his one concession to the heat, while his helmet hung from his belt. Many of the soldiers, busy tidying the battlefield or finishing the wounded Hadornens, had also removed their helms. Even Cogern, who normally would have blistered the troops for such a lapse, kept his silence. He also, Tregaron noted wryly, kept his helmet.

He glanced back at the wounded. The regiment had suffered three hundred casualties, a twenty-percent loss. It was a light butcher's bill considering the desperate nature of the fight, but still far too heavy. Tregaron took each dead and wounded soldier as a personal failure, his losing Karse's most precious resource.

The Hardornens had lost much worse than he, at least five times his numbers killed, one regiment destroyed, and another scattered. Still, Hardorn recruited the scum of five countries, and such losses were easily made good.

He bent to help one man who begged for water, taking his own canteen and holding it to the man's lips. Tregaron held the man's head while he sipped. He caught a whiff of punctured bowel. This soldier would never recover. His end would be agonizing as his own waste poisoned his body cavity.

"Do you wish mercy?" Tregaron asked, his voice gentle.

The soldier, perhaps only then realizing what he faced, sobbed once and nodded. "Hagan," the dying man whispered, "send Hagan. Third Battle, fifth company. He'll do it." Tregaron stood and summoned an orderly who sprinted to fetch the man's friend.

Havern waited at the end of the row. He seemed positively cheerful as he looked around at the long rows of gored and wounded soldiers. "Can I help you?" Tregaron asked, realizing as he looked at the man just how bone tired he felt.

"We'll have the Fires ready within the hour, Colonel," the Black-robe said.

"Must it happen now?" Tregaron replied.

"The Word and Will calls for a victory sacrifice as soon as the battle is won, Colonel. You know that."

"I know that the Battle Tithe plays merry hell with morale, sir," Tregaron said wearily. He held up his hand. "You may have the mercied men for your Fires, but only after their friends have released them from their pain."

Havern's face fell, falling into the mask of disapproval he wore when debating Solaris. "What the priests do in Rethwellan is one thing, Colonel, but here we follow the Word and Will literally. Those men too wounded to travel or otherwise unlikely to survive will go to the flames. Alive. Vkandis takes no pleasure in cold flesh."

"I never understood why Vkandis took pleasure in any flesh," Solaris said pleasantly.

Havern rounded on her. "Your deviance from the Word and Will has been repeatedly noted. After I'm through with you, Solaris, you'll be lucky to preside over an outhouse, much less an abbey."

Tregaron, recalling her rallying the regiment with the Oriflamme, felt his temper heat. "The Sun-priestess held her place and inspired the regiment. What did you do?"

Havern didn't bat an eye. "We got out of the way. We were the wrong tool for the job. You were the right one. We deferred to you on the matter of how best to conduct the fight. Now," he said maliciously, "you will defer to us on how to conduct the Fires. The army was given its dispensation to sacrifice those who would die anyway, rather than the hale. I will accept no compromise on that point.''

Solaris quietly slipped away and knelt by the gut-stabbed man, who still begged for water. She uncorked Tregaron's water bottle and gave him several small sips. Tregaron listened to the Sun-priest's tirade about duty and responsibility while trying vainly to hold onto the scraps of his self-possession.

Solaris stood and walked to the next soldier, who bled her life away from a gaping thigh wound. It wasn't until the gutted man sat up and felt his middle that Tregaron realized something bizarre had happened. Something far more important than the Black-robe's prating.

He turned his back and walked away from Havern as Solaris stood and went to the third man. The woman, who moments ago had been unconscious, moaned weakly and sat up. Tregaron caught a glimpse of Solaris' eyes as she knelt and placed her blood-covered hands on the man's exposed skull. Her gaze was far away, locked on a distant horizon, and she whispered to herself as she healed. Each time she knelt, her pupils shone with a golden glow and her hands were suffused in a warmth that looked like fire, but brought health, not hurt. Soon a dozen of the regiment followed her, whispering in hushed tones at the miracles as she healed each of the dying.

The story spread like wildfire through the regiment. By the time she finished, a thousand men and women were crowded around her, eager to see the prodigy. They stood silently, giving her space to work as she knitted flesh, healed bones, and restored health. After what seemed like an eternity she stood from beside the last.

The silent regiment gave way, opening before her to let her by. A few, braver or more foolhardy than the rest, reached out tentative hands to touch her cassock as she passed. Tregaron, trailed by the stunned and silent Black-robes, followed her as she took shaky steps toward the more lightly wounded.

She placed her hands on a man's slashed and splinted arm. Nothing happened. "It's gone," she said in a confused voice, "it's gone now."

"It's all right, mum," said the trooper, who looked old enough to be her father, "I saw what you done for the others. I'll heal all right by m'self."

She turned back toward the regiment. Tregaron saw the glow had faded from her eyes. Her self-possession seemed to return and she looked at Havern. "Now you have none for your Fires," she said in a weary voice. "The dispensation protects the rest."

Tregaron, overcome by the miracles and the restoration of those he thought he would see consumed, drew his battered sword and knelt before her. The regiment, following his cue, knelt as well.

"Command us, Lady," he said, "we are yours."

"No, sir," she replied with a soft, sweet smile. Her expression seemed transformed, as though she were in ecstasy. "You are not mine. You are Vkandis'. If He has chosen to work through me, it is through the worthiness of the cause, not of the vessel."

Havern cleared his throat. "Ahmmm . . ." he began, "I know we all think we saw something. . . ." He trailed off as a thousand hostile faces focused on him. "Um, yes," he concluded and retreated.

"Please rise, sir," Solaris said, her expression still beatific, "I am not the Son of the Sun."

Not yet, anyway, Tregaron thought as he rose. *Not yet.*

A Herald's Honor
by *Mickey Zucker Reichert*

Mickey Zucker Reichert is a pediatrician whose twelve
science fiction and fantasy novels include *The Legend
of Nightfall, The Unknown Soldier,* and *The Renshai
Trilogy.* Her most recent release from DAW Books is
Prince of Demons, the second in *The Renshai Chronicles* trilogy. Her short fiction has appeared in numerous anthologies. Her claims to fame: she *has*
performed brain surgery, and her parents *really are*
rocket scientists.

Rain pattered to the roof of the way station, rhythmic
beneath the low-pitched howl of the winds. Herald Judaia stared into the hearth, watching twists of flame
flicker through their collage of yellow and red. Though
her eyes followed the fire, her mind traced every movement of her mentor, Herald Martin. Already, he had curried his Companion, Tirithran, till the sheen of the
stallion's white coat rivaled the moon. His sword and dagger held edges a razor might envy, and he had soaped
his tack until Judaia feared he might wear the leather
thin as sandal bindings. The image made her smile
through a longing that had sharpened to pain. She imagined him struggling to buckle a back cinch the width of
a finger and mistaking Tirithran's bridle for a boot lace.

Judaia turned. For an instant, her dark eyes met Martin's gray-green ones and she thought she saw the same
desire in him that goaded her, as burning and relentless
as the hearth fire. He glanced away so quickly, his black
hair whipped into a mane and every muscle seemed to
tense in sequence. Movement only enhanced his beauty,

and the sight held Judaia momentarily spellbound. Her
mind emptied of every thought but him. The rigors of
her internship faded, insignificant beneath the more solid
and cruel pain of Martin's coldness. Unable to resist,
Judaia glided toward him, loving and hating the feelings
his presence inspired.

Apparently sensing her movement, Martin tensed.
Suddenly, he took several quick strides toward the door.
"I'm going to check on Tirithran and Brayth." He fumbled with the latch, uncharacteristically clumsy. The door
swung open, magnifying the drumlike beat of rain on
the way station's roof. Beneath an overhanging umbrella
of leaves, Tirithran and Brayth enjoyed the pleasures of
stallion and mare, their grunts punctuating the sounds
of wind and rain. Caught between Judaia and an even
more obvious passion, Martin froze in the doorway.

Judaia brushed back a strand of her shoulder-length
hair, wishing it looked less stringy and unruly. Its sandy
color seemed out-of-place framing dark eyes nearly
black. Still, though not classically beautiful, Judaia did
not believe herself homely either. She had kept her body
well-honed, even before the rigors of Herald training.
Her features, though plain, bore no deformities or scars.
Other men had found her attractive enough. Yet other
men had not mattered to Judaia since she had met Martin at the Collegium three years past. They had begun
their training together, year-mates, yet Martin had
passed into full Herald status and gone out on circuit a
year before her. Now, she learned from him. And maybe,
if he could turn his eyes and mind from preparations for
an instant, she might teach him something as well.

Martin remained still and silent for some time, seemingly oblivious to the rain that slanted through the open
door frame and left damp circles on his Herald whites.

Judaia studied Martin in the moonlight trickling between clouds and over the threshold. The first half of
their circuit had passed with routine ease, yet the Martin
she had seen direct tribunals, chastise embezzlers, and
calmly settle disputes seemed to have disappeared, replaced by an awkward child scarcely into his teens. The

transformation seemed nonsensical. She had never heard
of a chaste Herald. She had lost her virginity even before
Brayth had spirited her from Westmark to begin her
training. A handsome child of local nobility, Martin
surely had had his share of women, and Judaia had
heard Lyssa, one of the Seneschal's granddaughters,
bragging about Martin's prowess in bed. *Why, then, has
he spent the past five months finding every excuse in the
Sector to avoid me?* This night, Judaia decided, she
would find her answer, one way or another.

"Ah," Judaia said, her soft words shattering a long-
held silence. "I didn't know staring at love-making Companions could turn a man to stone."

Martin startled, suddenly and obviously aware of his
lapse. He closed the door with clear reluctance and
turned to face Judaia. Rain plastered black hair in ring-
lets to his forehead, and water dribbled along the crest
of one eyelid.

Martin looked so atypically undignified, Judaia could
not suppress a laugh. "I considered us lucky to get in
before the rain. I should have known Martin would find
another way to get himself soaked."

Finally, Martin smiled. He flicked away the trickling
raindrop and raked dripping locks from his forehead. He
headed for the fire, his wet Whites brushing Judaia's dry
ones as he passed, leaving a damp, darker line that the
warmth would quickly dry. He sat in front of the caper-
ing flames. Judaia took a seat beside him.

Martin fumbled dagger and whetstone from his pocket,
sharpening the blade for the twelfth time since its last
use. "Are you tired?"

"No. You?"

"Not yet," Martin admitted. The conversation seemed
to have come to an end, and he abruptly steered it in
another direction. Among strangers or while riding Companions, they always chatted with an easy fluency that
seemed to mock the choppy nervousness that character-
ized their more private moments. "You're doing well, so
far." He scratched stone over blade.

"Oh, yes," Judaia said, not bothering to hide her sarcasm. "I've gotten pretty good at riding around watching you work. I'm probably the Heraldic expert at observing Martin."

Martin glanced at the stone and steel in his hands as if noticing them for the first time. "I'm sorry. I guess I haven't been giving you much responsibility, and you *are* ready for it." Again, stone whisked over metal with a scraping hiss that set Judaia's teeth on edge. "Next time, *you* get to check the tax records."

Judaia had learned to care for her gear, too, and she put the appropriate amount of time and effort into the task. Martin's tending had become clearly excessive. "Tax records? Tax records be hanged. Hellfires, Martin. I want to make a judgment. By myself. No interference from you."

"A judgment?" Martin considered, whetstone scouring steel a dozen strokes before he spoke again. "All right then. The next judgment's yours and yours alone. I'd better warn you, though. We're getting toward the Borderlands, and those people have a different idea of justice and a woman's place."

"I can handle it." Though excited, Judaia could not keep annoyance from her voice. Martin's long closeness had fanned her desire from a spark to a bonfire. There could no longer be any doubt about the source of that need. *Lifebonded, no question.* Yet Martin seemed as oblivious to the ultimate sanction as he was to her readiness for a more active role in their Sector patrol.

Another long silence followed, interrupted only by the ceaseless gallop of the rain and the slash of stone against steel.

Judaia could avoid the need no longer. She clasped a hand to Martin's arm to halt the sharpening, staring directly at him. Martin stiffened, then ceased his work. His eyes darted from floor to dagger to fire. Finally, he met her gaze.

All of the emotion Judaia had suppressed came welling up at once. She did not waste words on caution or euphemism. Pent up frustration burst forth at once, and she no longer cared if she hurt or offended him. "What's wrong with you?"

"What?" Martin parted damp strands of hair from his eyes. Startlement at her outburst quickly faded to apology. "Look, I'm sorry. I guess I've been overprotecting you, but it is your first patrol and—"

Judaia interrupted, "That's not what I'm talking about, and you know it."

"What are you talking about?"

"I'm talking about you so free and confident out there." Judaia gestured vaguely northward, toward Haven and the towns and cities they had policed. "Then, every time we're alone together, you're currying Tirithran bald. Or you're cutting enough wood to fill six way stations summer to summer." She released his arm so suddenly, the whetstone tumbled from his fingers.

Now, Martin echoed Judaia's anger. "Well excuse me for being thorough."

"Thorough?" Judaia leaped to her feet. "Thorough! If you get any more *thorough,* you're going to whittle that dagger to a toothpick. You're not just being thorough; you're avoiding me."

Martin sheathed his dagger and put away the whetstone. "Yes," he admitted.

A blatant confession was the last thing Judaia expected to hear, and it completely arrested her train of thought. "What?"

Martin rose, again meeting Judaia's eyes, candor clear in his green-gray stare. For a moment, his shielding slipped, and she caught a glimpse of deep struggle, honor against need. Then, he hurriedly rebuilt his defenses. "Yes. I *am* avoiding you."

"Why?" Surprise dispersed Judaia's anger, leaving only confusion in its wake. "I feel . . . I mean we both know . . ." Words failed her, and she discovered an awkwardness as petrifying as Martin's had seemed.

"That we're lifebonded? Yes, I know."

Judaia could do nothing but stare, jaw sagging gradually open without her will or knowledge. At length, she managed speech. "You know? Then why are you avoiding me?"

"Because I made a vow to Lyssa that she would be my one and only, that I would never sleep with another woman."

Judaia did not know which shocked her more, her own disappointment, the tie to Lyssa, or the promise like none she had ever heard before. "Are you lifebonded with her, too?"

"No."

"Then why would you make such a promise?"

Martin shrugged. "She wanted me to, and I did. Lifebonds are uncommon enough I never expected to form one."

Judaia saw the hole in Martin's logic at once. Lyssa, she knew, had slept with many others, as recently as the night before Martin left to patrol the Sector. "Did she make a similar vow to you."

"Yes."

Judaia considered a tactful way to inform Martin of Lyssa's deceit and found none. Though she hated herself for the cruelty she might inflict, she chose a direct approach instead. He deserved to know the truth. "I'm sorry, Martin. Lyssa hasn't kept her vow."

Martin took the news too easily for it to have been a surprise. "Lyssa is not a Herald."

Judaia stared, not believing what she was hearing. More than anything in the world, she wanted Martin, and she knew now that he felt as strongly for her. Yet, the pledge that shackled him had become one-sided and the integrity of a Herald his undoing, as well as her own. "But it's not right!" she shouted, the agony of the thwarted lifebond writhing within her. "It's not fair."

Martin's eyes went moist, the green-gray smeared to a colorless blur. " 'Fair' is not the issue." Once again, he looked away, and this time Judaia applauded his decision to dodge her stare. "A Herald's vows," he said softly, "take precedence over desire. Honor always over right."

Suddenly, Judaia felt very tired.

*   *   *

Stormy night passed to crystalline day, free of humidity. Rainbows scored patches of sky and pooled along spiders' webs, but their beauty did little to raise Judaia's mood. She rode at Martin's side in silence. Overtended buckles and bridle bells reflected silver fragments of sunlight; clean whites and curried Companions shed the brightness until it seemed to enclose them like a divine glow. Birds flapped and twittered from the forests lining either edge of the roadway, feasting on insects drawn by the warm wetness following a gale.

Martin whistled a complicated tune written by his Bardic brother. He seemed to have forgotten the events of the previous evening, returning to his usual brisk confidence and grace under pressure. The normality of his routine only amplified Judaia's pain. The lifebond, already a noose, now felt like a noose on fire.

Brayth sensed the Herald's pain, Mindspeaking with a tone pitched to soothe. :*What's troubling you, little sister?*:

Judaia sighed, loath to inflict her sorrow on another, yet glad for a friendly ear. :*It's Martin.*:

:*What about Martin? He seems happy enough.*:

Judaia patted the Companion's silky neck. :*That's exactly the problem. How can he be so oblivious when I'm so miserable? Can't he feel the same pain, the same thwarted need?*: In explanation, Judaia opened her shields fully to Brayth, showing the mare the conversation in the way station and the mass of conflicting emotions it had inspired, at least in Judaia.

:*The lifebond is as strong in him as you. He feels it, too. But his honor is stronger even than the bond.*:

Frustration made Judaia sullen, and her next words came from superficial anger. :*Lady take his damnable honor. I hate it.*:

:*Do you truly hate his honor or the situation to which that honor has fettered him?*:

Uncertain of the question, Judaia gave no reply; but she did feel guilty for her lapse. Companions chose only those pure of intent, and devotion to duty came with the first Heraldic lesson.

Brayth continued questioning, *:Do you love Martin because of his honor or in spite of it? If he had made a similar vow to you, would you expect him to keep it?:*

The last, Judaia felt qualified to answer. *:Well, of course. But I'd never ask for such a vow. Or, if I did, I would keep my vow as well. Blind loyalty to one who deceives is simply slavery. Honor it may be, but an honor without justice.:*

Brayth shook her head, her frothy mane like silk on Judaia's fingers. *:Tell that to Martin.:*

:I already have.:

:Ah.: Brayth glanced back at her rider, a light dancing in her soft, sapphire eyes. *:Next time, sister two legs, you'll have to convince him.:*

As the Companion's words settled into Judaia's mind, the approaching pound of hoofbeats drew her from deeper consideration. She glanced at Martin, and the intensity of his focus on the road ahead cued her that he had heard as well. He signaled Tirithran to a halt, and Brayth stopped at the stallion's side. The broken pattern of the oncoming hoof falls and lack of bridle bells told her, without the need for vision, that the horse and rider were not Companion and Herald.

A moment later, a stranger appeared from around a curve in the roadway. He rode a stocky Border pony, its dark hooves drumming hard-packed roadway and its chestnut tail streaming. The thin man on its back wore a well-tailored cloak and tunic of plain design. As he drew closer, crow's feet and a shock of graying hair showed his age, and his carriage revealed high breeding. The pony slowed to a walk as he came within hailing distance. "Thank the Goddess, I've found you! Greetings, good Heralds."

Judaia nodded and deferred to her mentor. Anyone seeking would certainly have found them. They traveled the main roads. Their circuit, so far, had remained tame and routine; and they had lost no days, arriving in each town, village, and city at the expected time.

"What can we do for you?" Martin asked, apparently sensing the man's distress.

Judaia exercised her Gift, though weak compared with those of her year-mates, concentrating on the man's abstraction. She Saw a birthing room filled with clean straw pallets. She found four women in the picture. One clutched an infant tightly to her breast, gaze focused so intently she seemed not to notice that two others argued vehemently, clothes torn and arms waving. Another baby wailed, apparently frightened by the noise, though both combatants took clear and obvious caution not to harm the child. The fourth woman lay still on the straw, clearly injured; and two more infants sprawled limply near a corner. Stung to action by what she saw, Judaia Sent the image to Martin, bypassing the need for the stranger's slower, verbal description. Martin had a strong Communication Gift, which made the Sending easy, though he had little Sight to locate the knowledge for himself.

Still, though she formed an image, Judaia's Gift brought picture without sound. The need for haste drove her to request the important details first. Ordinarily, she would let Martin handle the situation; but he had promised her the next judgment. Though he could not have guessed the urgency that would accompany their next decision, Martin would not go back on his word. Now, Judaia cherished the honor she had cursed moments before.

The stranger had already begun his story. ". . . all giving birth on the same day—"

Judaia interrupted, delving for the necessary. "The women's fight. It's over what?"

The man broke off into a startled silence. Then, apparently attributing her understanding to Heraldic magic, he addressed the question. "The argument is over who gave birth to one of the babies, Herald."

Martin drew breath, but Judaia overran him. "Doesn't the midwife know?"

"She apparently got hurt in the struggle, Herald. She's unconscious, but alive. We have people tending her, but she might need a Healer. I'm afraid this can't wait until she's well."

Anger rose in Judaia against the bitterness that motherhood could inspire, every bit as strong as the bond of love so many lauded between woman and child. Horror touched her then, along with a possibility she did not have to know now but she asked for the sake of her own conscience. "Did the babies get caught in the battle as well?"

"No, Herald." The stranger seemed as horrified by the prospect. "Two stillborn."

Judaia had heard enough. "We'll meet you there." She signaled Brayth, and the mare launched into a gallop toward the Border Holding from which the stranger had come.

Not bothering to compete with the wind, Martin Mindspoke with Judaia as they rode. *:You took that over nicely.:*

Judaia sensed a touch of displeasure, though she could not feel certain. He hid it well behind a sense of pride at her budding competence. *:This one's my judgment, remember?:*

Now, Martin's discomfort came through more clearly. *:Are you sure you want this one? Something less serious might do for a start.:*

Brayth flashed around the curve in a stride and a half, neck stretched and head low for the straightaway. *:Are you breaking a promise?:*

:Never.: Martin recoiled from the possibilty, Tirithran matching Brayth stride for stride. *:Just giving you an out.:*

:I don't need an out. I can handle this, and the midwife needs you. The best I could do is carry her to a Healer.: Brayth whisked around another bend, and the Borderland came into sight, a patchwork of large but simple homes to accommodate the men with their multiple wives and myriad children. Crops and pastures dotted the areas between homesteads, and a small but ardent crowd surrounded a single building set off from the rest. Though Judaia's Sight had shown her only the inside of

the cottage, she knew this had to be the birthing room.
:*With your Gift, you might draw the midwife back to
consciousness or stabilize her enough that a Healer isn't
necessary. I can't do that.*:

Either Martin saw the wisdom in Judaia's words, or
he simply bowed to his promise. Eyes locked on the
approaching building, he did not bother to reply.

As the Companions' silver hooves rang over stone and
earth, a few members of the crowd glanced over. These
nudged more, until every eye eventually turned toward
the Heralds. A mass of voices rose in question, conversation, or attempts to inform, the whole blending into a
din Judaia did not bother to decipher. Some slunk away,
whispering among themselves. Judaia knew that many
of the Border Holdings considered Heraldic Gifts unholy
or the work of demons.

Judaia and Martin dismounted together, leaving the
Companions to tend themselves beyond the crowd. Ignoring the huddled mass of comments, Judaia pushed
through, the citizens parting to allow a path for the Heralds to get to the doorway.

The midwife sprawled just outside the door; apparently they had taken her from the crisis but feared to
move her far in her current state. Two men and a
woman hunched over her. These moved gratefully aside
as the Heralds came forward. "Head wound," one said
unnecessarily. "Can you help her?"

Martin replied. "If I can't, I can get her to help
quickly." He gestured Tirithran vaguely, then inclined
his head to indicate that Judaia should take care of the
problem inside.

Judaia reached for the portal, apprehension finally descending upon her as she tripped the latch. In the heat
of defending her need to judge, she had found no time
for self-doubt. Now finally on her own, consideration of
her weaknesses came unbidden. She had only the experience of watching Martin when it came to justice. Her
Gift of Sight would help her little here; it would take a
Communication Gift to delve into the complications of
situation and intention. Unlike Martin, Judaia could cast

only the first half of the Truth Spell; she could tell when a subject lied but could not force honesty the way he and the more strongly Gifted could. She would have to rely only on the first stage and on her own instincts, and the price for a mistake might prove the breaking of family and the severing of a bond between mother and child.

Too quickly, the door swung open. Again, Judaia saw two women arguing heatedly, their screams drowning one another's words so that the Herald could understand only a few broken phrases. The one nearest the door looked robust, her brown hair neatly combed despite the turmoil of childbirth. The other had curly locks hacked short, a hint of russet amid the darker strands. A naked baby boy curled, asleep, in the straw, clearly the object of their dispute. It pleased Judaia that they had taken care not to let their blows go wild enough to squash or harm the child. Against the far wall, a third female, more girl than woman, cradled another infant. The two still-born lay in a corner near the door.

"Stop!" Judaia said. Though she did not shout, the authority in her voice silenced the women. She seized on the hush. "My name is Herald Judaia, and I was sent to settle this dispute."

"The boy is mine!" the curly-haired one shouted.

"Liar!" The other lunged toward her, fist cocked to strike.

Judaia snatched the descending wrist in midair, wrenching the woman around to face her. "Rule one, no fighting." She hurled the arm away, and the woman staggered several steps. All three fixed their gazes on Judaia, the would-be attacker glaring. "Rule two, no one speaks unless questioned by me. You may call me Herald. Politeness has never displeased me." Judaia studied the women, guessing she would get the most unbiased story from the satisfied observer. "You there." She faced the quiet woman against the wall.

"Me, ma'am?" The youngster shook back mousy looks, keeping a firm grip on the baby that supported its head. She rose.

"What's your name?"

"Lindra, ma'am. Thirdwife of Salaman." She avoided Judaia's eyes, keeping her gaze low, at the level of the Herald's mouth.

"Is this your first baby?" Judaia hoped Lindra would answer in the affirmative. She seemed no older than fifteen, and Judaia hated to think the Holderkin stressed their women any younger.

"First live baby. Yes, ma'am." Apparently Lindra finally absorbed Judaia's words, for she corrected. "I mean, yes, Herald. I lost two others early."

"And you gave birth to the baby you're holding?"

"Oh, yes, ma'am . . . Herald. I'm certain of it."

The other two women fidgeted, obviously fighting the need to hold their tongues. Lindra's response bothered Judaia. The mention of certainty suggested exactly the opposite. A simple "yes" seemed far more natural, so Judaia prodded for details. "What do you remember?"

Now, Lindra met Judaia's gaze directly. When it came to defending her child, she could clearly gather the gumption and fire she otherwise lacked. "I carried twins, Herald. The first came out easy, but he was dead." She gestured the bodies in the corner, tears turning her muddy eyes moist. "She had to push around for the other. The stress of the first, and the pain . . ." She winced. "I fainted. I didn't actually see her take out my little girl, but I know she's mine, Herald. A mother can tell." She hugged the child closer.

The nearby fight stole all veracity from the latter statement, but Judaia let the observation lie. She saw no need to use the Truth Spell here. She had more obvious subjects for it.

The curly-haired woman had picked up the baby boy, clutching it with all the fierce tenderness that Lindra showed the girl. The other woman balled her fists, obedient to Judaia's rules though she clearly wanted to reclaim the child by violence.

Judaia placed a hand, both comforting and warning, on the woman's empty arms. "I speak for the Queen now. My decision here, no matter its end, will stand.

Who holds the baby while we speak will have no bearing on the judgment."

Judaia's words seemed to soothe the angered woman. Her fingers uncurled, and her manner softened. Still, the look she turned her curly-haired neighbor held venom.

Though she released her grip, Judaia kept her attention on the empty-armed Hold woman. "Speak your name."

"I am Keefhar, Firstwife of Kailer."

While the woman spoke, Judaia closed her eyes, focusing on the verse she would need to run through nine times. She pictured a fog with blue eyes, shaping the Truth Spell with a bent toward muting it. Gradually, a blue fog took shape about Keefhar's head and shoulders. As all subjects of the spell, she remained oblivious to it. Lindra seemed too fixated on the baby girl to notice. The third women squinted, rubbing her eyes, as if to blame the magical vapor on her own vision. Surely, none of them would have seen such a thing before nor known its purpose. "Keefhar," Judaia watched the blue fog closely. She had kept it sparse, which would make its comings and goings more difficult to evaluate. She relied upon her Sight to gauge the status of her spell. "Which baby did you bear?"

"The boy, Herald." Keefhar rolled her gaze to the infant nestled in the others' arms. The blue haze dispersed, indicating a lie. "The stillborn was hers." She jabbed a finger at the curly-haired woman. The fog returned, as bright as at its casting. About this, at least, she had spoken truth.

"She lies!" The woman indicated screamed.

Judaia dropped the Truth Spell, swiftly placing another on her only remaining witness. As weak as her power was, the double casting would cost her a nasty overuse headache, but she pressed aside consideration of consequences. She could tolerate pain as the price for a competent first judgment.

"The boy is mine!" the curly-haired woman shouted, the magical fog disappearing with her words. In her rage, the Hold woman discarded Judaia's rules as well as her request for manners. "The dead one is hers." Keeping one hand looped protectively around the boy, she used the other to gesture disdainfully at her accuser. The remnants of the Truth Spell did not return until after she finished speaking. Clearly, she had spoken all falsely.

Judaia imagined the crisp, blue eyes of the fog drawing closed, and the Truth Spell winked from existence. She kept her own eyes open and alert for movement, not trusting the women to remain at peace until she rendered her judgment. Her thoughts flew, bringing understanding of the cause of the argument and why the girl-child had been spared from the tug of war. The answer came with Martin's description: "Those people have a different idea of justice and a woman's place." Others had told her that the parents of girls paid dowries while a son's possessions and holdings remained his own. Since men married many times, a son brought wealth to a family, while daughters cost them dearly in wedding price.

The door opened, and Martin stepped inside. "The midwife will live—"

Judaia waved him silent before he could continue. The three Holderkin looked noticeably relieved, though whether glad for the midwife's health or for escape from the punishment that would have come with a charge of murder, she did not know or try to guess. She reached for the baby boy, and the curly-haired woman relinquished him with obvious reluctance. Keefhar smiled.

Judaia spoke. "In the name of the Queen, I make the following judgment: The baby girl shall remain with Lindra."

The women nodded, all apparently satisfied. Martin stiffened, but true to his word, he said nothing.

Judaia continued. "As to the baby boy . . ."

All eyes followed Judaia's every movement.

". . . he was born to Lindra and will remain with her." She handed the boy, too, to the youngest of the mothers.

Lindra smiled, cuddling the children, love making her dark eyes sparkle. "But I thought . . ." she started.

Judaia did not let her finish. "Many healthy babies are

born floppy and blue." With no further explanation, she left the birthing room to announce her decision to the elder whose slower pony should have arrived in the time it took to hear and judge. She left Martin to reinforce the finality of her decision. They would obey the word of a man in a way they never would a woman, even a Herald.

The ride from the Borderland Holding commenced in a silence far deeper than the previous one, but this time Martin seemed the more pensive of the two. He did not hum or sing, and his eyes remained fixed on the mound between Tirithran's ears.

Scarcely able to suppress a smile, Judaia waited for Martin's inevitable assessment of her work. It did not come. In fact, neither Herald passed a word until Martin drew rein in a quiet clearing alongside the beaten track. He dismounted there, removing the bitless bridle and bells from Tirithran's head. Judaia joined him, releasing Brayth as well. The Companions grazed on the boughs and underbrush while Martin prepared a meal in the same thoughtful hush he had assumed throughout the ride.

Finally, Martin broke the silence. "I spoke in private with the midwife."

Judaia leaned against a thick, rough-barked oak, nodding encouragement for him to continue.

"You gave only one of those babies to its rightful mother."

Judaia nodded. "Lindra bore the boy. The girl was Keefhar's baby."

Martin stared. "You knew?"

"Of course, I knew." Judaia met Martin's green-gray stare that appeared even more muddled than usual. Familiarity made the eyes beautiful, despite their indeterminate color. Guilt twinged through Judaia for the pain his silence must have caused him in the birthing room; he alone could have reversed her decision. But he had promised not to interfere with her judgment, and his honor had held him to that vow as strongly as to the other.

Martin seemed incapable of blinking. "You intentionally gave a baby to the wrong mother? Are you insane?"

"Maybe." Judaia plucked at the bark beneath her fingers, studying the fragments she pulled loose. "If you find considering the welfare of the children insane. Having a womb doesn't make a good or worthy mother. Bloodline isn't enough. No one, Martin, *no one* can grow in the hands of a liar or in a home without honesty, loyalty, and trust. As far as I'm concerned, Keefhar gave up her right to motherhood when she knowingly traded her child for another." Once again, Judaia met Martin's eyes, and she did not blink either. "Sometimes, Herald Martin . . ." She grinned. ". . . sometimes what's right is more important than the truth or any vow. Sometimes justice over honor."

Martin considered the words for some time. Gradually, his lips framed a smile, and he pulled Judaia into a friendly embrace that might become so much more. And all the awkwardness, at least, was gone.

A Song For No One's Mourning

by *Gary A. Braunbeck*

Gary A. Braunbeck has sold over 60 short stories to
various mystery, suspense, science fiction, fantasy,
and horror markets. His latest fiction also appears in
Future Net and *Careless Whispers*. His first story collection, *Things Left Behind,* is scheduled for hard-
cover release this year. He has been a full-time writer
since 1992 and lives in Columbus, Ohio.

1

Sweat ran down the young man's back and his ankle
hurt severely—he'd leaped from the window on impulse
and landed badly after the scullery maid discovered him
in the master's private chamber. She had simply opened
the door and walked in, her servant's eyes taking in everything—the bags of silver coins clutched in his hands,
the portrait set haphazardly on the floor, the exposed
secret cache in the wall, the broken-locked, opened lid
of the master's money box—before she thought to shout
an alarm to the others in the manor-keep, but by then
the young man had tossed a chair through the stained
glass window, perched himself there like a raven for only
a moment before hearing other loud voices and footsteps
thundering toward the room, then jumped. Though careful to bend his knees, the impact was nonetheless painful. It was a miracle he'd to made it to his horse without
losing more of the money, but make it to his horse he
did, and Ranyart—as fierce and strong a horse as ever
the young man knew—galloped swiftly away from the
manor, through the streets, past the city gates where the

guards and armsmen in the towers, too busy with their own private Harvestfest celebrations, were neither able to take up their crossbows nor lower the gate in time to stop him. He hoped they heard his laughter as Ranyart carried him away into the darkness of the forest road.

That had been several candlemarks ago, and now both ~~he and Ranyart were weary from the chase—and the~~ armsmen *had* given chase for a while before he lost them near the Westmark Hills. He was glad he had been alone this time, claiming to be a simple minstrel who wished only to entertain with song in exchange for a warm fire and a good meal; not only had his being alone enabled him to flee quickly without having to make excuses to anyone in whose company he might have been seen, but had such a disaster occurred while he was with a troupe, the other members would now be suffering for his actions.

And isn't that always the way, Father, he thought. *Whenever the rich find they've been bested by one of a "lower" heritage, they vent their wrath on others whom they deem undeserving of mercy, or kindness or understanding, let alone a chance to prove their innocence—and forget about individual worth; in the eyes of the rich, we are all the same: valueless fodder, so much human flotsam for them to treat with as much disregard or contempt as they please. I remember the way Lord Withen Ashkevron of Forst Reach treated you after those damned Herald-mages from Haven showed him what a Gifted one could do with metalworking. I remember how the bastards all laughed at you, and you were a good enough man to pretend you didn't hear the laughter or see the smirks. But did any of the gentry, any of the courtiers ever bring their trade to you again after that? No. Gods, how they killed your spirit. Half my life you've been dead, and I miss you no less now than I did on the day Mother and I had to watch the gravediggers toss your body in that foul, disgraceful hole. Damn them! Damn then all!*

The young man's name was Olias, a thief who secretly possessed a meager measure of both the Bardic and Heraldic Gifts. Often in his travels, when both money and food were running low, he would insinuate himself into the good graces of various traveling minstrel troupes, enchanting them with his storytelling and enviable abilities on the lute, rebec, and cornemuse (his fiddle- and pipe and tabor-playing, though not offensive to the untrained ear, left something to be desired in his opinion); inevitably, the leader of the troupe would invite him to travel and perform with them, which Olias was more than pleased to do, accompanying them from city to village to hamlet and hollow, playing for lords and ladies and peasants alike. Since he never wished to endanger the members of the troupes (who were always kind to him, despite their typically desperate circumstances), he took care to ensure his thievery would appear to be the act of someone with whom the victim was familiar. It seemed that every merchant and nobleman possessed their fair share of enemies, and it was surprisingly easy to discover who among them was the most envied or despised—as well as the names of those who harbored resentment—and thus lay the groundwork for his deception. Sometimes it was as simple as placing a few stolen coins outside the doorstep of his chosen scapegoat (always another member of the gentry or a successful tradesman, never one of the poor), making it appear that they, in their haste, had dropped some of their ill-gotten treasure as they ran from the sight of their crime; occasionally he would have to resort to more complex methods of duplicity in order to avert suspicion from himself or the other players—employing his mild Gift of Thought-sending to plant misgivings in others' minds—but the effect was always the same: None had ever accused him or any member of his temporary troupe of the robberies.

For Olias—lonely, angry, bitter, and distrustful—it was a good life.

Good enough.

The road he now found himself traveling was little more than a rutted tract of hard-packed dirt meandering through a skeletal tunnel of near-barren tree branches. This Harvest had been an usually cold one, and the trees, sensing this, chose to slumber earlier than many

of the people in Valdemar were accustomed to. Tendrils
of mist snaked from between the trees and lay across
the road like a blanket of living snow, shifting, curling,
reaching upward to ensnarl Ranyart's legs for only a
moment before dissolving into nothingness. Overhead,
the moonlight straggled through the branches, creating
diffuse columns of foggy light that to Olias' frayed
nerves became fingers of foggy light from a giant ghostly
hand that at any moment would fist together and crush
him. He was aware, as if in deep nightmare, of shadows
following along from either side of the road—silent, misshapen things, spiriting along with the mist for furlongs
until he snapped his head toward them. Then they would
disappear in slow degrees, mocking his anxiety, melting
back into the darker, unexplored areas of the night-silent
forest. These shadows called to mind far too many campfire tales and old wives' stories of the outKingdom and
the Pelagirs, with its uncanny creatures—which was not
all that far from here.

Unhooking his armed crossbow from its saddle-catch
(were some of those shadows moving even *closer*?), the
young man wiped the sweat from out of his eyes, then
leaned forward and whispered in Ranyart's ear. "I can't
speak for you, old friend, but I don't much care for this
stretch of road. I know that you're tired, but I promise
you that if you'll just quicken your pace and get us the
hell out of here, the small bag of sugar I have in my
pouch is yours."

In answer, Ranyart broke from his amble into a trot,
then a gallop, and soon they passed through a clearing
to emerge on a more inviting expanse of road where the
trees and mist and shadows were at a comforting distance, and the moonlight shone all around, crisp and
cold and clean, forming no phantom fingers.

But there was in the air a strong stench of burned
wood and straw, of fire-scorched stone and something
more; an odd, thick, sickly-sweet aroma that—though it
was not so mighty as to overpower the other smells—
seemed to be inexorably entwined with all the others.

Ranyart chuffed, shaking his foam-streaked head.

"I know," replied the young man, wrinkling his nose. "But we're both too tired to go any farther tonight, and there *is* a mild wind blowing against us; at least *that* makes the stink less offensive. We'll stop here until dawn and hope that the wind continues to blow in our favor."

Beneath him, the muscles in Ranyart's back rippled, as if the horse were shrugging its reluctant consent.

"Good. Then it's settled."

They made camp quickly, Olias taking care to find a nearby stream so Ranyart could quench his thirst, then turning his attention to building a fire and killing a pair of squirrels for this night's meal. He arranged his ground-bedding under an imposing old sorrow tree (thus called because its like, rare in these parts, was usually found in the distant Forest of Sorrows), then lay the crossbow within easy reach before attaching his dagger sheath to his uninjured ankle. As a further precaution, he slipped a small stonecarver's blade beneath his sorry excuse for a pillow, then removed the sugar from his pouch and gave it to Ranyart, almost smiling as he watched his horse devour the brilliant-white chunks.

When Ranyart had finished, he stared at Olias as if to ask, *Is that all?*

"I'm afraid there's none left, old friend. You'd think after all these years, you would have learned a little moderation."

Ranyart snorted once, loudly, then threw back his head as if quite insulted, and stalked off to the side of the road where he settled himself for the night.

"I'll remember this when you come begging for your morning oats."

Ranyart snorted again, but this time less indignantly—perhaps even with a touch of humility.

"You'll not charm me," said Olias. "I've known you far too long to—"

The rest of it died in his throat when he heard the sound of approaching hoofbeats, coming hard and fast from somewhere down the ghostly road he'd left behind not half a candlemark ago.

The back of Olias' neck prickled and his heart pounded against his rib cage.

Somehow, the armsmen had found his trail.

2

"*Hell to Havens!*" he hissed, throwing aside his blanket and grabbing up his crossbow, then rolling quickly to the right where a small, downward-sloped patch of land created a furrow just big enough for a man to hide himself. It was only after he was in position that he realized the sound was that of a *single* horse, carrying a single rider (a sound he'd trained himself to recognize). Perhaps one of the armsmen, in an attempt to prove himself to the others, had stubbornly pursued him this far.

Olias looked at the crossbow in his grip, and at the deadly, sharp, shiny silver tip of the arrow.

No. He wouldn't hurt this armsman, not in a way that could either kill him or cripple him for life.

He held his breath, listening to the near-frantic hoofbeats getting closer, and was wrenched from his concentration when the campfire hissed, then snapped loudly, spitting sparks upward, a few of which danced out into the center of the road, all but announcing his presence.

A careless fool's mistake, not dousing the flames.

No time to worry about that now.

Pushing forward on his knees and biting down on his lower lip to fight against the screaming pain of his wounded ankle, Olias scrabbled on his belly like an insect up toward the campsite and grabbed the quiver, slinging it over his shoulder and its strap across his chest, then Sent a silent call to Ranyart, who was at his side in moments, bending low the bulk of his massive body so Olias could snatch a coil of rope from one of the saddle hooks. Craning to see if the rider was yet in sight, Olias quickly disarmed the crossbow, slipping the silver-tipped arrow into the quiver and removing a grapnel arrow in its stead. Tying one end of the rope to its stem, he loaded the grapnel arrow into the crossbow and re-armed the firing mechanism. That done, he took a deep breath, rolled twice to the left, came up on his elbows, aimed at a large stone near the base of a tree across the road, and fired.

The grapnel caught solidly, and from the middle of the road it would be well-nigh impossible to see it unless one were specifically looking for such a thing, which the armsman most likely would not be, for—gods willing—he *must be* as tired as those he was pursuing.

Olias wound the remainder of the rope around his right wrist, making certain that the portion lying across the road was flat in the dirt and would not be seen until rider and horse were right on top of it, and by then it would be too late.

Slipping back down into the cramped furrow, Olias held his breath as the hoofbeats grew louder, closer, somewhat less fierce and slightly slower than before; he wondered why the armsman wasn't digging heels into the horse, forcing speed.

Still, it was running swiftly enough that the rope, when he yanked it taut, should trip the horse and cause it to throw its rider without permanently harming either of them.

The horse's hooves clattered against some stones embedded in the hard-packed ground as it bolted from the forest and neared the campsite. Olias grasped the rope with both hands now, winding it once around his left wrist and threading it through his grip, then rose to his knees and readied himself to pull—

—when the horse, nearly upon the trap, stopped dead in its tracks, hooves sparking against stones, one front leg in the air and bent at the knee—an almost absurd image, as if some wizard had frozen the beast in mid-motion—then slowly, mist jetting from its nostrils, began cantering backward.

The armsman had spotted the trap. *Damn!*

Disentwining his wrists from the rope as quickly as he was able, Olias pulled another silver-tipped arrow from the quiver and armed the crossbow, then struggled to

his feet (*Gods,* the pain in his ankle was agonizing!) and
limped into the road, taking aim at the rider.

"Let me see your hands, armsman, and may the gods
help you if—"

For the second time that night, the words died in his
throat.

The boy who sat upon the horse was no armsman; he
barely looked human. Even from this distance it was
obvious to Olias that the boy had been the victim of a
brutal beating. Most of his face and chest was covered
in blood and wounds, his lower lip looked to have been
half-sliced away by a knife's blade, and one side of his
face was so horribly swollen that neither his eye nor part
of his nose could be seen.

Olias snapped the crossbow to his side, pointing the
arrow toward the ground, and moved slowly forward,
one hand extended in a gesture of peace so as not to
alarm the horse.

It was only as he came up beside the gray mare that
he saw the rest.

"*Gods,*" he whispered. "*Who did this to you, boy?*"

The rider made no reply.

Not only had the boy been beaten, not only had he
been cut and thrashed and (judging by some of the
marks across his exposed stomach) whipped until nearly
dead, but someone had burned him, as well. Clumps of
ugly, flame-seared hair—looking more like pig's-bed
straw than anything that should be part of a human being's body—hung limply from the boy's head, made all
the more hideous by the contrast of its color against that
of the sickening, glistening, crimson-raw sections where
his scalp had been either sheared, pulled, or burned
away from his skull.

Olias swallowed. Twice. Hard and loudly.

Over the years since his father's death, Olias had
worked feverishly toward hardening himself against others' pain and misfortune. None had offered any comfort
or sympathy to Father in his time of need—nor to himself or his mother after Father's death—so he vowed
that none, no matter how pathetic, dire, or horrifying

their circumstances, would ever touch him that deeply again.

The next thought he blamed on weariness, for this boy whom he had mistaken for an armsman nearly reached into his core to wrest some small measure of tenderness ... but Olias, well-practiced in this particular art of self-defense, was able to quash the moment of vulnerability by concentrating on the skill that had gone into securing the boy to his horse.

His hands had been bound tightly together at the wrists and the bindings tied to the pommel of the saddle; there were no stirrup irons but the stirrup leathers had been left in place, used to tie the boy's calves to the saddle itself; he was belted thrice, two times at the waist—once to the pommel, once to the high cantle, using rings on the saddle meant for that purpose—and a third time around his neck. It was this last that threatened to move something buried deep in Olias' heart, for the opposite end of the leather strap had been split in two and each of the ends tied to the boy's ankles, as if he were a hog being bound for slaughter.

Olias leaned closer, sniffing the leather.

Beneath the coppery scent of blood and the charred aroma of flames and smoke, the scent of drenched hide drying was unmistakable. Whoever had bound the boy to this horse had soaked the leather straps, knowing damned well that as it dried it would shrink, tightening itself around the boy's neck and slowly crushing his throat.

Why didn't you just kill him? thought Olias. *What did this boy—barely a boy, more child than boy—what did he do that was so unspeakable as to warrant this kind of sick-making punishment, this . . . torture?*

Olias was still lost along such paths of thought when the boy turned his head downward—as much as the strap would allow him to—and opened his undamaged eye, which was so startlingly silver Olias felt a moment of awe tinged with fear.

"Ffrind-iau?" choked the boy. *"Caredig ffrind-iau?"*

Olias puzzled over the words. He'd traveled far

through Valdemar, and had (or so he thought) encountered all of its various languages—after all, Valdemar
was a patchwork quilt of a dozen different peoples es-
caping from a dozen different unbearable situations, and
each of them had their own unique tongue which naturally would undergo changes as the various clans began
to intermingle, but this boy was speaking in a language
Olias had never heard before. It might have been some
kind of primitive hybrid of Tayledras—Hawkbrother
tongue (some of the inflections were similar)—but he
doubted it; Hawkbrother tongue didn't have so many
guttural clicks, nor was it nearly as *musical* as this boy's
language. Under other circumstances, he probably
wouldn't have cared at all.

But despite his defenses, despite his not understanding
the words themselves, Olias Felt the pain and loneliness
and fear in the boy's plea.

He unsheathed his dagger and set about cutting the
straps, then lifted the boy (who was much, *much* larger
than he first appeared) from off the horse—and nearly
collapsed to the ground when the extra weight caused
the bones in his wounded ankle to snap.

:Ranyart!: Olias Called, trying to balance himself on
his other leg.

Ranyart ran up beside him. Olias managed to drape
the boy over Ranyart's saddle, then guided both horses
over to the campsite where he promptly collapsed to
the ground, clutching at his broken ankle and snarling
with pain.

The boy lifted his head, then pushed himself up and
slid slowly from Ranyart's back and stumbled over to
Olias.

"*Poen?*" he asked, gently placing one of his scarred
and bloody hands on Olias's ankle "*Cymorth poen?*"

"*Don't touch it!*" shouted Olias, throwing back his
head and wincing. "*Gods,* please . . . please don't! I—"

The boy closed his good eye, then tightened his grip.
A strange bluish glow appeared under the boy's hand,
quickly spilling outward to encircle Olias' ankle. And
before he could further protest or strike out at the boy,

Olias felt the broken bones and tendons instantly, pain-
lessly mend themselves. Moments later the boy helped
him to his feet and Olias was dumbstruck; the ankle was
fine. The boy had healed him.

Looking up, he watched as the boy set to work on his
own wounds, the same bluish light emanating from his
hands as he touched first his head, then face, lip, throat,
chest, and legs, finally grasping each wrist in turn to re-
move the bruises and strap burns. Each time his hands
brushed over a different area, more of his body glowed
with a shimmering soft blue light until, for a moment at
the end, he was encased in a spectral luminance; but in
an instant the light dissolved into his flesh and he stood
there, just a boy, far too large for his age but looking
healthy and unharmed . . . and least outwardly. Only
time would tell how much damage had been done to the
boy's mind and spirit by whatever filthy, sadistic cowards
had unleashed their brutality on him.

No wonder they tied your hands so tightly, thought
Olias. *They couldn't chance your healing yourself before
the horse had carried you far away from them . . . that
is, if they even* knew *about your healing powers. Were
they afraid of something else, odd one? Were they aware
of your powers, at all? Damn! What does it matter and
why should I care?*

Still, the thought persisted: Why hadn't they just killed
him? Didn't it occur to anyone that some other traveler
might chance upon the boy and set him free? Wouldn't
they know if that were to happen, the boy might come
back to seek vengeance?

The boy lifted his cherubic, smiling face to Olias.

Gods, thought Olias, feeling almost silly: *That* was not
the face of one who would go seeking vengeance.

"Th–thank you," said Olias, pointing down toward his
ankle. "It feels . . . feels fine. It feels *wonderful,* in fact."

The boy, his piercing, hypnotic silver gaze never wandering from Olias's eyes, simply smiled more widely and
nodded his head.

"What's your name, child? *Have* you a name?"

The boy cocked his head to the side, the expression on his face puzzled.

Sighing, Olias stood up straight and patted his own chest with both hands. "*Olias*. I am *Olias*." He pointed at the boy. "What's *your* name?"

The boy grinned, then stood up straight, patting his chest with both hands, and said, quite loudly, "*Olias!*"

Olias groaned, shaking his head. "No, no, no! *I* am Olias. *Me*. That's *my* name!" He pointed at the boy once again and raised his eyebrows in silent question.

The boy looked at him, opened his mouth to speak but didn't, then snapped up his head, eyes widening with understanding as he pointed to his chest and shouted, "*L'lewythi!*" Pressing his hand against Olias's chest, the boy whispered, somewhat hesitantly: "*Ffrind-iau. Chi, ti L'lewythi's ffrind-iau, ydhuch?*"

"Um . . . yes," replied Olias, nodding his head (for some reason, he sensed it was important to agree with the boy at this moment). "Yes, of course. *L'lewythi's ffrind-iau.*"

L'lewythi laughed, then embraced Olias (nearly crushing his rib cage—*gods,* the child was strong!), patting his back several times in a gesture of thanks and affection.

"You're . . . you're welcome. I think," responded Olias, pulling himself away from the boy and checking himself for internal bleeding, then pointing toward the fire where the squirrel-meat was roasting on a spit over the flames. "Are you hungry?"

The boy furrowed his brow in confusion, obviously no more familiar with Olias' language than Olias was with his.

Sighing, Olias rubbed a hand over his own stomach. "Hungry? Do you want something to eat?"

The boy tilted his head to the side, then shrugged.

His frustration growing, Olias took a calming breath and said, "*Rwy'n mynd I gael cinio. Gobeithio mai ty-wydd braf gawn ni?*"

Then gasped and promptly covered his mouth with his hand as the boy made a delighted sound, licked his lips, rubbed his stomach, and nodded vigorously.

Did I just invite him to join me in his own tongue? How in Havens could I do that—I've never heard this language before in my life!

The boy, perhaps sensing the other's confusion, touched a finger to his own mouth, then his head, then pointed toward Olias.

"You made me do that, didn't you? You . . . you *gave* your language to me for that moment, didn't you?"

"Ydhuch! L'lewythi cymorth ffrind-iau." He made his way toward the campfire. *"Bwuq!"* he said, laughing as he pointed to the roasting squirrels.

"Y–yes," stammered Olias. *"Bwuq."* It seemed that was the boy's word for *food*.

He proved himself to be a most pleasant and courteous meal companion, not taking more than his share of food and making sure that Olias had all that he wanted. Though there had been only two squirrels, it seemed to Olias that the layers of delicious meat on their carcasses were enough to have come from ten squirrels.

A candlemark later, when both Olias and L'lewythi were so full they couldn't eat another bite, it still looked as if they had barely touched the food.

Adding more wood to the fire, then crawling into his ground-bedding, Olias looked at L'lewythi and said (in his own language), "I don't know where you came from or what, exactly, you are, but I'm almost glad for your company—and believe me, I've not said *that* to another human being in a long, long while. You're welcome to stay here with Ranyart and me for the night."

The boy snuggled up against one of the trees, folded his hands in his lap, and leaned back his head . . . but did not—or *would not*, it appeared—close his eyes.

"I guess that means you're happy to accept the invitation," whispered Olias under his breath, then lay back, lute in hands, and strummed an old tune while staring up at the clear, starry night.

From time to time, Olias would chance a quick glance at his guest, and always the boy seemed to be fighting against falling asleep.

Why do you not wish to rest? thought Olias. *Are you*

frightened that your dreams will force you to relive what they did to you? Or is it something else, something you cannot express to me so that I'll understand?

He held his breath, momentarily opening his senses to the night as the wind changed direction and the stench of fire, smoke, and destruction grew stronger.

Out there, somewhere in the night, a great violence had taken place. Olias was able to Feel the lingering resonance of the destruction and brutality . . . and unspeakable terror. Closing his eyes and focusing on the sentient threads, he Sensed the presence of something powerful in slumber, something Otherworldly—no, not Otherworldly at all, but something that came from beyond the Otherworld, something he couldn't quite grasp and bring forward so that he might See and Understand.

Whatever it was, it was beyond any power he'd ever encountered, and somehow it was connected to this boy.

What are you, my strange lostling . . . and what did you do to deserve such a fate?

Then: *You're nothing to me, so why should I care? Each of us must deal alone with our demons. Don't count on anyone's help, lostling, because you'll not get it. Tonight you were lucky, but as far as I am concerned, come the dawn you are on your own.*

As if he had both heard and comprehended Olias' private musings, L'lewythi's face shadowed for an instant with a soul-sick hurt that made him look even more helpless and pathetic and so very, very sad.

Lest that look reach into his heart, Olias turned his face away, returning his attention to his lute.

Alone, lostling, we are all alone, from cradle to grave. Don't share your pain with me; I don't want to see it.

3

After a while—and without his being aware of it—Olias had begun to play "My Lady's Eyes", a sentimental song and one that he had always thought to be so much drivel, but it allowed a minstrel to show off his fingering. It had been his parents' favorite song. They had danced to it at their wedding.

Unexpectedly, Olias felt his throat tightening as unwanted tears began to form in his eyes. Swallowing back the emotions that were trying to surge to the surface, he laid the lute aside and forced himself to think of his blunder earlier tonight in allowing the scullery maid to panic him. He *could* have easily gotten past her and the others. After all, he'd taken time to walk through the manor-keep and decide upon his escape route, but for some reason, being discovered like that had unnerved him, and that had never happened before. What did it matter, though? That fat, arrogant, disgusting slug the servants called *m'Lord* was a lot poorer now than he'd been before allowing the minstrel into his home. Though Olias doubted the man would remain poorer for very long, he at least had the satisfaction of knowing that the bastard was stewing in his own juices tonight, cursing everyone and everything because he had been taken in by a common thief.

He sat up, rummaging around for the bottle of wine, and took three deep swallows, then looked over at his companion.

L'lewythi, looking exhausted and desperately in need of sleep, was still awake and staring at Olias, his face betraying his concern.

Olias began speaking to the boy; he couldn't stop himself. It was as if the spirits wandering this Sovvan-night were *forcing* him to talk.

"I was thinking about—" *No, best not tell him what you were* just this moment *thinking about. After all, a thief is a thief in any clan.*

"I was thinking about my parents. My mother was employed as an apprentice-seamstress at the manor-keep of Lord Withen Ashkevron of Forst Reach. My father was the village metalworker and blacksmith. I remember . . . I know this may sound odd to you— assuming you understand a word I'm saying—but of all things, I remember his hands the best. They were so large and powerful that when I was a child, I imagined that I could curl up in either of his palms and sleep there. They were rough hands, hard-callused and scarred, but his touch against my cheek was as gentle as angel's breath. I remember the way he would come home after a day's labors and scrub those hands until I thought he would scrape the flesh right off of them, and whenever my mother would say to him, 'Why do you wash so angrily?' he would show her one of his sad half-grins and say, 'It won't do for you to be touched by anything so dirty and hard,' and my mother would *laugh* . . . oh, gods, I miss hearing her laugh. If my father's hand so lightly against my cheek was the touch of angel's breath, then my mother's laugh was their song. And the love in their eyes whenever they would look at each other. . . .

"Neither of them were Gifted in any way; they weren't what I suppose you'd call particularly bright. They weren't educated, but they were good people, *fine* people, decent and honest and loyal. Don't misunderstand, each had their faults—Mother was often a little too worrisome, which annoyed Father no end, and *he,* gods bless him, could never seem to pay attention to anything besides his work for very long—conversations with him were a test of your patience, trust me—the man didn't know *how* to listen, and at times he and Mother argued over my upbringing and how to manage their money well enough to keep the creditors at bay . . . but they made certain that neither of them ever went to bed angry at the other. I once asked my mother why, and she told me that Father had this fear that were they to go to bed angry, one of them might die during the night and the survivor would be left with unanswered questions and unresolved regrets. I used to think that was funny until Mother told me that my father had once exchanged harsh words with *his* father, then stormed out of the house only to return the next morning and find that the old man had died in his sleep. 'He never got the chance to apologize,' she said to me. 'He never got to take it back. He's carried that sorrow with him for many years, and he wants to make sure that none of us ever has to face that.' " Olias, shaking his head, snorted a humorless laugh. "I always wondered why I never saw him really *smile*. I don't think he felt he *deserved* to smile, not after what happened with his father.

"Mother understood that about him, and she accepted it as best she was able, and did everything she could to give his heart some small measure of . . . of peace. Theirs was perhaps the most loving marriage I have ever seen.

"Then one day some Herald-Mage-trainees came to Forst Reach with Lord Withen Ashkevron's sister Savil. I found Savil herself to be a remarkably kind and pleasant woman, but some of her trainees . . . bah!—a more self-centered, arrogant bunch of brats I hope I never see!"

Absentmindedly, Olias picked up a nearby stick and began tapping it against the neck of his lute. "Among those Savil brought with her was a young man named Gwanwyn, who took great delight in amazing the courtiers with his metalworking prowess—and as much as I hate admitting it, his skill *was* impressive. Lord Ashkevron was suitably amazed that he called for a contest between Gwanwyn and my father. 'I wish for a new sword,' he said. 'One to rival even my armsmen's finest blades.' Until that night, my father had fashioned most of the swords used by Lord Ashkevron's soldiers, so few doubted that he would prevail. The only rule was that Gwanwyn *could not* employ any magic during the competition.

"I remember all the people. I was very young, so maybe there weren't as many as it seemed, but to my eyes half of Valdemar turned out for the contest. My father—he'd never been comfortable in large crowds—was nervous as a boy calling on his love for the first time, but Mother . . . Mother eased his anxiety as well she could, telling him that no matter the outcome, she would always love him. Dear, sweet, silly woman . . . as if love could be enough.

"I'm not sure how it happened, but I'm certain Gwanwyn cheated—he *must* have! He bested my father's efforts by more than half a candlemark—*no one* could have fashioned a blade that quickly *without* the use of magic, it just wasn't possible. Toward the end, when he began to realize that Gwanwyn was winning, my father became careless, and pulled his blade from the fire before it was ready for the hammer, and the first strike snapped the metal in two. He'd never made that mistake before, and I saw him die inside at the sight of those two halves lying on the ground before him.

"The people watching all laughed. *Gods,* I remember their laughter. It was such an ugly sound. Until that moment, I'd never realized that people you called 'neighbor,' people you called 'friend,' could take such delight in your disgrace. Only the Heralds were silent. My father was not a small man—he was perhaps one of the tallest men in the city—but I could see him shrink under the weight of that ugly laughter.

"When he walked away that day, he was looking at the ground. I don't believe I ever saw him look up again. They broke his heart and crippled his spirit. After that day, none of the gentry ever brought their business to him again. By the time he died, he'd been reduced to taking groom duties at one of the local stables. He never spoke much, except to thank the stable-master for his position. Of all the pains that he had to endure toward the end, the worst of it—though he would never say it aloud—was the way people looked at him. With such . . . pity. Distaste and pity.

"Mother died shortly after we buried Father. The grief and loneliness was too much for her. I tried, the gods know how I tried, to fill the void left in her life by Father's death. I would play for her at night—I'd always had a talent for music—but every song reminded her of Father. There is some grief you never recover from, I guess.

"I took to thieving shortly before she died. She'd become very ill and I knew she didn't have long left, and I was *damned* if her body was going to be tossed into a pauper's grave like my father's. I managed to steal enough to pay for a proper grave and marker, but I hadn't enough for a new grave for my father. To this day his body still lies in that pauper's field, and enough time has gone by that—though I can easily raise the price asked by the grave-diggers—I have . . . forgotten the exact location of the spot where his body was buried. I can't help but think that his spirit must be saddened by that, for I know how much he wanted to rest by Mother's side."

He picked up the lute and stared at it. "I will never forgive any of the gentry, any of the wealthy or the high-born for what they did to my parents. Never. They think they are so far above the rest of us, safe in their mansions. They are all the same in my eyes, and I in theirs—who am I, after all? To them? No one. Well, damn them all to hell, I say! I'll take from them what was denied my parents in life, and I'll do with the money as I please. If I wish to spend it on food and drink and the price of a woman in my bed, so be it. If I choose to give it away to beggars in the street, then *that* is what I'll do! And may the gods pity anyone who dares to try and stop me!" He angrily strummed the lute. "And someday, I swear, I'll make Lord Withen Ashkevron suffer for his betrayal of my father, and then I'll find Gwanwyn and I'll kill him. Slowly, so that he'll know the pain my parents suffered because of his pride." He strummed the lute once again, coldly and calmly, then lay the instrument aside lest he damage it in his anger.

He looked toward L'lewythi. "Damn you, as well, lost-ling. What is it about you that causes me to speak in an unknown tongue? What is it that made me want to tell these things to you?"

L'lewythi only stared in silence, looking more and more like some village idiot.

Olias groaned in frustration, then flipped onto his side, facing away from his guest.

Gods! At times like this I wish there were another place, another land, another world in another time where I could be rid of them all, where I wouldn't have to look upon the faces of Valdemar and see the ghost of my parents in everyone, in every place.

I wish. Gods, how I wish. . . .

4

He awakened sometime later to the sounds of rustling, and immediately drew his dagger from his ankle sheath and whipped around, brandishing the weapon.

L'lewythi was standing by the tree, his eyes closed, his arms outstretched, the fingers of his hands extending outward, then curling toward him as if he were beckoning someone.

Olias watched dumbstruck as threads of thin silver light danced around L'lewythi's fingertips, then reached out to encircle a small bundle attached to the back of L'lewythi's horse. The ropes holding the bundle in place untied themselves, the covering fell away, and the silver threads wound themselves around something that looked like a glass pipe—only this instrument was much larger than a pipe, easily the size of a man's forearm, tapered at one end and open at the other. Inside, the glass had been blown in such a way that several spheres, some larger than others, had formed along its length. The instrument rose from the horse, cradled in silver threads, and moved through the air to land gently in L'lewythi's grip. Smiling, the boy sat down once again and rubbed his hands against a small patch of ice near the base of the tree until the heat from his palms melted the ice sufficiently to wet his fingers. Laying the glass pipe across his knee, L'lewythi placed his fingers on the surface of the instrument. The spheres within began to revolve and whirl, some slower than others, some so fast they could barely be seen.

Olias couldn't tell how this was possible. The spheres were obviously part of the pipe, yet each moved as if independent of it.

L'lewythi began to finger the glass in much the same way harp players plucked at the taut strings of their instruments, but as he moved his fingers up and down the length of the pipe, each of the spheres glowed—not any single color, but all colors, one bleeding into the next until it was impossible to tell the difference between gold and red, red and gray, gray and blue, and with each burst of color and combinations of colors there came musical notes. The first was a lone, soft, sustained cry that floated above them on the wings of a dove, a mournful call that sang of foundered dreams and sorrowful partings and dusty, forgotten myths from ages long gone by, then progressively rose in pitch to strengthen this extraordinary melancholy with tinges of joy, wonder, and hope as the songs of the other spheres and colors joined it, becoming the sound of a million choral voices raised in worship to the gods, becoming music's fullest dimension, richest intention, whispering rest to Olias' weary heart as the light moved outward in waves and ripples, altering the landscape with every exalted refrain, voices a hundred times fuller than any human being's should ever be, pulsing, swirling, rising, then cascading over his body like pure crystal rain, and suddenly the rain, the music, was *inside* of him, assuming physical dimensions, forcing him to become more than he was, than he'd been, than he'd ever *dreamed* of becoming. Olias dropped down to one knee, the sound growing without and within him, and he was aware not only of the music and the colors and whirling spheres of glass but of every living thing that surrounded him—every weed, every insect, every glistening drop of dew on every blade of grass and every animal in deepest forest, and as the song continued rising in his soul, lavish, magnificent, and improbable, Olias Heard thoughts and Sensed dreams and Absorbed myriad impressions as they danced in the air, passing from spirit to mind to memory with compulsive speed and more sensory layers than he was able to comprehend, lifting everything toward a sublime awareness so acute, so alive, so incandescent and all-encompassing that he thought he might burst into flames for the blinding *want* underneath it all.

It was the closest thing to splendor he'd ever known.

L'lewythi lifted his hands from the pipe, but the music didn't immediately stop; instead, it faded away in degrees, one layer of sound absorbed into the next until, at the end, there was only the original note, pure and easy, sighing release like a breath rippling by.

Olias covered his face with his hands and took several deep breaths in an effort to still the pounding of his heart, then lifted his head and opened his eyes to daylight.

Daylight.

In a place he didn't recognize, barren of trees and bush. Ranyart was gone, as was L'lewythi's horse and the campsite, even the road.

"W–what . . . *what have you done?*" he croaked.

L'lewythi's only response was to smile, then turn and walk away, gesturing for Olias to follow.

The ground—mostly sun-browned mud covered in cracks—was much firmer than it appeared at first glance, though the terrain was far from level. They began ascending a hill and were met by a strong, steady wind soaring down, carrying with it the first stinging spatters of rain—yet the sky above was blue, the clearest Olias had ever seen.

He doubled his efforts to catch up with L'lewythi and continued climbing, blinking against the sea spray (not rain, after all) until the ground leveled off and he found himself standing at the top of a jagged overhang. Looking to each side, he was struck not only by the vast expanse of the cliffs upon which they were standing, but by their beauty, as well.

Silvery clouds rolled in above their heads, twirling and turning like banners in a breeze, moving quicker than any cloud formations Olias had ever seen, winding around one another and spinning in place. He opened his mouth to speak, and L'lewythi silenced him by placing a finger against his own lips. An odd noise caused Olias to shake his head: the sound of a million insects buzzing. Here atop the cliffs, the buzzing merged with the sounds of the sea and became clearer, more defined, not a buzz at all but the combined whispering of a million different voices speaking in as many tongues. Some were complex and excited, others low and monosyllabic, still others a combination of vaguely recognizable words that degenerated into animal clicks and whistling and yaps.

"What are those . . . those voices? Those sounds?" shouted Olias over the roar of the rushing waters below.

Again, L'lewythi raised a finger to his lips, then pointed out to sea.

The waters rumbled and churned, crashing against the base of the cliffs with the sound of shattering glass. The vibrations rocked upward through layers of stone and sand, shaking Olias to his bones.

Then, with stupendous force and thunderous volume, the spinning tower of silver clouds shot down into the sea, churning as it struck the surface and creating great, revolving waves of frothy spray before vanishing beneath the waters. The froth left in its wake formed a circle that spun around and around and around, its speed becoming frantic as it formed an ever-widening and deepening whirlpool.

The atmosphere crackled with power.

Olias covered his ears against the shrieking winds and watched as the whirlpool turned inside out, rising like a geyser. Atop the foaming fount appeared a shining white stallion with an opal mane, its front legs lifted high, heraldic, its belly the curve of the moon, the rest a silken fish scaled from chest to tail like a shower of silver coins.

The churning fount surged across the sea, the glorious creature riding the crest, its legs pumping, mane flowing in the wind. As it neared the cliffs, the fountain of water slowed and began to curve downward, the spray spinning off, lowering the creature until it hovered directly at the edge of the overhang.

Olias couldn't speak; the eyes of the creature demanded silence.

The creature threw back its head and opened its mouth. A soft, nearly imperceptible sound rose from deep in its chest, a clear, crisp *ping!* as if someone had flicked a finger against a crystal goblet. The sound—so much like the music L'lewythi had played earlier—grew in volume and, it seemed, even density, assuming a physical form invisible to the eye yet filling the air, enveloping Olias in a liquid-armor numbness, drugging him like a frosty sip from a Healer's herb cup but allowing him to maintain wakefulness as the geysering fount slowly shifted sideways, moving the creature until its face was inches from his own. The exalted sound, the wondrous lone crystal note sung in response to the call from L'lewythi's glass pipe, filled Olias' center, then suddenly split apart, becoming night stars that in turn became a symphony of musical notes even more unbearable in their purity than the music L'lewythi had created, and Olias realized that what he was hearing was the second verse to L'lewythi's song, a song of mourning, and rejoicing, a song meant for no one and everyone, but in that instant Olias chose to think of it as his, this chaste glory, this innocence, this music. A song for no one's mourning, sung only for him to honor the memory of his parents and all they had dreamed of. He hugged himself, dropping to his knees and rocking back and forth, the spuming foam covering him like lather. He was agonizingly aware of the swirling voices, the unknown languages shifting forward, dislodging themselves from his mind and themselves becoming tones. The first crystal note the creature had sung swam forward until it found its matching language-tone, and the two of them merged—a sharp sting in Olias' ears—and were translated—

—*"Pwy fydd yma ymhen can mlynedd?"*—

—into *his own* language—

—*"Who will be here in a hundred years?"*

Olias' torso shot straight up, his eyes staring into the unblinking golden disks of the creature's gaze.

"Gods," he whispered.

:*Greetings, Olias.:* said the creature. :*My name is Ylem. You should feel honored. L'lewythi doesn't bring many others to this place.:*

:*Where am I?:* asked Olias silently.

:*You are where you wished to be: another place, another world, another time. You are in a place that lies between Valdemar and the Otherworld, created by one who feels he has no place in either; only here can he feel some sense of home. You needn't worry about Ranyart. Were you able to cross through the veil that separates this world from Valdemar, you would find him only a few feet away from you.:*

:*I don't understand.*:

:*Perhaps, in time. . . .:* But Ylem did not finish the thought.

After the first merging of tones, the others happened quickly and easily. A note sung by Ylem would find its match in a language-tone, the two of them merging and translating in Olias' mind until he could not only hear the other languages spoken in their native tongue but understand them, as well.

Ylem leaned to the side, kissed L'lewythi's forehead, then whispered something in his ear.

Try as he did, Olias could not Hear what the creature was saying.

Ylem was in front of him again, hooves pressing against Olias' shoulder in a gesture of blessing. Then, releasing a triumphant crystal cry, the creature spun around, its tail snapping in the air, and sailed atop the fountain back out to sea, diving downward and disappearing beneath the waters—

—but not before Speaking one last time to Olias.

:*Take care, Olias, and realize if you can that you are not the only one in this place who has known soul-sickness and grief. Keep your anger near. You will need it—but not for the reasons you may think.:*

For several moments afterward, Olias could only kneel there, shaking.

Then a voice, a small, quiet child's voice asked, "Are you all right?"

Olias looked up as L'lewythi placed a hand upon his shoulder.

"Are we speaking in my language, or in yours?" asked Olias.

"Can you understand me?"

"Yes."

"Then what does it matter?"

Olias struggled to his feet, gasping for breath. "Where are we?"

"In the Barrens of my world," said L'lewythi, pointing

first to his head, then his heart, then spreading his arms in front of him. "I made it, I dreamed it. Do you like it?"

Olias rubbed his forehead. "I . . . I don't know. But so far, what I've seen has been . . . *gods*. . . ."

L'lewythi, now looking more like an overgrown child than ever, laughed a child's laugh, grabbed Olias' hand, and led him away from the cliffs. They stumbled down a sharp slope toward a pampas of richly green grass leading to a field where tall corn stalks brushed back and forth through the air. To Olias, everything smelled like lavender—which to him had always been the scent of his mother's skin, left there by the soap she bought from a local tradesman.

They moved toward the entrance to a grove, but as they neared it, Olias saw there were no trees beyond the few dozen that rose before them, arranged in two opposing rows, between which stood a stained glass archway.

Olias slowed his steps.

Something about this was familiar, but he didn't know why.

The trees were as tall as a castle's tower, each with a thick black trunk. The branches of each tree were obscured by onion layers of bleak blue leaves which collectively blossomed into human faces, each one turned skyward and staring up through milky, pupilless eyes. Every face wore the pinched, tight expression of concentrated grief, and as the wind passed through the trees, the faces opened their mouths and moaned deeply, steadily, mournfully.

L'lewythi looked upon them as if they were old friends.

Olias whispered, "They sound as if they're in pain."

"They are, but they're used to it. They're Keeningwoods, and this is what they do."

Keeningwoods, thought Olias.

And then: *the Forest of Sorrows!*

Looking backward, he began to see a pattern. L'lewythi had taken various parts of Valdemar and transposed them into this place the same way a skilled musician would transpose one theme into another. The Barrens could very well have been L'lewythi's version of the Border—Ylem's uncanny form attested to that, and Ylem itself could very well have been based partly on the legends of the Border's creatures, and partly on the Companions, the sea taking the place of Companion's Field, and here the Keeningwoods replaced the Forest of Sorrows.

It both made sense and did not.

Of course a child like L'lewythi would have to build upon things he already knew, and who in Valdemar didn't know of the Companions or their field, or the Forest of Sorrows, or countless other beings and places? (Some part of him shuddered inwardly at the thought of what a child might do with the concept of the outKingdom or the Pelagirs.)

Pointing toward the Keeningwoods, Olias asked L'lewythi, "Why do they make such an anguished sound?"

"To remind all travelers that there are only three things that really matter; people you love, your memories, and sadness." Such a wistful look in his silver eyes as he said this!

They passed under the Keeningwoods and through the archway, emerging on the threshold of a resplendent stone city where a raucous band of black-winged children flew past them, all smiling and greeting L'lewythi by name.

"They're my friends," said L'lewythi. "I like having friends. Even if I had to . . . make them up. . . ."

Just outside the city, they came to an ancient bridge made of sticks and bones. When they reached the middle, L'lewythi stopped and pointed over the side.

Beneath the clear, stilled surface of the turquoise water was a series of evenly spaced, hollowed boulders, each with a transparent sheet of glass attached to the front. Inside each of the boulders—which weren't boulders at all, Olias saw upon closer examination, but glass spheres like those within L'lewythi's strange pipe, only covered in moss and isinglass—sat a claylike lump. Some were shapeless blobs, others more human in shape, some were skeletal, others so corpulent their forms could barely be contained. Still others were merely hand-sized, featureless fetuses. All of the figures huddled with knees pulled up tightly against their chests.

None of them seemed complete. Their dark, sunken eyes stared blankly at the floating weeds and golden fish swimming by.

"You see them?" asked L'lewythi. "Don't they look safe?"

"No," whispered Olias. "They look imprisoned."

"Oh, no, no, I'd . . . I'd never do anything like *that*. I don't like feeling lonely, and I know that they feel the same way, so I made sure that the water is filled with stories and music to keep them company."

"Why do you want them to feel safe?"

"Because it's . . . it's nice to feel that way. I don't want them to be lonely. Lonely is cold. I don't like the cold. There's so much cold, sometimes. Don't you ever feel cold?"

"Most of my life."

"That's sad."

"No, it isn't. It's just the way that is. Your Keening-woods weep; I feel cold."

"But not here?"

Olias shrugged. "No, this is . . . this is fine." He looked down once more at the beings in the water. "How long will you keep them this way?"

L'lewythi stared down at his feet. "I guess . . . I don't—I mean, until. . . ."

"Until when?"

"Until I decide what to make out of them."

Olias stared at his companion, then said, very slowly, very carefully, "How did you come by this power? I've heard of no Herald-Mage who possesses such abilities. What . . . empowered you?"

"I don't know. My dreams, I guess. I dream a lot. Sometimes . . . I don't have a mother or father. If I ever *did* have, I can't remember. Mostly I live in the stables of my village. The grooms there are kind to me. They make sure that I have food and blankets." He stood a little taller, a little prouder. "I sweep up after the horses. I do a good job, the stable-master says so. I have a fine feather pillow. The stable-master's wife made it for me. She says I'm a nice boy, and it's a shame the other children won't . . . won't play with me."

Olias almost laughed at L'lewythi's referring to himself as a child. Perhaps in his mind, yes, but his body was that of the strongest armsmen. A child's mind in a warrior's body.

But . . . a stable-hand? Gods! Were they in a place such as Haven, a boy with L'lewythi's Gifts would be treated with the deepest respect and awe. No one would dare think to make a Gifted one sleep among the horses.

"L'lewythi," said Olias, slowly and carefully, "why were you made to sleep in the stables?"

"Because no one would take me into their home."

"Even though they knew of your powers?"

L'lewythi stared at him for a moment, then looked down at the ground and shook his head. "I never . . . never understood why I could do some of the things I could—*can* do. I thought they might be bad things, some of them, so I never . . . told anyone. I never showed them."

"But certainly there must have been . . ." Olias sighed, puzzling for a moment over how to say this. "There must have been people in your village who suffered, either from sickness or injury. *Children*, gods save us! Certainly there must have been children who fell ill and might have died if—"

"Oh, yes! There was one child, a little girl, who became so sick with fever that no one thought she would live if a Healer were not sent for. But I made her better."

"How, if no one knew?"

A bird—strangely metallic in coloring—flew overhead at that moment, and L'lewythi waved his hand toward it. Its wings went limp and its body began to plummet toward the ground, but a few seconds before it would have struck the earth L'lewythi waved his hand once

again and the bird—wrenched from its trance—frantically flapped its wings and, screeching, flew away.

"That's how I did it," said L'lewythi. "I can make
people sleep, or not see me. That's how I got into the
little girl's bedroom and made her all better. Everyone
in the village, they said it was a miracle, a blessing from
the gods."

"And anytime someone in the village needed healing,
you . . . you made them sleep or not see you?"

"Yes."

Olias nodded his head. "Did you cast this spell over
only those you helped, or did you—"

"The whole village."

"Everyone?"

L'lewythi nodded his head.

"That way I'd be *sure* no one could see me."

"Ah."

"I like helping them and no one knowing. It gives me
nice dreams sometimes, and sometimes when I feel lonely,
I'd think about the little girl and smile. And it's nice in
the stables, really, it is. I like it."

"I'm sure you're a fine stable-hand." Surprisingly,
Olias found that he meant it.

"But the other people in the village, they don't . . .
they don't talk to me. The other children tell me that
I'm too big and . . . and ugly, and no one wants to play
with a foundling—that's what I am. It makes me feel . . .
feel bad sometimes because I don't know where I came
from or . . . or anything. So when I finish sweeping at
night, I like to dream, even when I'm awake. And if I
dream hard enough, the dreams, they sometimes come
out of my head and become real. And the people in my
dreams, they're always my friends. Except for Gash—
you don't want to meet him. He's mean. And he always
wants me to tell him what he is. He says that if I can
ever do that, if I can tell him what he is, then he'll go
away and never come back. I try to guess, but I'm never
right, and then he destroys things. Don't be scared,
though, because he's never come around these parts."

Oh, you poor, simple-minded thing, thought Olias. *Has*

*the world treated you so wretchedly that even in your
dreams you invent one who torments you, who makes
you feel so alone and sad and worthless? Gods—did you
do so out of choice, or has your heart been so brutalized
that you simply think it's natural for someone to abuse
you?*

Unable to find the words which would adequately express what he was feeling, Olias reached out and placed
his hand on L'lewythi's shoulder.

Smiling, L'lewythi placed his hand atop Olias' and
asked, "Are you . . . do you like it here?"

"Yes, L'lewythi. I think it's very nice. I think it's
splendid."

The boy's face beamed at this mild praise. "*Really?*
Would you like to see more?"

"Very much so, yes."

"Are you . . . do you want to be . . . I—I mean—"

"Yes," whispered Olias. "I will be your friend."

He could have swum a hundred raging rivers then on
the memory of L'lewythi's smile. How strange it was, to
feel an attachment after so many years done; how
strange to feel some of the soul-coldness fading away.

But somehow, here in L'lewythi's odd world-within-a-
world, it seemed . . . right.

How strange, to feel affection for another human
being.

How strange, indeed.

*Dear Father, dear Mother, what would you think of
your boy now if you could see him? Lost in a place that
doesn't really exist, befriending a simpleton in whose
hands his destiny evidently rests?*

What would you think?

5

Once over the bridge the land became flat and hard
and dusty. As they walked beside one another, Olias and
L'lewythi spoke of their childhoods, of games and tales
and small wonders, of the animals they'd played with

and the places they'd seen, and it seemed to Olias that, as they spoke, some part of the world sang a song of rejoicing, of second chances and hope renewed, a Bardic ballad of two lifebonded friends meeting for the first time, and of the simple, untainted glory of learning to trust.

"I can see why you like it here so much," said Olias. "It must be difficult for you to leave."

L'lewythi touched his head, then his heart. "I don't leave, ever. It's always here, with me. Even when I'm gone."

The abstract wisdom in those words caught Olias by surprise. Could it be that L'lewythi was not as dim as people thought?

They came then to another section of the shoreline. The sea lapped at the edge of their feet, playfully, as if acknowledging their new bond and giving its blessing.

They came to rest on a large boulder, worn down by time, sea, and the seasons until its shape bore a humorous resemblance to a giant king's throne. Lying back, Olias allowed the sea mist to anoint his face, and felt even more at home.

"L'lewythi?"

"Hm?"

"Could you please tell me what happened to you—I mean, who . . . who hurt you? Who tied you to that horse?"

L'lewythi stared out at the sea, then looked down at his hands. "I . . . I don't know why I can do these things. I just know that I can. I play my glass pipe, and the music brings me here. It's so nice here, everyone's so good to me, they're . . . they're *happy* to see me. No one in Valdemar treats me this way, that's why I come here all the time, that's why I made this place, so I could go somewhere where people would be nice to me."

"I know, I understand that much, but—"

"I didn't mean for it to happen!" he shouted, eyes filling with tears. The sudden violence of his emotion shocked Olias, who was so startled he nearly cried out.

As L'lewythi spoke, his voice became louder and even

more childlike. Beneath every word his pain, deeper than Olias had imagined, came snarling to the surface. It was the panicked voice of a child, lost in the night, hands outstretched in hopes that someone kind would take hold of him and protect them from the darkness and pain and make the fear go away, a pain that asked, in its own way: *Please, please show a little kindness, a little tenderness.*

"S–s–somet–times, when I'm asleep, sometimes the dreams, they come out of my head and I can't make them do what I want because *I'm asleep and I don't know that they've come out!* I d–don't mean for it to happen, but it just happens sometimes. It's never been a bad thing before, but the other night . . . I was *so tired!* I'd worked hard and . . . and I was so tired! And when I fell asleep, Gash came out—and he's *so mean!* He hurt a lot of people in the village. He burned down some of the other stables and killed the horses, and th–th–then he, he started killing everyone. I woke up when I heard the screaming, but it was too late. *I couldn't stop him from killing everyone because I was asleep!* That's never happened to me before. When I woke up, Gash went back into my head, but he'd been so mean by then. And the people, they knew that it was me that had brought Gash into the village because a . . . a *Herald* was there, and he said he sensed that Gash had come from me. He . . . he tried to make them all understand, but they didn't. They all came after me and they . . . they *hurt me!* I mean, I've been hurt before—some of the other stable-boys, they like to hit me and call me names—but this time it w–was different. The Herald tried to stop them but there were too many. They hurt me for so long, and they screamed at me, and some of them even laughed like they were enjoying it. I tried to tell them that I'm not a bad boy, I'm not, I didn't mean for it to happen, but they wouldn't listen to me, they just kept hitting and spitting and then they burned me and . . . and . . ." He doubled over, clutching at his stomach, the sobs racking his body—deep, soul-shattering sobs as the grief and fear and confusion dragged rusty steel hooks across his body all over again. Then he fell backward, pulling his knees up to his chest and wrapping his arms around his knees, convulsing.

Olias climbed over to him, taking L'lewythi in his arms as the boy wept even harder, his next words coming in broken bursts: "I didn't . . . mean to h–hurt anyone . . . I d–didn't . . . I didn't. . . ."

"I know," whispered Olias, stroking L'lewythi's hair. "I know."

"I j–just wanted them to know . . . I wouldn't have . . . have done any of it . . . I wouldn't have dreamed another world l–like this if . . . if I could just tell Gash what he is, he'd go away, you see? And th–then m–maybe I could have a friend . . . just one, that's all . . . just one friend. . . ."

"You have one now. I will be your friend for the rest of our days, L'lewythi. There, there, take deep breaths, deep, there you are, hold onto me, that's it, hold on, I won't let go, I won't leave you alone, ever, I swear it on my parents' graves, *I swear it*! You'll never be lonely again, never—and no one will ever harm you from this day forward, not while I'm around . . . it's all right, shhh, there, there, go on, go on and cry, that's right, let it go, let it go . . ."

He leaned down and kissed L'lewythi's sweat-soaked forehead, then brushed back his hair and held him even tighter, rocking back and forth, feeling strong—and it was good to feel this way for someone after so long. The sudden rush of affection was dizzying, almost overpowering, but he didn't care. He could protect this boy, this sad, gentle boy who wanted nothing more than acceptance, something Olias himself had secretly wished for since the day he buried his mother—but instead of trusting others he had foolishly chosen to hide his loneliness behind a scrim of anger and bitterness.

It was then that Olias looked behind them and saw the wall of stone, an ancient ruin nearly overgrown with moist red vines. Sculpted into the wall was a woman's face. Her eye sockets were empty, raven-black ovals, and her mouth, opened as if calling out for some long-lost

love, was the entrance to a cave. It was a face which
held so much unspoken pain and grief that her expression alone would have been enough to move even the
hardest of hearts, but that is not why Olias' eyes began
to fill with tears.

The face was that of his mother.

Turning away, he stared into the distance and realized
that they had walked a straight path since leaving the
Barrens. He knew this because he could still see the
Keeningwoods from here. As he stared at them, they
seemed so much closer—at least in his mind's eye—and
his troubled heart grew even heavier, for now all of them
wore his father's face—and not the face he'd known as
a child, not the robust, labor-reddened, strong face of a
hearty man. No, this face was the same one he'd put on
the day of his defeat by Gwanwyn and never taken off,
even in death. This was the face of a broken-hearted,
disgraced man whose value had been diminished even
in his own eyes.

*Why, dear gods; can you tell me why even here our
grief haunts us? Can you make me understand why our
souls cannot find a measure of peace?*

As if in answer, a great rumbling came from the
depths of the dark cave.

Then the echo of even darker laughter.

". . . Gash . . ." whispered L'lewythi, clutching Olias'
arm.

There was no time to run. Already Olias could see
the thing's shape shifting forward from the depths of the
earth, moving toward the light, and bringing with it a
smell that was at first musty and stale like the odor from
a long-closed chest whose lid has suddenly been forced
open. The odor grew ever stronger, rancid and sickening,
the stench of bloated carcasses rotting under a blazing
sun.

Its step shook the ground, and when it at last emerged
from the cave, it had to bend over, it was so tall, thrice
the size of the tallest tower.

It was worse than any nightmare.

Gash was not one, but *two* soldier-creatures fused together. The first walked on reed-thin legs while the other grew out of its back, a torso whose head sat far above that of its carrier, with one twisted, grotesquely long arm that reached nearly to the ground, its misshapen bulk held upright by a pulsing black sack growing from between the carrier's shoulders. The shimmering gray skin had the jagged texture of rough stone, though not as dark. Its legs scraped together as it walked, loosing small clouds of chalk dust. The weight of the thing growing from its back forced the carrier to walk hunched over and in obvious pain. The bodies looked to have been once covered in armor that some terrible conflagration had melted to their skin.

The carrier looked at Olias and smiled, its pulverized lips squirming over rotted needlelike teeth. Its face was an abomination of all nature. Countless boils and leaking, diseased wounds covered its cheeks, and the sunlight reflected against the stone-sized tumors that buried its left eye. Its entire face was covered in a maze of something that looked like a spiderweb of hairless flesh.

When it spoke, it was in a voice filled with phlegm and corruption.

"Ah, a brave one," it spat. "I do so like brave ones. They die so well."

Olias couldn't move. L'lewythi had gone into some form of seizure, his body stone-rigid and still, his eyes rolled back into his head, exposing only the whites.

Olias thrust out his dagger, the only weapon he had. Against Gash's colossal form, it looked pathetic, a sad joke.

"You'll not need that if you can tell me what I am."

Olias gently set L'lewythi aside, then stood. "And if I cannot?"

Gash tossed back both its heads and released a mad, high-pitched, cackling laugh, then balled one of its hands into a fist and threw forth a fireball that slammed into the sea, hissing. "Then the next one will be for you. Now, look me in the face, boy, and tell me what I am."

Olias stared, long and hard and unblinkingly.

It seemed to him that both parts of Gash were as

familiar as everything else he'd encountered thus far. The carrier—brutal, cold-hearted—could well have been a perverted form of himself, of his soul, of what it might some day become; the other—so blank-eyed and vacant—very easily might be another form of L'lewythi.

But not one of his choosing, came the thought. *No; that is how others have seen him, how they have made him feel inside; hideous and freakish. The boy is Gifted, after all; those Gifts are raw and undisciplined, so he would be susceptible to others' unspoken perceptions. Is it so hard to imagine that some secret part of himself has come to view himself as other have—and not only that, but has done so without his even being consciously aware of it?*

If that is so, then why do you see yourself in the carrier? What is it about that thing, this place, the faces of Mother and Father that—

—he lowered the dagger to his side—

—as around him he heard the distant echoes of L'lewythi's song, plaintive and sorrowful and simmering with ethereal beauty—

—and like a seed becoming a root becoming a sprout becoming a blossom, the answer came to him as, one by one, the pieces of L'lewythi's painful puzzle fell into place.

"I know what you are," said Olias through clenched teeth. "You are loneliness, and grief, and the death of dreams. You are the sickness which taints the spirit, and the helplessness which breaks the heart. You are fear and cold darkness, doubt and regret. You are envy and avarice and the lies we tell ourselves to excuse our cowardice or selfishness. You are every cruel word, every unkind thought and act of violence ever brought into the world. You are the weeping of mothers over the bodies of their children, the blood of soldiers spilled in battle, the last gasp of the starving in the streets. You are this boy's misplaced anger and confusion, and you feed on his sadness. You are my father's disgrace and the thing which swallowed my mother's laughter. You are the blackness of my soul, all of my hate and lust for vengeance come to life, and in your diseased gaze I can see what my spirit might one day become. You are my weakness and failures—*all* weakness and failure . . . but most of all, you are jealous."

Gash snarled. *"Jealous? Of whom? And why?"*

"You are Pain, and you are jealous of us—not just the boy and me, but any human being who can forget for a while that you are real. You might be a part of our lives, but we can sometimes forget you exist. We can listen to music, or tell our tales, or dance in the waters as they lap the shoreline, or we can steal from the wealthy, or flee into the night where we meet a new friend. We can drink wine and eat fine food and sleep with chambermaids who pleasure us beyond imagining . . . or we can simply lie back and stare into the flames of a campfire and revel in the unadorned glory of the night stars. Ah, yes, we can forget about you and still go on living, but *you,* Gash, who are Pain and Grief and Loneliness, *you can never, for one moment, forget about us! You wish you could, but you can't, no matter how much you try.*

"And that is why you hate us so, and why you are jealous!

"Go away," said Olias, dismissing the monstrosity with a wave of his hand. "You no longer have any hold over this boy or me."

"Damn you, thief!"

"But a thief no more. From this day, I will protect this boy, and I will provide for him as best I can with what meager Bardic and Herald Gifts I possess, with honor and honesty, hurting no one. And if I can somehow make myself worthy, I will travel to Haven and ask the Herald-Mage Savil to teach me discipline so that I in turn might teach it to my friend.

"And you can be certain, Gash, that neither I nor L'lewythi will think of you very much at all."

Gash turned around and stormed back toward the cave, but with each step it took, some part of its body fell to dust.

"I am not the last of my kind," it screamed back at

him. "What created me can easily create others. You would do well to remember that, thief!" Then, turning to face him as its legs exploded into rubble, it gave one final, hideous grin, and hissed, "I'll remember you to your mother and father. I have them in my belly."

"No, you don't," said Olias. "But you *wish* I believed that."

What remained of Gash froze, unmoving, unspeaking, then cracked, broke apart, and fell to ruin.

When the sand and dust clouds died down, Olias looked to see that the woman in the wall was gone.

In the distance, the Keeningwoods were simply trees. No faces, no anguished sounds.

L'lewythi was still unconscious, but the seizure had passed. Olias knelt down and gently lifted his friend, carrying him as he would a newborn baby, walking slowly along the shoreline toward the bridge which would take them back through the stone city, then to the Barrens and cliffs beyond.

In his heart, he knew they could not stay here, no matter how much they might wish to. This had been a hiding place, a sanctuary of sorts for their wounded souls. Now that they had each other, neither would ever need it again.

But the ability that went into the creation of such a place—a world between worlds—*that* was desperately needed in Valdemar. To think of the suffering such a Gift could erase... !

Olias leaned down his head, pressing his cheek against L'lewythi's.

"You'll be safe now," he whispered. "I promise. We've done it, don't you see? In each other, we have found Home."

And I've not forgotten, dear Father, dear Mother; I've not forgotten how to care, how to love . . . nor how to fondly remember you, without rancor or regret.

I will make amends, somehow, for all the wrong I've done. I will honor the memory of your lives by living my own as well as I can, and with my friend by my side, I think that may be very well, indeed.

As the echo of L'lewythi's song found them once
again, Olias couldn't help but notice there were two ad-
ditional tones joining in the glory. One, sharp, loud, and
steady, was the sound of a blacksmith's hammer striking
down, proudly and confidently shaping steel into blade,
and the other, so pure and easy and light, was that of a
good woman's laughter, dancing across the heart, leaving
warmth and affection in its wake.

L'lewythi awoke soon after, and with silver threads
beckoned his glass pipe *come.*

His song—what Olias had thought of as a song for no
one's mourning—was even more transcendent than the
first time, and when they found themselves back at the
campsite where Ranyart and L'lewythi's horse were
waiting patiently, it was with renewed hope that they
readied themselves for their journeys—for there would
be many, of that there was no doubt.

They had much to do, and learn, and teach.

Climbing onto Ranyart, Olias looked at his new
friend, his dearest and most loving friend, and thought
that theirs would be a good life.

Good enough.

6

They say that if you travel the road between Haven
and the Forest of Sorrows on Sovvan-night, when the
Otherworld is so near, you might chance upon a pair of
riders resting at a campfire; they may invite you to join
them for their evening meal (which will be plentiful, for
none ever leaves their camp hungry), and later, if you
are so inclined, they will take up lute and pipe and sing
to you of another place, another land, another world in
another time where two broken souls found friendship,
and acceptance, and redemption.

They say you can see the spirits dancing as the riders sing.

They say you can hear the sound of the sea come so close you swear it's right behind you.

They say you can hear a blacksmith's hammer striking anvil, and a woman's laughter ghosting happily through the trees.

But most of all, they say, you will leave these riders as more than you were before, as if every sadness had been lifted from your eyes.

And their wondrous song will rest in your heart forever, as all true music should.

In loving memory of Edward King Shaw

Blue Heart

by *Philip M. Austin and Mercedes Lackey*

Philip M. Austin is currently an inmate at Soledad prison in California. About this story, he writes, "Misty Lackey is the one who made this story come alive. She deserves the majority of the credit and all of my thanks. [She] has been a good friend and mentor. She's been non-judgmental and helpful in so many ways. Through her good offers I've been able to dream of a future. A creative future without walls and bars. That dream is worth more than any monetary reward."

"There's a Herald to see you, Your Majesty," the page called quietly from the doorway of the Queen's private suite.

Selenay sighed and put down the silver pencil she had been using to scribe a design for an illuminated initial. "Can it wait until tomorrow?" she asked without hope. She was technically supposed to be asleep, not getting her fingers paint- and ink-stained, copying one of Daren's favorite poems. She cherished her time alone; all too rare and much needed. She understood why Elspeth *needed* that shed out in the back gardens, and the feeling of clay under her fingers. Her own hobby of calligraphy and illumination was very similar, intensely physical and requiring complete concentration, and gave her brief respites when she could forget the responsibilities of crown and country.

"He says to say that it's your shadow, Majesty," the page replied, clearly baffled by the enigmatic message.

But if the page was baffled, Selenay was not. She sat

up quickly and put away her implements. "Tell him to come in, and see that we're not disturbed."

"Her shadow" was an enigma; a Herald who never, if he could help it, appeared as himself. Very few people— Kerowyn, Alberich, her own husband Daren—even knew he existed, much less what he really looked like. This was a necessary precaution for his special and demanding duties. He, like Skif, was a spy and an assassin . . . her own special tool to use as needed, and always with reluctance.

When she did not need him, he sometimes requested leave—a day, a week, a month. She never asked him why. Usually it was innocuous, and he returned with tales of his Companion's doings—for it was often his *Companion* who wanted the leave, and not him. Sometimes, though, it was not; and when he reported for duty, his eyes told her she did not want to know what he had been doing, despite the fact that she must hear it. Whatever he did, he did it because she needed it done, whether or not she knew it. Never had she found a reason to even rebuke him for his private missions, and she knew that agonizing over whether to tell her before or after the fact must often cause him sleepless nights. He had requested leave some few weeks ago, and she searched his expression for some clue as to his mood.

But this time, he came as himself, an ordinary man with a pleasant face, unmarked and unremarkable, except for his haunted eyes. She relaxed as she read relaxation in his posture. So; it had been a true holiday, then, and not some secret mission of his own.

"Come in, sit down," she invited, brushing a strand of hair out of her eyes, and forced down the shiver that always came when he looked at her. She did not know his history; she did not know if *anyone* knew it. But whatever his past had been, it had left dreadful scars on his soul. "I hope you enjoyed your Midwinter holiday."

"Pilane appreciated it as much as I, if not more," he said with a smile, as he gracefully lowered himself into the chair. "He indulged himself in *his* passion *almost* as much as he wanted to!"

Selenay laughed. "Sometimes I think he Chose you

because you are the only Herald in Valdemar willing to sit and turn pages for him—*and* to take dictation from him and be his hands! But he is a most remarkable writer. I have copies of all of his books in my personal library, in fact." She relaxed a little more, sitting back in her chair. "I fear, though, I pay far more attention to the drawings and illustrations than I do to his scientific discourse."

"I won't tell him, Your Majesty," the young man laughed. "He does take his hobby quite seriously."

Selenay chuckled. "I'm sure he does. But what brings you here? Especially so late at night? You could— *should!*—have given yourself an evening of rest before reporting to me."

"I have a story to tell you, Your Majesty."

Selenay stiffened, folding her hands in her lap to hide their sudden trembling. She'd half expected to hear those words.

Too often, the story he had to tell was the dark and deadly result of what he *was*. For some reason, he preferred to give his reports as "stories." It was as if he tried to maintain some kind of fiction that *she* was innocent of *his* actions. She was not, and could never be. She gave him orders and the freedom to act; she was as culpable as the archer who looses an arrow. That she did not always know where it would land made her *more* responsible, not less.

"I thought—on a night like this one, in the deeps of winter—you would enjoy this," he continued, and smiled. "It is the story of the *Blue Heart,* Your Majesty; a regional legend of the mountains near White Foal Pass."

Selenay sighed, and relaxed again. Just a story, after all. . . .

And oddly enough, she was suddenly in a mood to hear a story.

"In those mountains," the Herald continued, "there is a small and isolated village. Its population is less than two hundred, and most of them make their living from the fine wool of the long-haired goats they raise."

"I know that wool!" the Queen said in surprise. "Very soft and fine, and *very* expensive."

The Herald nodded. "It is indeed. And it is with that wool that the story begins. . . ."

The trader examined the sample of wool cloth with pleasure and delight. It was soft as a puff of down, warm and light as a purring kitten, and a lovely shade of blue-gray. He'd never seen such cloth, nor anything of so fine a weave. *Plush* was the word he'd put to it, and he was already calculating his profits. He already had a customer in mind, a man of wealth and power in military and secular service of Sunlord Vkandis. Baron Munn—who had led his own private, household troops against the Unbelievers, and as a consequence was high in the favor of the Son of the Sun. The Baron made no attempt to conceal his fondness for luxuries, and he was a good, if choosy, customer.

"It will be hard to find customers for so unusual a weave, but I can take all you have at ten coppers the bolt," he said, expansively, with a condescending smile as if he were doing the rustics a favor.

But the village headman only shook his head sorrowfully. "Oh, Trader Gencan, that giving a mood we're not in," he said, just as condescendingly, and sighed. "It's a been a hard year, that it has. We need so many things, so *many* things, or there'll be no wool for next year, for we'll have had to eat our goats to stay alive." His voice hardened as he bent to the bargaining. "Thirty coppers it'll have to be, or nothing at all."

"What?" Gencan yelped, taken by surprise. Why—that was exactly what he'd expected to *sell* the stuff for! These mudfoots weren't nearly so green as they looked!

And neither was his former competitor, from whom he'd stolen—ah—*acquired* this trade route. Perhaps this was why he had not fought to retain it. There was nothing worse than a tradesman who knew the value of his goods!

He bent to the bargaining with a will, and sweated until he'd brought them down to something *reasonable*.

Something a man could make a decent profit on. Sixteen coppers a bolt was one copper more than he'd wanted to pay, but at least it allowed him a profit margin. . . .

They had just settled on that price, when he happened to look out the window and froze in surprise at what he saw wandering by.

"Who is *that*?" he gasped, wondering if he had somehow stumbled on a creature like one of the fabled Hawkbrothers. The headman followed his gaze and smiled.

"Our lovely butterfly," he said, with a smile of pure pleasure. "That's our butterfly."

"She's your daughter, then?" the trader replied, unable to take his eyes from the girl.

But the headman laughed. "No. Oh, no, Trader. In a way, she belongs to the whole village."

Now Gencan spared him a sharp glance. "The village? What's that supposed to mean?"

But now the headman frowned, just a little. The girl drifted out of sight, and Gencan was able to gather his scattered wits about him again. "It's a strange story, Trader," the headman said at last. "And not altogether a happy one."

Gencan pursed his lips and nodded sagely. "Well, then," he replied. "What say we drink to our bargain and you can tell me her story." He signaled to his servant to bring in the wine. "Nothing makes a bitter story more palatable than a good wine!"

He poured the headman a cup of the strong, smooth wine, then settled in to listen with as good a will as he'd bargained.

Leaving his caravan in the charge of his most trusted assistant, he rode out that very night, pushing hard for Karse. Eight days later he was kneeling, forehead to the floor, before Baron Munn. The cost of a private audience had been steep, but the results of this audience could make him wealthy beyond the income brought by any trade route. He would be able to retire and hire others to lead his caravans, while he directed them like a great lord with his retainers.

Baron Munn sucked at a plum pit, and looked down at him out of one half-lidded eye. The Baron was a massive, bulky man, but his face and limbs showed only the barest hint of the fat of soft living. He had been called "The Bull of the Sun," and he looked like his namesake in every way, down to the expression in his face. "Rise," he said at last, waving a hand languidly. "State your business."

Gencan only removed his forehead from the floor so that he could watch the Baron's expression. "I thank the great and wise Baron Munn for granting me an audience," he said, with every token of humility. "I am not even worthy to scrape the bottoms of the great one's—"

"Fine, fine," the Baron interrupted. "Get on with it." He selected another fruit and bit into it, licking the juice from his fingers.

"I have come to tell you of a young woman, Great Lord," Gencan said, quickly.

Baron Munn looked up from his half-eaten peach, pale eyes bright with interest.

"She is barely fourteen summers old," Gencan continued, "And just coming into the full bloom of womanhood. Her hair is the white of snow, of clearest ice, a waterfall of molten silver. Her eyes are the blue of a clear sky, of the finest sapphire. Her skin is as flawless as cream from the cattle of the Temple. Her face and her form are as perfect as that of a young goddess."

The Baron was truly interested now; he licked his lips and set his fruit aside. Oh, he was feigning indifference, but Gencan had not been a trader all his life without learning how to read people. He played his winning card.

"Such a lovely creature could only have been created by the Sunlord himself," Gencan continued piously. "And in the wisdom of the Sunlord, he has balanced all her virtues, by a single defect. He has given her the mind and heart of a child of no more than eight years. So she is now, and so shall she remain all of her life. Innocent, simple, trusting, and loving! She cannot know a lie, can-

not tell one. She cannot understand any but the simplest
of commands, or do more than care for herself as a child
would. Her needs are those of a child, her joys and fears
those of a child, and she will do anything she is told to
do by an adult."

Baron Munn straightened in his thronelike chair. Gencan watched as the light of interest and curiosity in his
eyes turned to the flames of desire, a desire that turned
his strong face into a caricature of himself. Now he
looked even more like a bull—a bull scenting a heifer.
And Gencan knew that the whispered rumors he had
heard about the Baron were true.

Baron Munn composed himself after a moment, pulling a mask of indifference over his features. He stared
at Gencan as if he were deciding on what he meant to
order for dinner. But his ragged breathing gave him
away.

"Tell me where this girl is, Trader," the Baron said
harshly. "I will send my people to see if all you have
told me is the truth." His hand, the strong hand that
had swung an ax it took two ordinary men to wield,
clenched on the arm of his chair. That ax itself hung
behind his chair in a jeweled sheath, lest anyone forget
what it was that had brought the Baron to power. "If it
is true, and I may have her, you will be rewarded."

His hand clenched again, and Gencan blanched, remembering how many heads the Baron had removed with
that ax, to the greater glory of the Sunlord. "If you lie,"
he continued, "I will make you my slave. My *emascu-
lated, deaf,* and *dumb* slave."

Gencan's mouth was suddenly very dry. "It is all true,
Great Lord, I swear it!" He ran his tongue over his lips,
and tried to keep from trembling with fear as he was
led away to wait.

In twenty days, the spies returned. Their reports of
the girl were even more enthusiastic than the trader's.
Baron Munn, in a fit of joy and generosity, rewarded
the trader with gold, gems, and spices from the South.

Spices so rare that Gencan had never tasted them, and could not resist trying them in his own celebratory feast.

Gencan died that night, a rich and happy man, never knowing that he had been poisoned by those spices from the South at the Baron's orders. There were other rich, powerful men who had the same appetites that the Baron had. The Baron did not intend Gencan to increase his profits by selling his knowledge to them as well. Gencan's own people, and all the Baron's spies but one, followed the trader into the arms of Vkandis.

Guided by his spy, the Baron led a handpicked company of men out of Karse and into the mountain lands disputed by his land and the land of Valdemar. Baron Munn did not trust any man to steal this girl for him. There was too much chance that she could be sold to another, taken away, or tampered with.

The late fall wind had a bite to it, here in the mountains. It whipped up the canyons and fled crying over the village with a hundred mournful voices, circling around the goat pens until the goats added their own plaintive bleats to the wind's cries.

And yet, compared to the mountains above, the village itself was relatively calm, protected by the mountains themselves and the trees that had been planted to shelter it from biting winds. The villagers were used to the winds, used to the deceptive cries. There was no reason to stop work from being done, not even a reason for children to stop their games. People simply wrapped themselves and their children a little tighter in their coats and narrowed their eyes against the blast. It was not even a reason to keep Mikhal from taking the older children up onto the slopes for their daily lessons in herbcraft and woodscraft.

But all work stopped when young Deke, the Watch-Boy, came pounding up the dirt street, arms and legs flailing, yelling that soldiers were coming—

—fast, on horseback—

—and lots of them.

The headman listened to Deke's breathless gasps of

warning. His mind roiled with shock and confusion. *Soldiers?* he thought desperately. *Why? Who would be sending soldiers? There's no reason for soldiers to come here!*

"They—they—they're coming from Karse!" Deke gasped around his panting.

And that was not good news. Soldiers from Karse were often no better than bandits. As the leader of the village, his was the decision; he had to do something, and quickly.

It was too late to get the people out of the village. He'd protect what he could.

"Run as fast as you can, Deke, up where the wild apples grow," he said. "Tell Mikhal to hide the children, and you stay with 'em. Don't you come back. You tell him not to bring the younglings back till he thinks it's safe and the soldiers are long gone. You tell him to hide *good,* you understand? Like the time we was looking for him, and he didn't want to be found. You tell him—*tell him*—we *don't want to know* where they are." He grabbed the boy's shoulders, and shook him once, and Deke's eyes got even bigger.

"You understand?" he said fiercely. *"You understand?"*

The boy's chin quivered, his eyes so big they filled his face. He nodded, bobbing his head on his thin little neck.

"Good!" the headman let him go. "Now go! *Run!*"

Deke was off, pelting away as fast as he could go, fear adding to his speed. As he vanished, the headman heard the pounding of hooves, and turned to see the first of the soldiers riding into the village. He stepped out to meet them.

Mikhal was the oldest man in the village; no one knew exactly how old he was, and he didn't even know himself. He was the village teacher and had been for more than forty years. Not the kind of teacher the priests were, in the ways of books and classrooms, but in the things a youngling in a mountain village needed, the ways of the mountains, the wild things, and the goats. Today, he'd brought the children up here to pick the last of the wild apples, making a game of it, but making sure they *learned* as well, and not just the acts, but the reasons behind them. Seeing that they took only half the apples on the trees, and none at all from the ground— telling them how the wild things, the ones that stayed awake for the winter, would need what they left.

But that lesson was shattered when Deke came pelting up the mountain path.

Mikhal listened carefully to Deke and saw the sense in the headman's orders. Calmly, methodically, and without any fuss, he gathered up the children, including the childlike butterfly, and led them away, down paths only he and the goats knew.

Then, down paths only he and the wild things knew. Only then did he tell them, in simple words they could understand, why he had hidden them away, and why they must stay hidden.

Even the wind shuddered away from the scream, a shriek of agony that went on and on forever before it finally died to a sobbing whimper. The headman's wife sagged back into the arms that held her firmly erect.

Baron Munn handed the hot iron back to the Captain of his Household Cavalry, and turned back to the headman. Four more men held him tightly, forcing him to kneel in the dirt but holding his head up by the hair so that he could not avoid watching.

"Now," the Baron said pleasantly. "Tell me where the girl is. No more lies. No sending my men off on wild-goat chases to look where she isn't."

"I don't know! I swear it!" the headman sobbed desperately. "I told old Mikhal to hide them all, and I don't know where he went! No one knows, no one *can* know, he's gone where only the wild things are! Please, by the gods, you must believe me!"

The man wept, great, racking sobs that shook his body.

"Oh, I do believe you," Munn said and smiled. "But one of these others may know what you don't."

He waved a hand at the villagers gathered under the swords of his men. They winced away.

"So, in case there is someone who knows, this entertainment will go on until I am certain that you are correct. And when your dear wife can bear no more, I shall choose someone else."

He signaled to his Captain, who handed him the iron, reheated to whiteness. "As pleasant a diversion as this is, my objective is still the same. I want the girl."

The headman's wife began to scream again, before the white-hot iron even touched her.

Hands on her ears, the girl crouched on her haunches, rocking back and forth. She tried to shut out everything, words, thoughts, all—

"They killed Headman Cracy an' his wife last night," Deke sobbed, his voice full of anguish. "Hurt 'em real bad afore they killed 'em."

She knew that. She'd known that long before Deke learned it. She could still feel the pain that had sent her to huddle in the back of the cave, racked with agony she could not explain.

Deke hugged his skinny arms to his chest, pausing now and then to wipe his nose and eyes with the back of his hand.

"They started on *my* pap and mam this morning!" Deke continued, his face screwing up into a mask of grief and bewilderment.

She knew that, too. And she knew that Deke's momma was only heartbeats from that same darkness that had taken Momma Cracy and Headman Cracy.

"Why they like that, Mikhal?" the boy sobbed, finally flinging himself into Mikhal's arms. "Why they gotta hurt and kill people? We never done nothin'! Why they gotta hurt my *mam* and *pap*?"

Mikhal pulled the boy to him, holding him close to his chest in a sheltering embrace. While the boy sobbed, Mikhal cursed under his breath.

The girl knew why. Mikhal cursed himself for sending Deke to spy on the village. Mikhal thought he should have gone himself.

"It's 'cause they're bad, Deke," Mikhal murmured be-

tween curses. "It's 'cause they want what we got, an'
just 'cause they *like* to hurt folks, an' this's a good excuse
to make somebody hurt. None of it's our doin', Deke.
None of it."

The old man kept his voice high enough for the other
children to hear. He was a teacher; even in the midst of
terror, he would teach.

"Ain't none of it our fault," he said, and the girl felt
his eyes probing the darkness, looking for her. "We just
gotta get through this, an' make sure it don't happen
again."

*They hurted Momma Cracy an' Poppa Cracy, hurted
'em an' kilt 'em.* The girl's thoughts were filled with confusion, terror, and anguish. *They hurted 'em, but it's
'cause they want* me. *They gonna hurt Deke's momma
an' poppa, they gonna hurt everybody till they get me!*

She rocked back and forth, tears burning down her
cheeks, trying to work out reasons and answers. But
there were no reasons, and she had never in her life
touched minds like these. Mikhal was right. Mikhal
was right.

But these horrible people wanted *her.* These people
were all her family, every adult was her Momma and
Poppa, every youngling a brother or sister. They all
loved her, and she loved them all. It was all she had
ever known, that love, that cherishing.

They're getting hurted, an' it's 'cause of me! She buried
her face in her arms, and faced the inescapable. *If—if I
go to 'em, they might hurt me . . . if I don't, they gonna
hurt everybody, an' maybe kilt 'em, too.*

Her traumatized mind kept trying to resolve the questions, and finally she groped her way through the fog to
an answer, and a decision.

She loved them. They loved her. They were being hurt
because of her. She could not bear that. And there was
only one way to stop the hurt.

She slipped away, as quietly as a mouse, running down
to the village to make the bad men stop.

*   *   *

Baron Munn stared at the lovely girl, completely enthralled. She was more beautiful than he dreamed, more vulnerable and tender, and her terror only served to make her lovelier in his eyes. That terror fed the hunger within him in a way that even the dying pain of her elders had not done.

She was perfect in every way.

She cowered at his feet, where she had thrown herself, weeping, placing herself between him and the woman he had been torturing, trying to hold him off with her soft little hands. Hands like fluttering doves, like white butterflies.

He took her face in his hands, carefully, and raised her eyes to his. Even weeping could not make her less than lovely.

Her eyes were as blue as the sky in winter, as a bottomless lake.

"The eyes are said to be the vision of the heart, and your heart is a heavenly blue," he said, running a hand over her molten silver hair. "What is your name, little dove?"

"P–P–Pilane," she choked out, silver tears coursing sweetly down her cheeks.

He smiled.

He ordered the villagers to make a cage in which he would carry her back to Karse. He ordered it carved and painted, and lined in layers of the village's fine wool, to keep her warm and sheltered and safe.

He had captured the butterfly. Now he would bring *his* prize, *his* Pilane, back to his barony for all to see, see and lust after, but never to touch. Only he would savor that touch, at his leisure, and savor what came after touching.

The villagers made his cage in a day and a night, all of them laboring until they dropped from exhaustion. He left as soon as it was completed, under cover of the first snow of winter. He headed for White Foal Pass at a forced march, driving his own men as hard as he had driven the villagers. He wanted the journey to Karse, to safe-haven, to be as quick as possible.

Behind him, the remaining villagers could only gather to mourn their dead, and to pray to the gods for their special daughter. They held no illusions about what was to befall her; her beauty would serve to enchant him only for so long—and when it palled, he would feed his desires in other ways. They prayed, then, for something, someone, to send her quick release—through rescue, or painless death.

When the stranger rode into the village, it seemed that their prayers had been answered, and a rumor that he was the messenger of the gods went through the village on the wings of the wind.

He certainly looked anything but human, riding a tall, handsome white horse with strange, knowledge-filled blue eyes. And he himself was garbed in pristine white, his face heartstoppingly handsome beneath silver-streaked hair. But most startling of all were his silver eyes, as filled with knowledge, sorrow, and understanding as those of his steed.

What else could he be? And even though he protested otherwise, *they* knew he was goddess-sent.

He listened carefully to their story with a troubled and angry face.

"I can stop them," he said, in a clear, edged voice, as sweet as springwater and as sharp as a blade of ice. "I *can* stop them. But the danger is great, and there is a chance that your Pilane will not survive."

"Better that than a life as *that* man's toy!" Mikhal snarled bitterly. "Her life will be short enough in any case in *his* hands!"

Behind him, the rest of the villagers nodded or spoke their agreement. Some wept, but all agreed. Baron Munn's actions had left them no illusions.

"Go to White Foal Pass, then, as soon as the snow stops," the stranger told them.

And then, he rode away.

That night, the light snow turned into a full winter storm, a blizzard the likes of which no one, not even Mikhal, had ever seen. Snow fell so thickly and heavily that it was a struggle just to get from house to house within the village.

Then it became too cold to snow; the wind strengthened, and whipped the snow already fallen into huge drifts. The cold grew deeper and deeper.

The blizzard lasted until moonrise the next night, then died.

At first light, the villagers put on their snow-staves, loaded up their sleds, and followed old Mikhal along the goat-tracks to the pass.

They found the Baron's soldiers and horses, frozen, as if they had been struck down by a cold more deadly than any man could imagine, and all in a single moment. They found the Baron with his hands frozen to the bars of the locked cage, his dead eyes staring into it, as if he had seen something he could not understand.

But Pilane was gone, without a trace.

They never found her.

The Queen wiped her tears away, and waited for her Herald to say something more. But as he sipped his tea, she shook her head.

"Is that all?" she demanded. "Just that? A mystery?"

"There is a little more," the Herald said, putting down his own cup. "One version of the story tells that the messenger took their prayers to the goddess, and it was She who made the storm and took the girl to her side. Another says that the man was only a man, but also a great and powerful mage, who used his magic to bring the storm and save the girl, and that he took her to his palace to live in peace. The last version says also that the man was a mage, but that he was heart-friends with the strange and mysterious Tayledras—that he begged their help, and it was *they* who sent the storm and took the girl to their homes above the trees, where she was loved, protected, and happy for the rest of her days."

"Tayledras?" the Queen replied. And she wondered; did Elspeth know of this legend? She was with the Tayledras, even now. Did she know the *real* ending to the story?

"The one thing that all three legends agree upon," the Herald continued, "is that whether it was a goddess, a mage, or the Tayledras, whoever took Pilane created a butterfly to take her place and remind those who loved her of her beauty, her goodness, and her own sacrifice to save them. They call it the 'Blue Heart' and it is a butterfly, they say, that lives only in early winter, after the first snow and only during the full moon. And they say this was done so that the memory of Pilane and all she was would never be lost to the mountains."

He sighed, and was quiet for a few heartbeats.

"And that ends my story, Your Majesty," he said at last.

"It's a lovely story," Selenay replied, lost in thought for a moment. Then something occurred to her, and she sat straight up in her chair. "The girl's name—it was *Pilane*! and that's your Companion's name!"

The Herald grinned a little shamefacedly. "It means 'butterfly' in a very old mountain dialect," he chuckled. "Which may be the reason why he has made himself into an expert on the little creatures."

But Selenay had another reason for laughter. "You mean that he had you two out in the snows of the mountains chasing a *legend*?" she laughed. "A butterfly—that is only a legend—out in snow and moonlight—in White Foal Pass?"

When she finished, tears of laughter were bright in her eyes, and she was holding her side.

"You—the most dangerous man in the Circle—chasing snow-butterflies in the moonlight!"

He hung his head sheepishly. "I am afraid so, Majesty," he replied. "And with your leave, I really must go."

The Queen waved her answer weakly from her chair, laughing soundlessly.

As he stood and turned to leave, the Herald placed a small package on the table beside her cup. "A gift, Your Majesty," he said. Then he was gone, the door closing behind him.

After several moments, the Queen wiped her eyes,

and got herself back under control. She picked up the package, curiosity overcoming her laughter. The Herald's gifts were rare, but fortunately were seldom as sinister as his "stories" could be.

Inside a wrapping of soft gray woolen cloth she found a carved, wooden presentation case for a hand-sized book, a case she opened with the key taken from the ribbon tied around it.

In the right side was a black-velvet-lined recess, containing a thin book. In raised silver letters on the elegant white leather cover were the words, *The Blue Heart* and beneath them, *C. Pilane*.

In the left side of the box was a glass-covered velvet-lined display case.

Positioned carefully on the black velvet was a butterfly. Each wing was no larger than her two thumbnails together. The wings were the color of molten silver, with an oblong blue spot on either side of the creature's slender body. Those marks, when seen with the wings fully opened as they were displayed, made the shape of a heart.

A heart as blue as a Companion's eyes, or the color of the clear winter sky.

Mercedes Lackey

The Novels of Valdemar

Tanya Huff